THE FUTURE HISTORY OF THE GRAIL BOOK ONE
FALL
OF THE
GREEN LAND
I0752164
PERCIVAL
J.G. FOLLANSBEE

THE FUTURE HISTORY OF THE GRAIL

Book 1: Fall of the Green Land

A novel

by J.G. Follansbee

Print ISBN: 978-1-7354656-7-8
E-book ISBN: 978-1-7354656-0-9
Seattle, Wash., USA
Cover art by Christian Bentulan
http://coversbychristian.com/
Edited by Melanie Austin
https://seattle-editing.com/
Proofread by Edith Follansbee

PROLOGUE

October 4, 3264, by the Old Calendar
The 77th year of the Treaty of Camelot

Merlin Ambrosius runs his gloved fingers across the sterile surface of the sphere. Pebbly knobs compete with ridges along grooves that cross and recross the surface like shallow canyons. Its luster ranges from pure chromium to a dusky pewter, with raised symbols and letters. Tiny jewels of red, blue, green, and a translucent white stud the exterior. Despite their lifelessness, Merlin senses a magic within, but he has no idea what's inside. As if contemplating hard, thankless work, the device sits leaden in its cradle, waiting for a command Merlin doesn't know.

The Grail is as lifeless as a lump of stone, but it is the key to saving the world.

The vid recorded the first time anyone had seen the Grail in a thousand years. What an exciting moment, Merlin reflected, one of the greatest of his long life. Brushing the back of his fingers over the trim white hairs under his chin, Merlin rewound the vid to the beginning. Taken on Summer Solstice Day, it was the best documentation of the device *in situ*. After almost sixty seasons of deciphering texts, poring over field reports, and trial and error poking and prodding, he'd reached the inner chamber of the Great Machine, and the Grail at its heart.

In the months after he'd made the recording, he'd discovered so much, but knew so little. He wasn't even sure the device was actually called "Grail." That was the best translation the sage-linguists could discern from the pre-Dissolution records they found. Reams of digital text, mostly unreadable, except for strange, almost mind-blowing hints. One spoke of a parallel universe, with legends that sounded eerily like his own reality. He dismissed the stories as mistranslations at best, fantasies at worst. He had a more important job.

He told the linguists to focus on the technical material. They needed to know how the Great Machine functioned. Despite the texts' fuzzy meanings and strange purposes, the word "Grail" stuck to the object in the vid. Ever since the Camelot com chans broke the news of Merlin's discovery, Arturus demanded daily reports of progress. Could Merlin repair the Grail? Could fixing the Grail repair the Great Machine? Once the Great Machine was working again, would the climate return to normal?

Merlin had no idea how to respond, but he hadn't been chief science advisor to three Viridian monarchs by answering, "I don't know." He fudged by sending videos and giving interviews to news chan anchors, though he detested their vacuousness. Meanwhile, he and his research team chipped away at the Grail's mystery in the compound below Apparatus Montis, the mountain home of the Great Machine. They moved the device to the lab, and slowly, one atom at a time, it seemed, the Grail revealed its secrets.

Until it couldn't.

The research season was nearly over. He'd planned to transport the device to his lab in Camelot. Instead, he stared at the empty space on his test bench once filled by the Grail. The black-clad visitor had come in the small hours, Merlin's favorite time for thinking through tough problems. The visitor belonged to a man and a woman who wanted something the Grail could bestow, though it had nothing to do with its technological power or ancient history. Merlin didn't want to give up the Grail, but the visitor was not a gentle, peace-loving individual. He threatened to kill Merlin, right there. His mouth still dry from the terror of that moment only an hour before, Merlin had no choice but to give up the priceless Grail.

What would he tell Arturus? He'd managed to keep the king at bay with a mixture of truth and exaggeration, claiming to be just days away from solving the Grail's mysteries and returning the Great Machine to healthy status. As was often the case in his long career, he decided to tell a half-truth. Someone took the Grail. The whole truth would have to wait.

CHAPTER 1: AN UNEXPECTED RESCUE

June 13, 3267, by the Old Calendar
The 80th year of the Treaty of Camelot

The forest mocked Percival for his faith. Dry, low-hanging spruce branches scourged him. Hemlock boughs slapped him in the face. Exposed roots tripped him for sport. Gaia gave life to the forest and everything else, and she took it from knights who lost their way. He'd watched everyone on his expedition fall to disease, starvation or despair. Percival, however, had to go on.

"Find the Grail," Arturus had said, "or we are all lost."

"I will find it, my lord," Percival said to himself, alone in woods thick as his flaming-red hair. "It's what I'm meant to do."

The vermin in the knight's beard grasped the hairs tightly as he stumbled. His clothes shed patches like molting fur. How many days had passed since he had last seen his human companions? How many weeks since his com had stopped working? No power, no messages. The setting sun was his final beacon, dimming like approaching disappointment as it sank behind the Range of Needles.

"You must find it." Arturus' graying face had the intensity of sun at noon. "The man or woman who owns the Grail owns the nation."

Percival thought of those words often, but the king's meaning always escaped him. A glottal growl stopped his reflection cold. The sound was layered: half-bark, half-bellow. It awakened a memory. A time before—centuries ago, it seemed, long before his acceptance to the Round Table, back when he was a teenager —he'd found spoor in the mountains on the edge of his mother's land. He'd gone home empty-handed on that quest, too, though he'd recorded the terrifying call. The sage-scientists declared it genuine. He'd been lucky to come back with a whole skin. As he stumbled forward in the forest twilight, somewhere east of Camelot, the growl had returned. He reached for his javelin, but he'd lost it the day before in a marsh. If the beast was pursuing him, he'd be an easy meal, though not much more than an appetizer.

The bestial voice rose into an anxious, restrained scream, coming from the direction of the dissipated sun. The western breeze carried Percival's scent away. The beast might not know he was near. So why the scream? Was it vocalizing fear? The earth trembled with the creature's advance.

Percival pressed himself against the trunk of a monster fir. The ridges of bark dug into his spine. He thought the tree might vibrate in sympathy with his terror and give him away. He wanted to live. He'd avoided the despair of a few of his companions, who'd wandered off into the desert or mountains one by one to end their drain on the expedition's resources. Others died from disease. More died from attacks by trolls and ordinary two-footed predators. Only Percival remained. He lived because the expedition's story was important. His death was a luxury Viridiae, the "Green Country," his country, could not afford.

The slow *thump-thump* stopped. In the violet darkness, Percival heard the questing beast inhale sharply. Only the wide trunk of the tree hid him from his predator. The beast barked, and Percival reflected that its call was less like the baying of a brace of hounds, and more like the plaintive cry of a chorus of mountain lions. The sound resonated in Percival's heart, but it was discordant. It sounded the way Percival felt—afraid. What could frighten a mutant heavier and longer than three horses lined up nose to tail?

Another sound penetrated the forest, bouncing between the rock walls of the narrow ravine, trapping Percival and the chimera. Percival's ears pricked at a human voice, distant and diffuse. The beast cried a second time, its pace quickened by anxiety. Confident he was safe from its jaws, Percival dared to peer around the fir's trunk, hoping to catch a glimpse of it. Percival missed seeing the whole animal, but he caught the fleshy, arrowhead shape of its tail's tip. It swished.

For a moment, silence cloaked the forest. The final wisp of breeze had dropped away, but Percival's breathing quickened again. What if the beast had slunk into a position better for an attack on him? Unlike animals formed by natural selection, the beasts were descendants of animals designed for the pleasure of people, and therefore, like people, unpredictable. It might circle back. It was an ambush predator, like a cat.

The lost knight fell to his haunches, the remnants of his hope for survival evaporating. He couldn't call for help. Running was impossible. The beast wouldn't listen to pleas for mercy. His mouth resembled the eastern desert, his stomach a hollowed-out tree. Exhaustion prevented tears.

Nothing happened.

Don't toy with me! Percival thought to himself. He deserved to die with a little dignity. He was a knight, a favorite of Arturus. He started to laugh. What a useless thought! The beast hates knights who pursue it with the relentlessness of a rising tide. Why shouldn't it torture human prey as revenge for living a life of fear?

Another *thump* came through the spongy ground, but this sound was different. It didn't belong to the beast. Again, Percival pressed against the tree. A jingle of metal mixed with the panting of a horse ridden hard. The rider called out, but the words were lost among the branches.

Percival knew her voice.

Relief flooded him. He never expected rescue. The expedition had lost touch with Camelot nearly a year previously. Batteries for its com equipment wouldn't charge, and the survivors were left with navigating by the sun and stars. They had no idea where to go, except west. By pure accident, a beast-hunting knight had found Percival.

Or was the rider searching for the expedition and not the beast? The thought gave Percival pause. Everyone wanted to find the Grail, but the competition was fierce, especially among the knights at Court. Not only would the winner save the nation and repair the Great Machine, he or she would enjoy fame forever. Animated light paintings and sculpted monuments would seal the memories. The material rewards would be pretty good, too.

Percival understood the covetousness and jealousy of his peers when it came to glory. The betrayal of his expedition was his evidence. Hearing the clink of the dame knight's armor and the heavy hoofs of her warhorse, he wondered if she was his enemy, not the beast.

He debated what to do. Arturus needed to know what happened. The king himself might be in danger. Even thousands of kilometers from home, the expedition heard rumors of incipient coups and revolts. Percival could not risk capture by a rebellious cabal. He had to survive, not only to inform the king, but to keep the search for the Grail alive.

The drumbeat of hooves forced Percival's hand. He reached into his last reserves and bolted. He ran like a rabbit, dodging the starlit, lichen-encrusted rocks. He jumped ankle-breaking holes while scanning for an overhang or a cleft big enough to conceal him. Glancing over his shoulder, he saw the mounted knight bearing down on him, the polished steel of her breastplate reflecting his panicked image. Percival whimpered; he'd never outrun the horse. He kept going, until a low-hanging branch caught him in the chest like a tournament lance, throwing him to the ground. He rolled onto his back, stars orbiting on the edges of his vision.

The knight dismounted. The point of her sword touched Percival's throat. A millimeter more and he'd bleed to death.

“Why are you running?” In the pitch darkness, Percival couldn't see her face, but the familiar voice calmed him. She wouldn't kill him.

“Answer me, or Dame Lancelot du Lac will slice you in two.”

The threat puzzled Percival. Didn't Lancelot recognize him? The sword pressed further into Percival's neck. He felt a trickle on his throat, but he wasn't sure if it was sweat or blood.

"Did you see it?" Lancelot said.

"See what?"

"The beast, damn you."

Percival swallowed, but not too hard. The sword point hadn't moved. "Yes, I think so."

An electric torch blinded Percival. "Which way? I have to know!"

Percival glanced in the way he had come. The beam of light followed his gaze. Lancelot jumped on the pawing horse.

"Wait!" Percival cried.

Lancelot ignored Percival, wheeling the horse around to continue her chase.

"Please! I'm Percival Rathkeale."

The armored warrior reined in her horse, confusing the animal. It wanted to run, but Lancelot paused, as if considering the information. "Not possible. He died weeks, maybe months ago."

"I swear I'm Percival. I'm the son of Eleanor Rathkeale. My sister is—"

"Shut up." Lancelot shifted. Her distressed animal bellowed, as if arguing with its master. It was trained to kill, and it smelled a victory.

"I'm the only one left," Percival said. The torch beam danced on him. He lifted his hands to his eyes to block its painful brightness. "What are you doing? Don't you believe me?"

The beam narrowed on Percival's face as Lancelot drew nearer. "I thought you might be a troll, but trolls don't have facial hair."

Percival shuddered at the mention of the creatures. "They killed three of the expedition."

"What expedition?"

"The last Grail Expedition. The one King Arturus III sent out in the spring."

"Twenty knights and squires went on that jaunt. Where are the rest of them?"

"All dead."

"Except you."

Percival nodded.

"Don't lie. Arondight is thirsty tonight."

Percival glanced at Lancelot's blade. "You know me. I wouldn't harm anyone, except Viridiae's enemies. I swear I'm the only survivor. The last one besides me died a week ago, and I'm lost. What is this place? Am I close to Camelot?"

"In a word, no. Judging by your scrawny state, you'd never have made it."

Lancelot backed away a step and sheathed her blade, evidently believing Percival's claims. "Gaia's blood, you are Percival. You have the man's guileless face."

The prone knight sat up, and the standing knight switched off the torch. The darkness enveloped Percival, like a glimpse of death, though ill-defined shapes appeared as his eyes adjusted. Percival, Lancelot, and the horse were in a small clearing.

Lancelot drew close to Percival, who could smell the dame knight's sweaty leather jacket. "What did it look like?" she asked.

"The Grail?"

"Well, that, of course. But I mean the beast."

Percival related his encounter.

"Damn, I knew it was close. I was within meters! And now you ..." Lancelot cursed in frustration. Percival had interrupted a hunter's pursuit, and the quarry escaped. Lancelot leaned against a rock that stood like a threatened bear. "You're lucky, Percival. Virtually no one alive has seen a questing beast. Heard them plenty, but rarely seen one."

"I remember. You told me this when I was a squire."

Lancelot seemed not to hear. "Not even the sage-scientists, with their fancy cameras and recorders, have gotten a good look. I've wanted to capture one since I was five. I've only found bones."

Lancelot removed gear from her horse's pannier. In a moment, an electric fire glowed, and Percival edged nearer. He was grateful Lancelot had chosen to stay with him, instead of continuing her hunt, but he was unsure of Lancelot's mood.

"Hungry?"

Percival, who had eaten nothing but grubs and roots for days, offered a restrained nod and accepted the handful of dried beef. He selected the biggest piece and gnawed on it.

"You said you saw it?"

"The beast? Just a glimpse, like I said—"

Lancelot chuckled. "No, the Grail."

Percival shook his head. "I saw its resting place, but it was gone. It was like knowing your lover had just been in the room, but had left before you got there." He'd reflected on that feeling for weeks.

"So near, and as far away as the moon. I know what you mean." Lancelot looked at the ground.

Lancelot gave Percival a wool blanket. Removing her horse's saddle, she laid the saddle blanket on the ground for herself, propped her sword on a boulder, and drew her cloak tighter. She sat cross-legged in front of the warm, glowing fire. Percival studied her round face, wide-set eyes, and the brown-black hair gathered in a tight braid that fell down her left shoulder.

"Sir Percival, are you afraid of failure?"

Percival did not know the answer. Was Lancelot, one of the greatest knights of the Round Table, speaking of herself, or him, or someone else?

"You're lucky," Lancelot repeated without waiting for Percival's response. "You saw the questing beast. And you've missed the changes."

"Changes?"

"Better to see for yourself. Tomorrow." Lancelot stretched out, laying her head on the saddle as a pillow.

Lancelot's desire for sleep lasted only a second or two. Her horse let out a gurgling scream followed by a sickening crunch of bone. Thunder coursed through the ground as its broken body fell. A barking growl supplanted the pounding of the questing beast's feet. The knights scrambled away, surprise driving them into the dark. Percival caught a glimpse of the beast's intelligent eyes reflecting the electric fire's fading glow. Like a cornered animal, it had attacked, rather than wait for the inevitable. By killing the horse, it had evened the chances it might prevail. If it slashed the air to the left with its razor teeth, it would kill Percival. If it moved the opposite way, Lancelot would die.

"My sword!"

Lancelot's stifled cry focused Percival's attention on the weapon, still propped on the rock, but below the beast's bobbing chin. It sniffed, knowing its enemy was near. Was its eyesight poor? Was the light too little for it to see its mortal enemies? What about its hearing?

Percival and Lancelot were separated by ten meters, the beast between them. Every fiber of Percival begged him to run, but he held still. The beast paused, as if working out a decision.

"It can't kill us both," Lancelot whispered.

Percival disagreed, but stayed silent. The beast wasn't malevolent, but it was also terrified, and it would destroy the threat to its life, if it could. But Lancelot was right about one thing. Two knights, one beast. The chances for one to survive were decent. For two?

"I'm going after my sword, but around the beast's flank," Lancelot said. "Stay put."

Two seconds passed. Four seconds. A snap from Percival's left. The beast had what it needed. It charged in Lancelot's direction, passing near enough to Percival for him to smell its scaly skin. The fire's light glowed with the power of a near-dead candle. The sword waited. Percival ignored Lancelot's advice and ran the ten paces, grabbed the scabbard, and drew the sword. It was as heavy as his javelin, but the weight was more concentrated. In his weakened state, he feared he couldn't swing it properly.

The beast screamed, perhaps frustrated, perhaps triumphant, and Lancelot appeared, taking the empty scabbard in her hands. Shock transformed her face, and the beast snapped its jaws. The strike missed, and Lancelot scrambled away, crashing into the broad trunk of a tree. She fell, holding her wrist, and the beast snapped at her again. Lancelot dodged.

"Percival!" She was angry, as well as fearful.

The emaciated knight lunged from his hiding spot, using his weight to drive the point of Arondight into the beast's flank. The sword traveled only a few centimeters into the tough hide, but the pain distracted the creature. Percival let go of the hilt. The point of the blade stuck in the beast's skin like a thorn. The beast's head flailed as it reached for the steel. It lost its balance and crashed to the ground. Lancelot had a half-second to get out of its way. The crash knocked the sword out of the beast's body. The creature scrambled to its feet and thundered off. The fight was done.

Lancelot gasped for breath in the thin mountain air. She collapsed at the base of the tree. Percival joined her.

"Thank Gaia it's not my sword hand." Lancelot worked her injured wrist. Her fingers opened and closed. "Just a light sprain."

Percival fought back tears of relief. He'd seen slow deaths for weeks and nearly met his own quick death. Neither kind was noble.

"It's like fighting the whole damned Lucian army," Lancelot said. Her face was streaked with dirt and the remnants of her terror, as if waking up from a nightmare. Then she turned on Percival. "What the fuck were you doing? How dare you take my weapon. I had it all worked out!"

Percival edged away. "But the beast spotted you. Another meter and it—"

"How many times did I tell you and the other cretinous squires at The Keep never to touch Arondight? She was made for me, and no one else." Lancelot slid her sword gently into the scabbard, highlighted with inlaid oyster shell.

"I'm sorry."

Lancelot sighed. "I might never see a questing beast again. Damn the luck." Her temper cooled, as if the chill air absorbed it. She folded her arms. "I suppose I owe you one."

"Just get me back to Camelot. That's enough for me."

Lancelot nodded.

Percival doubted the beast would return. The knights would

not pursue it, at least not now. Percival's breath came out in shudders as his beating heart calmed. He would live a while longer.

Lancelot added another battery to the fire. Percival stared into the elements, designed to simulate the hypnotic effect of a true camp blaze. The Earth couldn't afford the carbon load in the atmosphere from a plasma fire. No one was even sure the Grail would bring the world back into balance, if it was ever found. Percival, like dozens of other knights, had failed, but the quest would go on, if Camelot and Viridiae survived.

CHAPTER 2: BROTHER AND SISTER

Percival confronted the burned-out shell of the bakery, like a monument to a forgotten war. The battle scars were fresh, and smoke drifted over the boulevard into the blue sky. Broken display fixtures, aluminum trays for loaves, and shards of glass carpeted the sidewalk. Men-at-arms carrying single-shot pistols and short swords stood at each end of the barricaded street.

"Another bread riot." Lancelot dismounted and led her spare horse around the debris.

Percival followed suit, descending from his animal borrowed from a farmer on the road back. Neighboring buildings suffered collateral damage, if not outright arson. "We heard reports of unrest when communications were good, but they were hard to believe."

"Believe it. The fall harvest was much worse than expected. The sage-climatologists say the agricultural decline is happening faster than expected. It's not raining enough or too much. The seasons are changing too early or too late. Everyone's sure the Warming has returned."

"What about the grain reserves?"

"Arturus is holding them back for a real emergency. Or a war."

"This looks like an emergency to me."

"The price of bread might be the trigger."

The bakery was in the suburbs of Camelot, a sprawl of independent towns and small cities below a walled city that had grown up around a hilltop citadel. Collectively, the residents called it the lower town. Percival had walked the broad boulevard in this neighborhood a hundred times, and it was always full of people. The day after the bread riot, the only sounds were the crunching of glass under his feet and the buzz of militia drones over the wrecked scene.

"Who started the riot?" Percival said.

Lancelot wore a blank expression. "Hungry people. Desperate people."

Once past the bakery, however, the street came back to life. Lancelot's arrival sparked a raucous parade. Old men on horseback, rich matrons in automated cars, and skinny girls and boys by the dozens exited electric trolleys to mob her. Next to Arturus, she was the most famous person in Viridiae, and far more accessible to the average citizen. She had dominated tournaments for years, winning trophy after trophy in everything from jousting to archery. The throng forced her and Percival to slow their pace, and she waved in appreciation.

Percival trudged along behind. The throng loved Lancelot, but Percival noted a change in their affect, compared to the day his expedition left nine months before. Viridians were a patient, disciplined people, able to sacrifice and adjust to adverse circumstances. The loss of the Grail had shocked everyone, and the populace, taking its cue from the king and the Round Table, had been confident all would be well. Arturus sent his best knights and smartest sage-scientists to find the Grail, and when the first expedition came back empty-handed, he sent another, and another, including Percival's, which had also failed. The worry etched around the eyes of the otherwise smiling faces of Lancelot's fans revealed their mood, along with the aftermath of the bread riot. Percival wondered how much more they could take.

The people hardly noticed Lancelot's pale and bearded companion, who resembled a servant to the dame. Percival had discarded his rags for spare livery worn by Lancelot's attendants. He admitted a twinge of envy for Lancelot's adulation. "It's like they've forgotten me."

"They've probably just forgotten what you look like. You're not exactly the picture of health."

Percival scratched the fleshy skin of his jaw.

"Besides, no one's heard from you for months. You might as well be dead, as far as the masses are concerned. And I wouldn't thump my breast for attention, just now."

"I don't understand."

The warriors' entrance into the city morphed into a procession as a few citizens realized Percival's identity. Word had already reached them that he'd survived. Well-wishers shook his hand and called out welcomes. They asked if he'd found the Grail.

He apologized and said no. The welcoming grins transformed into crestfallen frowns. Percival's embarrassment deepened.

"Be careful what you say. You'll soon have a target on your back," Lancelot warned. "You're the first person the mob and the ignoramuses in the court will blame."

"For what?"

"The failure of the expedition. You've survived, but you've come back empty-handed. You must've done something wrong." Lancelot grinned at her sarcasm.

Percival failed to grasp Lancelot's humor, but politics was not Percival's strong suit.

They reached the eastern gate in the outer curtain wall of the old city. Percival noticed a marshaled group of wagons and horses.

"It's the next expedition," Lancelot said. "They're leaving in a few days."

Percival was incredulous. "Shouldn't Arturus wait until he hears what happened to the spring expedition?"

"I doubt he thinks he has the time." Lancelot turned up a side street.

Percival halted. "Aren't we going to report to Arturus?"

"I had to pull strings to get ten minutes with him. I'm not going to present myself with a half-starved, filthy vagrant as my gift."

Percival scratched his armpit.

"And you'll want to speak with a visitor."

"I'd rather go to the citadel."

Lancelot threw up her hands. "Can you relax for five minutes? Don't you want to see your sister?"

A lump rose in Percival's throat. "I suppose." He'd barely thought about Dee over the last few months. He'd pushed the mental image of his twin away, thinking that his homesickness would overwhelm his sense of duty and paralyze him.

"I thought so. I sent her a message."

The tidy townhouses and neat shops inside the curtain wall reflected their proximity to Camelot's citadel, the seat of Arturus' power. By now, the news feeds had spread word of the knights' arrival, and the people in this neighborhood were congratulatory, but more restrained. Somehow, the rowdy welcome in the lower town cheered Percival more. The attitude of these fashionably dressed urbanites contained a touch of skepticism, even pity. Behind their smiles, were they drawing their bows to loose arrows at the metaphorical target Lancelot mentioned?

Lancelot's three-story townhouse resembled others on the street, with the exception of the shield painted with red stripes on a white field mounted above the front door. They left the horses in care of a liveryman at a stable shared with neighbors who could afford horses. Propriety required knights, bureaucrats, or merchants to keep the animals for business reasons or for show. A few polished electric cars roamed the city, owned by the hyper-wealthy. Even fewer public cars, wearing scrapes like war scars, offered rides to middle and lower-class people willing to splurge.

Opening her front door, Lancelot called down a short hallway and removed her riding coat. A dour woman half Lancelot's height greeted her mistress, took one look at Percival, and held back a scream. Lancelot offered a quick explanation, and she pointed wordlessly at a room with a bed and an *ensuite*.

Percival was alone in the room, and he made straight for the shower. He let the warm water stream over his head and body a full ten minutes. In near ecstasy, he soaped himself like a cyprian after her shift in the bawdy house. He scrubbed every crevice of his dirt-caked body. Eventually, a pounding woke him from his daydreaming. He emerged from the shower dripping and naked.

"What do you think you are, some sort of male naiad?" Dee threw him a towel.

Percival wrapped himself. He stared at his twin sister. She'd seen him nude before, but he was surprised by her shocked gaze.

"Lancelot was right," she said. "You're half dead."

Dee Rathkeale's reaction didn't stop her from embracing Percival. Her strength energized him, like the hot water in the shower, and he felt her joy at seeing her brother alive after three-quarters of a year. Of all the million people in Camelot and its suburbs, Percival was duty bound to report to Arturus, but he only desired to see his sister. She was his rock in a city that often perplexed him. He would do anything for her.

"You've got to lose that." Dee pointed to Percival's beard. Behind her was a muscled man with powerful hands, introduced as a barber. Thirty minutes later, Percival had a smooth face and a simple, neat haircut. He donned fresh clothes, which rounded out his feeling of renewal.

The housekeeper shooed him toward the solar, complaining about the menagerie of six-legged critters Percival had imported. He countered that he had driven the invasion into the sewers. An acrid smell of bleach replaced him when he left the bedroom.

In the solar, Lancelot greeted Percival and Dee with honey wine. The dame knight was dressed in comfortable trousers and a form-fitting tunic and belt that set off her broad shoulders. She'd showered and tied back her hair. Dee was less athletic but no less striking in her casual pants and blouse. Her hair was deep red with brown low-lights, giving away her status, apart from her gender, as Percival's fraternal twin. His hair, in contrast, was a fiery red, said to be the same red as his dead father's.

Percival recalled the last time he saw Dee, the day his expedition departed Camelot. Each had fought back tears as they waved their goodbyes because they had relied on each other in the years after arriving at the city. Before an invitation to Camelot by the king himself, they'd grown up on their mother's land far enough from the capital to feel sheltered from the intrigues at court and the teeming masses of the lower town. Nothing important was said, done, or decided by either without a quick check with their twin.

Lancelot became a close friend to both after Percival graduated the military academy known as The Keep. "I'm glad to see you reunited. I've been meaning to ask you something."

"Yes?" Dee said.

"Your mother Eleanor named you 'Dindrane.'"

"That's how I sign my name," Dee said.

"But Percival calls you 'Dee.'"

"That's because she hates her name," Percival said. "When we were kids, I teased her once with 'Plain Jane Dindrane' and she ran away crying. After she slapped me, I never called her that again. She told me to call her 'Dee'."

Dee laughed. "You know how some names just seem to fit a personality? 'Dindrane' was unadventurous and flat. 'Dee' had more energy."

"I've seen that energy in action. Be sure to show Percival some of your recent paintings."

"'Perce.'"

"What?" Lancelot tilted her head.

"That's what I call him. No one else has that privilege."

Percival face flushed. "You didn't exactly ask permission."

"Well, then," Lancelot said. "You're fortunate to have such a tolerant sibling, Dee."

The housekeeper, who also cooked Lancelot's meals when she had guests, invited them to the table. Pangs of hunger nearly overwhelmed Percival, though he'd eaten good camp food on the way back to Camelot. Lancelot's table was laid out with simple, but tasty dishes: farmed salmon, fresh vegetables from the community garden, and another carafe of the amber-colored wine. He thought twice, though, before reaching for the bread. It was a huge rustic loaf flanked by a bowl of butter.

“I thought there was a shortage of wheat,” Percival said.

Lancelot noted Percival's reticence. “Most people in the upper city keep a reserve of flour these days. The better-off families in the lower town do the same.”

“What about the riots?”

“The poor, the ones who can't afford a reserve. Or much else.”

“And Arturus won't feed them?”

“Believe me,” Lancelot sighed, “The arguments at the Round Table are endless.”

“Students at the university are agitating for the release of more grain reserves to keep bread prices affordable.” Dee kept her eyes down out of respect for Lancelot in her own house.

Percival assumed Lancelot was less sympathetic to the students than Dee, who had close ties to the school community.

“This is why finding the Grail is so important, and getting more important by the day.” Lancelot finished off her wine. “Society is getting more unstable. It's fine to put more grain in the hands of the people, but we need to get the Great Machine working again and set the climate to rights. That's the long-term solution.”

“And what if we don't find it?” Dee said. “Maybe it's gone forever?”

Percival shook his head. “I don't believe that. I know it's out there.”

“But you didn't find it,” Dee said. “Maybe it's been lost. Maybe we have to adjust to new circumstances.”

“Let's hope not,” Lancelot said. “The sage-scientists say the results of failure would be disastrous. Millions of deaths, for one thing. The end of our way of life, if you can believe them.”

“I saw its resting place, but it was gone.” Percival's eyes glowed with intensity. “We were betrayed. I'm certain of it. I have evidence. Hard evidence you can hold in your hand.”

“That's what you've been saying since I found you, Percival, but you haven't offered me any details.” Lancelot's eyes were hooded. “You'll see Arturus in the morning. Your story better be good.”

"I'm sorry, Lancelot. I'm so grateful for your rescue, but I feel that I need to tell my story to the king himself before anyone else."

"Don't you trust me?"

"I'm not sure whom to trust. Fully, anyway."

"Not even your twin sister?" Dee said.

"You could never betray Camelot, Dee. Of all people, I know that you'll let me do this my way."

CHAPTER 3: A HURRIED EXPEDITION

Lancelot anticipated a tense moment with Arturus as she and Percival exited the black staff car in front of the palace. Viridiae's elected king was running out of options to find the Grail and save the country, and when he called one of his closest advisors for advice, he expected an immediate answer. When Arturus had summoned Lancelot earlier in the week, she was unreachable. He was incensed, said lower-level courtiers. Lancelot hoped the fallout wouldn't color this morning's meeting with him and the newly returned adventurer.

The royal steward announced the two knights to the gathering in a spacious reception hall. Heavy drapes like hooded eyes cut the window light by half. Arturus and his aides huddled over a map of North America spread on a square table. Viridiae and its thrice-as-large neighbor, the Lucian Empire, dominated the geography, with a half-dozen petty states on the edges to the north and south. Under ordinary circumstances, Lancelot could approach a similar gathering as an equal with minimal ceremony. However, she was in the doghouse, and she waited for recognition.

A few in the group greeted Lancelot with a silent nod, but a full two minutes passed before Arturus lifted his eyes from the map. Arturus had heard the steward's introduction, but he deliberately waited as a kind of message to his servant. His choleric attitude signaled a subtler idea. Lancelot saw Arturus once or twice a week, and each time, the king's appearance alarmed her. Arturus' face was wan, his skin sallow. His illness had sapped him. Almost a decade had passed since she pledged fealty and service to the king, days after his election to Viridiae's throne. Then, he was tall, strong, with luxuriant hair that fell to his shoulders in braids. Today—

"Did you find it, Dame Lancelot?" Arturus spoke while shifting his eyes to a tablet.

"I'm sorry, my lord?"

"The questing beast. That's what you were chasing when we summoned you, correct?"

"Yes, my lord, I was after the beast, but I found only signs." A white lie would save Lancelot the trouble of a long explanation.

"If you weren't one of my best knights and my friend, you'd be out of a job."

"Yes, sir." Lancelot cleared her throat, and motioned Percival to her side. "If I may, sir, I found something else."

"Sir Percival." Arturus' skeptical look at Lancelot switched to a warm grin for Percival. He extended his hand, a signal for the red-haired knight to approach. Percival stepped forward, dropped gracefully to one knee, and kissed Arturus' signet ring. The overnight transformation from walking wounded to confident soldier impressed Lancelot. Arturus touched Percival on the shoulder, urging him to his feet. "We are indeed glad to see you."

"As are we all, my lord." Mordred Lothian's basso voice filled the high-ceiling room. The other advisors' faces tightened.

Percival eyed Mordred. "My lord king, thank you for seeing me at this early hour. I fear I must report to you—"

Arturus raised his hand. "I'm sorry, Percival, I'll have to postpone our discussion. I know you are anxious to discuss the results of your expedition, but we are at an important moment."

Percival pressed forward. "I see that you are about to mount another expedition to find the Grail. I feel that you must—"

Mordred interrupted. "I'm sure His Majesty will forgive your presumptuousness, Sir Percival, given your physical and mental state after your ordeal."

The red-haired knight glared at the king's prime minister.

Lancelot feared for the youth. Mordred was as close to an heir as Arturus had. The black-haired, handsome son of one of Viridiae's most powerful women, Morgause, did not take challenges lightly.

"I'm surprised Lancelot didn't tell you, Percival," Arturus said.

"Sir?" Lancelot was uncertain what he meant.

"It's in the briefing paper for this meeting. Didn't you read it?"

Lancelot admitted she had not. Lancelot hated reading reports, though she usually looked at the executive summary before a senior staff meeting.

"Chasing magical creatures is a high priority," Mordred said, turning up a corner of his thin, sarcastic mouth. "We've received fresh intelligence. The Grail may be in the far northwest on an island known as 'Koda.'"

"The new expedition already planned to look in the region," Arturus said. "We've sped up the timeline. It's going to the island immediately."

Percival looked at Lancelot doubtfully, then addressed Arturus. "Sir, we were certain about the Grail's location when my expedition departed. However, the information proved—"

Mordred interrupted again. "This new information is extremely reliable, Sir Percival. The Regarder Order is our best network. Your information was of lower quality."

"We have to follow every lead, Percival," Arturus said. "The fate of Viridiae depends on it. It's unfortunate that your expedition failed, perhaps due to faulty information."

"There's more to it than that, sir."

Lancelot wanted to caution Percival, but the young knight was determined.

"I'm worried about—"

"An investigation will begin immediately," Mordred said.

"I would appreciate it if you did not interrupt me, Lord Mordred."

Lancelot touched Percival's arm.

"Enough," Arturus said. "Sir Galahad's expedition leaves today. I'll see it off in two hours. All of you will join me at the departure ceremony to wish it success."

Lancelot, Percival, Mordred, and the other advisors bowed as Arturus left the room. The dame knight breathed out.

* * *

Lancelot escorted Percival to a crowded private lunchroom where they met Dindrane. Like Percival, she was a member of the King's Household, a large, but selective list of citizens Arturus thought worthy of special access. Connections helped. The twins' mother, Eleanor, was an old friend of Arturus before he became king. She also interned in the entourage of Arturus' mother, the old queen, before she died.

Dindrane picked at a salad of apple cubes, raisins, and yogurt. "Mordred has a stick up his ass," she said after hearing her brother describe his encounter.

Percival growled. "Do you still think Mordred is the handsomest man in the kingdom?"

"He's ugly as sin." Dindrane did not meet her brother's eye.

Lancelot stopped herself from laughing out loud. "Careful, Ms Rathkeale! It's sometimes better to speak the truth in whispers."

"He's got something against me," Percival said. "He said there'd be an investigation. What is he talking about?"

"Standard procedure whenever there's a disaster like yours, Percival," Lancelot said.

"Does Mordred think I did something wrong?"

"Remember what I said about a target on your back? I'd say he wants to make sure you get just enough credit for surviving, but nothing more. He doesn't want any heroes competing with him for Arturus' attention."

"A reporter came knocking on my door this morning," Dindrane said. "Looking for Percival."

Lancelot watched Percival's face grow pained, as if the ordeal of the past few months was catching up with him. He should be wolfing down his shepherd's pie, Lancelot thought. Instead, he seemed as sick as Arturus.

"I'm sorry, Dee," he said.

Dindrane shrugged. "I was interviewed a few months ago, before my first big gallery show. I can handle the media."

Lancelot sighed. She remembered having that much confidence when she was Dindrane's age. "What did you tell them?"

"Only that Percival was reporting to the king today. The reporter kept asking if I knew what happened on the expedition." Dindrane bit into an avocado sandwich.

"And you said..."

"The truth. He wants to talk to His Majesty first."

Lancelot studied a screen on the wall of the lunchroom. It showed a live feed from one of the com networks, including preparations for the ceremony. The sound was off, but the crawl mentioned Percival's visit to the palace and a "secret meeting" with Arturus. Lancelot folded her arms and considered the situation: Another expedition had failed, with Mordred saying, "I told you so," in so many words. He would use the investigation to find a sacrificial lamb. He would use any scandal or perceived scandal to his advantage. Percival needed protection. "If either of you are approached by media people again, refer them to the royal communications office."

"Okay."

Lancelot collected her plate and utensils. "If Dee's finished with her salad, let's go out to the square and see how the preparations for the new expedition are going."

Lancelot, Percival, and Dee followed a stream of people heading for the main square in front of the palace, which served as the venue for all of Viridiae's major civic ceremonies, from coronations to annual celebrations of the end of the civil war that created the nation. Opposite the palace was the cavernous structure that hosted sessions of the elected and appointed Knights of the Round Table. Administrative offices and military headquarters took up the two other sides of the public space. Banners, draped and flying, decorated the buildings. Thousands of spectators from the upper city and the lower town mingled, while armed militia watched from strategic points. Drones with cameras floated high enough to appear benign, like disturbed pigeons. Security was always tight for these events, out of caution against Lucian agents.

Lancelot had no role in the preparations, though she was treated with respect and deference, given her position and closeness to Arturus. Scattered applause from the crowd greeted her. Others commented on Percival's gaunt aspect in whispers. Dindrane was a cipher to most people, except for connoisseurs of visual arts, and intimates who knew about her esoteric powers.

Lancelot liked visibility and wanted to show support for her king and his policies. And she wanted to support her son Galahad, even as she felt nervous at his impending departure. Too many expeditions had departed, never to return, or with only one or two survivors returning. Galahad had never led an expedition prior to this one.

Sir Galahad du Lac-Corbenic touched his cheek to Lancelot's. “Madam, I'm glad you came.” The gesture was friendly, if not entirely loving. The knight, dressed in his father's family livery for the occasion, dismissed a pair of assistants. “I'm very busy right now. Do you have a question?”

“I wanted to introduce you to Sir Percival and his sister Dindrane,” Lancelot said. “I think the three of you were born the same year.”

Galahad greeted Percival with a wide smile. “I admire your survival skills, Sir Percival, though I'm sorry that none of your colleagues made it back. Is there something I should know before we depart?”

Percival straightened his back. “I wish you the best of luck, Sir Galahad.” Percival bit his lip. “I wish I could say more right here, but—” He glanced at the crowd. “—there are too many ears who should not hear.”

Lancelot and her son exchanged looks, and her anxiety spiked. Why didn't Percival want to share what he knows, if there are dangers? Instead of objecting, she told Galahad a brief version of how she'd found Percival, though she left out Percival's rambling about some kind of betrayal. “Percival's sense of duty is single-minded."

"He's just stubborn," Dindrane said.

"A pleasure to meet you as well, Miss," Galahad bowed slightly. "I'm sorry I won't be able to see your new work at the Viridian Arts Society, at least until I get back."

Dindrane smiled. "I'll give you a private showing, especially if you discover the Grail."

"I'm hoping your sources are dependable, Galahad," Lancelot said.

"My informants," Galahad said, "are confirming what Mordred and his Regarders have learned about the Grail's location."

"The Regarders sent us on a wild goose chase!" Percival's blurted declaration caught the group by surprise, including himself. After saying the words, he seemed to shrink into himself. Dindrane took his arm. "I'm sorry," Percival said, "I shouldn't have said that."

Speaking low to avoid the ears of casual gossips, Galahad said, "I'm afraid of the same thing, my friend, but the best evidence now points to the north and the island." He shrugged. "I'm obliged by Arturus to try."

"I wish I were going with you," Percival said.

"You're in no condition to travel anywhere," Dindrane objected, "much less a godforsaken island."

"If you were a little stronger, Sir Percival, I'd welcome you on our journey," Galahad said. "Your lovely sister is correct, though. And unfortunately, I have to say goodbye for now. The ceremony starts in ten minutes."

Lancelot received a message broadcast over the com network asking people to move behind portable barricades. A voice announcement followed. Trumpeters appeared on a palace balcony. After a brief fanfare, three mounted knights, one of them Galahad, all in polished armor, rode into the square in front of the balcony. All had ceremonial lances with large pennants. A group of 20 or so solemn men and women followed on foot. They lined up a few paces behind the riders. At a barked order, the knights lowered their lances in salute, and the retinue bowed their heads. The trumpeters blew another fanfare, and Arturus appeared, along with Mordred and others. Lancelot wondered if she ought to be on the balcony with her king, but she wanted to say good hunting to her son.

At a distance of more than hundred meters, Arturus appeared tall and strong. He was dressed in a light coat, though the sun made the plaza warm. He spoke of heroic journeys, the legacy of past generations who had built Viridiae and its society after centuries of chaos, and of the expedition's mission: to secure the future of their nation, their children, and their children's children. "The Grail will be found, and Viridiae will fulfill its destiny as a protector of the earth."

With that, he waved in blessing, and the trumpets sounded a third time.

The mounted riders, Galahad included, raised their lances, and turned toward the square's main entrance, which led to the eastern gate, where the supply wagons were parked. With Percival and Dindrane beside her, Lancelot watched as the short parade of adventurers marched by. As Galahad passed and he nodded in respect, if not love, to his mother, their eyes met. Lancelot felt a sharp pain in her breast. Had she done the right thing, a quarter-century ago? What if she'd decided to raise him, she thought, as most women would? The old doubts persisted, even though she dismissed them every time they came up. Galahad was a beautiful young man and a proud knight. His father and grandfather had done a wonderful job.

A moment later, the parade was gone. "Come, Percival," Lancelot said. "The king is waiting."

CHAPTER 4: A PIN AS EVIDENCE

Lancelot planned Percival's interception of Arturus in the palace as if she were laying an ambush. Earlier in the morning, Arturus put off a discussion of Percival's expedition, but neither he nor his courtiers had suggested a date or time. Percival's outburst in the courtyard was far more than a symptom of exhaustion. With Percival and Dindrane behind her, Lancelot hurried along the ancient dressed sandstone corridors she'd patrolled as a freshly minted soldier 20 years previous. Running up a flight of marble stairs, waiting at the landing for her guests to catch up, she heard Arturus' voice around a corner. He appeared, trailed by Mordred and a few others, including Gawain, Mordred's brother.

"What a pleasant surprise, my lord!" Lancelot lied. "I was just showing off some of the palace's architectural features."

Arriving a second or two later, Percival gasped for breath. Dindrane removed her jacket.

Arturus appeared confused, then his visage softened, as if he discerned Lancelot's true purpose. "The citadel's history is even more interesting, Lancelot. The original stronghold was made of wood, but my grandfather had it rebuilt of stone. The nine turrets represent the nine provinces. I grew up playing Knights and Lucians there."

Mordred's gaze lingered on Dindrane. She gave no hint of whether she'd noticed.

"Which reminds me, Majesty," Lancelot said, "Percival is quite anxious to make his report to you about his expedition."

"I already said there would be an investigation," Mordred said, dragging his attention away from Dindrane.

Arturus lifted his hand. “I can hear from him informally. We were just on our way to my private office. Percival, if you're up to it, we can talk. You can join us, Lancelot.”

Lancelot bowed, along with her companions. She indicated Percival's sister. “This young lady is Dindrane Rathkeale, Percival's sister.”

“Yes, I remember. A pleasure to see you again, Ms Rathkeale.”

Dindrane bowed slightly at the waist.

“It would be a great favor to me, my lord, if Dindrane could join us,” Lancelot said. “She is caring for her brother as he recovers.”

The twins exchanged glances.

“Very well,” Arturus said. “Mordred, you should listen in.”

“Happily, sir.” Mordred's smile was forced.

Percival coughed. “Sir, I'd prefer a private discussion.”

Arturus dismissed the demand. “Mordred is a trusted adviser. His Regarders will be in charge of the investigation, so he will want to know your story as well.”

Percival lowered his eyes, relenting.

“That said, let's keep the crowd to a minimum, shall we, Lord Mordred?”

Mordred whispered to his brother, and Gawain departed, lips parted in a sneer.

Arturus' private office was intimate and friendly. Printed books on polished wooden shelves gave the room an intellectual air. The furniture was spare but comfortable. A large western window let in the day's fading sun. Dindrane was drawn to a light tapestry on the wall opposite Arturus' massive desk.

“My father's portrait was created by Ganieda, Merlin's sister,” Arturus said.

“Yes, my lord, I know.” Dindrane spoke without turning Arturus' way. The hint of animation in Arturus II's features was meant to keep the viewer's attention. “Ganieda is my teacher.”

“Well, then perhaps one of your tapestries will grace our dreary palace's walls someday.”

Lancelot said, “Where is Professor Merlin, if I may ask?”

“My chief science advisor is where he ought to be, at the Great Machine in Apparatus Montis, trying to make it work without the Grail.”

“Is he making any progress?”

“None that he's reported to me.”

Lancelot wasn't surprised at Merlin's trouble. Although the Grail was a critical piece of hardware, no one fully understood how it worked within the Great Machine, nor how the Great Machine itself controlled the earth's climate, or more importantly, why it stopped controlling the climate after the Grail disappeared. The machine was like a spring-powered clock that had wound down. No one knew how to rewind it. Merlin and his researchers couldn't even recover the massive machine's true name from the ancient digital records, corrupted after a thousand years.

A steward brought in tea and coffee. Arturus invited everyone to sit on sofas and chairs surrounding a low, wooden table.

Arturus took a chair emblazoned with the royal crest, a stylized combination of eagle, salmon, and conifer cone. “Well, Sir Percival, I'm anxious to hear your tale, provided it's not too long.”

Percival sat on the edge of the sofa. He brought his hands together in supplication. “First, Majesty, please let me say that I take responsibility for the failure of the expedition. We reached our destination, but—”

“Relax, Sir Percival,” Arturus said gently. “No one is blaming you, least of all me.”

“With respect, sir,” Mordred said as he leaned back on the sofa, his right leg crossed over his left, “we should reserve judgment until the investigation is complete.”

Dindrane cradled a cup of tea.

Arturus rested his elbows on his knees, his hands folded, as if in prayer. “Percival, tell me the story.”

“Sir Kevin Pacifica's expedition was a disaster from day one. I think he suspected black magic played a part in what happened.”

Percival looked at Mordred. Lancelot got the hint. Mordred's mother, Morgause, was rumored to practice the darker arts of the theurgist.

"Horses went lame, wagons broke axles, communications equipment failed, and nearly all of the 25-member party fell ill." Percival glanced at his hands. "Everyone felt a nagging sense of unease, as if we'd forgotten something important back in Camelot."

Mordred interrupted. "Perhaps if we had listened to the Regarders' skeptical evaluation of Sir Kevin's evidence for the Grail's location, we might have avoided a disaster."

"Now who's prejudging, Sir Mordred?" Lancelot said.

"Go on, Percival," Arturus urged.

A tap on a side door stopped the young knight from continuing. A woman of exquisite beauty and grace stepped in. At least, that's how Lancelot viewed her. Any time Guinevere entered a room, Lancelot felt a surge of energy that made her breathe faster. Everyone in the room rose to their feet.

"I'm sorry for interrupting your meeting, my lord husband, but I haven't seen you since returning from my family's demesne three days ago." Guinevere acknowledged the others in the room with a warm glance.

Arturus eyes sparkled, and he reached out to her. "I'm so very sorry, dear love. The preparations for Galahad's Grail expedition took every minute of my time. Did you receive my messages?"

"I did, but nothing compares to your kiss in the morning."

Lancelot knew that kiss as well, but when she witnessed the ordinary, even chaste expression of Guinevere's affection for Arturus, she felt as if a spear pierced her heart. The pain was all the greater because Guinevere had confided to her that while Arturus was a good husband and king, Guinevere reserved her passion for Lancelot.

"It's a pleasure to see all of you again, including you, Ms Rathkeale," Guinevere said.

"I'm honored, my lady." Dee beamed at the recognition.

"May I listen in, husband?" Guinevere said.

"Of course, dear love. I'll ask you for your views later, if you don't mind."

Guinevere agreed. Her family was one of the most powerful in Viridiae, though it had lost everything in the civil wars nearly a century before. She was widely regarded as an insightful politician, and she influenced all of Arturus' important decisions. Cynics claimed she turned his decisions to benefit her self-interest, which weren't always the same as Arturus'.

Percival continued his story. Lancelot, however, could not concentrate, even as the young knight described weeks of pouring rain in the mountains, a desert crossing that killed most of the animals, and a month of losing their way in badlands. Instead of listening, Lancelot fought the urge to drink in Guinevere's scent. Her heart hammered with a desire to touch her, even if it was just a handshake or a brush of her arm. Lancelot prayed her face didn't flush as she recalled their last encounter in Guinevere's bed. Lancelot shook her head to break the spell.

Mordred cleared his throat. "Are you alright, Lancelot?"

"I'm sorry. I have a slight headache."

Percival described signs of Lucian patrols. The party feared an ambush. "Our water was gone, and our food was gone. We were just about to decide to turn back, when we met a fit man with bronze skin and a broad face who spoke a language unlike any I've heard. He knew some Folk Tongue, and he offered to take us to a local hamlet, where we traded most of our working electronics for supplies."

"Go on," Arturus said.

"We explained our purpose, and he told us he had met another, smaller group of 'people from the west.' That's what he called them."

"That's odd," Guinevere said. "There are no other expeditions, at least from Viridiae."

"They were also looking for the Grail. He'd encountered them a week before."

"Really," Mordred reminded Lancelot of a diplomat who knew all the details of a secret treaty but was obliged to fake ignorance.

"Did he say more about these western people?"

"Only that they resembled us in clothing, manners, language, and electronics." Percival's excitement mounted. "But Majesty, I haven't told you the most important thing. The bronze man, whose name was 'Napayshni,' said he had guided the other group to a cave deep in the badlands. He'd been to the cave before, and said it was nothing special, but the group appeared quite interested. He took them there. They thanked him and gave him some money. Napaynshni shrugged and left. A day or two later, he began to worry about them. He went back to the cave, but they were gone."

Mordred frowned. "Majesty, I'm not sure this anecdote is meaningful. We know that the Lucians are looking for the Grail. It's also possible a private Viridian expedition passed through the area."

"Aren't all Viridian expeditions supposed to get approval, Lord Mordred?" Guinevere said.

"Indeed."

Percival eyed Mordred suspiciously. "Lord Mordred, Napayshni was told to expect us. He was paid to keep a secret."

Lancelot began to understand what Percival had meant by a betrayal.

"Interesting." Arturus rested his chin on his knuckles.

"I'm certain," Percival added, "that the other group knew about us. They may have shadowed us part of the way to the badlands. Maybe all the way from Camelot."

"That is pure speculation," Mordred said.

"What did you do next, Percival?" Arturus said.

"We asked Napayshni to take us to the cave. It was large enough to shelter two or three people. A narrow shaft in the back led into darkness."

"Sounds like an old mine," Lancelot observed. "Possibly a gold or silver mine."

"You obviously did not find the Grail." Arturus didn't hide his disappointment, though the fact wasn't news.

"No, sir, but the other group was sloppy. Their latrine was

unburied and garbage was piled in a corner. The food wrappings were Viridian. They came, or they were at least supplied, by people here."

"I'm skeptical, my lord," Mordred said. "What would a competing expedition have to gain?"

Lancelot laughed. "I'm shocked, Mordred. Haven't you heard of fame, glory, riches, and other kinds of nonsense?"

Guinevere turned the conversation back to the subject. "Did you document all this, Percival?"

"I have photos and video, my lady."

"Where is this evidence?" Mordred demanded.

"I've hidden it on the com network, sir."

Lancelot gained new respect for Percival, who'd taken precautions against enemies who might discredit him. He was an intelligent young man.

Mordred was incensed. "I insist you turn over this evidence immediately to the Regarders. This could turn into a criminal matter."

"Against whom, my lord Mordred?" Guinevere said. "Sir Percival, who ought to be hailed as a hero?"

"You'll get your evidence in due time, Mordred," Arturus said as he studied Percival. "Did you find any more information on the Grail. That's the important thing."

Percival sagged. "No, I'm sorry, sir." He breathed out. "There is one more thing, my lord, but I fear..."

"You have nothing to be afraid of, Sir Percival, if you are telling the truth."

"I asked for a private meeting. I'd like to repeat that."

Mordred's eyes flashed.

"Noted, my young friend. Please continue."

"We found something that troubled us more than anything." Percival reached into a pocket and removed an object wrapped in a dusty cloth. He unfolded the cloth, revealing a polished cloak pin the size of a large coin. The pin was decorated with the Lothian family crest.

The group stared at the pin in shock. After a deep breath in and out, Arturus broke the silence. “Well, Mordred, what do you make of it?”

“I'm not sure what you mean,” the Prince of Lothia said evenly. “It's a cloak pin.”

“Don't you recognize it?”

“With all due respect, Majesty, the province of Lothia and my family's lands cover hundreds of thousands of hectares. A million people live under our jurisdiction.”

Percival gnashed his teeth. “I've seen this pin on some of your staff, Sir Mordred.”

Mordred reddened. “Sir Percival, you are skating on thin ice. Be careful what you say next.”

“It is a lovely pin, I must say.” Guinevere broke the tension. “Plain, but well-made.”

Lancelot added, “I've seen them in Camelot's marketplaces, mostly in the lower town. They're made by the hundreds in Lothia. Isn't that correct, Mordred?”

“Indeed, Dame Lancelot.” Mordred relaxed, thankful for the cover.

In contrast, Percival eyes lit on everyone in the room, even Dee. He pointed at the pin. “This is evidence of treason!”

“Stop right there, Sir Percival,” Arturus held up his hands.

“But sir—”

“This is evidence of nothing, except that someone who owned it was careless and dropped it.”

“You mean they walked all the way to the badlands in the middle of the continent and dropped this as if it were trash?”

Arturus stood up, his face as stern as the stone walls of the palace. “This meeting is over. I thank you, Percival, for bringing your story back. You will turn over your records to the Regarders and follow their further instructions.”

Dee slipped her arm under her brother's.

“I'll take that.” Mordred reached for the pin.

Percival snatched his hand away. His face was full of contempt for the prime minister. “Not until I get a signed order requesting it. Until then, I'll keep it safe with me.”

“Gentlemen,” Guinevere said. “Our country has enough troubles. Let's allow the process to go forward. The truth will come out.” She addressed Arturus. “My husband, you look tired.”

Arturus's palm rested on his forehead, as if he'd come down with Lancelot's feigned headache. He looked at his queen as if he wanted to speak, but couldn't, because of the other people in the room. Guinevere took his hand and led him through a private door to their residence.

Lancelot put her hand on Percival's shoulder in reassurance. Mordred, however, faced the young knight down.

“You came within a millimeter of crossing a line, Percival. You do not want to be my enemy.”

Percival did not blink, but Lancelot feared that his exhaustion might undermine his judgment. “Don't you have someone to harass or arrest or something, Mordred?”

The head of the Regarders Order narrowed his eyes at Lancelot before he departed with a last glance at Dee.

Percival closed his eyes. Dee drew him closer.

“I lied, Percival,” Lancelot said. “At least, I didn't speak the whole truth.”

“I don't understand.”

“I meant it when I said that I had seen hundreds of these pins in the markets. Most of those are iron, or pewter.”

Percival studied the pin again.

“Yours is high-quality silver,” Lancelot said. “The Lothian family gives these to trusted servants as rewards. They're uncommon, and they're unlikely to find their way into just anyone's hands.”

Percival nodded.

“Something happened out there, Percival. And it originated in Viridiae, maybe even here in the palace.” Lancelot wasn't willing to say what she was thinking about Mordred or the Lothian clan.

CHAPTER 5: A FATHER DISCOVERED

After the briefing, Dee was stopped in the vestibule outside Arturus' office by an aide to Guinevere. The aide handed Dee a message: *Please take Sir Percival to my personal physician for an examination immediately. I have sent word to her. I am concerned about your brother's health.* Dee felt the same way, but her brother had that useless pride that required young men like him to suffer through anything without complaint. In reality, he could barely keep himself standing. He eyed a chair against the wall with envy, as if he wanted to prevent an embarrassing collapse but didn't want to show weakness. Dee thought his attitude pretentious.

"The queen is ordering you to the doctor." Exaggeration might persuade her brother, Dee gambled.

"She doesn't have any authority over me. I report to—"

"Don't be stubborn, Perce. Anyone can see you're ill."

"But I've never met her before today. Why would she care?"

Dee didn't have an answer. Guinevere had a reputation for generosity, but Dee's mother warned that altruism in the palace was rare as hen's teeth. A member of an ancient Viridian family, Guinevere maneuvered for influence and allies. Offering a service was a way of investing in the future. "She thinks you're brave, Perce. She likes you."

Brother and sister arrived at the clinic that served the palace compound. A nurse ushered Dee and Percival into an exam room. Percival rested on a padded table with his shirt off.

"I'm sorry, Dee."

"What for?"

"When we came to Camelot, you told me I would find the Grail."

Dee had several dreams over many months that featured Percival presenting an otherworldly object to Arturus. Ganieda, her mentor, interpreted the object as the Grail, though no one could be sure with dreams. A purely symbolic analysis was acceptable —a desire for a higher plane of existence, for example—but Percival took the interpretation literally.

"I didn't dream you would find it on your expedition, only that you would find it someday." Dee wanted to encourage Percival, though his near-death experience argued for a more cautious view. "It's not as though you have to achieve all your goals this afternoon."

Percival's shoulders slumped, as if he carried the weight of the world. "I failed, Dee. I failed you. I failed the country. I failed the earth."

"Stop blaming yourself."

"Who else can I blame? I'm a knight. My job is to protect my people, my country, and the planet's biosphere. We need the Grail back in its place in the Great Machine. I didn't do my job. I left people to die."

Before Dee could object, a middle-aged woman with a kind but imperious air introduced herself. She examined Percival from head to toe, impressing Dee with her thoroughness. After consulting Percival's medical records, the doctor pronounced Percival healthy, but underweight and suffering extreme fatigue. She also suspected an incipient case of delayed-stress illness. She prescribed immediate rest.

"I don't need any rest." Percival climbed into a public car at the end of the appointment. Dee couldn't afford it, but her brother was dead on his feet. "I have a job to do."

"You're making things worse for yourself, Perce."

"I should be with Galahad. He'll need my help."

She steadied her brother as he stepped like an old man up the one flight of stairs to his apartment near The Keep. She wondered why Perce was so keen on killing himself. Perhaps his devotion kept him going when everyone around him died. Guilt might be a factor, too, going back to their adolescence.

Dee knew she was now in charge of her brother, at least until he recovered from his ordeal. She could call on Mother for help, but she was several days travel away, and Percival might recover by then. Or he might not. Her throat caught in a panic. How could she nurse Percival, complete her commissions, and follow the disciplines Ganieda demanded? She couldn't just set aside her life because Percival was sick. She stopped herself, remorseful for complaining, albeit silently, about a temporary inconvenience. She loved her brother more than anyone in the world, maybe even her mother, but she had her own life to run, a life growing more complicated by the day. She allowed herself a little resentment, as long as she kept it in an emotional compartment with the key hidden.

Percival's apartment was cold and dank as a tomb. While he was away, Dee had checked it every couple of weeks, watering the single houseplant given as a housewarming present by their mother. She paid the rent and the bills, though she shut off the heat. Fortunately, the bed had clean sheets and a pair of blankets. She helped Percival remove his clothes, and he was asleep as soon as his head touched the pillow.

The cooler was empty and the cupboard bare, save for a few cans of soup. On her com, she ordered two fresh apple pies for delivery, one for herself and one for Percival. She brewed chamomile tea in case Percival needed it for sleep. He wouldn't touch his pie until the morning, but a day-old pie was as good as fresh from the oven for him. That was one difference between them; Dee hated leftovers or stale food.

She messaged her roommate, saying she planned to stay the night at her brother's place. That wasn't unusual. Dee was without a lover, a state she found exhilarating, given the tawdry romantic dramas she witnessed among her peers. She wouldn't mind a little time for herself to think.

In the course of undressing Percival, she'd pocketed the pin with the Lothian crest, and now she examined it. The eye of the mythical creature was a small blue sapphire. Whoever had lost this pin was probably frantic to have it back, if only because of its beauty. Dee thought back on Mordred's denial of its importance, and she marked Percival's skepticism. Mordred was a handsome man and a patron of several artists in Dee's circle. A purchase by him saved more than one artist from an eviction or bankruptcy. His power, though, made him dangerous. Though she brushed off his inquisitive look in the hall before the meeting, she remembered it, and she couldn't help feeling pleased. She didn't need a man to boost her ego, but it didn't hurt when one admired you.

The pies arrived, and Dee ate while catching up on the news. The main story was Galahad's expedition, which had already suffered minor setbacks. Galahad said the breakdowns and oversights were expected, and they wouldn't affect the expedition's progress. Dee shut off her tablet and found a nightdress she kept in Percival's apartment for emergencies. She slept there occasionally to get away from the pressures of life. Crawling into bed beside her brother, she listened for his breathing. A tiny shudder reassured her he was still alive.

How many times growing up did they comfort each other after a fight with their mother or during a raging storm? They would talk for hours, puzzling out their problems. Throughout their lives, one question hung over them: What happened to their father? It was eventually answered, evidenced by a dark shape on a table in one corner of the bedroom. Ambient light from the street made it visible, though it was little more than a shadow. Their father's helmet, crimson red in daylight, but black as jet in the corner of the bedroom, was a reminder of their first, and last, encounter.

* * *

Dee rose with the first hint of morning light. She did not feel rested. Images crammed her mind most of the night, preventing restful sleep. Percival looked as if he'd hardly moved after laying down his head. Dee showered, dressed in spare clothes, and ate a light breakfast of yogurt and fruit. She had an early appointment with Ganieda.

Few people walked the streets of Camelot in the minutes before dawn. Ganieda lived in a modest townhouse in an older section of the lower town near one of the city's first stone gates. She turned the large shed in her back garden, carefully tended with flower beds and fruit trees, into an art studio. For Dee, it doubled as a classroom for learning the arts of theurgy.

The elderly Ganieda was a few years older than her brother Merlin. Dee had known Ganieda for five years, ever since her sophomore year in college. Dee thought Ganieda was ancient then, but she saw an accelerating pace of decline. Other people marked the change in elderly relatives, and even middle-aged parents, since the loss of the Grail. Arturus seemed to age by the day, but people said it was the stress of kingship.

"Before you get back to your tapestry," Ganieda said, "it's time for your exercises."

Dee joined Ganieda on the pillows in a corner of the main room set aside for Gaia and her contemplation. The elder's joints creaked, but she managed to tuck her legs under her body, while Dee easily dropped into a comfortable cross-legged position. The exercise was part meditation, part visualization, part relaxation.

Over the years, the exercises had helped Dee accept her abilities, even as she resented the luck that had given her those abilities. The Old Civilization had allowed people to modify their DNA to please their vanity, and the consequence echoed a thousand years later. As she developed a newly discovered talent for tapestry art, she channeled her dark energy into creating visual pieces that stunned audiences. Over time, Ganieda had showed her how to balance darkness with positive forces, as well as the practical techniques of color weaving.

Ganieda had done the same with Dee's mother, before the rape ended Eleanor's ambitions.

After the exercises were done, Ganieda asked Dee to remain

with her in front of the shrine to Gaia. "You're troubled, my dear."

"I didn't sleep well last night, that's all."

"How is your brother?"

Dee shrugged. "Resting."

Ganieda rose from her pillows. Her house dress swished on the wooden floor. She poured hot water over a tea strainer. She handed the cup to Dee. "Your dream returned, I take it."

Ganieda's perception always shocked Dee, as if the old woman could read her thoughts. Dee nodded. "It's more like a memory, because it really happened."

"I want you to tell me every detail. The tea will help."

"I've told you the story a hundred times."

Ganieda lifted her finger, which Dee knew was a sign to obey.

Dee sighed. "It always starts the same. A powerfully built man named Brenin comes to my mother's house unannounced. He's riding a strong horse and wearing simple traveling clothes. He says he's going to meet my father Sir Adnan deGrosse. Brenin seems to know us, including Mother, but I've never seen him before."

"Eleanor kept you and your brother apart from society in that cottage after she found out she was pregnant by deGrosse. It must've been lonely, just you, Percival, and your mother."

"Sometimes," Dee said. "But Percival and I loved playing in the forest. By the time Brenin came, when we were 15, we knew more about that area than Mother."

"And Brenin was different than other visitors."

"Yes. He had personal business with Sir Adnan, but he asked Mother permission to let Percival and I accompany him."

"How did you feel about that?"

"Very mixed feelings. Mother had always been vague about our father. She closed up whenever Percival or I asked about him. One day, Percival researched Sir Adnan, and found out he'd been exiled by Arturus II after raping a woman at court."

"That woman was your mother, and you were the children born of that awful event."

"Mother hated Sir Adnan. That was clear. But Percival and I were curious more than anything. We both wanted to go with Brenin. What children wouldn't want to meet their father, even if he was a criminal? Mother allowed us to go with Brenin, but she was terrified."

"Eleanor trusted Brenin. Go on."

Dee felt the tea doing its work. Whenever Ganieda wanted Dee to explore her emotions and memories more deeply than was possible with ordinary spiritual exercises, she gave her the tea, which was her own mix of rare herbs and forest fungi.

"After three days, Brenin, Percival and I reached a place Brenin called 'The Lake of Souls.' It's deep in the Range of Needles on the king's land. We followed the tarn's shore to a broad alluvial plain that resembled a sea of grass. We arrived late in the evening. Venus and Mars dimmed overhead. Percival and I pitched camp while Brenin scouted the area.

"Purple sky outlined the spires of the Range of Needles in the distance. Waves driven by the wind pressed against the lakeshore, which was the site of a major battle between Viridiae and the Lucian Empire 50 years before. I could feel the spirits of the dead. There were thousands of them, all wailing in sorrow.

"I remember talking with Brenin on our journey. He held something back in his conversations, I thought, a secret that might change my life, like a new variable in one of the calculus problems Mother gave us for practice. Brenin returned from his reconnaissance, and we slept. When I woke up, Brenin was gone."

"That must've been scary," Ganieda said.

"I remember being a little scared, but Brenin was so nice with us, looking out for Percival and I as if we were his children. He even spent an hour with Percival during the trip helping him with his javelin technique. Percival loved throwing that thing, and he was good at it. I never felt in danger from Brenin."

"Tell me more, Dee."

"We waited for Brenin until the sun rose above the mountains. The tension proved too much for Percival. He grabbed his javelin and headed toward the open plain. I went with him. Fifty meters from camp, my throat tightened, as if a prophecy was coming true. I heard a strange noise. Thunderheads crawled up the mountain slopes, undergirded by an ash-gray line of clouds that marched across the Lake of Souls' agitated surface, like a phalanx of soldiers. Shouts, at once angry and demanding, floated across the prairie. A shaft of sunlight pierced the broken overcast.

"I pointed to where the damp grass was pushed aside by a running horse. We followed it up a creek bank to a low rise and saw a knight on horseback. The horse was Brenin's. The mounted warrior was the same size as Brenin, but fully armored, helmeted, and he carried a compound lance. I thought back to the canvas-covered gear on the rump of Brenin's horse as we rode to the lake. The man shouted a challenge, but I couldn't make it out in detail. Percival and I crouched, edging toward Brenin, whose animal bellowed its eagerness for battle. Percival pushed down the grass obscuring our vision, and I saw the vulture.

"The featherless head of the dead-devouring bird crested the helmet of Brenin's enemy, an enormous man encased from head to toe in crimson armor. A broadsword was strapped to his saddle. The breath of his oily black, armored warhorse steamed the air ahead of him."

Under the influence of the tea, which enhanced her memories like a magnifying glass, Dee's hands grew sweaty and her muscles tensed. Ten years had passed, but the vision of that moment on the plain next to the Lake of Souls brought it into the present, as if it were happening to her again.

"You're safe with me, Dee. It's important that you remember every feeling, every word."

"Brenin called to the warrior. 'Sir Adnan deGrosse, I say again, surrender or I will kill you.'

"DeGrosse removed his helmet. I recognized him right away, even though Mother never showed us pictures. Percival had found a few on the com net. They were many years old, and they showed a young man with piercing eyes, a thin mouth, a thick neck, and hair like a solstice bonfire. He hadn't changed, except for his age and scars of battle.

“I looked at my brother's hair, a darker shade from our mother's side, but still an intense red. Mine is darker, closer to Mother's, but no one could mistake where we got the traits.

“DeGrosse seemed unaware of our presence. 'You are a liar,' he called out in a drum-like barotone. 'You call yourself Brenin, but that is not your name. Tell the truth, liar. Why are you here?'

“'For justice, long-delayed.'

“'Justice?' DeGrosse appeared puzzled. 'What are you talking about?'

“'For Eleanor Rathkeale.'

“DeGrosse grinned, teeth yellow but even. He worked his jaw, considering his response.

“'What about her? She's nothing to me.'

“I remember controlling my breath, as if I was meditating, but deGrosse's answer struck me as untrue. He was holding back his true feelings.

“For his part, Percival's fist strangled a clump of grass as he watched the confrontation.

“DeGrosse shifted in his saddle. 'That was fifteen, sixteen years ago, Brenin. I'm no lawyer, but the statute of limitations has run out. You're too late.'

“'For the law, but not for justice.'

“'You wanted her, too, as I remember. Still like her, eh? What did she promise you? What she wouldn't give you the first time?'

“My jaw dropped. Were Brenin and Mother more than acquaintances?

“'She's promised me nothing, deGrosse. On the other hand, I bear some of the burden of what happened after you assaulted her—'

“'Another lie! She asked for it.'

“Brenin's horse shook its head.

“'The king was weak,' deGrosse declared. 'I was wasting my time and treasure on him. Exile was the better option. Don't look that way at me, Brenin. What choice did I have? Rot in the citadel's bowels? Or be a free man?'

"Ganieda, my mother was—is—a woman with a powerful mind and soul. She was unafraid of deGrosse. She called him out in public and presented all the evidence, even the most personal details, fearing nothing for her reputation. It cost her most of her friends, though the old queen stood beside her. However, the old king, Arturus II, hesitated. DeGrosse was an unmatched warrior and popular among the people. Without waiting for Eleanor's accusation to play out in the courts, Arturus II banished the rapist. As Arturus' vassal, deGrosse accepted the sentence with no remorse or regret.

"'But you came back,' Brenin said on the plain next to the Lake of Souls. 'Why?'

"DeGrosse shrugged in his armor. 'A man gets homesick. My parents are dead. Most of my friends were killed in battle. I went to the Freezing Sea at the top of the world to kill Viridiae's enemies. But the people who sail that ocean are as cold as its water, and full of ingratitude.' DeGrosse shifted. 'Your turn, Brenin. Tell me why *you* are here.'

"'You are not welcome.'

"DeGrosse laughed. 'I'll tell you why you're here. You were complicit in the whitewash of what you call a crime and you're trying to make up for your stupidity.'

"Brenin ignored the provocation. 'If you come peaceably with me, and admit to your crimes, I'll use my influence to restore your good name. Viridiae still honors your service.'

"'Bow my head to you and the rest of your supplicants at Camelot? Not a chance.'

"'Do it for your children.'

"DeGrosse was perplexed. 'That woman's whelps? I've left a dozen across the continent. What are they to you?'

"As the men argued, I wanted to announce myself. I wanted to stand before DeGrosse and spit in his eye. Not only had he raped my mother, he'd ignored me and Percival, never taking responsibility for what he'd done. I held back though, gathering my strength. Something told me I'd need it. Thunder rolled down the mountains to the plain.

“'I am their protector,' Brenin said.

“DeGrosse slapped his thigh and guffawed. 'You'd find fewer lies in a brothel.'

“'I've met them. They are… what you could've been.'

DeGrosse hissed through his teeth. His horse stamped its hooves, sensing its master's agitation, or the unsettled darkness in the sky above it.

“Brenin said, 'Eleanor is willing to forgive you, if you acknowledge your children, pay for your crime, and leave her and her children alone.'

“Ganieda, I felt as if I'd been struck by one of the lightning bolts that flashed silently in the mountains. Mother had never suggested a compromise. Then I saw it. Mother feared for Brenin's life.

“'Why should I agree to this? I'm going to kill you, Brenin, just like I killed all the knights you sent against me.'

“I drew a breath. 'I know who Brenin is, Perce. I know what's going to happen.'

“'How?'

“'I just feel it. It's like it was always meant to happen, and I can see it before anyone else.'

“'What's going to happen?'

“'One of them will die.' I felt like a cat, still, quiet, ready to strike, but what would I do if...

“Brenin's horse moved a few paces left, then right, as if the mounted man struggled with a decision.

“'I am not the old king,' Brenin said. 'Times are different now. Viridiae is stronger. I may die here, but many will follow me. They will find you, Adnan deGrosse.'

“DeGrosse's expression twisted into a grimace. 'You'll die like all the lackeys you sent against me. Get ready!' DeGrosse donned his helmet, closed his visor, lowered his lance, and charged.

“Brenin did the same.

“The two warriors met with a crash, and Brenin was unhorsed. A kilometer distant, a thunderstorm broke with a bolt of lightning cloud to ground. DeGrosse, still mounted, reeled from Brenin's blow. As his challenger lay sprawled on the grass, deGrosse paused to catch his breath. His destrier pawed the ground, eager to run. Collecting himself, deGrosse lowered his lance and his horse leaped forward.

"I watched, frozen in place. I felt like a rock pounded by the tempest-driven waves. DeGrosse bore down on the stunned, weaponless Brenin. What could I do? Percival made his decision. I knew his mind like it was my own. He saw a helpless figure, a friend to his mother, a seeker for justice, about to be killed by a rapist, a blackmailer, and his father.

"For me, that realization brought no feelings of affection, or even curiosity. That was long gone. The man in the red armor was a machine bent on killing a guest in my mother's house—my house—a man who loved my mother, who'd been kind and courteous, and who was the most important citizen of Viridiae.

"Percival stood up, grasped his javelin, slipped his forefinger and middle finger into the amentum's loop, and threw the missile as DeGrosse rode straight at him. Brenin was sandwiched between. The wind, behind Percival, carried the javelin further than I had ever seen him throw it. I pulled Percival back down to the grass, but he watched the javelin fly straight, true, and into DeGrosse's shoulder.

"DeGrosse roared in pain. Confused, his horse turned enough to avoid a collision with the wounded Brenin. DeGrosse fought to regain control of his animal, but it reared, throwing him. The steel point of the javelin had found our father's flesh. Blood dripped from gaps in his crimson armor. Enraged, he snapped the javelin in two where the wood met the metal point, and he marched toward the son whom he did not know.

"DeGrosse halted. Perhaps he looked into a kind of mirror, and he saw himself on the verge of manhood in decades past. He opened his mouth, as if wanting to say something. By the look on his face, it was a question, not a threat or a warning. *Who are you?* In a moment, however, deGrosse dismissed his thought, drew his sword, and strode toward Percival.

"Percival did not know how to defend himself.

In Ganieda's studio, clear morning light stream through the sun window in the roof, Dee covered her face. Her body shook with fear. She believed she was back on the plain, watching her father bear down on her brother. Ganieda took her hands as tears fell from Dee's red eyes. The old woman's strength calmed her.

"You must go on, my dearest friend." Ganieda squeezed Dee's clenched fists. "We can only heal when we know ourselves."

"On the plain, I stood apart from Percival. DeGrosse ignored me. A teenage girl is not a threat, I suppose. I planted my feet with purpose. The wind blew my waist-length hair in all directions, as if I were a naiad submerged in the Lake of Souls. My tresses swayed in the current. My arms reached out for the air-breathing mortals of the land. I cried out, and the air exploded.

"A lightning bolt descended from the charcoal cloud above and struck the steel dart stuck in deGrosse's shoulder. For a full second, his entire body glowed blue-white, then faded to a dark red, except for a coal black stain on his breastplate.

"DeGrosse lay on his back. Rain fell on his face, filling his eyes, streaming down his temples into his tangled hair. Percival fell to his knees beside the fallen knight. I stood behind my brother, shaking in the cold, fired with adrenaline. DeGrosse mouthed words.

"'Tell Eleanor ...' DeGrosse's breath came in gasps.

"I didn't want to hear Mother's name spoken by deGrosse.

"DeGrosse smiled, even as his body convulsed. I'm convinced he heard my thoughts. Was he proud? Disgusted? Indifferent? I couldn't tell, but he was thinking something I couldn't fathom. It was in his eyes. A moment later, that light left him.

"My mind had turned inside out. I had just helped my brother kill a human being."

Her story done, Dee collapsed into sobs, laying her head on Ganieda's breast. The elder stroked Dee's auburn hair, encouraging her emotions to drain away. Dee collected herself after wiping her eyes.

"It was soon after that that Brenin told us that he was the

king's son, who's now our king today. Brenin was grateful to us for saving his life. He invited us to become official members of his household. Mother consented, and almost ten years later, Percival went on the expedition to find the Grail, and I'm an artist and theurgist-in-training."

"Dee, what do you think you learned that day?"

"I have a power almost no one else has. I knew I had something before that day. When I was a few years younger, I killed a spider on a log by wishing it dead. Children are so cruel. But I learned I would do anything to protect my family."

"That's why you're here, to learn to accept and control a terrible burden," Ganieda said. "I'm convinced you'll succeed, though it will be painful for you."

Dee embraced Ganieda, but her heart chilled. Like that moment at the Lake of Souls, she caught a glimpse of the future. She knew she would kill again.

CHAPTER 6: AN UNWELCOME ASSIGNMENT

Sorting out the events of the day took herculean effort as the sun beat down on Dame Lancelot's broad straw hat and her strong palfrey. Morning had barely broken when an encrypted com message came through asking her to attend a meeting of the Privy Council "at her earliest convenience," which meant immediately. Trouble was coming. She slipped on her service uniform and spurs and presented herself at the palace gate. She arrived moments after Lord Mordred and the other council members. Lancelot inclined her head first to the flag of Viridiae and then to Arturus, who sipped a coffee.

Guinevere stood beside Arturus, whispering to him. Her eyes met Lancelot's, and her serious expression raised alarms.

Arturus took a seat at the head of an oblong table. The others followed his lead. "I hope you've read the briefing paper in your com accounts."

"I studied it in detail, Majesty." She'd learned her lesson after Arturus' previous reproof. The assessment was discouraging.

"Any thoughts at this point?" Arturus expected his senior staff to know as much or more than he at the beginning of a meeting, rather than waste time waiting for slower minds to catch up.

As Arturus' First Minister, Mordred was the first to speak, as protocol demanded. "Your Majesty, Sir Galahad is an honorable knight and a highly intelligent man, but he has never managed a large undertaking of this type. I am disappointed, but not surprised by the troubles he's encountered."

Mordred's brother, Gawain, always in attendance as Mordred's chief lackey, nodded in agreement.

"As I recall, Mordred," Arturus said, "you wanted us to mount a new expedition as soon as possible once you confirmed your new information on the Grail's whereabouts."

"But only after we believed that Sir Kevin's expedition had been lost, sir."

"Which reminds me," Arturus interrupted. "How is Sir Percival? I'm told he was dangerously sick."

"My husband," Guinevere said, "I asked Dindrane, his sister, about his health. She tells me he is recovering and anxious to take up his duties again."

"I'm glad to hear it. We need all our knights healthy and strong. That said, he should take it easy until he's 100 percent again."

"I'll relay the message, my lord."

"He's a strong man of refreshing virtue, my lord," Lancelot said. "I will probably be meeting him in the lists within the week."

Arturus chuckled. "You'll no doubt defeat him, Lancelot, as you have all challengers that I remember."

"As Galahad might in the melee," Mordred continued, steering the conversation back to the issue, "Dame Lancelot's son has found himself assailed on all sides, if not by armed adversaries, then by bad luck and poor management."

Lancelot bristled at Mordred's mention of her relationship to Galahad. It stirred up memories of an old, irrelevant personal scandal that Lancelot wanted to forget.

"It seems to me you're blaming the wrong person, Mordred." Lancelot referred to the report on his tablet. "The wagons were built with substandard materials and the food packaging was defective. Why don't the Regarders investigate the vendors?" The last question was directed at Gawain, Mordred's chief deputy in the Order.

"Our agents are already interviewing the manufacturers." Gawain's dark features reminded Lancelot of a henchman in a popular historical drama. It was about evil oil men who brought about the Dissolution, when the world fell apart.

"No one could've predicted the weather would turn the roads to mud." Lancelot watched metaphorical vultures circle the table. What did Mordred want?

"He could've taken the ancient concrete road to Perditon and its port. The old road is usable most of the way. Instead he chose a shorter route, as the crow flies, and he's already behind schedule."

"I seem to remember that you pressed for an early departure," Lancelot said.

Mordred fumed. "If you are attempting to blame me—"

"Gentles." Arturus lifted his hand. "We have a problem to solve."

"Nobles," Guinevere said, "as you know, there are bigger issues. The people are already grumbling about this expedition. They've seen one disaster this year, and all previous expeditions have failed. The government might not survive another failure. Back-benchers at the Round Table have already called for a no-confidence vote."

"What do you propose?" Arturus reserved his gentlest tones for his queen.

"The equipment problems can be fixed. The sage-scientists have forecast dry weather for the next few weeks. Perhaps shoring up the expedition's leadership with a fresh face would give confidence to the people and heart to Sir Galahad?"

Mordred grinned, as if he'd planted the idea in Guinevere's mind and was pleased with himself that the opportunity had risen so soon.

Arturus nodded. "The question is, whom should I send?"

Mordred was ready to burst out of his chair, but Guinevere interrupted. "May I suggest a short break while you consider the idea, my husband?" She didn't wait for Arturus' assent. She examined the coffee and pastries on a side table.

Mordred cocked his head, as if her suggestion was unexpected.

Other things on her mind, Lancelot sidled up to Guinevere as Arturus chatted with Mordred. “I miss you, Guin.”

“Not here, Lancelot.” Guinevere's tiny smile gave away her pleasure. She forced herself into a serious mien. “You have more important things to think about.”

Lancelot brushed her finger against Guinevere's. “What's more important than lying in bed with you?”

“Stop it. Look at Mordred.”

Lancelot glanced over his shoulder. “He's sucking up to the king like he always does. What do you suppose he wants now?”

“He wants to replace Galahad. He wants to lead the expedition.”

“So?”

“Are you blind?” Guinevere rolled her eyes. “He's wanted the throne ever since Arturus' illness began, but most people don't like him or trust him.”

“He's oily as an old horse trader.”

“He sees the expedition as a way to curry favor with the population and, more importantly, the Round Table. If Arturus should die, the Round Table knights elect the new king.”

“You sound as if you're just as anxious for him to die,” Lancelot said.

Guinevere faced her lover squarely. “He's my husband and my king. I want only what's best for him and my country. My family's history with his grandfather is not relevant.”

“You brought that up, not me.” Lancelot sighed. “What do you want me to do about it?”

“Volunteer to co-lead the expedition.”

Lancelot's jaw dropped. Though she wanted the Grail found as much as any Viridian, she had already done her part. Acting on information from Galahad's private sources, she had traveled to a huge lake surrounded by mountains in the eastern desert. The lake was so salty, it was impossible for anyone swimming in it to drown. The air itself corroded the metal of her weapons. The Grail was said to be in the ruins of a temple in the abandoned city on the lake's shores, but the building was empty, stripped bare over the centuries. Lancelot returned empty-handed, her duty done. “I'm not interested.”

“Would you rather see Mordred in Arturus' place?”

Lancelot laughed. “I'd rather go on another hunt for the questing beast.”

Guinevere ignored the wisecrack. “Mordred would be a terrible leader. He cares only for personal glory.”

“Why don't you volunteer?”

“Be practical. I may be a knight of the Round Table, but how would it look if I suddenly left my husband's side?”

She'd also be gone for months, perhaps years, an idea that made Lancelot shudder. “I'd be away for a long time. Would you miss me, Guin?”

“Of course, I would. But we have to think of the country first. We need to keep Mordred off the throne.”

Though Lancelot trusted Guinevere's loyalty, her appeal to “country first” rang hollow. She rarely acted without weighing the benefit to herself or her family.

Arturus knocked his signet ring on the table to call people back to the Privy Council meeting. “Lord Mordred has something to say.”

“Thank you, sir. An efficient, well-run government is my first priority, but the long-term health of the nation and the planet is everyone's concern. I've volunteered to replace Sir Galahad as the expedition's leader. I'll depart—”

“Replace?” Lancelot was surprised. Mordred had gone too far. “My lord,” Lancelot turned to Arturus, “Galahad does not deserve humiliation.”

The king's face was pained. He did not want to choose between Mordred and Lancelot.

Mordred lifted a corner of his mouth. “Majesty, one would expect Lancelot to defend Galahad. He is, after all, her son.”

The reference rankled Lancelot further. She moved her hand

toward her dagger. After she gave up Galahad to his father's family, backbiting courtiers used her decision against her. They had no sympathy for an ambitious female knight, despite the Viridian ethic of equal opportunity for all sexes. Was he truly aiming for the throne? Would he even wait for Arturus to die or abdicate? Her fingers did not find the blade. She had surrendered it at the palace gate, per security protocols.

"I have a better idea, sir," Lancelot said. "I would like to volunteer as the expedition's co-leader. Let me repeat: co-leader. I can leave immediately."

Guinevere's eyes sparkled in approval.

Mordred went red. "Majesty, Lancelot is not qualified—"

"I think it's a brilliant idea," Guinevere said. "Lancelot is the most popular knight in the kingdom. Naming her as co-leader would please everyone and give Viridiae confidence in Sir Galahad and the whole venture."

Arturus' eyes shifted between Mordred and Lancelot. His mind turned this way and that, weighing the costs and benefits. He relied on Guinevere for her political instincts.

"Mordred," Arturus said, "you are too important to Viridiae to leave the palace just now."

"But, my lord—"

"We just lost an entire expedition, save Sir Percival, and the circumstances are not entirely clear. I don't want to risk losing one of my best knights."

Arturus' praise undercut Mordred objections. "Of course, my lord. Thank you." The prime minister shot a dagger look at Lancelot.

"Lancelot," Arturus said, "we're grateful, as always, for your service. You'll leave today."

* * *

The encampment of Sir Galahad's expedition was on a plot of land he owned a half-day's ride from his manor house. Lancelot halted her horse as the twilight turned purple. Next to her son's tent, a wainwright's apprentice disassembled a wagon. Half the expedition's wagons were in pieces or lined up for a repair. The apprentice and his journeyman boss worked under lights powered by a bank of solar cells, which fed electricity to other parts of the camp as well.

In the gloom of his tent, its interior lit by a low-wattage bulb, Galahad looked up from a traveling desk. "Mother, it's a pleasure to see you." He rose and they touched cheeks. Galahad's good manners were legendary.

"I'm glad to see you, too," Lancelot said, "though I didn't expect to see you so soon after your departure from Camelot."

"I thought we'd be boarding the ship for Koda by now. The Fates had other ideas."

Galahad offered water from a cask.

"I suppose you've seen the orders from the palace," Lancelot said.

"Of course."

Galahad betrayed no emotion, though his voice was flat, as if he were struggling to suppress his feelings. Lancelot's heart went out to him. "You may not know that Mordred wanted the job."

"That arrogant bastard?" Lancelot said. "He's a menace to the kingdom."

"He's loyal to Viridiae and the search for the Grail."

"And what of his loyalty to Arturus?" Galahad didn't wait for an answer. "Mordred is interested primarily in himself. He takes credit for the Regarders' discoveries, and he rams his opinions down our throats."

"Arturus was anxious to keep him in Camelot."

"'Keep your enemies near?'" Galahad's tone was testy. "That doesn't explain why he sent you."

"I volunteered. Arturus also wanted to take command away from you and give it to Mordred. You don't deserve embarrassment. I'm more than satisfied with co-leader."

Galahad sniggered. "I'm a country knight that spends too much time with books and tablets. I send com messages around the world about a missing gadget when I should be in my armor patrolling the Lucian border. Don't disagree. I know that's what the court thinks of me. If you believe Arturus was generous by naming you co-leader instead of sacking me outright, you're more naive than I thought. I went from head of the expedition to sharing that role. 'Co-leader' is just another word for 'demotion,' as I see it."

The accusation stung Lancelot. She had spent much of her life at court, and she believed she knew its ways, constructive and destructive. Arturus really did mean that Galahad was still in charge. On the other hand, she could understand how a man given as much responsibility as Galahad might see her appointment differently. "You may have had some administrative trouble, but you're the country's foremost independent expert on the Grail, after Merlin. You know more than anyone in the Regarders."

Behind all the drama lay the inescapable fact that they were mother and son.

"Galahad, son, I'm here to support you, not the other way around."

Galahad looked up from his tablet, his expression on the edge of contempt. "'Son,' is it? Are you expecting me to refer to my so-called co-leader as 'Mother'?"

"That's not—"

"You sent me away after I was born because I was in your way."

Lancelot was taken aback. "I was a teenager. I made a mistake. I was never meant to be a mother. I was meant to be a warrior. I would never be home, never hold you, never fix you breakfast, kiss you before you went to school." A pain worse than a sword wound pierced her heart. "I handed you over to your father and grandfather because I wanted what was best for you."

"And you expect me to accept you here with no reservations? How do I know you won't find a way to push me aside again?"

Lancelot swallowed. She understood his bitterness. She remembered the day when Galahad's grandfather came to the hospital. His father would not come. The old man looked at her as if she were a monster. In the years that followed, she barely heard from Galahad until he entered the military academy at The Keep.

"You must believe me, s—, I mean, Sir Galahad. I'm here because I want the expedition to succeed. I want you to succeed."

After a moment, Galahad's face relaxed. "Would you like to meet my people?"

The offer was a relief to Lancelot. He'd accepted her, for now.

They walked side by side, a middle-aged female warrior and a young, smart, brown-haired, brown-eyed scholarly man who, in another life, might have taken an appointment at Camelot University. She met the researchers and support staff, and she tried to praise Galahad without appearing to symbolically truss him up for roasting. She signed her autograph on a ten-year-old keepsake tournament program that mysteriously appeared from a trunk. The walkabout cheered people up.

In front of his closest assistants, she asked Galahad how she could be helpful. He lifted his tent flap and invited her inside. The message both sent was clear: We may be co-leaders, but Galahad is still making the decisions.

Behind the scenes, Lancelot exercised her influence. As an officer on Arturus' general staff, she had the legal authority to redirect certain kinds of resources in the national interest, such as parts for the wagons and new communications gear. She worked her contacts at military suppliers, and within a few days, wagons arrived with high-quality rations. Galahad was grateful. Without her intervention, the expedition might have stalled for weeks.

The journos circled the camp like flies on roadkill, looking for the latest scandal to report to their readers and viewers on the news chans. Lancelot distracted them with her charisma while talking up the latest research on the Grail's location. Criticism on the com network social boards died down. Arturus messaged godspeed when Galahad announced the expedition's return to the journey. With clearing weather and drying roads, the expedition made up time, and it arrived at the rural port of Grey Harbor only a week behind schedule. Spirits were high as the wagons, horses, and adventurers organized themselves at the staging area next to the windship that would take them to Koda.

Despite their good morale, the expedition members, including Galahad and Lancelot, needed a rest. Worried relatives met the expedition at the dock and work came to a halt. The weather was deteriorating, and the windship's captain would not leave port in poor conditions. Galahad allowed a delay of twenty-four hours before loading began.

Lancelot was assigned lodgings at the waterside town's best hotel, a three-story affair with one two-room suite for VIPs. When she opened the door to her room, Guinevere greeted her. They fell into each other's arms.

"How?" Lancelot said.

"A public send-off from the queen would dispel any lingering doubts about the expedition," Guinevere said. "I took the fastest route via the old concrete road."

"Arturus?"

"Totally in support."

"You wanted to surprise me. Guin."

"Well, yes."

Lancelot scanned the empty hall with its parallel banks of doors guarding the hall's emptiness. "Does anyone know you're here?"

"I have the room next to yours."

"Your security detail—"

"Hush, Lancelot. We're consulting on plans for the voyage to Koda. I told them the meeting might last all night." She grinned.

"But Galahad would be here for a planning meeting." Lancelot frowned. "There's too many holes in your story, my love. We're in a small town. Tongues wag."

"No more than in Camelot, and we've been carrying on for years. Stop worrying."

Though her reassurances were far from convincing, Lancelot was thrilled to see Guinevere. She'd ordered food and wine and the simple meal was sumptuous for the exhausted dame knight. A few minutes later, they satisfied other kinds of hunger.

* * *

Lancelot gave in to her curiosity about a preliminary report on Sir Kevin's expedition, the one Percival survived. As he promised, he'd turned over his personal records to the Regarders.

"Mordred is determined to make this out to be about how he was right and Sir Kevin was wrong," Lancelot said.

Guinevere propped up her head with her arm. "Maybe that's the case. The Regarders are respected by everyone. They don't make many mistakes."

"You can't tell me that a bunch of forest rangers don't screw up too."

"The Regarders are knights, not rangers," Guinevere said. "Arturus' grandfather pledged to put protection of the land, the air, and the water above all things. The Regarders put an end to the illegal felling and theft of timber from the King's Forest. In their care, the forests are healthier than at any time in memory."

"Yes, we have a lot of pretty trees, Guin. How did that mission grow into an agency that collects intelligence on everything from how much water we drink to how much shit we expel?"

Guinevere laughed. "You're exaggerating."

"I'm not. These days, the Regarders enforce environmental regulations that cover every human interaction with the air, land, and water. That includes our feces."

The queen shrugged. "The Regarders accomplished their mission. Success is rewarded."

"Some people think they summarily execute environmental criminals caught red-handed. They also hunt and kill trolls." Lancelot had seen the corpses of the mutants during her hunt for a questing beast.

"A fearsome reputation is useful," Guinevere said.

"If they're so good, how come they haven't found the Grail? Even Mordred knows it's essential to keeping the world's environment stable." Lancelot's distrust of Mordred and his Regarders was on full display.

"Everyone is trying, love. The Regarders are only human."

"Mordred undercuts others' efforts. He wants the glory for himself."

"He's supporting Galahad's expedition. Remember what he said about the new evidence for the Grail's location on Koda? It's very good."

Guinevere was right, but Lancelot disliked Mordred for his arrogance. Arturus and Guinevere had no sons or daughters. Rumors persisted that Mordred was the unacknowledged son of Arturus by Morgause, his lover prior to his coronation. Even if the rumors were true, under Viridian law, no first-born son or daughter, legitimate or not, automatically ascended to the throne. Technically, Viridiae's monarchs were elected by the Round Table, but Mordred would be impossible to beat when it came to a ballot.

"Why are you defending him? Lothia was no friend to your family in the civil wars, as I recall."

"It's true. Lothia switched sides for Arturus the Great and abandoned Cameliard."

"If it weren't for Lothia—"

"The Leodegrance family would've prospered, instead of falling into penury. I was told the story again and again by my grandmother." Guinevere smiled. "That's all in the past now. I'm the wife of Arturus the Great's grandson and I'm the queen of Viridiae. I'd say we've recovered our place in the kingdom. Wouldn't you?"

Lancelot wasn't so naive to think that a blood feud ended at the marriage altar. The Leodegrances may have returned to their status previous to the civil wars, but that didn't mean the clan had forgiven Lothia. That's what made Guinevere's tolerance of Mordred so strange. Did they have a private truce? Or a secret arrangement? Lancelot preferred to observe palace intrigue, rather than participate, unless her position was threatened. She wondered if that moment was around the corner.

CHAPTER 7: A CEREMONY OF LIGHT

On her way home from Ganieda's studio, Dee stopped at Percival's apartment, and he was moping, as usual.

"Have you seen what they did?"

"Who?" Dee rarely checked the daily news before she got home.

"The king! Mordred, the whole bunch of them. They've sent Lancelot to take over Galahad's expedition."

Dee glanced at the report on Percival's tablet. "It says she's to be Galahad's co-leader."

"It doesn't matter. I should be there."

Dee shrugged. "To do what? Get in the way?"

"You don't know what you're talking about."

"In case you hadn't noticed, you're recovering from a near-death experience. The doctor says you're getting better, but you're to stay on leave until she gives you permission to return to duty. The queen asked me to keep an eye on you."

"I don't follow the queen's orders and I don't follow yours. I feel fine! I've already gained five kilos. I got friends to bring me some weights for strength training." He pointed to the weight set. "The only thing I can't do is riding and throwing my javelin."

"It'll come with time."

"You sound like Mother."

Dee allowed that Percival was right. Though she initially dreaded the responsibility for looking after Percival, thinking she might have to spoon-feed him, figuratively and literally, she found herself putting on the brakes to keep him from moving too fast. "The doctor said you need to give yourself time to heal."

"I'm almost there, I'm telling you." He flopped on his frayed couch. "Another couple days of staying indoors and I'll go crazy. A run every day isn't enough. Do you know how much interesting programming is on the com during the day?"

"No."

"This much." He formed his forefinger and thumb into a zero. "And now Arturus and Mordred are disrespecting Galahad. He's a good knight. I know him. I want to help him."

Percival's last statement made Dee suspicious, then alarmed. "What do you mean?"

Her brother sat up and folded his arms. "Nothing. I'm just pissed about everything."

"Are you still upset about the way your expedition went?"

"What do you think? A couple of Regarders investigators came by today and asked me a bunch of questions. I didn't like their attitude. It was like they were trying to blame Sir Kevin for the failure."

"What about you?" Dee feared that Percival, as the only survivor, might suffer blame.

"I didn't like their attitude about me either. They kept asking me if I'd seen the Grail. Or if I'd picked it up and lost it, like some kid losing a toy. I was in charge of the military escort, and there were only two of us. What could I have done wrong?"

The Regarders would think of something. Dee's brother tended to ignore or simply not see the nuances of court intrigue. Black and white were his favorite colors, in a manner of speaking. "If you don't feel that you did anything wrong, then you have nothing to worry about."

"You don't understand. I do feel that I screwed up. I could've done more to save Sir Kevin and the others, but I didn't. The thing is, I have no clue what I could've done differently. We simply ran out of food and water. We had no power for navigating. People were dropping like flies. I survived, and they didn't."

"Did the Regarders ask you about the betrayals you talked about?"

"They were very interested in that. It's just that, I'm not sure about it anymore. I was so out of my head that all I remember is feeling like someone in Camelot was watching us and found the Grail before we got to the cave."

"What about the evidence you brought back?"

"They wouldn't talk to me about it. 'Still being analyzed,' they said."

Percival's moodiness was a sign to Dee that he was not ready to return to his duties as a military knight. She gathered her jacket. "I'm going home. I have a lot on my mind too. Your complaining is giving me a headache."

"So what's going on with you?"

Dee was glad Percival asked. At least he wasn't so wrapped up in himself that he forgot she had a life too. "I got a text from the queen." Dee couldn't help but smirk proudly.

"Well, is she your new best friend?"

"She asked about my work. And how you were feeling."

"And you said?"

"Better, but still stubborn as a mule."

Percival folded his arms.

"I'm tired. I'm going home to bed."

As Dee opened the door to leave, Percival called out to her. "I need to find the Grail. I will find the Grail."

Dee returned to the sitting room and kissed her brother on the forehead. She felt the bone of his skull beneath his pale skin. "I know you will. It's your destiny."

* * *

A few days later, Dee's "first light" ceremony for her new work attracted far more people than she expected. For most of her short career, her light tapestries had hung in the student galleries at Camelot University or the school's one professional-level gallery as part of an annual fourth-year show. She showed her portfolio to the handful of mid-level private galleries in the capital, but no one showed any interest. One day, she received a com call from the leading pro gallery; Would she consider a special one-week showing as a test?

A few months later, three dozen people chatted amiably and sipped Napene wine in the gallery as they waited for the unveiling. Dee couldn't sleep the night before and she showed up at the gallery hours early pumped with caffeine. A young woman with a name tag saying “Edlina Catalpec” greeted her.

“I'm so glad to meet you. May I call you Dindrane?”

Dee recognized her as one of Ganieda's newer students. They'd met briefly at a gathering in the elder's studio. She looked professional and understated in her evening dress, as if she understood the need to ensure all attention was on the artist and her show.

“Dee is fine. Where's Judson?”

“You can call me Lina, if you like. Judson's at his other gallery. He asked me to help you with any last minute problems.”

“I'm so nervous, Lina.”

“You've nothing to worry about, Dee. All the staff thinks tonight will be a huge success.”

Dee still didn't quite believe what was happening. She wanted everything to be perfect. So did the gallery owner; he had sent out hundreds of invitations to buyers and connoisseurs in Perditon and other major Viridian cities. He was taking a gamble on Dee.

Finally, the first people arrived. Dee wiped the sweat off her hands with a cloth napkin and took up her place in the darkened display room. Ganieda was in the audience, as well as her circle of arts friends. Judson Ball walked in and introduced Dee. A balding man with a friendly, exacting manner, Ball couldn't stop giving Dee suggestions on everything from the placement of the light emitters to her makeup choices.

After a brief thank-you speech, Dee touched a key on her tablet. The room lit up with the “first light” of the unveiling. Colors and forms danced on the wall, coalescing into a scene from Viridian history, the accession of Arturus the Great, the first monarch of the new state of Viridiae. The weaving of light streams, together with their subtle animation, brought a gasp from the audience. *Coronation* was Dee's largest work by far, taking up the entire five-meter wall.

Applause burst from the audience.

Dee was shocked on the one hand and gleeful on the other. She'd never seen this kind of reaction from an audience that wasn't her close friends, instructors at school, or Ganieda. They were all supportive, but Dee was skeptical. They might be polite, while yawning behind her back. After all, she'd done that very thing behind her fellow students' backs.

That wasn't the case on this night, as evidenced by Ball, who was beside himself. A few minutes after first light, he approached Dee with eyes as wide as a toddler's on Winter Solstice morning. Someone had already offered twice the listed price for *Coronation*.

Dee did a quick calculation. She was stunned. Even after Ball's hefty cut, she'd have money to live on for months.

Ball wasn't ready to sell yet. He thought he could get triple the list, maybe more.

That's when Queen Guinevere arrived.

The limousine pulled up to the gallery door ten minutes after first light, and a footman—really a member of her security detail—approached Ball asking for Dee, who identified herself. The footman glanced in the direction of the car, and Guinevere exited by a rear door. She was dressed in a casual evening costume.

Mordred followed her, dressed in a similar manner.

The gallery owner nearly fell over. Dee and Lina slipped their hands under Ball's arm to prevent a scene. He'd been very open with her about why he'd accepted her work. She was a member of the King's Household, which meant she had connections at court. He also thought she had great talent. It was a perfect combination, despite her youth.

“Majesty,” he said to Guinevere, bowing his head. “What an amazing surprise.”

“I'm sorry to just turn up without RSVP'ing.” Guinevere's apology was sincere, if a little forced, to Dee's mind. “Lord Mordred and I were having dinner at the Knight's Arms, and I remembered Ms Rathkeale's opening. We were only around the corner."

"No need to apologize, ma'am." Ball recovered from his faint. "We're thrilled and honored by your presence and Lord Mordred's. May I introduce Ms Dindrane Rathkeale."

"She and I are already friends," Guinevere said. "I hope the opening is going well, Ms Rathkeale. I've heard about your work."

Dee was almost as stunned to see Guinevere as Ball, though Dee's brief conversations at court and her occasional participation in court events helped her feel less disoriented. Dee thought the queen's use of the word "friends" a little presumptuous, but she wouldn't push back. "I'm flattered that you came, ma'am. Please call me Dee."

Mordred hung back a step, as if measuring each word of Guinevere and Dee's conversation.

Ball interrupted. "Forgive me, ma'am, but may I offer some refreshment? We ordered fine Napene wine for the occasion."

"Actually, Mordred and I have only a few minutes. May we see Dee's work?"

"Of course, please come this way."

Lina led the way through a small hallway that helped eyes adjust to the darker display space. The stunned crowd bowed their heads at the monarch's wife, and she took a seat on a long backless couch to gaze at the tapestry. Mordred stood behind her and to her right.

"Extraordinary," Guinevere said.

Dee watched the queen, alert to whether she offered obliged praise or genuine interest. No doubt about it: The queen was dazzled.

Mordred was pleased as well. For the first time since arriving, he spoke. "Mr Ball has lived up to his reputation for talent spotting. This is quite good, if I may say so."

"Oh, of course, you may say so, Lord Mordred." Ball bowed slightly. His breath came in slight pants. Lina handed him a glass of wine, which he gulped. "I've been honored and pleased to find fine work for your manor house in Lothia."

“Mordred told me about you, Mr Ball,” Guinevere said. “I agree with his assessment.”

Ball inclined his sweating head. “You're too kind, ma'am.”

“I'm curious, Mr Ball. How much are you asking for it?”

Ball named the list price. “Unfortunately, ma'am, another patron has offered more, and I believe we have a sale.”

“You are deservedly fortunate, Mr Ball. And Dee as well.” Guinevere rose, though her eyes remained on Dee's tapestry.

“That is to say, ma'am, that the sale is not finalized. The work is technically still on the market, in a manner of speaking.”

Lina winked at Dee. Ball was attempting to bid up the price.

“This would make a fine addition to the decorations in the main receiving hall, don't you think, Lord Mordred?”

“Indeed.” Mordred caught Dee's eye, and she saw genuine admiration. “I believe you have a long career ahead of you, Ms Rathkeale.”

“Thank you, sir.” Unlike the calculating praise of a politician, Mordred's sentiment came from a place of sincerity. He had shared a piece of his heart with Dee, and it cheered her.

Guinevere leaned over and spoke softly to Ball.

Dee feared his knees would give way, and she took his arm again.

“That's more than generous, ma'am.”

“It's probably not enough,” Guinevere said, “but my purse isn't limitless.”

“I'll have the purchase agreement ready in the morning.” Ball almost spat out the words, afraid the queen might change her mind.

Guinevere extended her hand to Dee. “Congratulations. You deserve high praise.”

“Thank you, ma'am.”

Mordred offered his hand as well. He lowered his eyes in respectful courtesy. “My congratulations as well.”

As Mordred held Dee's hand, a tremor overcame her. She studied the prince's angular face, and noticed how the lines weren't as sharp as they might be if he was cruel or thoughtless. Like anyone who wanted to survive at court, he didn't always say what he meant, but his mouth had an honesty to it. Perhaps he regretted necessary dissembling. His eyes were clear and sharp, suggesting an intelligence that wasn't appreciated by most people around him, except for those who knew him best. Dee felt a desire to be in his orbit.

"It seems that you will be spending more time at court, at least while you oversee the installation of *Coronation*," Mordred said. "You will bring grace and a spirituality the court desperately needs. I do hope we will have a chance to discuss your artistic process and inspiration. I'm truly curious."

Dee's heart raced at the invitation. As First Minister, Mordred had nearly the same power and influence as the king, with only slightly less responsibility. Though he was only ten years or so older than Dee, gray hair flecked his temples, and she imagined his shoulders tight from carrying the burdens of state. She blushed as she realized that she wanted to massage those cares away. "I'd be happy to discuss my work. My teacher, Ganieda, has been so generous to me."

"Ah, Ganieda. I have two of her light tapestries, one in my personal quarters in the palace. I see that she has influenced you."

"I would not be here without her."

"Mordred?" Guinevere moved toward the gallery door.

Mordred bowed slightly to his queen, but lingered with Dee. "How is your brother? Recovering?"

"He gets better every day. He'd be here tonight if his doctors hadn't told him to avoid strain."

"He'll be back in the saddle in no time, I'm sure of it. Goodnight."

As Mordred passed Guinevere on the way to the car, the two women's eyes met. Guinevere worked her jaw, as if chewing a tasty morsel. "Be careful, my dear. His fire burns hot, and careless women are often burned."

For an instant, Dee hated Guinevere for stepping into her business uninvited. The emotion vanished when she understood the comment was meant as a friendly warning, rather than snark. Dee did not respond, instead catching a final glimpse of Mordred as the limo's door closed behind him.

CHAPTER 8: JOURNEY TO PERDITON

Lancelot signed the customs papers aboard the windship *Dolphin*, the temporary home of the expedition for the voyage to Koda. A stiff breeze blew cold from the north, where the rugged island lay off the coast 4,500 kilometers away. As Lancelot contemplated the uncertain weeks ahead, a breathless messenger halted in front of Lancelot and asked her to come to Galahad's tent immediately.

Fearing bad news from Camelot, Lancelot hurried to her co-leader, imagining all kinds of disasters, from Arturus' sudden death to an accident maiming Guinevere. Lancelot's lover had left in the middle of the night. Though Lancelot was not one for emotional scenes, the parting was difficult. Months might pass before she saw Guinevere again. Lancelot hoped the coming adventure aboard the *Dolphin* and at Koda would distract her.

Galahad finished a com call as Lancelot pushed back the tent flap. Galahad's face was flushed, and his eyes were frantic.

"What's wrong?" Lancelot said.

"A Grail has been found."

The news stunned Lancelot. Was the expedition called off? Did the Regarders find it? "Wait a moment. 'A Grail'? Don't you mean 'the Grail'?"

"In this business, you hedge your bets. Don't forget what happened to Percival."

As the Regarders' investigation continued, more and more doubts were raised about Sir Kevin's expedition. The Viridian media were calling it a fool's errand. Arturus' critics at the

Round Table asserted that a dozen sage-scientists, knights, and servants had died for nothing.

"But you think there might be something to this rumor?"

Galahad nodded his head gravely. "The report says it's near the Great Machine in Perditon."

Perditon was Camelot's second city, a port on the enormous estuary that split Viridiae nearly in two north to south.

"Most of the evidence on the Grail's whereabouts put it hundreds or thousands of kilometers from the Great Machine, as if it had flown away on one of the ancient turbine planes."

"This one's different."

"Reports like this one are rare. I feel we have to investigate. The city is only a couple of days away. Arturus agrees. I'm going to Perditon."

Lancelot did not relish the idea of visiting the teeming city. In many ways, it was the opposite of Camelot, a hell to the capital's heaven. "You're leaving now?"

"Actually, I'd like you to go with me." The request seemed painful to Galahad. "I can handle myself, but the chances of success are greater with two than with a single individual."

"Shouldn't I stay here and keep things going?"

"The expedition's on hold until we sort this out. I think I can leave things with subordinates. We should be back in a week or so."

Lancelot doubted Galahad's decision, but her son had shown good judgment since departing their mountain encampment. Now was not the time to challenge him.

"The animals should be unloaded. The risk of illness goes up when they're confined."

"Agreed. I want my warhorse, in any case. You should unload yours as well. I wouldn't bother with your heavy armor. It's no good in an urban fight."

* * *

A torrid breeze lifted the edges of Lancelot and Galahad's

cloaks. Spring announced itself with a rainstorm, but it didn't clear the dull, gaseous stench. The crumbling city inhaled oxygen and exhaled corruption. The flat clop of the knight's horses on the bridge to Perditon echoed in the indifferent or unfriendly looks of the throng.

The crowd's gloom left Lancelot uneasy. Galahad brushed the hilt of his sword, Secace, for reassurance. Boats passed under the bridge, like guards walking a curtain wall, the vessels guided by unseen hands. The bridge traversed the water border separating the Old Civilization city—what was left of it—from the rest of Viridiae.

A knobby-kneed, ragged girl approached Galahad. She carried a canvas bag and a water skin weighing at least as much as she. "Batteries for your com? Water for you? Guaranteed clean!"

Galahad's faux-leather saddle creaked as he dismounted his horse. Spatters of mud stained the white wool of his wrap. Lancelot followed her son's lead. They'd decided that Lancelot would appear as Galahad's bodyguard. That suited Lancelot, who was a better fighter than Galahad. The younger knight, however, knew the territory, having visited the city before.

"Clean water?" Galahad said. "How do I know you're not lying?"

"It's bottled by Recovery, Recycle, Repair, and Repurpose, Inc!" The girl pronounced each word like an actor in Camelot's best troupe. "It's honest water, and good for you."

Lancelot admired the girl. She had found a way to survive, even if she was bony and filthy.

Galahad said, "How did you come by batteries, girl?"

"The See-Oh himself."

"Who's that these days?"

"Chief Executive Officer Olc." The girl looked at Galahad and Lancelot as if they were rubes. "You know him, don't you?"

Galahad examined the thumb-sized energy pack the girl held up like an offering. The required salvage label seemed wrong, though that wasn't unusual. "You're well-connected. I'm impressed."

"See-Oh Olc is Perditon's richest man. He makes our city work." A shadow overcame her confidence. "He has to know everybody. And everything."

"I've never met him."

The girl held up the batteries. "Please, sir, do you want batteries or not? Discount for a twelve-pack. I have to sell them, or..."

Brabus Olc earned a handsome profit from recycled tech. He also ruled Perditon with an iron hand. Galahad waved his com ring over the girl's ring, which hung around her neck on a thick string. Surprised by the readout, he said, "Your prices will empty my wallet."

"Quality filtration isn't cheap."

The water's sweet taste reminded Lancelot of her hunger. A line of food stalls anchored the city end of the bridge.

"Which one of those towers is the Banker's Redoubt?" Lancelot knew the answer. She and Galahad had discussed how to approach Olc. The girl was confirming information, and Lancelot wanted an excuse to give her a coin.

She pointed at the tallest. "Are you going to see See-Oh Olc?"

Lancelot and Galahad glanced at each other.

"If you meet Mr. Olc, tell him Penny will pay her debts on time this month." She swallowed, as if nervous.

Lancelot thought about giving her two digicoins, but changed her mind. She didn't want her to be noticed, unlike herself and Galahad, who stood out in the shuffling street life like a rose bush in a field of bramble. "If I see him, I'll tell him you're one of his best reps."

Penny ran off, swallowed by Perditon's horde.

* * *

Lancelot bought measures of oats from a vendor and slipped feedbags over her and Galahad mounts' heads. The Banker's Redoubt rose out of Perditon's haze three kilometers distant, flanked by other decaying towers of the ancient city. Mother and son needed their own recharge. At a table in front of a tiny restaurant, Galahad enjoyed stir-fried vegetables and flat bread. Lancelot chose a meat dish.

"Meat is impure, and slows you down, Mother," Galahad said. "Granddad told me that every time he cooked. 'You need a clear head, and a clean body, inside and out.'" Galahad grinned at the memory.

Lancelot didn't respond, though her appetite began to fail her. "You're not saying I'm somehow unclean, are you, Galahad?"

Galahad stopped in mid-chew. "Of course not, Mother. I was just repeating something Granddad Pellas said."

The son of Sir Elliot of Corbenic and the grandson of Sir Roger Pellas had his father's broad face and his grandfather's intelligent eyes. Did Galahad's touch of arrogance come from herself, Elliot, or his grandfather? The family traced its origins to before the Dissolution, when the world fell apart, but Lancelot hardly knew Galahad. As well as giving up his body to the Pellas clan, she gave up his mind, or rather, the chance to influence his mind.

"I like a good chicken leg as well as stir-fry," Lancelot said. "Humans were meant to spread their food bets."

"Meat makes me retch," Galahad said. "I once had to eat a morsel of pork at a farmer's wedding. I kept the chunk in my mouth until I had a chance to spit it out."

"Wouldn't that insult the farmer?"

"I went out behind the barn and spat it into the sty."

"Who taught you that? Your grandfather?"

A shadow passed over Galahad's face.

"I'm sorry, Galahad, I shouldn't have said that."

Galahad paid the bill and left the table. Lancelot sighed and followed her "master" to the horses.

The two knights led their animals down a long, decrepit boulevard toward the city center. Lancelot sensed pairs of eyes on her multiply exponentially. Some were human. Some were electronic or biologic, salvaged from the detritus of the Old Civilization, a product of Perditon's main industry, recycling.

"Granddad Pellas was a kind of recycler," Galahad recalled, apparently recovered from his momentary peevishness. "He told and retold the same stories for as long as I can remember."

White-bearded, stooped, and intimidating, Pellas told the boy Galahad how Joseph Arimathea invented the technology that halted the Warming. Humanity sparked the climate disaster, but the scientist found a way to stop it in its tracks. The great machines Arimathea designed—twelve in all around the world—kept the Warming in check. Arimathea himself installed one of the machines in the mountain range west of Perditon.

Lancelot and Galahad crested one of Perditon's seven hills and paused in the heat. Clouds obscured the mountains, including Apparatus Montis, the site of the climate machine. Below Galahad was the city, veiled by dust kicked up by people, animals, and the electric-powered carts favored by the elite. Galahad owned one, but never drove it. Granddad Pellas hated them. "They reminded him how the Old Civilization destroyed the world."

"That's a long time to hold a grudge," Lancelot said.

"Granddad Pellas said I would one day save the world."

Lancelot gauged that her son believed his grandfather. Mothers and fathers often planted the idea of saving the nation into the heads of boys and girls destined for knighthood, even before the Grail was lost. Lancelot never had a chance to discover if she would transmit the same ideas to her son, though she had seen enough of battle and politics to know that the myths had as much substance as fog.

"If we find the Grail, your grandfather's prediction might come true."

"Are your batteries holding their charge, sir?"

Appearing out of nowhere like a sparrow, Penny stood beside Galahad, eyes expectant. He checked his batteries' level. "I should find a recharging station."

"There's one a block away. May I show it to you?"

"I bet it's owned by Brabus Olc."

Penny tilted her head. "I get a referral fee, if that's what you mean."

"And what's the percentage you kick back to See-Oh Olc?" Lancelot said.

"That's a company secret."

Galahad laughed. "Fine. Lead on."

Penny ran ahead to claim a space for him at the busy kiosk. Before Galahad and Lancelot could catch up, a hooded figure pushed her aside. Penny tripped into a mound of offal, and a cart swerved to avoid her.

Lancelot touched the pommel of Arondight.

Galahad lifted his finger to warn her off.

The hooded figure, male by his height and the set of his shoulders, plugged in a pair of devices. Galahad tied his horse to a post, lifted Penny to her feet, and instructed her to stay out of the way.

To the hooded man, Galahad said, "I believe you cut into line, sir. Can you wait your turn?"

"Fuck off." The figure kept his back to Galahad.

"The girl was holding my spot."

"That insect?" The figure grunted with a mealy voice reminiscent of a teenage thug. "She's cheating you and See-Oh Olc."

Lancelot watched her son carefully. Though she did not raise him, she'd met him more than once in the lists. She prided herself on reading her opponents' moods, which could be turned to advantage, if they were distracted or discouraged. Galahad had a simmering frustration, unrelated as it was to the specific insult, like a bug bite irritating a sunburn. Lancelot put it down to a life's work of searching for the Grail, and failing.

Standing before the hooded bully, Galahad breathed out. "You're in my spot, sir."

The figure turned. Lancelot did a double-take. She could see only the figure's chin because of the covering, but it was almost feminine, as well as hairless, but not as if it was shaven.

"Well then, pretty boy," the figure said. "You're the newcomer I've been sent to find. Square-jawed and golden-haired, just like the photo." The figure ignored Lancelot. "When I saw the picture, I thought you were a character from one of the chan shows, you know, the ones with the demi-gods that beat Lucians and trolls once a week." She looked Galahad up and down. "Guess I was right."

A pang of jealousy infected Lancelot, who enjoyed her celebrity. She liked being the center of attention, but she was a supporting player in this drama.

"I'm instructed to take you to my boss," the figure said.

"Sir." Penny pulled at Galahad's cloak, as if warning him away.

Galahad studied the hooded figure, as if considering his options. His Grandfather Pellas wrote to Lancelot a few days after his father, Sir Elliott, died. *He is a member of a great family. He will be a Knight of the Round Table. He is a child with a destiny. And he will be tested, every day.*

Lancelot learned what her son's grandfather meant by "destiny." He believed Galahad was fated to recover the Grail and repair the Great Machine. First, he had to find it. It wouldn't be easy.

He'll have to climb mountains of one kind or another.

Grandfather Pellas wasn't quite right in the head, Lancelot thought. Destiny was something you made for yourself. It wasn't handed to you on a platter. On the other hand, opportunities to succeed sometimes dropped in your lap, and it was up to you to make something of them.

Galahad had his doubts. He confided in Lancelot during their trek to Perditon. "I feel like I've looked behind every tree and under every rock on the continent. I'm starting to wonder if Granddad's stories were just stories, like chan shows."

"First things first," Galahad said to the armed figure by the kiosk. "You cut in line. You owe this young lady a fee."

"Save me your protect-the-weak clichés."

"And then you can pay me the common courtesy of identifying yourself. My name is Sir Galahad du Lac-Corbenic. This is Dame Lancelot du Lac."

"I am called Aideen."

Lancelot stifled a gasp when the figure lifted off her hood. The face was more angular than most young women, even masculine. The thuggish figure's height and bulk argued against her gender, and her eyes glowed an unnatural turquoise.

Galahad spotted the sword hilt at the figure's side. "I'll say this one last time. Apologize to the child."

Aideen snickered. "I'd say you're interested in dying today, pretty boy. Happy to oblige."

An image of her dying son flashed in Lancelot's mind. He'd earned a reputation in the lists and on the battlefield as an excellent fighter, but Lancelot knew his great weakness. He was technically brilliant, almost perfect in his war style, but he had trouble breaking free from training. He avoided improvisation in the heat of the moment. Lancelot wished she'd had a chance to teach him to trust his creativity. When she stepped forward, ready to defend him as his titular bodyguard, Galahad waved her away. He wanted the fight for himself. He had something to prove.

The crowd around the kiosk backed away. They gave the belligerents room in an impromptu fighting pit. Lancelot's anxiety spiked. She did not like Aideen.

The female warrior pulled her single-shot pistol, but Galahad was ready with a kick, knocking it out of her hand. She gripped her wrist, more from shock than injury.

Galahad had left his brace of pistols secure in their holsters on his horse. There was no time to retrieve them, but he drew Secace from the sheath on his hip. It was a good choice, Lancelot realized. The short sword worked best in urban streets; thugs with weak egos preferred longer swords, in Lancelot's experience. Aideen was no exception. Keeping his eyes on her, Galahad rolled his cloak into a thick shield around his arm. Lancelot smiled to herself. Perhaps Galahad had learned some improvisational tricks after all.

Aideen attacked. Galahad dodged the first blow and ducked as she swung around. He slapped her with the flat of his blade. If he knocked her down, she might yield. Lancelot suppressed an urge to cheer. Aideen was stronger, however, than she expected for a woman around nineteen, Lancelot guessed. She'd trained hard. Lancelot thought of other dame knights at tournaments. Lancelot was almost undefeated in the lists, and she still competed in her forties.

Aideen's thrusts and parries were strategic, giving Galahad pause. Lancelot was dying to intervene, but Galahad upped his game. He dodged another swing and stepped inside her reach. Apart from her mail shirt, Aideen was defenseless when he was this close. A short stab and she was dead, but Galahad held back.

"I can kill you whenever I want, Aideen," Galahad said. "You're good, but inexperienced, and you have the wrong weapon. I don't want to hurt you."

"You've insulted me, and I'm going to cut off your head."

Aideen spun away, raging. She swung again, and her blade came within a millimeter of Galahad's neck. Lancelot closed her eyes. Galahad would have to risk injuring her, or else Aideen might get lucky. Galahad feinted, then drove his sword at the inner muscle of her upper sword arm. The blade cut through the thin shirt, but Galahad pulled his thrust before it did real damage. Lancelot cheered inwardly. It was a brilliant, humane move. She'd judged him too harshly for his stereotyped style, remembering that a tournament fight was far different than real combat. Aideen screamed in pain and dropped her sword.

Galahad pushed her to the ground, and held his blade to her neck. "Apologize to the girl."

Aideen spat an incomprehensible word.

"Now, do your job, and take us to Brabus Olc."

* * *

The remains of Banker's Redoubt loomed over Lancelot, Galahad, and Aideen. The com system displayed wayfinding icons as they drew nearer the 60-story structure, half-wrecked by age, salvagers, and the occasional typhoon. An advertisement for an Olc-branded project accompanied each icon, but they were unobtrusive, even pleasant. Most of the ads promoted his recycling ventures or repurposing enterprises.

Lancelot's belly tightened when the trio descended a ramp, along with the horses and gear, into a level beneath the high-rise. It was too much like a cave, which made her nervous. The low ceiling was balanced with good lighting, however, and the presence of other visitors' horses eased her mind. Electric carts occupied marked spaces along a concrete wall.

"Put your pistols and sword in the public weapons cabinet. Your other blades, too." Aideen indicated a heavy steel box with several lockers. "It's safer that way."

Aideen's manner had changed during the hike to the Banker's Redoubt. She had relaxed as if she'd reached a goal. The fight with Galahad might've have been a way to prove her status or her value, but to whom?

Galahad knew his manners. He followed the host's rules. Lancelot hesitated, then complied, more to show that she was Galahad's obedient protector. Aideen did not give up her weapons.

A brushed steel door slid open next to the cabinet, inviting passengers.

"I'm taking you directly to Olc's headquarters." Aideen held her com ring over the reader.

A panel indicated several floors beneath them. However, the elevator rose with a fluid quiver. Aideen kept her sword hand near the hilt.

"How is your arm?" Galahad was nervous. Lancelot mirrored his anxiety. She disliked enclosed spaces with little room for maneuver.

"I heal fast." Aideen was calm as a pond.

The elevator opened to a foyer. On the opposite wall, salvaged sculpture flanked double doors embedded with tiny tiles in abstract forms. Lancelot felt under-dressed in her dusty maroon cloak. One of the double doors opened. The moment and setting called for courteous behavior, as if the two knights from Camelot were visiting a nobleman's house.

Open as a meadow, the grand room rose three times the height of man or woman. One wall offered a 180-degree panorama of Perditon beside a salt-water estuary. Apparatus Montis guarded the estuary's far shore. Three- and four-masted sailing cargo vessels similar to the *Dolphin* dotted the bay like toys in a bathtub.

Not even Camelot's tallest defensive towers reached this height. The decayed city and its layers of grime and mildew lay 150 meters below, the details lost and unimportant. Lancelot felt as if she were flying.

Aideen stepped away into a shadow, unobtrusive, but menacing.

"May I offer you a whiskey? Or would you prefer something brewed?"

The voice belonged to a pudgy man, a head shorter than Galahad, with powerful hands. His eyes were bright and mischievous, but he had the gravitas of a government minister.

"May I call you Galahad, instead of Mr Du Lac?" Olc winked. "I've never been very good at ceremony."

"You could've simply invited me." Galahad glanced at Aideen and accepted a glass with a finger of amber liquid.

"And your companion?"

"My bodyguard."

Lancelot was glad Galahad didn't name her. He knew it might raise more questions than it answered, though Lancelot concluded Olc knew far more than he let on. He didn't show it.

"You are welcome in my home, madam."

Lancelot nodded and stepped back, but not into a shadow. She wanted to be seen, and if she was lucky, feared by Olc and Aideen.

"Sir Galahad, I ask your pardon," Olc said. "I didn't intend for you and Aideen to fight. I sent her to meet you, but she can be ... aggressive."

Dressed in stylish black highlighted by gold jewelry and accents, Olc moved to a spot on a long sofa, antique, but in mint condition. Another bit of salvage, Lancelot surmised, as her son was invited to sit. The See-Oh of Brabus Olc Recovery, Recycle, Repair, and Repurpose, Inc., sprawled on his furniture like a cyprian, tempting and threatening. Lancelot knew her court manners, but Olc's gaudy sophistication put her off. She felt as if she were asked to a dinner, but no one explained which fork to use.

"I didn't expect to meet you in person so quickly, Mr Olc,"

Galahad said. “You're a busy man, I imagine. My informant said only to come to the city.”

“Brabus, please. I certainly expected, or at least hoped, to meet *you*.”

Lancelot wondered if Galahad's informant was Olc himself behind layers of security.

“How is that, Mr Olc?”

“Let me tell you a story, Sir Galahad. I know of your life's mission.”

Lancelot detected a skeptical note. Galahad grasped his tumbler of whiskey tightly.

“I also know you're frustrated in your quest,” Olc continued, “as is every other knight in Viridiae seeking the device known as the Grail. Of all of them, you are the most single-minded. Some would say obsessed.”

“If the Grail isn't found soon, the world will slip into another Dissolution,” Galahad said.

“I believe you will fulfill your destiny, my new friend. I think I can help, but I doubted you would come at my invitation. Who am I but an ordinary businessman? Not in your circle, so to speak.” Olc indicated a tab. “I arranged for one of your informants to tease you into coming.”

“Just like you teased me by nearly having me killed?”

“Over-reach on Aideen's part. I have apologized for her.”

“I'm curious, Olc. Why are her eyes turquoise?”

“Among my many ventures is a research arm that's attempting to revive some of the genetic manipulation techniques of the Old Civilization. To put it bluntly, she allowed herself to be—what's the ancient phrase?—a guinea pig.”

Galahad grasped his meaning. “Is she trapped here?”

“She chooses to stay.”

“She's trapped.”

“Not at all. She's free to leave Perditon at any time, though her strength and skill will wane without the treatments.”

Lancelot did not understand Galahad's curiosity about Olc's sidekick. Perhaps it was the same impulse that led him to behave kindly to the waif who offered the water and batteries. Galahad's outward formality hid a compassion for the weak or the abused, and Aideen qualified, as far as Galahad was concerned. In a flash, Lancelot understood. Galahad felt abandoned as well, despite a loving grandfather. A fresh wave of guilt washed over Lancelot. Would he have had the same empathy had she raised him herself? It was impossible to know, but somehow, she doubted it.

"Let me be straight with you, Galahad.," Olc continued. "I may have found the Grail. However, I've been unable to recover it." Olc chuckled. "It's apparently not my destiny."

"I don't understand. You know where it is." Galahad's hand swept over the room. "You have far more resources than I. Why are you having so much trouble?"

"I'm a materialist, Sir Galahad. But I'm not so dismissive of the unseen realm as you might think. Destiny is an acknowledgment of influences beyond our understanding. It cuts both ways. I'm willing to place a bet on your destiny, and profit by it. We both win."

Satisfied with Olc's answer, Galahad said, "Where is it?"

"In time, my friend. First, I want to discuss an offer."

"You mean a trade? I'm not on a quest for a bargain, Olc."

"Life is a bargain, Galahad. You give up something to get something, whether it's your daily bread or the Grail. It's all a matter of the price."

"The Grail is more than an object, Olc." Galahad set his whiskey aside. "It's a symbol of humanity's dedication to restore the planet to health after polluting it for so many centuries. Viridiae needs the Grail back in its place. That's how humanity can be redeemed."

"That's what your grandfather told you, didn't he? Your grandfather also told you that you were the instrument of that redemption."

Galahad bristled at Olc's sarcasm.

"Unlike you, I have more prosaic designs on the Grail."

"I'm not interested in trading for it, Olc."

"Rest easy, Galahad. At least let me pitch my offer. It's the courteous thing to do."

Galahad could not resist an appeal to knightly virtue. Lancelot agreed. The fate of Viridiae was at stake.

CHAPTER 9: DESCENT INTO DECAY

Recovering their arms, Lancelot and Galahad climbed into a salvaged electric cart with Aideen and Olc. The vehicle gleamed as if newly made. Viridian law forbade manufacturing the carts from scratch, due to the damage mineral and ore extraction inflicted on the land in pre-Dissolution times. Olc, however, recovered Old Civilization transportation technology, and he added a trendy shine.

The trip to the mining site passed other Brabus Olc ventures. The cart's open windows let in the acrid smell of burning acetylene as robots cut apart salvaged steel fed to solar-powered furnaces and mills. Industrial hammers pounded molded shapes out of flat plate. Cranes lifted long bundles of extruded rebar onto flatbed trucks, their teamsters staying tight one behind the other like segments of a millipede. Though Lancelot traveled all over Viridiae and into the wilder parts of the Lucian Empire, she had never seen the factories that turned the detritus of the Old Civilization into the articles Camelot and the rest of the country needed to thrive. The forges of Perditon were her country's invisible lungs and heart.

The road led south away from the city, past neighborhoods of shanties and tenements. As the kilometers ticked by, the dense humanity thinned to a kind of gauze separating the city from the countryside. Olc's cart slowed and turned up a drive toward a gate. Signs in red and orange warned of danger to life and limb. A smaller sign required a check-in at the guard shack. A uniformed man, who stiffened into a semblance of respectful attention, waved the group through.

A vague odor of decay hung in the air, muting a collection of wilted flowers and burnt-out candles. “A makeshift memorial,” Olc said, “to my employees who've encountered whatever killed them.”

Two massive steel doors screeched as they opened. Just inside, another shack, empty, but big enough for two supervisors at desks, welcomed the travelers. When Olc stepped through the door, a screen flickered, asking for credentials. Like a tour guide, he said, “We're standing at the edge of what the Old Civilization called a 'landfill.'”

Aideen stood near the supervisor's office, glancing down a corridor black as ink. The air had the moist smell of decay.

“I work a dozen of these landfills all over Viridiae,” Olc said, “but this one is different. It's the biggest I've ever seen, three square kilometers. And it's at least a kilometer thick, though only a hundred meters lay above the normal elevation.”

The mound had more volume than the entire citadel of Camelot and its walled city combined. “It's a giant hole in the ground filled with trash,” Galahad said.

“It's not just any trash. For one thing, the landfill has an asphalt cap, a meter thick. We usually strip mine these landfills, but it was cheaper to bore into its side, like the old ore mines.”

“Why did the Old Civilization cap it and not the others?” Lancelot said.

“Probably to shed water. There's also a synthetic rubber liner underneath the landfill, probably to capture seepage. The whole thing sits on a basalt dome. This structure was purpose-built for containing the worst kinds of refuse, the type that turns groundwater into poison.” Olc picked up a fingernail-sized clump of metal, his eyes shining. “There's more gold, silver, and refined rare earths here than anywhere else on the continent. Only the Lucians have access to this much, and they don't care about protecting the land.”

Galahad held the amalgam of irregular shapes, dull colors, and reflective pinpoints. “You said something about a creature or predator."

"Someone tried to mine this landfill before, or at least they tunneled into it, looking for something. My engineers found the tunnels by accident."

"And they found this creature."

Lancelot thought of her hunt for the questing beast, and how it nearly killed her and Percival.

"They found something," Olc continued, "but I don't know what it is for sure. The first engineers did find a gallery, like a cave dug out of the compacted matrix. The metals interfered with the com signals, but we got this image."

Olc waved his com ring across the screen, about the size and shape of a large picture book or small atlas. The still image was fuzzy, but the roughly spherical shape was multifaceted, like a crystal, reflecting the miners' lamps, while glowing with a life of its own.

"My gods," Galahad said.

Lancelot nearly laughed. Her son reminded her of a boy of eight or nine, presented with the toy he'd always wanted. She'd sent him gifts for Winter Solstice, but she never saw him open them.

Aideen lost her angry edge as she gazed at the image on the screen. "Could it really be the Grail?"

"I've lost count of how many times I've asked myself that question," Olc said. "I admit a wave of feeling too, when I first saw the image. Despite its poor quality, it's one of the most beautiful things I've ever seen. It fits the description as well."

Lancelot was more skeptical. "Excuse me, but an out-of-focus snapshot isn't proof. Why do you suppose it's here, Olc?"

"I think it's an early prototype or a failed working design that was thrown out as a dead end. The Old Civilization was wasteful beyond belief. I'm betting there's plenty of value for me."

Lancelot reflected on the bargain Galahad and Olc struck. Galahad would recover the Grail and Olc would acquire any technology attached to the object. "What happened to your engineers?" Lancelot said.

"We don't know. They never came out. We presume they are dead. We sent in a rescue party, but they disappeared as well. Some of its telemetry suggests they were knocked around before they went silent."

Aideen spoke up. "That's when people started talking about an animal or monster."

The Grail had no sister, as far as anyone knew, but it was a functioning keystone relic of a more technologically advanced past. That's why Viridiae wanted it. Merlin reported that the rest of the machinery around the Great Machine was in good condition. Galahad would keep the working Grail device, but Olc could have the other equipment to recycle, repurpose, or sell.

"Do you have a map?" Galahad said.

"It's already in your com."

The map, akin to a sketch, appeared in Lancelot's com as well. "It's a half-day's journey in and out."

"You can leave in the morning," Olc said.

"I don't think I could wait that long," Galahad said. "I'll leave now."

"Hold on." Lancelot retreated, realizing she'd overstepped her role. As far as Olc was concerned, she was her son's functionary. "I mean, Sir Galahad, we should discuss this. We didn't plan on an expedition down a mine shaft."

Olc opened a locker. "We have emergency supplies here. They're meant for rescue operations. Take whatever you need."

"I'm going with you, pretty boy," Aideen announced. Uncertainty colored her declaration.

Sensing she was part of Olc's plan, Lancelot said, "Why, Olc?"

The businessman shrugged. "Insurance. You and Sir Galahad may be the knights destined to find the Grail, but I always hedge my bets."

* * *

The tunnel into the landfill, wide at first because of the boring machine, narrowed after a half-kilometer to space enough for an electric cart. It constricted after a half-dozen twists and turns to a passageway that forced the orange-helmeted knights and Olc's bodyguard into a crouch. All three wore salvaged and repaired night vision goggles. Lancelot squinted in the fuzzy green light, wondering if her eyesight was failing. The walls radiated a mossy glow like the embers of a chemical fire, highlighted by bits of metal that focused the heat into points, resembling stars in the night sky. Water dripped on everyone's head and their liquid-shedding coveralls. It dribbled down the tunnel walls. The stink was worse than the open sewers of Perditon's slums.

Lancelot started to think she'd made a mistake going into the tunnel, but she couldn't just let Galahad go in with Aideen while she waited outside.

"Aideen, what did Olc offer you?" Galahad said. "In exchange for the genetics?"

"Power. Strength. Influence. The usual temptations."

"Did you get what you wanted?"

"Yes, but..."

"Go on."

They came to a fork, and decided on the bigger tunnel.

"Actually, I lied just now," Aideen said. "Partly lied. I came to Perditon to get away from my parents. They wanted me to go to Camelot University. Spent thousands on tutors and youth sports. It was suffocating. I hated it. I hated them. I got some money for my 18th birthday. I spent it on a ticket here."

"Olc didn't force you to do anything, did he?" Lancelot could forgive many things, but not a man forcing himself on a woman.

"No, he has asshole qualities, but not that. Olc fancies being my mentor. I tolerate his ... quirks."

Lancelot understood. Aideen did what she had to do to survive, much like Penny, the water girl. While Penny was afraid of Olc, Aideen's attitude suggested a grudging admiration.

The tunnel abruptly ended, as if an old-style prospector had given up on a vein of ore. "The map says it goes on."

"What now?" Lancelot handed her companions water bulbs, and drank from her own.

"We've followed the map exactly," Galahad said. "Maybe there was a cave-in."

"Maybe that's why the engineers didn't come back. Crushed by thousand-year-old trash."

The collapse idea made more sense than a demonic creature to Lancelot. A time or two over the past hour, she believed she'd heard, or felt, a rumble through the tunnel floor. A fearful worker might imagine the tread of a monster or the paranormal. Even after a millennium, the mountain of refuse would settle, especially if water were plentiful. Lancelot wondered if voids formed, as they did in limestone as water and gravity worked their will on the compacted shells of sea creatures.

Galahad ran a gloved hand over the blockage. He pulled at the man-made scree a fragment at a time. Lancelot and Aideen pushed the detritus to the side. More material tumbled down from above. Shards of metal and plastic piled around the explorers' boots. A hole appeared, or rather a glow around a rough circle of oily black.

"I think we've found the gallery," Galahad said.

The explorers opened up a space large enough to crawl through. The gallery was bathed in deep green light so dense that Lancelot thought she was swimming in a pool of bio-luminescent plankton. The air was pestilential, according to the portable sensors. She adjusted her oxygen mask and goggles. She saw the bodies. "Five dead."

"Two engineers and three rescuers," Aideen said. "I recognize them."

Lancelot examined the bodies, arranged as if they died waiting for retrieval. "I don't see any oxygen bottles. You'd think the rescuers would've been better prepared."

"They wouldn't be the first rescuers to die from the same causes as the initial victims," Galahad said.

"Methane? Carbon monoxide?"

"Gaia knows what sort of evil is cooking in here. Olc should've known, though."

The gallery was irregular in shape. A low ceiling alternated with a nave-like cavity above a shallow pool. Dripping water echoed around the open space. Galahad picked his way around broken glass, jagged edges of torn steel, and lengths of wire. Nothing moved, suggesting nothing lived, except invisible, exotic bacteria or viruses.

Galahad gasped, a sickly sound coming through his mask. Lancelot followed his gaze and saw the Grail.

Her son fell to his knees. Was this moment that emotionally charged for him? She was awed, but not overwhelmed. The Grail was a goal, a mission, not a pilgrimage. Galahad behaved as if seeing a miracle described in the texts of the old monotheistic religions. Was it an instinctive reverence that brought him down to the disgusting floor of the cave? Or was it a child's amazement at seeing a dream incarnate itself into a thing that could be touched and held, like a long-sought gift on Winter Solstice Day? Lancelot let herself enjoy the comedy of it. After so many searches, Galahad had found the holy of holies on a high-tech dung heap.

"I hope it's worth all this trouble," Lancelot said.

Aideen knelt next to the helmet-sized device. "I had this idea of strange machinery all around, with wires and tubes and switches and blinking lights, like in the chan fantasy shows. This thing looks like it was dropped here like a deflated kick-game ball."

"A little respect, please," Galahad said.

"Sorry, I forgot it's your destiny to find the Grail."

Aideen's cheekiness had no visible effect on Galahad, but Lancelot imagined him hurt, while keeping his silence. Lancelot brought out a padded bag supplied by Olc. The device was smooth and warm, despite a layer of grime. Galahad caressed it.

Lancelot felt a rumble. "What's that?"

A chunk of the gallery wall loosened and fell, like a tiny avalanche.

"We need to go," Aideen said. "Now."

The three explorers leaped toward the burrowed entrance they'd created. Aideen pushed Galahad and Lancelot through.

He cradled the precious Grail in its bag, as if it were an infant. Ahead of them, chunks of metal resembling Olc's screen in the shack dropped, threatening to block their escape. They charged through the narrow tunnel, the green illumination poor at highlighting ankle-breaking divots on the floor.

A massive slab of metal leaned down, ready to fall. Galahad and Lancelot raced past it, but she felt a whoosh of air as the roof let go. The pressure of Aideen's palm on Lancelot's back, which reassured her against the emerald gloom, lessened, and she turned around. The fall buried Aideen, leaving only part of her arm visible.

Lancelot grasped her bleeding hand. "Aideen! We'll get you out." Only hours earlier, Aideen had tried to kill her son, and he'd threatened to kill her. However, she went into the tunnel with them, welcoming a dangerous adventure. She'd become a companion. For a moment, they all shared a common goal, to find the Grail. Aideen did it because she wanted to. Lancelot did it because it was her duty. Galahad did it because he had to.

Mother and son pawed at the junk until Lancelot came to a metal box crushing Aideen's shoulder. Her grip on Lancelot's hand weakened and then relaxed into an endless sleep.

Aideen's death saddened Lancelot, but she had seen many companions die on the battlefield. All the same, a tiredness crept up on her. The Grail, she reflected, was a killer, sure as a Lucian ambush. How many knights had failed to return from a quest for it? Look at Percival's expedition. One survivor out of two dozen. The Grail might kill again if they didn't run.

She tugged at Galahad, and she saw the tears welling in his eyes. What connection did he have to her? They were of similar age and both alone in the world. After his grandfather died, she received one of his few letters to her. It talked mostly about the estate—he'd left virtually all his property to him—but it contained one line Lancelot would never forget. *He was the most important person in my life.* She had no idea whom he turned to now for friendship. Another rumble brought Lancelot back to the moment.

After a kilometer, the tunnel widened, and the rumbling stopped. Breathing hard after a dead run, the knights stumbled forward, carrying the memory of Aideen's last touch, as well as the precious package. Lancelot tore off her goggles, seeing natural light for the first time in what felt like years. A worker sprayed soapy water on them from a hose. Olc agreed to a basic decontamination procedure. Another worker stood by, waiting for the missing explorer.

Olc approached Galahad. “Do you have it?”

“Yes.”

“Is Aideen coming?”

“No.”

Olc pursed his lips. “I see. Like the others?”

Galahad nodded.

“She was a ... valued employee.” Olc held out his hand for the bag.

Galahad shook his head. “We agreed.”

“I only meant to hold your burden for a moment while you rested.” Olc's face was pained. “But ...”

“We're leaving,” Galahad said. “Thank you for your help.”

Lancelot didn't like Olc either, and they had what he wanted. She guessed Galahad's mind raced ahead to his next task, returning the Grail to the machine on Apparatus Montis.

“Aideen sent me photos and recordings from the gallery.”

Lancelot thought of Galahad's silly obeisance before the Grail. “So?”

“There's nothing there, nothing of value, besides the Grail itself.”

“I guess you lost out on the bargain.” Galahad pushed past Olc. “Tough luck on the lack of return on your investment.”

“Wait. I'm not done. I can offer more.”

Galahad stopped.

“May I see it?”

Galahad removed it from the bag. In the late afternoon sun, the object gleamed less, but displayed more detail. Intricate embossed lines encased it, like a coarse, but tightly woven fabric. Its feathery lightness puzzled Lancelot, as if it were hollow.

"No one has seen this technology up close for a thousand years," Olc said. "Even Merlin is uncertain how this works, or how it fits into the machine in Apparatus Montis. All the sage-scientists know is that it's critical to keeping the planet's climate from spiraling out of control."

"I'm going to put it back where it belongs, Olc."

"Just give me five minutes with it, Galahad. I want to know its secrets."

"Does it matter?"

"Aren't you curious? What exotic metals and compounds it contains? Gold? Platinum? Gallium arsenide? My researchers still don't know how the Old Civilization made things. I want to know."

Lancelot's awareness turned to the pistols in her belt and Arondight on her hip. Would Olc try to take the Grail? There were no guards nearby, except at the gate shack.

"I'll give you anything for it, Galahad. I'm the richest man in Viridiae. Name your price!"

"How do you put a price on saving the planet? We have a job to do."

"I forgot. You have a destiny." Olc was on the verge of pleading. "I have a destiny, too. I supply the technology that we can't be rid of, com units and electrical power and lights at night. It's hard work, and I need help. Galahad, work with me."

Until now, Galahad had worked entirely alone on his search. Some people, Lancelot reflected, could never admit that life was a team effort. What did Galahad have to show for his investment? Almost nothing, and Olc had found the Grail in a place Galahad had never considered. He owed Olc.

"Let's be partners, Galahad," Olc said. "Share and share alike. With your reputation and my contacts, we'll conquer the whole country. We'll make Viridiae richer and stronger. That is your real destiny!"

All the talk of destiny made Lancelot wonder about hers. Guinevere came to mind, but how their futures were intertwined, she couldn't say.

In Galahad's hands, the Grail looked heavier, as if it took on mass generated by Olc's persuasiveness. And cupidity. Was Galahad selfish, Lancelot thought, believing only he had a destiny vis a vis the Grail?

Olc continued his speech. “Listen, Galahad, your grandfather understood the Grail's importance to Viridiae. He didn't mean for you to keep it to yourself. The Grail belongs to everyone. Make your grandfather proud and let me unlock its secrets. I won't harm it. I'll examine it, take images, record its behavior, maybe even duplicate it. Then you can take the original to Apparatus Montis. Imagine how you'll be honored and remembered for all you've achieved.”

An appeal to vanity. Olc was good at that.

Lancelot fantasized of riding her best horse through the streets of Camelot, soaking in the people's adulation. She loved the cheers of the crowd. Galahad however, craved one thing only, his grandfather's love. Would the old man have approved?

Finally, Galahad said, “You must promise not to change it or damage it, Olc. It has to be fully functional when the caretakers at Apparatus Montis re-install it.”

Olc's grin was as wide as the estuary that separated Perditon from the western mountains. “Of course, Galahad, of course.”

Olc left instructions for his miners to do all they could to retrieve the bodies of Aideen and the others. Lancelot, Galahad and Olc returned to the city. Galahad kept the Grail in his hands every moment. When they arrived at the Banker's Redoubt, the dirt, sweat, and oily smell persuaded Lancelot to bathe and let Olc's servants clean her clothing. Galahad followed suit, and he looked grand in his white woolen cloak. The knights let Olc lead them to the floors below the parking garage and stables.

“My research facilities,” Olc said. “Security is important to me, and there's no place in Perditon easier to defend.”

Or hard to escape from, Lancelot thought. The trio passed brightly lit rooms with white-coated technicians manipulating liquids and machines the nature of which Lancelot could only guess at. They opened the door to one of the labs, finding sage-scientists who eyed the Grail with the same greedy affect as Olc. With a gravity Lancelot appreciated nonetheless, they took the object out of its protective bag and placed it on a pedestal.

“The first thing we'll do is a full recording session, pictures, electromagnetic emissions, even sounds it might make,” Olc said, “for posterity's sake.”

Lancelot and Galahad had little to do but watch. An hour passed, then two. Incrementally, imperceptibly, the mood in the lab changed. Excitement morphed into puzzlement then dismay. Olc argued with his employees, demanding more tests, more images. The knights kept their distance, though Galahad never allowed the object out of his sight. It was like a part of his own body. Olc raged, and Lancelot wished she hadn't left her weapons in the locker. At last, wearing an expression that reminded her of the day she gave up her son, Olc approached.

“We found some writing on the ... Grail,” the See-Oh said.

“What does it say?” Galahad said. “Instructions on how it works?”

“We've gone over the translation a dozen times. It's hard to understand.” Olc rubbed the bottom of his chin, still disbelieving what he'd been told.

“Well?”

“The words say something like, 'For demo purposes only. Not functional.'”

“What?”

“There isn't a single working circuit in it, beyond a few light emitting diodes.”

Galahad blinked.

“It's not what either of us is looking for,” Olc said.

The humor of it overwhelmed Lancelot. She guffawed so hard she reached for a wall to keep from falling and embarrassing herself. It was a sample, a show piece, a facsimile. She stopped laughing when she remembered Aideen.

The edges of Galahad's mouth turned down in disappointment. Another dead-end for him. Another false lead. Another failure. A false Grail, this time. Galahad thought he was smart enough and trained enough to see enough before he tripped over the fakes, the replicas, the copies.

Lancelot felt ashamed of her laughter. The light had gone out of her son's eyes.

What Galahad found in the landfill never occurred to him as a possibility, but it offered a new puzzle. What did "demo" mean? "Demonstration," maybe? Why would you build the most important invention in 10,000 years as a spectacle or an exhibit? Much of the Old Civilization was unexplained.

Olc handed Galahad the padded bag. The object was inside. "This belongs to you. It's got some recycle value, but..."

Six people died for the device, believing it was something it was not.

The three spoke little as they rode the elevator to the garage. Olc appeared as if the incident was all in a day's work. Lancelot felt a mixture of contempt and admiration for the pudgy See-Oh, who let tragedy go like an old scab.

The weight of the world was on Galahad's shoulders.

The elevator door opened to a commotion. A child screamed, and a heavyset man in a faded uniform dragged her toward Olc. The child was Penny.

"Mr See-Oh, I swear I was going to pay you, but..."

Penny was caught shorting the loan enforcer on her installments.

"Sales have been terrible this month. The new batteries didn't hold charges, and people wanted their money back."

Lancelot noticed that her com charge didn't last as long as it should.

"No excuse, kid," Olc said. "Money owed is money owed. You know what happens to stiffers."

Penny's face went white. "Please, just a few more days, Mr See-Oh." She glanced at Galahad. "Sir, you must be the See-Oh's friend. Tell him to trust me. You know me. I'll get the money."

The idea that Galahad might be Olc's friend struck Lancelot as delusional. On the other hand, he was standing beside the businessman like a colleague. “Olc, is punishment necessary?”

“This isn't your business, Galahad.”

Lancelot found the urge to make it her business. In a way, Penny reminded her of Aideen, independent and ambitious. She didn't know what the punishment might be for Penny, but she guessed it was something a child shouldn't suffer. Or anyone. “Olc, you said the Grail, I mean, this object, had some recycle value.”

“A little.”

“Will it cover the child's debt?”

Olc eyed the knight, doing the math, and, Lancelot guessed, the value of staying on the good side of two Round Table knights. “It could.”

Galahad pushed the bag into Olc's hands. He approached the guard, looking him in the eye. The guard glanced at Olc, and released his grip on Penny.

“Thank you, sir. Thank you.” She made as if to scramble off.

Galahad snagged her ragged dress. “Not so fast. Now you owe us.”

Penny's expression changed from relief to fear.

“Saddle the horses. We're leaving.”

“But, sir--”

“Do as I tell you or I'll take back my offer.”

Penny's glance went round among the faces of Lancelot, Galahad, and Olc.

“Maybe we'll have better luck next time, Galahad.” Olc departed, the guard trailing him.

Lancelot doubted Galahad would ever see Olc again.

Her options down to one, Penny struggled to put the heavy saddle on Galahad's horse. The knights came over and helped her with both animals. Lancelot showed her how to cinch the saddles tight without irritating the creatures.

“You're a terrible groom,” Galahad said to Penny, “but I need help at my farm.”

“You're kidnapping me?”

“I'm offering you a job.” Galahad saw her doubt. “Two meals a day, a pallet in the barn, none of Olc's punishments."

Penny said nothing, though Lancelot guessed she was again weighing her options. She'd learned not to jump at chances too quickly.

When Olc's guard appeared at the exit to the street, Lancelot thought Penny was wiser than her years. She moved her hand slowly to her single-shot pistol.

"See-Oh Olc wants you to have this." The guard held out the padded bag.

Galahad opened it and saw the False Grail.

"The See-Oh says it's of no use to him."

Lancelot remembered the pain on his face when he informed him of Aideen's death. Did the False Grail remind him of her? Did he want to forget?

Galahad nodded in thanks, and the guard stepped aside.

On the street, Penny spoke up. "What if I don't like the job?"

"What job?" Galahad was distracted.

"At your farm."

"You can always come back to Perditon."

Penny took in the squalor of the half-dead city. "I guess I owe you a few day's work."

Lancelot was glad. Galahad had scored a success, after all.

CHAPTER 10: DISOBEDIENCE

Percival paced in front of a window in his apartment that overlooked a busy street. Watching people and carts moving freely in Camelot intensified his boredom and anxiety. He was bound to follow Arturus' orders to rest at home, and though he woke up tired in the morning and often napped during the day, he itched to get back to unfinished business.

"Your landlord won't appreciate the groove you're wearing into the floor." Dee sat in Percival's only comfortable chair, swinging her leg impatiently.

Percival ignored her taunt. "Have you been following the news from Perditon?"

"Everyone's seen it."

"A secret trip to the city. They disappear for a couple of days. The com channel talkers go crazy with made-up stories. And this False Grail thing happens."

"People are wondering if the Grail even exists and we're all doomed."

Percival tapped absently on the window glass. "No, it's out there, but I'm stuck here."

"Lord Mordred and the Regarders believe it's out there too."

"I don't trust him. He knows more, and he wants more than he's letting on. What's up with you and him, anyway?"

Dee looked away. Percival had read the comments thread on the com about Guinevere and the First Minister's visit to the gallery for Dee's opening. The gossips chattered about Mordred's interest in the up-and-coming artist.

"He's just a potential patron, that's all. I have to be friendly with all of them. Don't believe everything you read."

A plausible answer, but it wasn't the whole truth. Percival wasn't in the mood, however, for teasing out the real story. His mind kept returning to the Grail, and his failures. Galahad's expedition seemed on the verge of failure as well. Disease had erupted among the horses at Grey Harbor. Several had died. An idea formed in Percival's heart. The new delay gave him an opportunity.

"What are you thinking about?"

Dee could almost read his mind.

"Nothing important."

"You have that look you got when you were going to do something forbidden by Mother."

The mention of his mother elicited a sharp pain in Percival's chest. It gave him a chance to change the subject. "Have you heard from her?"

"I've kept her up to date. What about you?"

"Nothing."

"Have you called or texted her?"

Percival pursed his lips. He'd barely spoken to her since his graduation from The Keep. At least she'd attended. Of course, communication was impossible for much of Sir Kevin's expedition, but Percival had received nothing since his return. "I don't know if I should. She's ..." Percival shook his head, unwilling to broach the subject.

"I know you and her are still—"

"I don't want to talk about it. I just need to get out of here."

"What do you have in mind?"

"Gaia in Heaven, what do you want from me?"

Dee raised his shoulders defensively. "You don't need to take my head off. I just know you're planning something and it's probably wrong or possibly illegal."

"How long am I supposed to stay cooped up in here when I should be helping Lancelot and Galahad find the Grail?"

"As long as it takes to get better. Arturus said to stay home.

Guinevere's doctor said the same."

"They didn't mean to put me in a cage. Can't I just go riding for an hour?"

"I'd say 'yes', but that's not what you have in mind."

Dee could be so exasperating. He needed her to support him, to be his best friend, as she always was. Sometimes best friends looked the other way. She wouldn't this time.

"If I tell you, will you snitch on me?"

"It depends. If I think you're wrong, or you're going to hurt yourself, I might."

"Then I'll keep it to myself."

Dee threw up her hands. "Fine! I won't report you, but you have to tell me the details, just in case I have to organize a rescue."

Percival relaxed. "I'm thinking of going to Grey Harbor and see if Lancelot and Galahad will let me come with them."

"You're even dumber than I thought. They won't let you near their expedition."

"Why not?"

"First, you'd be disobeying the king. That's bad enough. They'd be aiding and abetting too. That's a crime."

"Not if I snuck aboard the ship."

"You have truly lost your mind."

"I can't stay in here forever!" Percival needed to get out of Camelot. He wanted to search for the Grail, by himself if necessary. He needed to redeem himself for surviving Sir Kevin's expedition. The old knight was the last one to die on the trek home. He asked Percival to keep up the search. The Grail had to be found. The nation and the planet depended on it. He believed Percival was the man to do it. He had to bring it back to Camelot.

"What are you thinking about now?" Dee said.

"An old man, a failure, not much different from our father, except that Sir Kevin was a good man in every way that Sir Adnan was not."

"You're not escaping Camelot out of guilt, are you?"

"I'm going because I have to go. It's the only thing I know how to do."

Dee thought for a moment. "I don't blame you, Perce. I'd go crazy, too. Just take it easy and don't hurt yourself."

"Thanks, Dee."

"Find a way to tell me you're alright. Or I'll worry too much."

"I will. I'm planning to stop at a friend's place on the way." Percival explained his next step.

"If I don't hear from you in three days, I'll report you," Dee said.

Percival loved his sister because she believed in him. For most of his life, he had only her and his mother. He would do anything to promote Dee or protect her.

"I've got to get back to the studio." Dee gathered her jacket. "Ganieda tells me people are knocking on her door every ten minutes asking about me."

"Fame must be fun."

"I'm not sold on it."

Brother and sister embraced. Percival watched for her to appear on the street below his window. He waved, and she was gone.

He skipped into his bedroom. He threw a change of clothes into a pack and slung it over his shoulder. He studied his new war javelin, meant to replace the one he'd lost in the forest, but he couldn't take it with him. It would cause too much gossip on the street. Once out the door, he ran to the royal stables. He felt as he'd been sprung from a jail cell. The sun was bright and the air warm with freedom. He roused a stable boy from a nap and borrowed one of the riding horses, promising to return it in an hour. He regretted the lie, but he needed time to get away.

Percival rode down side streets toward Camelot's western gate. His route took him past the Judson Ball Gallery, where Dee had her "first light" show. He'd wanted to attend, but she insisted he stay home. He agreed, in part because too many people might gather around him, rather than focus on her. As he walked his horse past the gallery window, it appeared empty, save for a young woman sweeping the floor. Percival couldn't resist stopping. He dismounted, tied the horse's reins to a post, and stepped into the gallery.

"I'm sorry, sir, we're closed." The young woman was firm, but friendly. She had light blond hair to her shoulders, which set off her gray-green eyes.

"The door was open," Percival said. "Sorry."

"I was just about to lock up." The woman looked at Percival funny. "I recognize you. You're Sir Percival, Dee Rathkeale's brother."

Percival looked over his shoulder. "Yes, I am. Do you mind keeping your voice down? I'm not really supposed to be out."

"Okay." The woman looked wary, then grinned, as if she'd caught on to a game. "My name's Lina. Your sister and I met at her show's opening night."

"I think she mentioned you. Look, I'm on my way ... out. But I couldn't come to the show. Do you think I could look at the tapestry?"

Lina brushed past Percival. Her hair smelled of rosemary. She locked the gallery door and gestured Percival to follow.

He was happy to do so.

Lina flicked a few switches and Dee's *Coronation* lit up. The light tapestry awed Percival for its intricate colors and fine movements, but he couldn't help looking at Lina as well. What was it about her? Dee had only mentioned her in passing, but she was as magnetic as the art.

"I can only stay a minute, Sir Percival. I have a class tonight, and I haven't read the materials. You can come back tomorrow. We open at 10 a.m."

"I won't be in town. I mean, I won't be available." Percival kicked himself for revealing too much, but Lina made him forget where he was and what he was doing.

Lina touched him lightly on the arm, a signal that she wanted him to leave. "If you come back, I'll give you a full tour."

Percival moved toward the door. "I'd like that."

A moment later, Percival was back on his horse. He blinked a few times, wondering why he'd come to the gallery. A public car honked at him, and he remembered. In a slight daze, he spurred the horse out the western gate, and into an enormous green space reserved for mushrooms and other wild foods. The woodland and meadow, called the People's Preserve, was rough and wild, but its morels and huckleberries were prized by every kitchen cook and restaurant chef in the city. He thought of his mother's property near the King's Forest far up in the mountains.

The memory was loaded with nostalgia and sadness. The last time he saw Eleanor's land and house was a few days after the death of his father, Sir Adnan deGrosse. In the aftermath, Percival was sorry for his father's death, despite the noble reasons, and he was certain his mother would be relieved, but he was fearful of how she would take his next decision.

For as long as he could remember, she'd hated all knights. The mere mention of them would start a fight. She believed all knights who espoused chivalry and courtesy were nothing but hypocrites, and in the case of Adnan deGrosse, criminals. Percival respected his mother, but he also respected Arturus, and he wanted to follow him. He wanted to become a knight.

Percival did not like arguing with his mother. She had a way of bullying people if she didn't get what she wanted. She owned property in the nearest town. When her tenants were late on their rent, she would threaten to evict them. But a knight asked for what he wanted with courage, calm, and courtesy.

"Mother, His Majesty has invited me to join his household as a page. He's promised me a place at The Keep if I obey the rules and serve him with honor. Dee is invited too. I'm going. That's my decision."

"You're not even sixteen yet. You're my child, and I forbid you to go."

Percival found more courage. "Are you telling me that I should turn down an invitation from our king?"

Eleanor trembled with rage. Percival also sensed fear, but of what, he couldn't tell.

"Mother, Gaia in Her goodness has opened this door. I promise

I'll be the best knight I can be. I'll serve the king and make you proud. Maybe I'll even find the Grail."

For a moment, Percival thought Eleanor might be softening. He was wrong.

"If you leave, I will never speak to you again."

The conversation was over. The abrupt end brought tears to Percival's eyes, but he'd made up his mind. He didn't really believe his mother would close her world to him. She was just angry. That's what Dee said. But since then, his mother had been true to her word.

On the trail in the People's Preserve, Percival's eyes watered at the painful memory, but he never regretted his decision to follow his own path. He loved being a knight, and though he'd failed in his last mission, other people still seemed to respect him. He found the idea hard to swallow, but people were hard to figure out, sometimes.

It didn't take long for Percival to recover himself. His palfrey was strong and sleek. The horse ambled lightly over the trail, enjoying the relative liberation of the People's Preserve. Energy returned to Percival as if he were a bank of solar cells soaking up the rays pouring down from heaven. He thought of the girl in the gallery, Lina. He hoped to see her again.

* * *

A few hours later, Percival stopped at the crest of a rise offering a westerly view. The sun was a hands-breadth above the horizon. His mood dimmed as the solar disk dropped. The light shone thicker. Shadows stretched further. The air temperature fell. He had doubts about his decision to leave Camelot without permission. He didn't like tricking people or asking Dee to lie for him. He pulled on a light coat, and he stopped at a place where the trail to the ridge met the main track through the woodland. He could still go back to the city. Or he could visit a man he respected and ask his advice. He was a knight of the Round Table and a member of the Regarders Order. Percival headed into the gathering darkness.

Just as the sun dipped below the hills, he came upon private land adjoining the public forest. The road passed a compact, well-kept farm with a large, long barn, a few outbuildings, and a red house with a broad porch sheltering two spindly chairs. Percival saw no animals, apart from a destrier that chewed on clumps of grass in a pasture. A vague smell of urine floated from the outbuildings. Since the loss of the Grail, crops for vegetable protein failed to make predicted yields, and the demand for meat was rising. The farmer had expanded his swine operation as prices rose, despite the tight limitations on animal protein production. The silence puzzled Percival.

Sir Alan Christopher Bors de Gannes was nowhere to be seen. Percival called into the house with no answer. He walked his borrowed palfrey to the barn, tied him to a post, and let him snack on leftovers from a hay bale. The ground was mucky from a recent shower, and Percival had a hard time making way to the rear of the house without slipping on his ass. There he found a man with a gloved hand resting on the butt end of a shovel. The blade touched a mound at his feet.

"Chris!" Percival called out.

Bors lifted his head to see who had called to him. He tilted a straw hat away from his eyes and allowed a smile. He lay the shovel on the ground and used his teeth to take off the leather glove. He reached out with his right hand and took Percival's warmly.

The stump of his left arm was thin but tanned.

"Percival Rathkeale, as I live and breathe."

Sir Bors was genuinely happy to see Percival, as if the young man was a cool glass of water after hard work. Droplets of sweat gathered on the farmer's temples.

Percival reviewed Bors' work. The mound was long and low, the dirt freshly turned. "I'm afraid to ask, but..."

"Yes, it's a grave."

Percival tensed. "Not Elaine? Not Agravain?" Percival feared the worst.

"No, both are healthy and strong, but not here. Wife and son are off visiting relatives." He named a small town a couple of hundred kilometers away.

"Then who is it?"

"I doubt you knew her."

"What happened?"

"Come on, let's go to the house. I stink, and I need a beer."

Inside the farmhouse, Bors pulled off his shirt, revealing a bandage that wrapped around the lower half of his torso. Dots of dark red seeped through.

"Chris, you're hurt!"

"I'm fine, but you can help me with changing the bandage."

Percival forgot about his troubles. A thousand different questions crowded his mind about Bors. He worried for his old instructor, who had taught a series of classes in forest law. They'd struck up a friendship after discovering a mutual interest in long hikes.

The wound was a five-centimeter gash just below his rib cage. The stitches were even and tight and surrounded by black and blue.

The shower and fresh dressing renewed Bors. He offered Percival a cold beer and suggested they sit on the porch. The air was cool but still. Both men wrapped themselves in a light blanket. Night insects called and bats ate their fill.

"What brings you out here?" Bors said.

"After seeing the grave and your wound, I'm not sure it's really important."

"I'll tell you the story if you tell me why you've come. I haven't seen you in a year. You were on Sir Kevin's expedition, right?"

Percival told a short version of Lancelot's rescue, his semi-exile at home, and his desire to join the new expedition against the king's wishes.

Bors did not immediately condemn Percival's idea of leaving Camelot. That was why Percival wanted to talk to Bors. He knew the farmer and warrior would hear him out. Bors had a reputation as a practical man who didn't accept received wisdom. On the other hand, he didn't always jump to a friend's side if he thought the friend was wrong.

"Big decision," Bors said. "It's hard to go against the king."

"But I'd be doing it for the country and the planet. Just like the Regarders are sworn to do."

Bors nodded. "I'll have to think about it. In the meantime," he said, raising his bottle, "let's drink to Odilia Malehaut, may she rest in peace."

Percival listened as Bors began his tale.

CHAPTER 11: A HUNT FOR TROLLS

On a blustery day three days before Percival's visit, Sir Bors touched commands on the ranch robot's controller with the thick, calloused thumb of his right hand, wedging the device against the stump of his left arm. He added whistles and shouts to the squeals of his sows and boars. Odilia Malehaut, Bors' tenant and occasional farmhand, goaded the animals through a gate.

"Are you going to obey those orders, Bors?" Dil maneuvered her mobile chair to extricate herself from the fetid mix of mud and pig dung. "The bureaucrats at Camelot always underestimate a troll's cleverness." The dog-sized robot scooted out of her way.

"My first job is getting the livestock under a roof before the weather gets here." Bors observed the signs of another deluge, confirmed by the forecast from Camelot's observatory. Bors thumbed another command.

Bors closed the livestock gate behind him with his good hand. Dil inched her chair forward to hold the gate closed while Bors wrapped a salvaged piece of electrical wire around the posts as a makeshift latch. Bors owed Dil, though her bitterness at her *de facto* exile wore on him. At least once a day, she railed against the powers that put her out to pasture, vowing revenge, though Bors could not imagine what use to Camelot a paraplegic knight might be.

Underneath the whirring blades of a wind turbine, Bors blew off chunks of mud from the robot herder's treads with a power sprayer. "Sir Gawain's instructions are straightforward enough, Dil, and he speaks with Lord Mordred's authority. There are suspected trolls poaching in the forest. Gawain wants me to investigate and liquidate."

"Great Gaia, Bors. How many times do I have to tell you? What the message doesn't say is as important as what it does say."

"Alright, read between the lines for me."

"They want you back at court, man, even a one-armed swineherd like you."

Bors shook his head. "I'm not interested in court life, but I promised Mordred to stay in the Regarders. I have a duty."

"You ought to say 'no'. It's not safe for a knight without backup, even one as good as you."

"I'll be fine."

"So you're going?"

"I swore an oath to protect the land and the people. Refusing is not an option." He held a door open while Dil's chair crawled through. The robot remained outside. "Besides, it's only a couple of trolls."

Dil winced.

"Gaia, I'm sorry, Dil." A troll had put Dil in her chair.

"I let my guard down one time, and the bastard slices through my spinal cord with a short blade. It was as much my fault as its fault." Dil sighed and fingered her war knife, though she'd never use it again in a fight. "If it weren't for you, Bors, I'd be a corpse. Or a half-corpse with no place to live."

Dil had no family, so Bors took her in and gave her the cottage at low rent. He wasn't sure where the money came from, but it wasn't his business. Bors' wife Elaine objected, arguing that the cottage be converted into a getaway for overworked corporates. The family needed the cash.

"I know it's just trolls, Bors, but it smells of bigger things, things that might overwhelm you."

"I can take care of myself."

"What's your plan?" Dil's skepticism was marbled with worry.

Bors fingered the key code on the armory door. "Start at the last known kill. See if there's any obvious trail."

"It's been two days. The trail's gone cold. Maybe you should start at the known troll nests? Or maybe delay a start and ask Gawain's office for more details?"

When she was whole, Bors thought, she was less cautious. Go with what you know, she taught. She'd lost more to that troll than her legs. Her anger and grief had eroded Bors the student's faith in Dil the master.

Bors stepped into the vault, which was too narrow for Dil and her chair. He donned his lighter, fiber-based armor that covered his bulky shoulders, torso, upper legs, and upper arms. With practice, he learned to secure everything one-handed. He'd lost his left forearm and hand when a one-ton warhorse at full gallop stepped on it. He'd seen coarser meat in a sausage. He'd tried a prosthesis, but the gadgets were worse than no arm at all.

"Trolls are smarter than most people think, Dil, but they'll leave something at the site."

"Suit yourself, but I'd look for a nest, even a cave."

Bors opened a tall cabinet and removed a sword. Like the plate armor, he left his heavy long sword, Terror-Cause, in its place, and removed Reach-Into-The-Enemy's-Heart. He unwrapped the lighter weapon from a tightly woven cloth and examined the blade. He smiled to himself and wiped it with a polishing cloth, careful not to touch its cutting edge.

He also tucked a single-shot, muzzle-loading pistol into his holster and tuned his com set to the Regarders' frequencies. Bors tested the grip of Reach and moved the long blade in sweeps, warming up his arm and body, stepping through the routine Dil had taught him, though he had added variations of his own to compensate for his lost limb. He missed the warrior's life at times like this, when he could focus on strength and grace, grateful that he had not lost his skills even as his thirties ticked off. He liked his present situation, however, raising a son and sleeping with a beautiful woman every night, though she spent more time than he liked with her parents in Cameliard.

"Your *remise* is too slow, Bors," Dil said. "And your balance is off. Perhaps you should practice a day or two before heading out."

"You have no enthusiasm for this assignment, do you, Dil?" Bors relaxed from his attack stance. "The Dame Odilia Malehaut who was my teacher would've told me to practice by killing a troll or a Lucian knight."

Dil shrugged. "Life in a wheelchair puts aggression into perspective."

Bors slipped Reach into the scabbard on his hip.

Tears of the Dead neighed.

Bors approached his black mare, touching its rump. "I'm sorry, girl. Heavy warhorses aren't much use on forested ground."

The animal whinnied again, as if protesting. Bors stroked its forehead and kissed it. "We'll ride together again soon. I promise."

"I'll let her out for a run when the rain stops, Bors." Dil had not mounted a horse since her injury.

Bors slipped on the backpack he'd prepared in the morning. He ran a cloth over the chromed Regarder badge. In the center was a golden tulip, the ancient symbol of environmental protection. The Order's motto on his badge, *Defendat super omnia Terrae*, roughly translated to "Protect the Earth over all things."

"Be careful, goddamn you." Dil said.

"It's just another troll hunt, one more job among a thousand."

"I wish I were going with you."

Bors tapped his friend's shoulder. "Take care of the place, Dil." The knight flipped the cowl of his coat over his clean-shaven head, and walked into the rain.

* * *

The concrete road—a relic of the percussive impact of humans on the land before the Dissolution—hugged a river that flowed out of the mountains. The road angled into an adjoining dell and vanished beyond a felled tree covered in moss, the man-made slabs smothered by maple and alder, hemlock and fir. The log marked the boundary between private land and the lands protected by the Crown. Bors was one of only a handful of people legally allowed to do so in this section of the preserve. Not even Arturus could take animals, plants, or ores from the preserve and its mountains without the Round Table's consent. Button-sized drips of rainwater collected on the new leaves and thumped Bors' cowl when they didn't hit his prominent nose.

A creature emerged from the forest. Bors tensed and lifted his gun. A doe and her fawn nibbled at new shoots of salal. Bors breathed out. No threat here. He sat on the middle step of three molded stairs blanketed in sprawling moss the color of Elaine's eyes.

Before leaving the farm, Bors discussed tactics with Dil. "Do you believe what they say?"

"About what?"

For a second, Bors saw the tall Odilia Malehaut towering in the saddle of her warhorse. Her hair was white-silver, and it cascaded to her shoulders in waves. Her voice was breathy, like a wind through a pass.

"It's said the hearts of trolls are black."

"I can tell you they're as meaty and bloody as a man or woman's."

"I mean black in the psychological sense, that they have no empathy."

"Son," Dil said, "when I was active in the Regarders, I didn't concern myself with a troll's mental state, except whether it was trying to kill me or not. In the former case, I killed it first. In the latter case, I killed it anyway. I thought of them as vermin, with a bigger brain, admittedly."

"They're an offshoot of humanity, after all. Doesn't that entitle them to a measure of respect, even rights? There's sage-scientists at Camelot University who think their intelligence is equal to humans."

"Maybe, but I've never seen it."

In the clearing where the fawn appeared, Bors unpacked his shelter, sleeping gear, and electric fire. He needed his rest for the coming slaughter.

* * *

The first sign of troll appeared around noon the next day, but not as Bors had expected. He'd located the site of the last-known kill. To Bors' disappointment, the trail was cold; grasses and fungi had already sprung up around the area where the animal, a large deer, was butchered. That said, broken branches and other clues pointed toward the foothills.

The rain had stopped overnight, but a wind had come up, sweeping through the dense firs as Bors climbed the trail. A crack echoed now and then, as rotted branches gave way and fell. The thin track followed a rushing rill, and Bors marked its contrast to the desert lands on the other side of the mountains split by the River Colum.

If she were with him, Dil might've seen the troll before Bors did, before it had a chance to swing its cudgel and catch him in the shoulder of his good, whole arm. The blow ejected the gun from his hand and knocked him into a tree. He dodged the rushing troll just in time for it to crash into the ancient fir. They struggled around its rising roots, but the troll found purchase a half-second before Bors. When it tackled him, the knight's unprotected head hit a stone. When he came to, he was sitting next to the ashes of an illegal camp fire, his one wrist lashed to a sapling as thick as his forearm.

Reach-Into-The-Enemy's-Heart was out of reach. His pistol was nowhere in sight.

Despite the knock on the head, Bors' mind was clear. By this time, he had seen dozens of trolls, buck and bitch, dead and alive. This buck's gray-black skin was scarred and filthy, but he looked comfortable in the evening chill, as if he were on a tropical beach. He brushed his matted, sandy hair away from his widely spaced eyes, the pupils black as onyx. The sage-scientists had given his kind a name: *homo sapiens mutans*, Mutant Man.

“Why haven't you gagged me?” Bors could think of nothing

else to say.

"To whom will you call out?"

Not to Dil, Bors thought.

"If you do decide to make noise, I'll kill you."

"Like you did the king's wildlife?"

"You would do the same if you were starving or needed medicine."

"Why don't you kill me now?"

"I'm not a murderer."

Bors fought an urge to recount the warriors' bodies he'd seen mutilated by trolls. He restrained himself from arguing with his captor, however, knowing a cool head and patience would see him through his predicament.

His jawed dropped, though, when the troll removed a finger length scroll from the pocket of his ragged and torn shirt. Unrolling the paper, the creature withdrew a thin length of charcoal, and he made a series of careful marks.

No one had ever reported a troll taking notes, as far as Bors knew.

"You accuse us of murder constantly." The troll called itself Mang. "You, on the other hand, are the real murderers."

"How so?" Bors knew the troll's answer. Getting it to talk might distract it. The knight needed time to loosen his bonds. The troll had done half-a-job on the knot that held Bors fast to the tree.

"That's the thing with you smooth-skins," the troll said. "You're oblivious to what you created, and how you hate it."

Bors, like most people, thought of trolls with contempt as well as fear. As part of his training, he'd learned about the DNA mods. Before the Dissolution, when the world fell apart, doctors learned to modify DNA in living people to cure disease. A few people decided to add tiger stripes or fur to their bodies. Two or three generations later, the trolls appeared. The mods had infested the gene pool, launching a branch of the human race.

"Hate is a strong word." Bors tugged at his binding.

"You don't pity us, do you?" The troll scratched an insect bite.

"Pity should be reserved for dumb animals, not human beings."

When Bors was seven years old, his mother took him to see his aunt. She was so pregnant, Bors worried she might burst. She asked him whether he was excited about having a new playmate. He was. Later, he'd heard the baby was born, but within a few days, his parents stopped answering his questions about his new cousin, as if it had never been conceived.

The birth of a troll brought shame on a family. Bors' cousin had been left in a designated place in the forest in hopes that it would be found by a bitch, or even a buck, to raise as its own. The family never spoke of the babe again.

Bors rarely thought about his lost cousin, except when hunting trolls.

The knight positioned his body to hide his successful effort at loosening his bonds. "If trolls stopped poaching animals and fouling streams and land with their waste, Viridiae would leave them alone."

"You expect us to starve ourselves? You discard your whelps in the forest in hopes they'll survive, but when they do, you try to kill them. And now, as your land is dying, you come to us for food."

Bors had not thought much about how the bush meat had found its way into Camelot. His instructions were to find and eliminate the trolls killing wildlife. That word, the plural "trolls," doubled back and hit him. Bors cursed himself for forgetting the fact. Despite their aversion to groups, they disliked solitude. They worked in pairs whenever possible. "Where's your partner, Mang?"

The troll said nothing, but Bors saw the change. The creature shrank a little into itself. It's expression morphed from defiance to loss, or fear of loss. Bors resented the troll's emotions. He didn't want it to *feel*. If it knew empathy, destroying it was harder. If it was as intelligent as he, implied by the dusty scratching on the scroll, killing it might be murder.

"Where is she?" Bors caught Mang's eye. What if the creature was his cousin? What if it had somehow learned to read and write, and it found a mate, though the pair could never have children? Dear gods, Bors thought, what if we're wrong about that too?

Bors tore himself away from his doubts as he gently tugged on his bindings. The Regarder had a job, a mission, an oath, even as he regretted his goal. He meant to slay a creature that had no respect for the land, even if it were a kind of cousin, separated from Bors by a thousand years and the mistakes of a dead civilization. "Let me go, Mang, and I'll let you find her."

The troll laughed. "Letting you go would be like letting a snarling dog loose to tear me to shreds." He reached into a soiled bag, a Viridian castoff salvaged by Mang or its partner.

Bors launched himself shoulder-first into his captor's ribs. He heard a *crack* as the two tussled. Bors found Reach, got to his feet, and swung it in a tight arc. The tip of the blade sliced the tough skin of Mang's lower back, but only enough to split the epidermis. Mang yelped and took off at a run. It had the advantage of knowing the terrain, and as the chase quickened, Bors understood that it was running for its partner, as well as its life.

The path ahead made a sharp curve around a cliff face. Bors stopped. The rain started again, the droplets the size of a sparrow's eggs, and he fought off a shiver. The spot was a perfect place to ambush the knight as he made the turn. "Mang, let's talk." The troll was near. He could feel it. He thought of the marks on the paper. "We can trade. Your life for that document. It's a record, right?" Bors guess on the scroll's contents was a gamble. He was tasked with eliminating the troll, but if it was smart enough to keep records...

"Why should I trust you?"

The voice was to Bors' rear. Had he missed something? "I'm turning around to face you, Mang. I respect you that much." The troll was three meters away, pointing Bors' pistol at his head.

"You think I'm no better than a rodent."

They're vermin, Dil had said, *with a few more gray cells.* "I've a job to do, Mang." A fear pricked at Bors, the kind that makes you wonder if you've made a huge mistake. "My job is to kill you, but

I get to decide when. I don't have to do it right now."

Mang's hand held steady, but the rain pouring onto its head flowed into its eyes, and it blinked. Bors charged. The creature was nimble enough to avoid him, and it took off down the trail again.

Bors wondered why the troll hadn't shot him.

The twists and turns kept Mang just out of Reach's range until the troll tripped on an exposed root. It fell sideways onto its broken rib and screamed. Just as Bors caught up, it lifted the pistol and fired over the knight's head.

Bors raised the steel blade. He plunged it into the creature's chest below its sternum. The troll lived long enough to grab the blade with its hands, ignoring the slicing pain in its palms as it struggled to pull it out. Bors held firm, an image in his mind of a broken Dil in her wheelchair. The troll's eyes rolled up and it let out a gurgling final breath.

* * *

The liquidation occurred in the thin transition zone between the forest and cultivated land on the border of the preserve. When Bors withdrew a gore-smeared Reach and oriented himself, he saw his barn and his house and his warhorse Tears of the Dead in his pasture, and he thought of his wife, his son, and Dil. His breath shortened. Mang was within shouting distance of its partner. The scream was a warning.

Bors imagined the worst: His wife, home early, surprised by a troll, beaten to death, and his son, his brains bashed out on a fence post, and Dil, out of her chair, defenseless. The downpour darkened the gloom, and Bors steeled himself. He used the subtle drumming of drops on the roofs of his house and barn to cover his approach. No lights illuminated the house, despite the slow turning of the wind generator, and he sighed with relief; Elaine hadn't come home, and she would have his son Agravain with her.

That left Dil. Tears of the Dead was sheltering under a tree, which meant Dil was not in her cottage. Crouching low, moving with deliberation, he approached the barn, and he saw the light in the crack between the door and the threshold. He heard nothing, and he began to doubt his assumptions. Was she inside? Did she forget to turn the light off before leaving? Was she a hostage, trussed up like one of his pigs after slaughter?

Bors circled to a window and peered inside. He saw Dil in her chair at a desk making notes in a ledger. He thought of Mang's notes, which were now in Bors' possession. The barn window gave him a decent view of its interior, and he saw no sign of a troll. He relaxed and trudged around to the door, knocked, and opened it.

Dil looked up in mild surprise. “Bors! I didn't know you'd be back so soon.”

“Neither did I.”

“Success?” Dil closed the ledger and placed it in a pocket on her chair.

“Partly. I got one of the two.” Bors noticed the door to his secure armory. It was open.

Terror-Cause was gone.

A reflection flashed and the enormous war blade took a finger-sized chunk out of the heavy post at Bors' head. He rolled away and drew Reach. Its blade was smaller and shorter than Terror, but the troll did not know how to use a longsword. It was designed for work in an open battlefield, not a barn.

The shaggy-haired, half-naked, knobby-skinned troll was a meter taller than Mang, and her eyes were red with rage and fear. She loomed over a frightened Bors, who eyed the blade that could slice him in two, with a twinge of shame at how he'd been ambushed. The barn animals squealed, lowed and crashed against their pens in agitation.

“Dil, help me!”

“Why should I?”

The answer shocked Bors, but it made the situation clear as crystal. His mouth drooped open as he wrapped his head around the facts. Dil and the troll were working together. She probably worked with Mang, too.

"I've nothing to gain by helping you, Bors, and everything to lose. I'm sorry this happened, but I didn't expect you back so soon."

"You knew I was outside?"

"I guessed as much." Dil gestured to the troll. "Sharon was outside when she saw you kill her partner. I figured you'd come here, scared for your family or me. I opened the armory and she hid. Pretty simple."

Bors processed Dil's story. She had betrayed him, but why? "You're involved in the poaching."

"Indeed. Camelot may have discarded me like a lame horse, but I still have connections in the capital, and it was a chance to get a little revenge. Arturus' precious rules are made to be broken."

"Mang and Sharon brought you the bush meat." Bors talked while keeping one eye on the troll, who edged side to side, looking for a chance to strike. The knight considered ways to flank it.

"My dear Bors, I wouldn't be dumb enough to accept illegal carcasses here. I simply arranged the transfer. I brought the parties together and stuck it to the king and his cronies."

"I still don't understand why, Dil." Bors pushed back the pain of Dil's deception and dishonesty. "We fought trolls together. You've killed a dozen. You called them animals. Are they your pets now?"

At the word "pets," Sharon's eyes flicked to Dil, as if she were on the verge of a revelation.

Dil noticed the discomfort. "Any idiot could see trolls are intelligent, maybe more intelligent than the morons at Camelot. How else could they coordinate their attacks on us? They're human, just a different kind. History is filled with people who blind themselves to their enemy's humanity to make killing them easier. I decided to turn it against my enemies at court. A little scandal to show I've still got what it takes to make things happen."

"You broke our most sacred laws, Dil, protection of nature and her creatures. That's our duty." Bors didn't quite believe he was quoting chapter and verse for a part-time job.

"All the more reason to shock the self-righteous parasites at court."

Bors loved his mentor, but he took his obligations seriously. "Once I take care of Sharon, I'll have to take you in, Dil." The promise rang hollow to the Regarder, not only because he was uncertain whether he could defeat the troll with one arm and a sword too short for the job, but because he couldn't see himself handing Dil over to the Lord General of the Regarders for punishment.

"You forget it's two against one, Bors."

A mad troll and a paraplegic retiree against a one-armed knight? Did Dil really mean to kill him?

The knight glanced about, thinking another troll might be in the shadows. Sharon swung Terror-Cause. She wasn't used to its weight and length, and the arc was slow. Bors dodged it and jumped toward a corner of the barn with empty pens.

"Call it off, Dil. If it kills me, the whole Order will look for it, and when they find you—"

"They'll what? Banish me again?"

Sharon came after him and swung again. The blade splintered slats of wood and Bors bolted past the creature, thrusting with Reach. The angle was awkward, however, and he only pricked her skin. The creature roared in pain and brought the blade around. It whooshed over Bors' head as he crouched, and he scrambled to find room to work.

He slipped on a dollop of cow dung and fell backward toward Dil. He regained his balance, but a sharp pain jolted him. He eyed his side, just below his rib cage. Blood seeped in the gap between his fiber armor plates. Blood was on Dil's war knife. His blood.

"I'm sorry, Bors, but I can't let you live."

The pain in his side rose like a storm. He lifted Reach-Into-The-Enemy's-Heart against her, his urge to self-defense instinctive. He examined Dil's face, set in the way he'd seen so many times during training, in skirmishes, in battle planning, before a melee with a Lucian army. She'd made up her mind, and nothing could dissuade her. Her decision was fully conscious: She would betray her oath and her friends.

How would he fight two enemies?

Sharon answered the question. She raised Terror-Cause above her head and roared in anger, eager for the killing blow. Bors watched the broad blade, decorated with gold filigree and etched with animals and flowers, follow a crescent over his head like the sun in clear blue sky. Bors, Reach still in his hand, lightheaded due to his wound, stepped aside as if drunk, fully aware of the consequences of his move, and Terror-Cause found flesh, but not his. He cried out in anticipation.

The blade met that place on Dil's body between shoulder and neck, cutting her body in two until the blade struck the back of her mobile chair and stopped cold. No sound came from her. Bors brought his body round, arm at maximum leverage, and Reach found the troll's torso and its heart. The creature dropped to the hay-covered floor of the barn and lay still. The racket from the animals stopped.

Bors let go of Reach, which quivered like a nervous bride in the troll's corpse, and he stumbled toward the door. He knew Dil and the troll were dead, but he wanted to get away. A monster had tried to kill him. His mentor had tried to kill him. He needed to see Elaine and his son.

He never made it to the door.

* * *

Percival pictured Bors lying in a heap in the shit and mud of the barn floor, bleeding to death. Bors had passed out, and a half-hour ticked by before the automated search drone found him. The Regarders' communications command center had received a medical alert via Bors' com set. The medics pronounced his survival a miracle. A millimeter or two deeper, and Dil's knife would've nicked Bors' aorta.

"I've made plenty of mistakes in this business," Bors said, "but who'd have thought trusting your teacher and mentor was one?"

The clean-up crew hauled away the troll carcasses for incineration. They wrapped Dil's body in a cloth and left it at the farm. Within a day, an investigative team rolled up the bush meat ring.

"Are we wrong about the trolls, Percival? Are they human? Do they deserve to die when they break our laws?"

Percival didn't know. He rarely thought about those kinds of questions. He wanted one thing only. He wanted to find the Grail and restore the kingdom to health.

Bors patted his friend on the shoulder. "You have a way of reminding people what's important. My little adventure is just a lesson on the way." He sighed. "I don't know what you should do, Percival. Disobeying your sovereign is a serious offense, but you have to follow your heart, and your intent is noble. Arturus is a forgiving man."

"What about you?"

"I'm a pig farmer. I'm not going anywhere. Elaine wanted to come back and nurse me, but I told her to stay with her relatives. My wound looks worse than it is."

Percival had a hard time believing Bors' claim, but he didn't dispute it. "I'm glad you have what you want, Chris."

The elder knight tapped his finger as if unsatisfied with the response in his mind. "Pig farming isn't all it's cracked up to be. You know something, Percival, I enjoyed that hunt, at least up until I had a knife stuck in me. I envy you."

"Then come with me. We'll find the Grail together."

Bors laughed. "Spoken like a young man who knows nothing about life."

"That's not fair."

"Sorry, Percival, I respect you like a brother." Bors paused. "When are you leaving?"

"In the morning."

Bors considered an idea. "Tell you what. The pigs can take care of themselves for a couple of days. I'll have a neighbor check on them. It'll be nice to saddle up Tears-of-the-Dead and pretend to go on a quest. I'll accompany you to the ship and wish you luck on the voyage."

Percival's heart thrilled. He couldn't imagine a finer companion.

CHAPTER 12: THE PRINCE OF LOTHIA'S DREAM

Dee shrank before the commission presented to her by Lord Mordred. The idea of tackling such a large physical space dismayed her. Sage-architects called the Great Audience Hall a basilica, a long, narrow structure with a flat ceiling flanked by columns. The wall above the western side aisle covered half a hectare, or so it seemed. But Mordred was correct. Almost a century ago, shortly after the death of Arturus the Great, an artist had composed a dark and confused two-dimensional fresco for the space.

"The old work is embarrassing. I think you can do much better."

The lantern-jawed first minster sat with Dee and Ganieda in the basilica's central aisle. They were like ants against the broad, vaulted roof above them.

"My lord, I've never done anything like this."

Dee's normal self-assurance faded into apprehension. She looked to Ganieda for support. The teacher had come to the meeting at Mordred's request, and Dee was glad to see her. Doubts made her hands shake.

"The pieces in the gallery show were my largest, and this is three or four times the size." Dee swallowed, fearful of embarrassing herself in front of Mordred and Ganieda.

"Lord Mordred was thoughtful enough to seek out my opinion, my dear." Ganieda folded her hands on her lap. Dee's eye caught the ring of emerald and lapis lazuli on her left hand, which signaled her office of preceptor in the Society of Theurgists. "I told him you have more than enough talent and ability."

Ganieda was always going on about how Dee never gave herself enough credit.

"You still don't agree? Ganieda warned me that you would be stubborn." Mordred's short laugh underscored his belief in Dee's prospects for success. She read it as an amused shrug, or the dismissal of an obvious exaggeration.

The laugh had an unexpected effect. Unlike the job, the man did not intimidate her. The realization surprised Dee. Mordred was famous for his ruthlessness, but he was offering a gift in that cavernous hall. Dee sensed he had not proposed anything like it to anyone else. If she agreed to the job, she would be near him for months. He was carving out a space for her in his life. The chink of vulnerability in his emotional armor endeared him to her.

"I'm hopeful you'll accept the commission, Ms Rathkeale." He glanced at her, then away. Did he worry that she would refuse it?

"Of course, my lord." She wanted to reassure him, and the potential of seeing more of him felt right. "If I seem reluctant, it's my mother's training. She always advised me to think carefully about big decisions. I hope you understand."

"Madame Rathkeale sounds like an extraordinary woman."

Dee heard relief in his sigh.

"Tell me," he continued, "do you have any thoughts on a subject for the painting?"

She didn't, but before Dee could speak, the muffled tapping of a woman's shoes on marble echoed in the hall. A man bowed to the woman. Dee recognized Gawain before he slipped into the shadows. Coming toward Mordred and Dee was a middle-aged matron dressed in casual, all-black clothes. Her face was framed by a widow's veil. The gray in her hair balanced the black strands perfectly. She wore a ring on her right third finger in the shape of an all-seeing eye. The iris was garnet. The pupil was polished obsidian.

The matronly woman's ring with the black pupil signaled a mind that absorbed everything around it, while it reflected nothing. The stone was reserved for the most powerful theurgists. Under the lady's gaze, Dee wondered if the stone and wearer devoured light, like the invisible stars the sage-scientists said powered the galaxy.

Dee fingered her own theurgist's ring in the shape of all-seeing eye. The iris and pupil were both white onyx. It was the ring for a novice, symbolizing the blindness of one who wishes to see, but cannot. Not yet.

Mordred reached out to take the lady's hand. "I wasn't expecting—"

"Your office told me I might find you here, son."

"Ms Rathkeale, this is my mother, the Lady Morgause."

"Madame." Lifting her head from a slight bow, Dee saw his forced smile during his introduction fade. He was inwardly rattled by his mother.

"A pleasure to meet you, Ms Rathkeale."

Morgause addressed Ganieda. "How is your brother, Merlin? Still tinkering with his toys?"

The tone shocked Dee. Ganieda was a dignified, intelligent woman worthy of respect.

"Morgause." Ganieda bowed in greeting. "You are the soul of courtesy for asking."

Ganieda's tone was just as sarcastic. What was happening?

Morgause grunted as she sat in a chair Gawain brought over. "Ms Rathkeale, my son has high praise for your artistic talents."

Dee observed Mordred roll his eyes, but the comment brought her up short. Mordred had spoken to his mother about her. It confirmed Dee's suspicions of Mordred's romantic interest, but Morgause hadn't formed an opinion about it. Dee offered her own tiny smile. At this angle, he had a strong resemblance to Arturus, though his brow, eyes, nose, and cheeks were all his mother's. The resemblance fueled gossip about Mordred's paternity.

"I'm honored ma'am by his esteem," Dee said, "but I'm still a student, technically. Art for the palace ought to be done by Viridiae's best artists and craftspeople. In fact, I was thinking that Sir Qua—"

Mordred looked stricken, as if fearing Dee had changed her mind.

Morgause interrupted. "Forget the polite modesty, Ms Rathkeale. I've watched your career from afar. You're young, of course, but you have an exciting freshness. I think you're perfect for the job. I know you won't disappoint us."

Ganieda allowed a small smile.

Dee managed only a raspy, "Thank you."

"Have you and Mordred discussed potential themes or subjects for the work?"

"We were just coming to that, Mother. Something historical would be fitting, don't you think, Ms Rathkeale?"

Mordred's idea made sense. The other sculptures and paintings in the hall and the aisles were all historical scenes or people, including a monumental piece depicting Arturus the Great showing mercy to his enemies at Cameliard. The painting hung over his tomb in the apse.

"I wonder if it would be cheeky,"Morgause said, touching her finger to her lip, "if Ms Rathkeale painted something that highlighted our family, the Lothians."

Now Ganieda rolled her eyes.

Mordred's mood darkened. "I'm prime minister, Mother. Such a work would be viewed as arrogant. If I'm to gain Arturus' trust, I can't highlight myself."

"I do not understand why the king does not trust you, as you say. You are the elected prime minister, chosen by the Round Table to enact the government's policy under the direction of the king. He confirmed your appointment."

"He did not let me lead the Grail expedition. He gave that job to Galahad."

Dee wished she could shrink to the size of a gnat.

"Your time will come, my son. Perhaps someday, you will

work the levers of power single-handed."

"Mother!"

Ganieda put a finger to her lips. She was stifling a laugh.

"All I'm saying, Mordred, is that you deserve the king's complete trust and loyalty. After all, you are his—" Morgause stopped herself, remembering Dee and Ganieda's presence. "You are his prime minister. Confidence goes with the job."

"I have a suggestion," Ganieda said. "Perhaps a piece that honors Arturus's family history might cement his trust in you."

"Indeed, Ganieda. On further consideration, I agree with my son that it shouldn't be about our family. On the other hand, your great-grandfather, my grandfather, played an enormous role in the final victory that created the Viridian nation. Arturus the Great persuaded him to join his cause during a tournament at our home. Seems to me that a tournament scene featuring Grandfather and Arturus I offers wonderful opportunities for color, action, all sorts of things the founder's grandson would appreciate. What do you think, Ms Rathkeale?"

The question snapped Dee out of her desire to hide. She was back on familiar ground. Dee thought the lady's idea sound, if ordinary. On the other hand, she didn't like Morgause's tone, suggesting that Dee was a functionary, rather than a creative, independent artist. She might be a student, but she had her own ideas. Isn't that why she was here? Or was this meeting a subterfuge by Mordred intended to give his mother a chance to size up Dee? Morgause's status at court was far higher than Dee's, apart from her vocation as a theurgist, and they wouldn't normally cross paths. Dee judged Morgause to be an intelligent woman, ambitious for her son, but with a chip on her shoulder. Dee couldn't resist speculating to herself on its source. Perhaps Arturus had rejected Morgause as a potential queen?

"I'd have to research the details of their meeting, the place and time and so on," Dee said.

"Of course. It's only a suggestion. Viridiae's history goes back to the Dark Days after the Dissolution. I'm sure there are plenty of subjects to choose from." She turned to Mordred. "I'll leave you three to discuss the matter. Good day to you, Ms Rathkeale. Ganieda."

Morgause offered an aristocratic nod to the three others and departed.

"Well, Lord Mordred?" Dee stared straight at him. "Did I pass muster?"

"I beg your pardon?"

"That was a test. You have a great deal of respect for your lady mother and you told her I would be here, available for inspection."

Ganieda clucked. "Dee, I don't think that's quite fair."

Mordred chuckled. "I did say you were coming, but I didn't present you as if you were a horse to be purchased."

Likely true, Dee thought, and she felt a little ashamed at her accusation. "I apologize if I offended."

"No apology needed," Mordred said. "My mother is a strong-willed woman. She knows what she wants, and she does not suffer fools. I've learned not to disappoint her."

"I'm not that much different than your lady mother, my lord."

Mordred grinned at Dee's comment. "I knew that to be the case the moment I saw you in the gallery. You have a confidence in you that reminds me—" Mordred stopped himself, as if he were about to transgress.

"I remind you of your mother, is that it?" Dee laughed. "I'm flattered. She is comfortable with power."

"She craves it, in fact."

His answer begged a question: What did Dee crave? She loved the adulation at the gallery opening, and if she pleased Mordred and Morgause, her career could soar in no time. Was Gaia tempting her? "You mean she craves it for you, my lord."

"Viridiae has never had a woman as chief of state, though there's no law or custom against it. We're a young nation, but my mother has many enemies at the Round Table. They trace their dislike of her, even hatred, to the Civil Wars, when her grandfather switched sides from the Concordium to Arturus. Her grandfather, you see, was a traitor, in their eyes. Betrayed people never forget their betrayers."

"He was not a traitor to Viridiae. correct?"

Mordred shrugged. "His side won. After he changed allegiances. Therefore he was not a traitor. That doesn't stop families on the losing side from nursing private jealousies and vendettas."

"But those feelings don't extend to you," Dee said, amazed to think a family could harbor grudges for a century.

"Fortunately, I've made my own reputation. Thankfully, my own grandfather was a loyal servant to the Crown. And my... father was a respected man loyal to Viridiae before he died."

"I'm sorry."

"I was only a baby just learning to walk. My mother has always seen Camelot as my second home, even my destiny, you might call it." Mordred made the comment as he eyed an elevated platform of stone on one end of the Great Hall, in front of the first Arturus' resting place. On the platform, a simple, carved wooden chair acted as a throne when Viridiae's kings formally welcomed ambassadors and honored ordinary citizens. Historians said Arturus the Great sat in the chair when he proclaimed the Viridian state.

Dee also saw frustration in Mordred's look, as if he thought he belonged in that chair, not the current occupant. How did that insight surface in Dee's heart? He would never admit such ambition out loud. Viridians were free to speak their minds, a cultural inheritance from the Old Civilization, but Mordred was a calculating man. She appreciated yearning for success, because she nurtured her own dreams.

"What would you like to see me paint, my lord?"

"Ms Rathkeale, I'd be honored if you would simply call me 'Mordred' in our private moments."

"My friends call me 'Dee.'" The diminutive of Dindrane was reserved for her brother, her mother, and her closest friends, and she was not ready to count Mordred among those, but she felt as though a relationship with this man was inevitable. And desirable.

"I think I should excuse myself." Ganieda rose from her chair. "Dee, my lord, please let me know if I can help further."

Mordred watched Ganieda leave.

"Please, Dee, I hope we will be friends for a long time. I am a picky man when it comes to friends, and I'm thrilled to be called one of yours. To answer your question, my wish is a subject that honors Viridiae's spirit, perhaps something about our sacred stewardship of the land, or perhaps our knights' quests to find the Grail."

The mention brought to mind Percival. He'd texted Dee privately about his walkabout in the People's Preserve. He had something else in mind, though, she was sure.

"I'm not sure I want to paint about failure."

"A good point. Perhaps the subject could inspire hope in the people that the Grail will be found and Viridiae's natural health restored."

Dee liked the thought, though she had no idea how she'd execute it. "A fantasy of some kind?"

"A dream for the future." Mordred's face assumed a faraway look.

"I'm curious, my lo—I mean, Mordred."

The prime minister grinned.

"What is your dream?"

"A simple question, and a difficult answer."

"I'd love to hear more."

"I'm so glad."

For an instant, Dee thought Mordred was about to take her hand, but he didn't move.

"As prime minister, my dream for Viridiae is a return of its natural health, to see forests and fields teeming with healthy populations of animals and trees, and its people happy in the Green Country. As head of the Regarders, I dream of a citizenry that believes as fervently as I do that no one is above the earth, and that we are all stewards of a great gift to humanity."

"Lofty dreams."

"They are the only ones that matter."

"But you have other dreams."

"You are perceptive. This is why I like you so much."

The sentiment sent a thrill through Dee's body, and she enjoyed it. As Mordred looked at her, his features softened. A moment later, they went hard again.

"My mother has a dream for me. You must not tell anyone. Please promise me."

Dee believed he was sincere in his desire to share something he normally kept to himself. At the moment, she understood his loneliness. "Of course. I swear to secrecy."

"She wants me to lead Viridiae."

"I don't understand. You already do."

Mordred laughed. "I'm sorry. I've said too much. I'm content with my role in government."

Dee saw this as a lie, but she chose not to call him out. Why embarrass him? A silence fell between them that became painful. "You have another dream, don't you?"

A hint of anguish pinched Mordred's face. At that moment, a page came into the Great Hall and approached. Mordred lost his relaxed mien as the page bowed and asked him to attend Arturus in his office. He stood from his chair. "Thank you, Ms Rathkeale, for taking on this commission. I have complete confidence in your abilities. I'm looking forward to your proposal." He nodded formally, and followed the page out of the hall.

In that moment, Dee saw a different man than the haughty, precise politician and family scion she'd met at the gallery. He had high ambitions for his country, and for himself. His mother was a driving force in his life, but she was as much trouble as help. He loved her and feared her. Above all, he was lonely. And he was attracted to Dee.

She couldn't remember a reference in his official online biography or the palace gossip to a woman in his life, certainly not a mate. How could this be so? He was a handsome man with power and wealth. He had opened up to her, however awkwardly. Dee felt warmth and curiosity about this tall man who wanted to confide in her. Should she nurture these feelings? Or was she too much the commoner? Her family was middle-class with a little property. He was the prime minister of a large country with an estate and a castle. A mismatch in some eyes, mostly likely Morgause's. As Dee studied the blank canvas of the Great Audience Hall above her seat, she decided Mordred had to appear in the work that would someday dance over it.

She knew his secret dream, and it gave her a certain power. He wanted to fall in love with her.

CHAPTER 13: THE DOLPHIN

Rain gave Grey Harbor its name, and Lancelot cursed the rain and the place. The local veterinarian claimed the unrelenting downpours had nothing to do with the influenza that had sickened most of the horses. Lancelot disagreed. The damp was unnatural, and it made the illness virulent, in her opinion. Five of the animals had to be put down. The knight's warhorse, Beric, had escaped the illness. The trip to Perditon probably saved its life. Lancelot kept it apart from the sick mounts. However, it was listless and bored, reflecting the mood of its owner.

"How much longer, Galahad?" Lancelot gulped the dregs of Napene wine in her glass.

"The epidemic has to run its course. Another few days."

Galahad sent Penny, the girl from Perditon, home to his estate with the False Grail. He hoped it might offer clues on the location of the true Grail, but he didn't have the time or the equipment at the quayside camp to study it. Brabus Olc promised to share his measurements and images. Of course, the expedition might discover the true Grail on Koda. If it did, the artifact from the Perditon landfill would be nothing more than a curiosity. For her part, Lancelot considered the trip to the Old Civilization city a waste.

"I thought the sage-scientists in Camelot had developed a cure for the horse flu."

"They're working on it, so I'm told, along with cures for swine and cattle diseases," said Sir Bors, who sat at a table with Lancelot and Percival in Galahad's tent, while the latter worked at his desk. "Merlin's researchers found a document in the Great Machine's archives that discussed a process called 'vaccination.'"

"The sage-historians believe it could also be used in humans," Percival said. He nursed a mug of strong tea. "We read about this in my History of Science course. The process was lost after the Dissolution."

Percival and Bors arrived at the expedition's camp the day after Lancelot and Galahad returned from Perditon. Lancelot was glad to see Percival, but she scolded him for disobeying Arturus' direct orders. Technically, Lancelot was supposed to report Percival as absent without permission, but she couldn't bring herself to send the com mail. Galahad hadn't reported the violation either, as near as Lancelot could tell. Sitting in Galahad's tent, the rain pelting the fabric roof like pebbles, she sympathized with Percival's sense of imprisonment at home. Perhaps Bors and Galahad felt the same way. It wasn't discussed in the open.

Unlike Percival, Bors' presence was a mystery to Lancelot. He'd left his farm in the care of a neighbor, but instead of returning after delivering Percival, he stuck around to help with the sick horses. His wife and child were still visiting relatives. A hint of trouble at home? Lancelot didn't like it. He was a Regarder, after all, and he belonged to Mordred. A spy?

Lancelot fingered the empty wine glass. There's nothing worse for a man or woman of action than inaction. You start to imagine things, and that leads to trouble.

"Where is Merlin?" Lancelot said. "Has anyone seen him?"

"Isn't he at Apparatus Montis, caring for the Great Machine?" Percival answered.

"That's what they say, but he rarely makes an appearance at court or on the com channels." Lancelot said. "He's more myth than reality these days."

Galahad lifted his tablet stylus. "He probably wants to keep a low profile. He's managing expectations."

"What for? He's a national hero, adviser to Viridian kings, the last living link to Arturus the Great." Lancelot's mood soured further.

“A few people in Camelot blame him for the loss of the Grail,” Galahad said.

“That makes no sense,” Percival said. “He's the caretaker for the Great Machine.”

“The Grail was lost on his watch, so to speak,” Galahad said. “It vanished while he was—still is—the head of the group that's minding the Great Machine and trying to learn more about it.”

“Are you saying he had something to do with the Grail's disappearance?” Bors lowered his bottle of local beer, listening attentively.

Galahad lifted his hands. “I'm not saying I agree with gossips and conspiracy theorists. The tiny bits of evidence are purely circumstantial, but the rumors have circulated for years, and they never seem to go away.”

“It's just people looking for someone to blame. It's like saying the fox took the chickens when it was really a weasel,” Bors said. “What would be his motive for lying?”

Bors' eyes lingered on Lancelot a moment too long, and the dame knight didn't like it.

“I can think of a dozen motives,” Lancelot said. “Reputation, for one. He was Arturus the Great's science advisor. He was appointed when he was only 19, for Gaia's sake. Arturus II kept him on when the Great King died. Our Arturus did the same when his father died. Merlin is like a holy relic. They say his mind is as sharp as ever. I heard a rumor that he discovered an elixir of life that keeps him alive long after he's supposed to depart this vale of tears.” She ran her fingers like a comb through her golden brown hair.

“You make him sound like a magician, rather than a sage-scientist,” Percival said.

“It's just a rumor, but he'd be in his, what, early one-tens?”

“There's dozens of people a hundred years old and more in Viridiae,” Lancelot said. “Another result of the Old Civilization's obsession with DNA.”

“I know an old woman who says she's 120 years old.” Bors grinned. “She says Arturus the Great fucked her on the way to one of his battles. I bet that isn't in the history books."

Bors laughed at his own joke. Galahad smirked. Percival turned beet red. Lancelot did not laugh.

"You're a boor, Bors." Lancelot said. "Or is it boar?"

"What are you talking about?" Bors face scrunched in puzzlement.

"Never mind. I would've thought a pig farmer would grasp a little word-play."

Bors harrumphed. "I know what kind of game interests you."

Now Lancelot was perplexed. "You're not making sense, swineherd."

Bors fingered his empty bottle. "I think you do." He belched. "What's she like, O Champion of Champions?"

The reference to one of Lancelot's titles earned in the lists didn't connect, until she remembered the last national tourney, when Guinevere bestowed it at the awards ceremony. In an instant, Lancelot was on her feet. She knocked over her wine glass, which crashed on the portable wooden floor of Galahad's tent. Galahad and Percival stood, ready to stop a fight, though Bors remained seated, laughing.

"I don't like what you're implying Bors. Guinevere and I—"

"'Guinevere and I' A little familiar, isn't it? Not 'The Queen and I'? Not 'Her Majesty and I'?"

"Shut up, Bors."

"No, let's talk about your relationship with the wife of Arturus."

"You're not stupid enough to object to two women—"

"I don't care who you fuck. I care that you're compromising my king and queen. It's disloyal and endangers both of them. They have a thousand enemies, not to mention the Lucians, who'd love to make hay out of your stupidity. Don't you see that?"

Lancelot restrained her rage. Rumors about her affair with Guinevere were rampant at court, but no one had ever thrown it in her face until now. Instead of growing angry, she did what she promised Guinevere she would always do.

“You know it's not true, Bors. We're friends, that's all. I'm not surprised a pig farmer would spread that kind of manure among his companions.”

“You're such a bad liar, Lancelot.” Bors leaned back in his chair. “A pimp has more honor than you.”

Lancelot lost her temper. She drew her dagger, but Percival grabbed her arm before she could lunge. Bors had enough time to jump up from his chair, but Galahad stepped between the belligerents.

“Stop it. Gaia's breath, you're behaving like children. Mother, give Percival your weapon.”

Lancelot had no choice. A fight at the moment might end the expedition, and she'd be blamed. On top of that, the truth about her and Guinevere might be revealed in a way that would hurt the queen.

“Bors, apologize to Dame Lancelot.”

Bors sneered and nodded, but said nothing. Instead, he slipped out of the tent.

Lancelot would remember his insult to her and Guinevere. The truth of it was irrelevant.

* * *

The weather cleared soon after the argument. The list of things to do exploded. The vet declared the remaining horses healthy. Bors took over the purchase of new animals, while Lancelot supervised the camp's dismantling. The frenetic activity kept the simmering conflict between Lancelot and Bors from boiling over. The dame knight reminded herself that Bors would go back to his farm when the *Dolphin* set sail, and she wouldn't see him again until the expedition returned. The knowledge cheered her as the last of the gear was lowered into the ship's hold. Intramural fights never ended well.

Lancelot reported her completed task to Galahad as the expedition's leader met with the ship's captain, Michael Libb, a thick-chested man in his early forties. Lancelot fancied his intense eyes.

"We've got a window for good weather starting tomorrow, Mr Corbenic," Libb said, "and the Camelot Observatory predicts northwest winds for several days. We'll be sailing in damn near perfect conditions."

"Any chance we can make up some of our lost time?"

Libb's lip curled skeptically. "*Dolphin* isn't one of those ancient oil-burning monsters that can make 30 knots in a headwind. We can do 14 knots on a good day, which happens pretty much never."

Galahad nodded. "When do we leave?"

"High water is at dawn. As soon as the cook's lackey stows the breakfast dishes."

A call took Galahad's attention. Lancelot introduced herself to Libb.

"Well, then, it's nice to meet the knight that has cost me a fortune over the years."

"How so?"

"People keep convincing me to wager against you in the lists. The sports chans say you're getting old, if you'll pardon the expression."

Lancelot didn't take offense. There were days when she felt the best masseuse within a thousand kilometers couldn't touch the knots in her lower back. She found time every day for yoga stretches, but staying in good physical shape was getting harder and harder. "Maybe I should retire as a winner?"

"My friends would hate you for it, because it would mean fewer drinks on me." Libb laughed with the mirth of a man with many friends.

When *Dolphin* wasn't chartered for special runs to Koda, she sailed a regular route between Grey Harbor and a dozen other ports large and small on the eastern edge of the Peaceful Sea. *Dolphin* was a 60-meter steel-hulled schooner with four steel masts, each around 15 meters in height. A sailor, sitting on a wooden slat suspended by a rope, painted the highest point on the mast. He was hardly more than a smudge in the clear, blue sky. Lancelot remembered a term—"fore-and-aft"—which referred to the way the sails lined up along the ship's keel. Fore-and-aft was a popular configuration for coast-hugging ships, while the mega-cargo ships that sailed on the east-west trade routes preferred square sails, which worked better far away from the coasts. Lancelot learned all this from Libb over coffee, which the mariners drank by the liter.

"I'm looking forward to the trip, Captain. I've never been to sea before."

"It could get rough. The weather in the northern latitudes isn't kind. Ever had trouble with motion sickness?"

Lancelot thought a moment. "Not so far."

Dolphin also had a secret. Among the expedition members, only Galahad was allowed into a special room below deck toward the stern of the vessel. Even he was given just a glimpse of the compartment's contents, and he promised not to reveal what he saw. Galahad did say it reassured him in case of trouble. Lancelot suspected a large projectile weapon, perhaps something salvaged by one of Brabus Olc's subsidiaries, but she had no real idea.

As she reflected on the coming voyage, a boy came pounding down the long curve of *Dolphin*'s main deck straight for Lancelot, begging her to come to Galahad's office. Lancelot walked with urgent briskness to the shack where her son had set up a temporary headquarters after his tent was dismantled.

"He's coming here." Galahad's face was calm, but Lancelot heard mild alarm.

"Who?"

"Arturus."

"Good Gaia. Why?"

"I don't know. He wants to see the ship? He's the king. He does what he wants."

"Within reason," Lancelot said. "When?"

"Tonight."

Dolphin was a cargo ship, not a yacht. Lancelot had dined in the captain's mess once. It was the size of a large closet. It could never hold an entourage. The cook was excellent, though. "You'd better tell Captain Libb."

"I already have. Seven for dinner. Arturus, Percival, Bors, Libb, you, myself." Galahad stopped his recitation.

"That's six."

"And Guinevere."

* * *

Lancelot found herself growing more attached to *Dolphin*, her master, and her crew after the meal with Arturus and Guinevere. Libb brought out a small table and placed it on the ship's broad fantail. He was the son of a retired diplomat who'd served Arturus' father, and in the pleasant breeze off the river, he was garrulous and well-informed. *Dolphin* was already clean as a new sword; the idle time enforced by the horse influenza was filled by the crew of ten and its squad of maintenance robots with polishing brass and touching up paint. Libb's brilliant cook served a delicate dish of fresh sole, potatoes and oysters. Napene wine was plentiful. Everyone, even Bors, was affable.

One thing was missing from Lancelot's point of view: Arturus's motivation for the trip to Grey Harbor. As the host and guests finished a bowl of fresh peaches and cream, Arturus asked Lancelot and Guinevere to join him for a brief stroll on *Dolphin*'s weather deck. That was the signal for the others to depart for their quarters, onshore in the case of the knights, to the master's cabin in the case of Libb. On the wharf, a contingent of armed guards shadowed the knight, the sovereign, and his lady as the last rays of the sun left a purple twilight in its wake. The lights of the town twinkled a ten-minute walk up the quay.

Arturus said, "Let me repeat my wishes for a safe journey and a successful recovery of the Grail."

"Thank you, Majesty." Even in the dimness, Arturus' face was lined with care. Worry and his illness were taking their toll on his body.

"For once, Lancelot, forget the formalities. It's just you, me, and Guinevere."

The request warmed Lancelot's heart. It reminded her of the days before Arturus was elevated to Viridiae's throne, when both of them were merely soldiers of equal rank and duty. Dinner back then would have been full of songs, more food than they could eat, and a splitting headache the next morning from the fortified ale.

"Of course, my lord." Lancelot had pledged her fealty to Arturus as her liege. That never went away. "I think you're here for more than good wishes."

"Yes." Arturus fixed his eyes on the horizon where the sun was only a memory. "Do you remember Percival's claim that his expedition had been betrayed?"

"You told Mordred's Regarders to investigate."

"They haven't reported back. However, I have received information..." Arturus glanced at Guinevere.

"We have alternate means for learning what's going on in the realm," Guinevere said.

"I take it the information is troubling you, my lord," Lancelot said.

"I can't tell you everything, Lancelot, and I'll ask you to be judicious in what you say to Galahad. He's the expedition leader. He ought to know, but I probably wouldn't take it farther than him."

"Of course."

"It's about Gawain."

"Mordred's brother," Lancelot said.

"He was seen along the route of Sir Kevin's expedition by hard-scrabble ranchers in the eastern wastelands," Arturus said. "He was within shouting distance of Kevin."

Lancelot wondered why Percival, as part of the expedition's security contingent, hadn't spotted him.

"Gawain does nothing without first clearing it with Mordred," Guinevere said.

"Or Morgause," Arturus added.

Guinevere crossed her arms. "We're sure the First Minister is up to something."

"I'm not going to accuse Mordred of anything," Arturus said. "He may simply need his own independent sources of information. But Percival might be right. Someone may not have wanted Kevin to find the Grail, assuming it was even out there. Maybe Mordred wanted to get there first."

"But what about the loss of all the expedition members, except for Percival?"

"That's still a mystery, though I'd guess poor planning or leadership. Kevin was not the sharpest arrow in the quiver. Percival is lucky to be alive."

"What do you want me to do?"

"Nothing. Stay alert."

"Bors is a Regarder." The farmer knight was a good soldier. Lancelot respected that, even if he was a prick. Percival seemed to like him, though Lancelot couldn't imagine why. "If he's reporting back to Mordred—"

"—then he's doing his job." Arturus said. "I would expect nothing less."

Lancelot would be glad to see his back once *Dolphin* cast off.

"I'm tired." Arturus sighed. "My darling, are you ready to turn in?"

"May I have a few minutes with Lancelot?"

Arturus eyes lingered on his wife, then on Lancelot. "Of course. I'll say my goodnights."

Half the guards accompanied Arturus to the royal tent. Half remained behind, waiting for his queen.

Lancelot longed to take Guinevere in her arms. She wanted to take in the scent of her hair, the silky feel of her skin. The dame knight had to satisfy herself with a loving gaze, although Guinevere did not return it. "Is something wrong?" Lancelot wanted to add "my love" to her question, but she remembered that sound carried better over water, and hidden ears might hear.

"There's always something wrong, Lancelot. That's the nature of governing." Guinevere ran her hand along *Dolphin*'s cap rail. "But I understand your question. Arturus has never felt more threatened. On the one hand, Mordred is loyal and competent. On the other, he sharpens his knives. His mother turns the stone."

"Then dismiss him. Send him home."

"Politics has never been your strong suit, Lancelot." Guinevere grinned. "His family is among the most powerful in Viridiae. I am married to Arturus because of Lothia."

Next to Lothia, Guinevere's was the most powerful family in the country. "I've always known that your marriage to Arturus was meant to counter Lothia's influence," Lancelot said. "But isn't it also true that Arturus loves you?"

"He does, and I love him."

The statement hurt Lancelot, but she kept her tongue.

"I love him for Viridiae's sake," Guinevere said, "and I will defend him with my life."

Lancelot would do the same, because it was her duty. Arturus was also her friend.

The baby's breath of breeze swayed unkempt hairs in Guinevere's simple coiffure. "Our country is in danger, Lancelot. Arturus is ill. The country is ill. There are rumors and rumors of rumors coming from every corner and crevice, inside and outside the palace. The Lucians. The Round Table. People are frightened. Something may have to be done before it's too late."

Lancelot listened, but she saw only the outline of Guinevere's profile, with its convex shape and snub nose. Lancelot wanted to kiss it.

"Good night, Dame Lancelot, and safe voyage." Guinevere touched her cheek to Lancelot's. To prying eyes, it would appear warm, even intimate, but chaste. The touch sent a thrill into every cell of Lancelot's body. She watched Guinevere disappear into the darkness on shore, followed by her guards.

Lancelot did not want to move from her spot on *Dolphin*'s deck, as if staying would preserve the moment. After a time, she sat on the deck, back against a hatch, staring at the stars overhead. After a while she closed her eyes and dreamed of the night she and Guinevere spent in Grey Harbor's best hotel. In the dream, Guinevere repeated, *"Something had to be done."*

A commotion woke Lancelot. Dawn was breaking. The crew and expedition members bustled about. Galahad stood over his mother. "I thought you were too old to pass out from drunkenness."

"I didn't. I simply fell asleep after a stroll. The night was beautiful."

"Well, the weather's changed, and the tide is ebbing. The captain wants to leave."

Lancelot's eyes widened as another man came up to Galahad.

"The horses are happy. Looks like we're as ready as we'll ever be."

"Your gear is aboard?"

"Yep. Thanks again for letting me come along. It'll be fun."

Lancelot watched Sir Bors head back in to the bowels of the *Dolphin*. Under her cloak in the cool morning, she felt the hilt of her dagger.

CHAPTER 14: THE DEER PEOPLE

Thirty-two days later, *Dolphin* slipped into a sheltered bay at Koda. She was towed over the glassy water by the captain's launch. As they watched the rowers dipping their oars in the cold sea, Percival, the other passengers, and each crew member listened at the rail as the bosun at *Dolphin*'s bow called out numbers. A lead weight sank as the seaman tossed it ahead of the ship. When the weight touched bottom, the mariner called out the mark on the line attached to the lead. Anything less than six meters risked a grounding, and Captain Libb was a cautious man. When the depth reached eight meters, he called out in his rumbling baritone for the rowers to halt, and he ordered the anchor dropped.

The splash had a melancholy quality for Percival. The voyage had proved an unexpected joy. When *Dolphin* cleared Grey Harbor, Libb set the mainsail, foresail, and outer jib, and the long, sleek vessel leaped forward, much like its namesake. To port, the horizon stretched in a flat line. To starboard, the continent's mountains broke the horizon's edge. A northwest wind blew night and day, steady and bracing, signaling its origins in the far north. The breeze filled *Dolphin*'s new white sails, giving her an unearthly aura, as if the old myths of a heaven with angels had come to life on the gray-blue water.

Fascinated by the intricate dance of mariner, robot, and ship's master, Percival absorbed the spectacle of her operation like a sponge. Within days, he'd learned the names of each line, each sail, and every part of *Dolphin* from the deck to the mastheads.

Dolphin was shorthanded, and Percival filled gaps wherever he could. He reveled in the labor of hauling on a line in coordinated fashion as a leader sang a song to make the work easier.

I thought I heard the Old Man say,
John kanaka 'naka tu rye ay,
Today, it is a holiday.
John kanaka 'naka tu rye ay,

Tu rye ay, oh, tu rye ay,
John kanaka 'naka tu rye ay.

We'll work tomorrow, but not today,
John kanaka 'naka tu rye ay,
We'll work tomorrow, but not today,
John kanaka 'naka tu rye ay,

Tu rye ay, oh, tu rye ay,
John kanaka 'naka tu rye ay.

Haul away, oh, haul away
John kanaka 'naka tu rye ay,
Oh, haul away an' earn your pay
John kanaka 'naka tu rye ay,

Tu rye ay, oh, tu rye ay,
John kanaka 'naka tu rye ay.

No one had complained about Percival's novice presence. They appreciated every strong back.

The Peaceful Sea lived up to its name. Libb claimed he'd never seen it so benign over so many weeks. Libb confessed to his nervousness about its unexpected calm, but Percival took its tranquility as a good omen. One flat note marred Percival's happiness. Dee had sent him a long com message. She detailed the commission for the light painting in the Great Audience Hall, and she hinted at a budding interest in Mordred. Percival always left Dee to her friends and lovers, but until now all were her equals in class and age. Mordred was different. He was powerful, at least ten years older, and one of the richest men in the kingdom.

Though brother and sister were fraternal twins, Percival was older by a few minutes. Even that small difference led to an expectation on his mother's part for a brotherly watch over his sister. Perhaps Eleanor's expectations compensated for the absence of a father. Percival couldn't help feeling guilty that he was not in Camelot to intervene if things got dangerous for Dee. His impulsive decision to join Galahad's expedition might be a huge mistake, vis a vis his sister. Before *Dolphin* left Viridiae's com system behind, Percival wrote a supportive note back, warning Dee to stay out of court politics, if she could. "It'll swallow you like a monster," he wrote.

In *Dolphin*'s saloon, Galahad huddled with his staff, going over maps of Koda, pinpointing possible locations of the Grail. Percival admired Galahad's single-mindedness, though the dusky gathering space reminded him of the exile to his apartment after Lancelot's rescue. At the pre-departure dinner, Percival was ready to apologize to Arturus for his disobedience, but the monarch had either forgotten it or ignored it. The king had other things on his mind than disciplining a young knight eager to serve his country.

The only human aboard *Dolphin* in any trouble had been Lancelot. As soon as *Dolphin* cleared Grey Harbor's bar, Lancelot had found a secluded place and vomited over the side. Percival had never seen his friend so ill. Each time he approached her to offer tea or a word of compassion, Lancelot gave him a dirty look from a pale, pathetic face.

"The crew says to keep your eyes fixed on the horizon," Percival suggested. "That'll ease the symptoms."

"Fuck the crew."

"Captain Libb might let you bunk closer to the middle of the ship. That helps reduce the motion."

"Fuck the boat."

"If you prefer to be miserable, I'll leave you alone."

Lancelot groaned. “How is it that I'm the only one with this cursed sea sickness?”

Percival took pity on the dame knight, so powerful in the saddle and weak as a baby on the ocean.

Lancelot held her head in her hands. “This headache is going to cleft my skull in two.”

“The headache might be dehydration,” Percival said. “If you come on deck for some fresh air, I'll bring you some ginger tea from the mess. Cook says it's a medicine for motion sickness.”

Lancelot didn't want to move, but she agreed, and Percival found her a place on a hatch cover out of the sun with a view of the horizon. Lancelot relaxed, but Percival's mood darkened.

“Are you alright, Percival?” Lancelot sipped. “Maybe you need some of this tea.”

Percival held a long pause. “I was just thinking about my sister.”

“Write to her. She'd probably like that.”

“I can't get a carrier wave from our com network. Too far away.”

Lancelot eyed her companion. “Tell me about her. She and I haven't spoken much, until recently, at least.”

“She's an artist.”

“I don't know much about art.”

“Our mother wanted her to be a scientist. She wanted me to be a scientist too.”

“You're worried about your sister,” Lancelot nodded. “And now you're thousands of kilometers away and can't help her if she gets into trouble.”

“Thing is, Dee is more likely to protect me than I would protect her.”

A realization came over Lancelot's face. “Ah! I've heard that your sister has some unique abilities.”

“Mother used to let us roam our property by ourselves, even when we were little. One time, when I was about 14, I took a long hike by myself to our boundary with the King's Forest. We'd heard rumors of trolls in the area, but Mother wasn't worried.”

"Good. Most mothers worry overmuch."

"I got lost and ran into a troll nest."

"Gaia's blood. What happened?"

"I don't remember much, but I do remember that I was thinking about Dee at the time. We were almost carrying on a conversation, but not using words. I felt as if she were walking with me, but she was dozens of kilometers away at our mother's cottage. Anyhow, I think I surprised the buck, and it attacked me."

"You survived, obviously."

"It was Dee. After the incident, I went straight home. I was scared and hurt, though only cut and bruised. About a kilometer from the cottage, Dee showed up to meet me. The first thing she said was, 'Did I kill it?'"

Percival described the look on Dee's face, determined and merciless.

"You said she was several kilometers away," Lancelot said. "Does her power have a range?"

Percival gaped. "You talk as if Dee were a weapon. She's my sister."

Lancelot shrugged. "I have to know about these things. I'm Arturus' military chief of staff."

Percival sighed. "I suppose there's a range. I don't feel as strong a connection to her when I'm this far away."

"Did she kill the troll?"

"I don't think so. She says she can feel when I'm in danger, and that she can act to protect me, but she doesn't know how it works."

"But is it possible she killed it?"

Percival thought back to the spider on the log near their cottage. Dee had nearly killed it before Percival stopped her. A twinge of pride held Percival back from answering Lancelot. Percival was the warrior, trained to kill, if necessary. Dee was not a soldier, but she could do things most soldiers and knights only wished for.

"It's possible."

"She's getting training for this, I hope," Lancelot said. "She needs discipline and discernment."

Percival explained Dee's tutelage by Ganieda. "Dee wants to study theurgy."

"Theurgic practice will give her the tools to use her ability wisely. I just hope she's not tested before she's ready."

"How do you mean?"

"I've known too many people thrown into life-threatening situations before they could handle themselves. I'm thinking of squires who went into battles and were cut down before they could even swing a sword." Lancelot grew solemn, perhaps at a memory. "I hope that doesn't happen to Dee. I like you and your sister. Losing one or both of you would break my heart."

* * *

In the sheltered bay at Koda, five hundred meters off the starboard beam, a broad bight below forested hills was kissed by rhythmic waves. Except for the northern latitude's chill, the scene was idyllic.

"What do we do now, Bors?" Percival asked

"You know how to swim, don't you?"

The burly knight's wound at the hands of Odilia Malehaut during the affair with the trolls had healed nicely, and Bors cared for the animals with the expedition's hostler. Bors had made a previous passage to the Hot Lands south of Viridiae, and early in the voyage, he'd supervised the placement of a spare sail to direct wind into *Dolphin*'s hold, giving the horses fresh air and blowing out the stink. Every day, a horse was rotated into a clean stall, allowing robots to clean out the fouled stall. Large barrels of drinking water and bales of hay kept the beasts healthy in their comfortable slings.

In the mild swell of the bay, the mariners removed a hatch cover and assembled a small crane.

"I can't say I'm going to miss this tub," Lancelot said, as the captain's launch came alongside.

"A little help here," Galahad called out. "We have to ferry

everything to the beach. We've only got a few hours before dark."

No one was spared the duty of moving the expedition's gear from the boat to the beach. Bors and the hostler had the toughest job, coaxing the horses to swim. Lancelot volunteered to encourage her warhorse Beric to lead the parade. The animal was trained to ford rushing rivers. Bors brought all the animals to the open hatch in the side of *Dolphin*'s hull. Lancelot, in a small boat next to the *Dolphin*, took Beric's reigns. The big mare jumped the two meters into the water, making an enormous splash that nearly swamped Lancelot's dinghy. The other horses, following their natural herd instinct, jumped one-by-one. All made it to the beach unhurt. By nightfall, tents were up, fires lit, the wind generator turned, and the two dozen knights and support people settled in for the night.

Captain Libb wished Galahad luck and promised to wait as long as necessary for the expedition's return.

Waking early, Percival explored the immediate area around the campsite. In the millennium since the Dissolution, the rising sea level had swallowed many coastal towns of the Old Civilization, submerging and destroying ancient port facilities. Galahad's expedition had made landfall about a kilometer south of small city's ruins. A few thousand souls may have called it home. He could only guess at its size, however, because nothing was left of it except concrete foundations of buildings large and small. Lichen and moss encrusted the crumbling, molded forms, echoing the decay of Perditon, but offering no hint of the buildings' purposes. Their regular spacing formed the ghost-like outline of a street plan. Enormous firs and cedars appeared to march down the steep, surrounding hills to the water's edge.

Hunger reminded Percival of breakfast, and the expedition's cook, though not as sophisticated as *Dolphin*'s cook, brought forth heaps of pancakes and mounds of scrambled eggs made from powder. Galahad and his staff again huddled over a map. An hour later, the expedition broke camp. After the expedition's trouble reaching Grey Harbor from Camelot, the members had plenty of practice loading and unloading the animals, and they set off inland.

The travel was easy under the low-angled sun. Everyone was told to wear their heavy coats due to the changeable weather, but it seemed a misplaced concern to Percival. As the trail took them into a gap between two hills, one of the hostler's helpers started to sing.

The singing stopped when the singer's throat was cut by an arrow. He fell to the ground, and a moment passed before anyone realized what had happened. In an instant, a storm of arrows and spears rained down on the party, which was strung out in single file.

"Ambush! Bors! Percival!" At the head of the column, Lancelot drew Arondight and spurred Beric, but there was almost no room to maneuver the big horse and the broadsword in the narrow gap.

"Damn her," Bors said to Percival. "Why wasn't she watching for bandits?"

Percival had no time to defend the dame knight's lack of vigilance. A body flew from a rocky outcrop onto his horse and pushed him to the ground. He landed on his back, knocking the wind out of his lungs. Percival looked into the sky. Blinded by the sun, a hooded figure raised a spear shaft and brought it down to Percival's chest. He dodged the blow and tripped his assailant, pulling his dagger from his boot. Before he could slash the enemy's leg, the attacker ran away.

A high-pitched whistle caught everyone's attention. In seconds, the attackers withdrew to each end of the cut, trapping the expedition. Other attackers stood above them, crossbows drawn, out of reach.

An aged man whose gray beard reached his collarbone approached Lancelot. The man wore leather and fur from head to toe. Dignified, but not haughty, an animal skull and antlers decorated his head. Lancelot held Arondight with both hands, ready to strike. If she attacked, a younger man next to the elder was in position to stab her with his stone-tipped spear. The spearhead's flint was as sharp as Lancelot's steel.

"Do you know the Old Words?" The elder's speech was hesitant, as if he were unsure if the words were correct.

Galahad stood up and approached the elder. The old man's bodyguard shook his spear, as if reminding Galahad of the threat.

"I don't know these 'Old Words,' sir, but I understand your words. Do you understand mine?"

"I do, but they come strange from your mouth. They sound like the others' words."

"Others?"

"The ones like you that came before."

The remark caught Percival by surprise. Who could these "others" be?

"Why did you attack us?" Lancelot snarled. "We've done nothing to you."

The elder regarded Lancelot dismissively. "I will not speak to you. I will speak to this one, who treats an old man with respect." He nodded at Galahad.

Galahad glanced at a shocked Lancelot and shrugged. He turned to the elder. "My name is Galahad. We are from Viridiae. We seek the Grail."

"That is what the others said."

Galahad's expedition had competition. The wounded hostler moaned.

"Our man is hurt," Galahad said. "One of your arrows struck him. We need to help him. He's losing blood."

"Come with us." With that, the man with the skull and antlers turned to leave.

"Aren't we going to fight, Galahad?" Lancelot was incredulous.

"Why are you so anxious for slaughter, Mother? We're here to find the Grail, not kill innocents."

The old man grinned, showing yellowed, but healthy teeth. "You called her 'Mother.'"

"She has that privilege."

The man laughed and gestured the group forward. Two of the old man's companions came down from the hill and unfolded a simple stretcher made of skins, as if they expected to carry wounded. They loaded the hostler gently into the stretcher. Percival and the rest of the Galahad expedition had no choice but to follow.

In the space of a short hike, the mood among the Viridians changed from jubilant to sour. The expedition was now under the control of strangers, as if they were prisoners of war. Percival had never seen people like these. They weren't from aboriginal stock. During the long voyage to Koda, he'd read a com book that described the region's history. Prior to the arrival of Europeans almost 1,500 years in the past, a people with tan skin, broad faces, and narrow eyes had inhabited the area for thousands of years. After the Old Civilization decimated them with disease and forced removal, their numbers dwindled to almost nothing. Isolated settlements survived the Dissolution, mostly on the mainland.

These people on Koda, however, though tanned and scarred from a life in the open, had features much like Percival's. One had hazel eyes and sandy hair, but they had none of the metal tools, steel blades, single-shot pistols, or small electronics salvaged from the Old Civilization, unless they kept them hidden. His curiosity nearly overwhelmed him, but when he turned to ask a question of one of his captors, he was only nudged forward with the point of a spear.

When captor and captive cleared the gap between the two hills, they came to a group of huts tall enough to sit in, but not stand. An elderly woman greeted the old man, who removed his headdress, kissed her hand and touched it to his forehead. Percival did not understand the meaning of the gesture, but it seemed that the old woman was also a leader of the group.

"I am Jarn. This is my wife, Mem. The Deer People have allowed us to lead them this year." Mem opened the animal-skin flap covering the opening of one the huts, which occupied the center of the camp. "Please, Galahad, join us. We would be honored with your mother's presence as well."

Lancelot huffed.

"We're honored to be your guests." Galahad bowed.

"Our healer will help your man."

Galahad moved to follow Jarn inside, but one of the young men reached out to Galahad's sword, still in its scabbard. The move startled Lancelot, and she fingered Arondight. For an instant, the uneasy truce was on the verge of breaking down. The elder Mem barked a command, and the warrior, a dark-haired, thick-chested youth who could easily beat any Viridian recruit in The Keep's wrestling arena, lowered his weapon.

"We'll leave our weapons outside, Jarn," Galahad said, undoing the buckle for his scabbard.

"But..." Lancelot stopped herself, and followed her son's lead.

Percival and Bors seated themselves outside the door of the hut. The younger knight could hear the conversation inside.

For a few minutes, nothing was said, as if the four people —Jarn, Mem, Galahad, and Lancelot—were gathering their thoughts. Perhaps Galahad thought waiting for his host was wise considering he was in a weak position as a stranger on Koda. A young woman brought in tea, and Jarn spoke first.

"You are like the others, but you are not them."

"I don't understand, Jarn," Galahad said.

"Days ago, a group of men came to our camp. They were dressed much like you, and spoke with your manner of speech."

Percival observed that Jarn grew more comfortable with what he called the Old Words.

"They were friendly at first, if a little wary of us. We welcomed them, and shared food and drink. One of them offered their own drink, a terrible tasting liquid. He shared it with our young men and women. Mem and I thought little of it. That was a mistake. We don't know exactly what happened, but one of the visitors tried to have sex with a woman of the Deer People without her consent."

"I'm sorry that this happened, Jarn," Galahad said. "It's against our laws. We will punish him severely, if we catch him."

"It is too late for that," Mem said, speaking for the first time in the old language. "The woman killed him. Wolves gnaw at his bones now."

"Rough justice," Lancelot said.

"But you must now understand why we attacked you," Mem said. "We could not take the chance that one of your people might try the same thing. We had to prevent that."

"But you stopped the attack, Jarn."

"We're not murderers. You were helpless. If you had fought more, though, we would've killed all of you."

"Thank you for not doing so," Galahad said. "And thank you for the tea, but you said something just now I didn't understand."

"Go on," Jarn said.

"You mentioned the Deer People."

"That is what we call ourselves. In our language, we say—" At this, Percival's ears failed him. "The words 'Deer People' are not correct, but close enough."

"Are all of your people here with us now?" Galahad said.

Percival estimated the group of men, women, and children at about 100 souls.

"Yes," Jarn said, "except for two hunters searching for meat. They've been out for 10 days."

"Please forgive me, Jarn and Mem, but my people and yours almost seem, well, related."

"I will tell you a story." Jarn seemed pleased to settle into a storyteller role. "Mothers have told this story to daughters, fathers have told this story to sons, for more than 30 generations. The people who came before us were part of the Old Civilization, but they disliked its way of life. They thought human beings had forgotten what humanity meant. They had forgotten that nature was not a tool. The earth and air and water was not something to be dominated or conquered or used for profit. Even when some people in the Old Civilization tried to repair human beings' relationship with Gaia, our grandfathers and grandmothers thought they were foolish."

"They thought there was only one way to repair the rip in Gaia's family," Mem continued. "They formed small groups and found wild places and disappeared into the forests, or onto the ice, or sailed to islands where nobody lived. The people who called themselves the Deer People threw away everything, even their clothes. They walked barefoot and naked into the forests on this island. They gave themselves to Gaia, and they used knowledge she gave them to survive."

Jarn cleared his throat. "When my father and grandfather told me this story, they said most of the first Deer People died or went back to the Old Civilization after only one year. Giving up familiar things and feeling hungry and cold all the time was too much. But a few people kept going, and they survived. They are our ancestors."

"An amazing story," Galahad said.

Percival agreed silently. He glanced at Bors, who listened with the same intensity.

"What about the Dissolution, when the whole world fell apart?" Lancelot said. "That must've made things harder."

"It was a blessing," Mem said. "My mother said to me that the people of the Old Civilization fought among themselves over the resources they had polluted, and the pollution led to their destruction. But they left the Deer People alone. To them we were unimportant, even insane. We survived. They didn't."

"I don't mean disrespect, but how do you know this is all true," Galahad said. "It's been a thousand years since the old nations and technologies died out."

"All you have to do," Jarn said, "is look at this island. Do you see anything left of the Old Civilization?"

Percival thought of the crumbling concrete foundations of the ancient town.

"But people come to this island, right?"

"Not often. We're distant from most settlements. A small community of Revered Ones lives on the mainland, and they trade with us once or twice a year."

"Revered Ones?" Lancelot said.

"The people who lived in the area before, going back thousands of years," Mem said. "They belong here, and we're thankful for their tolerance of our presence. We're still strangers in their eyes."

Mem must mean the aboriginal people, Percival thought.

"I wish we could listen to more of your story, Jarn and Mem, but we are here for an urgent purpose."

"The Grail."

"The Old Civilization did try to fix what it had done, as you said," Galahad said, "but one of its Great Machines, the one in our country, is no longer working, because an important piece of it was lost."

"Or stolen," Lancelot said.

Jarn sighed. "We know all about the machines. They were intended to fix the climate. It was one of the things our ancestors thought was foolish."

"Do you still think that?" Lancelot said.

"It may be, but that is in the distant past, and we prefer not to judge. All we ask is to be left in peace and to live our lives as we choose."

"We want nothing more than that as well," Galahad said, "except for any knowledge you might have of where we might find the Grail."

"We don't know where it is exactly, but I can take you to its most likely location."

Percival's heart beat faster.

"We'd be grateful for that," Galahad said.

"But you must know something. The group that came before you—"

"The group with the man our woman killed," Mem added.

"They are going to the same place," Jarn said. "They may already be there."

"We'll take that risk," Lancelot said.

Galahad and the Deer People's co-leader narrowed down the potential location of the Grail to a rugged range of mountains on Koda called the Backbone. The area was three days walk from the camp. The next morning, five young men and women, along with Jarn, joined the expedition for the trek.

Percival's heart warmed at the long goodbye between Jarn and Mem. They spoke to each other in hushed tones. Tears flowed freely. Jarn made a small speech in their own language to the rest of the community—really an extended family—and Percival picked up a few words, such as "yes," "day," and "mother." Jarn promised a short trip and a quick return. The words bore a closer resemblance to Viridiae's language than Percival thought at first, and he wondered if the original Deer People had come from his part of the world.

Lancelot mounted Beric and led the column. Having learned her lesson from the Deer People's surprise attack, she asked Bors and Percival to ride the flanks as much as they could. The rough, sloping ground was perfect for ambush, though Jarn assured Lancelot that his band was the only local humans for walks of several days. He'd seen no sign of the other Viridians since their departure from his camp.

The first two days of the trek were uneventful, even dull. Percival's com found no signals from the outside world. He attempted to make friends with one of Jarn's retainers, who happened to be the guard who had prodded him with a spear after their capture. After offering small gifts and smiles, Percival learned his name: Nealla. He was Jarn's grandson, but he seemed uninterested in knowing more about Percival.

The tension broke in the evening of the second day, when Nealla appeared with a snared rabbit, freshly killed. Using gestures, Percival asked to see it, and within a few seconds, he skinned it, a skill he'd learned prowling his mother's property. Nealla laughed and they cooked the meal over Percival's electric fire. Though he disdained Percival's technology whenever Percival tried to demonstrate, Nealla was fascinated by the fire. Back at the Deer People's camp, Percival saw clear evidence of ashes from burned wood, and he imagined Bors, the Regarder, the sworn protector of earth, air, and water, itching to write a carbon ticket for illegal emissions. When Percival asked him about it, Bors said he had no jurisdiction beyond Viridiae's border, no matter how egregious the crime.

The travelers found shelter in a cave open to a steep-sided valley. Jarn insisted on building an old-style plasma fire, and Percival found himself mesmerized by the dancing, forbidden flames. Viridians and Deer People gathered together to face its warmth, and Percival regretted his lack of experience working with such a magical substance. Over the past thousand years, however, a deep-seated taboo had grown over letting carbon loose into the atmosphere deliberately. Percival doubted he could start a blaze without Gaia reacting with death and destruction.

As the group settled in for the night, Lancelot cleaned and sharpened Arondight with a polishing cloth. Percival watched her stroke it almost lovingly.

"Such a beautiful blade, Lancelot. Who made it?"

"My aunt Nimue."

"The Lady of the Lake? Didn't her mother make Excalibur for Arturus the Great?"

"Indeed." Arondight's gleam caught Lancelot's reflection. "The family forges the finest swords on the continent."

"Do you remember the first time you used it?"

"Yes. The incident with DeMaunt."

Percival nodded. While Percival was a student in The Keep, Sir Melvin DeMaunt had accused Lancelot of cheating during a tournament. DeMaunt was the son of a prominent nobleman, who was an important political ally of King Arturus. At the tournament, Arturus sided with Lancelot, which enraged the volatile Melvin. Queen Guinevere also played a part, but Percival couldn't recall the details.

"Will you tell me the story, Lancelot?"

CHAPTER 15: LANCELOT AND DEMAUNT

The pounding on her door at 4 a.m. woke Lancelot to a crisis, and when the page spoke, her throat closed in worry and fear. The dark and skeletal DeMaunt was a violent man, and she imagined a confrontation between him and Guinevere that did not end well for the queen. Lancelot rushed to Arturus.

The king handed a scroll to Lancelot as if it weighed a thousand kilos. "The queen has disappeared."

The writing on the scroll was small, precise, and thick. *You and the court have insulted me for the last time. Lancelot is a liar and a cheat. You do not deserve the throne. Come and fight me at Turrim Monte. – DeMaunt*

"The queen could not have gone willingly, my lord. DeMaunt kidnapped her." Lancelot checked her arm as it sought Arondight, her new war blade.

"I hope that's what he means."

Lancelot startled. "How could he mean anything else, sir? Your wife is loyal to you. I would swear to it."

Arturus turned up a corner of his mouth. "Loyalty is a thin thing, easily broken when interest serves another purpose."

"My lord, whose interests would the queen have other than yours?"

"Lancelot, a marriage to a monarch is not like other marriages. I love Guinevere, and she loves me as a man, I believe."

Arturus ran his thumb nervously over the papery skin of his hand. “The queen is also the most politically astute woman I've ever known. She could run this country. Her father is elderly. She will soon be head of her house. Leodegrance is on a par with DeMaunt's. She would not let her feelings for me as a man obscure her feelings for my role as elected leader of Viridiae.”

Lancelot could not believe her ears. Her friend and king was on the verge of accusing his wife of running off with a traitor. “No, sir. I don't believe she would do this. DeMaunt forced her to come with him. She is his prisoner. Kidnapping her would force you to protect your reputation, as a husband and a king.”

Arturus regarded his favorite champion. “I agree with you, Lancelot. This is a direct challenge to me as the legitimate head of Viridiae's government. It's also a challenge to me personally, but the dignity of my office matters more than my personal honor, meaning I can't send an army after DeMaunt. Or Guinevere.”

Lancelot nodded, less in understanding than acknowledgment.

“In fact, I consider this… incident a state secret.”

“Sir?”

“You are still my champion, right?”

Lancelot stiffened. As an officer, Lancelot had sworn an oath to defend the Great Charter, whomever sat on the throne. She had also sworn a private oath to Arturus to defend his person, including his reputation. “Of course, sir. You're my king, and my friend.”

Arturus drank from a cup of coffee. “I don't mean to question your word, Lancelot. I'd like to keep this private. I'm asking you to bring Guinevere back without anyone knowing she was gone.”

* * *

As Lancelot rode her palfrey to Turrim Monte, the DeMaunt family's stronghold, Arturus put out a story that Guinevere had rushed to her father's side after he fell ill in the middle of the night. Lancelot had twenty-four hours to bring Guinevere back, thirty-six at the most, before the court and the com nets suspected a ruse.

What if she could not accomplish her mission? She expected to fight DeMaunt to the death, possibly her death. What did DeMaunt have to gain by killing Arturus, or his champion?

And what of Guinevere, if she had gone with DeMaunt willingly? Would she resist Arturus' demand that she return, if Lancelot won?

Lancelot knew one thing for sure: She would support her friend. A distant relative of Arturus the Great by marriage, also called "Strong-Arm," Lancelot was welcomed by an aging Arturus II. Sent to an outpost on the River Colum, Viridiae's eastern border, Lancelot took over the under-manned garrison after its commander was killed in a skirmish. With a few men-at-arms, she turned back a Lucian incursion, and she was awarded her old commander's place at the Round Table. Arturus II died within a year.

His son, called Arturus Longshanks, could not accede to the throne without the consent of the Round Table. Lancelot, a close friend of the prince, was always in his camp, but the country was uncertain. Arturii had ruled for two generations. Could it accept a third? The elected and appointed knights struggled to reach the super-majority to confirm Arturus as king until "Gaia shall receive him unto her bosom," the Great Charter declared.

"Stay close to Arturus," Nimue advised. "He is the only choice who can hold the country together. The kingship is his birthright."

Finally, Lord Bagley DeMaunt, Melvin's father, brought his northeastern faction to the majority, and Arturus took his seat as the head of government. No one quite knew why Lord DeMaunt had thrown his weight behind Arturus.

On the road to Turrim Monte, Lancelot barely noticed how the sickly stalks of the early summer corn resembled the thinning fingers of the king. The thinly leaved trees along Lancelot's route mocked her preoccupation with Guinevere. Court politics carried little weight with Lancelot, at least for the moment. She was on a mission to rescue Guinevere from a kidnapper.

A well-worn horse trail away from the main road emerged at a turbulent stream in front of the DeMaunt's stone keep. To reach the castle's main gate, she'd have to cross a bridge. Twenty men-at-arms waited for her on the other side, though DeMaunt was not among them. Lore described the wood and iron bridge as made of the melted-down swords and gun barrels of the family's defeated enemies. Lancelot saw nothing on the rusting girders that resembled grips, guards, or blades.

She counted her breaths, imagining each rise and fall as a product of her will. In command of every atom of creation within a thousand klicks, Lancelot squeezed her knees with the lightest pressure, and her warhorse Beric edged onto the bridge.

"Stop right there." One of the men, a hands-breadth taller than the rest, wearing mail and a broadsword, stepped forward. "No further, please."

"I ask permission to cross your bridge, sergeant."

"Not granted, ma'am."

"I am Lancelot, on the king's business. I—"

"I know who you are. I've seen you on the com net and in the lists, and the three red bands on your shield prove who you are."

"Then you know why the king and the Round Table gave me those bands."

A flicker of apprehension crossed the sergeant's face. "They are the color of your enemy's blood. I heard you say it in an interview."

"You do not wish to be one of my enemies, do you, young man?"

Beric nodded, as if agreeing with its mistress.

The sergeant licked his lips. "My orders are to let no one cross this bridge, except the king himself."

"I come instead of him. I am his champion." Lancelot urged Beric forward another step. Knight and mount were already halfway across. "I ask politely for the last time. Please allow me to pass. I have business with Sir Melvin."

"I'm sorry, dame knight. I cannot." The sergeant touched his pommel, and the other guards gathered behind him.

"Very well, sergeant. I admire your loyalty and your discipline. To honor you and your squadron, I will fight you on foot." Lancelot dismounted Beric, knowing that if DeMaunt's men charged at this instant, she was a dead woman. Nothing happened.

Lancelot screamed her war cry, pitched over years of practice to inflict pain on an enemy's ears and terror in his heart. The soldiers hesitated, long enough for Lancelot to take off the head of the corporal and slash the arm of a nearby man. The sergeant and the other soldiers drew their single-shot pistols and fired. All missed except one, and the bullet glanced off Lancelot's fiber-reinforced chest plate. Lancelot killed two more of the soldiers, but the sergeant brought down his sword on Lancelot's helm, dazing her for a half-second. Lancelot brought Arondight around and slashed the sergeant's leg. The man yelled and fell to the pavement. The other soldiers, leaderless, broke and ran.

Lancelot halted, aware of her rising blood lust. Beric neighed, wanting to carry its mistress to further kills, but the animal stayed in place. The knight, however, knew her true mission, and she centered herself, quieting her desire to inflict death on all her country's enemies. At her feet, the blood of the crying, dying sergeant and his men dripped between the bridge's planks to the rushing stream below.

"Is Arturus a coward, a weakling, or both?" The echoing voice was DeMaunt's, but it came from everywhere, as if amplified or broadcast.

Lancelot scanned the flat, open ground between the bridge and Tirrum Monte's closed main gate. "Arturus sent me." She raised her voice to her invisible foe. "You have taken Guinevere. Release her to me. I'm taking her home."

"You're so sure of yourself, Lancelot, just like Arturus, and just as blind."

Lancelot's neck prickled. Something was wrong, but the fault was fuzzy, like the low clouds blurring the silver-gray landscape. "Where is Guinevere? Have you hurt her?" The thought of her queen injured or worse by DeMaunt enraged Arturus' champion, but she forced herself to breathe easy. An angry warrior made mistakes.

"Lancelot." It was Guinevere's voice.

"My lady!" Lancelot spun around, distracted by her siren's call, trying to pinpoint its location. Guinevere's contralto was as obscured as DeMaunt's tenor.

"Lancelot, I'm well." Guinevere said. "I don't want you hurt. Go back across the Bridge of Swords. I'm afraid for you."

Lancelot's frustration boiled. "Arturus ordered me to bring you back to Camelot. He asked me to say that he loves you and that you belong at the capital."

"We're both captives, Lancelot du Lac." The new voice, disembodied like the others, was familiar.

"Lord DeMaunt?"

"My son is half-mad. He doesn't understand what he's doing."

"Lancelot, go home! I don't want you to die," Guinevere cried.

A knight in full battle armor, its visor down, its lance down, rode out from behind the keep's perimeter wall. The armor was the same worn by DeMaunt at the tournament. Something was odd about him, though. Lancelot didn't have time to figure it out. The destrier galloped straight for Lancelot, its rider bent on impaling the champion.

Lancelot tossed aside her shield and Arondight and remembered DeMaunt's habit of aiming low for his opponent's belly. Lancelot played at freezing with fear and surprise. She had only milliseconds to act. The lance head extended a meter in front of the enemy horse's head. At the last moment, Lancelot pushed the lance head down into the soft ground with her gloved hands. Now a lever, it lifted the enemy knight off its saddle. Lancelot heard the snap of the warrior's arm coming out of its socket. He screamed and fell to the earth.

Lancelot grabbed Arondight. "Yield, DeMaunt, or you're dead."

"Lancelot, behind you!"

Lancelot lifted her head. She thrilled at her queen's race toward her, and she heard the pounding of hooves, like thunder in the mountains. Another knight bore down on Lancelot. The lance point entered the inside of Lancelot's right leg, where only mail, not plate, protected her. It ripped through the upper muscle. The pain was excruciating as the lance tore the skin before stabbing the turf and breaking off. The haft of the lance slapped Lancelot's backside like an angry parent.

The horse flew past Lancelot, and DeMaunt lifted his visor and brandished his sword. "I'm going to kill you now, you cheater, you thief, and then I'm going to kill your master."

The pain in Lancelot's leg brought her to her knees, though Arondight remained in her hand. The prone knight she had unhorsed was unconscious, his visor knocked open. Lancelot didn't recognize him, but he'd been sent as a feint while her true enemy attacked from the bridge. DeMaunt bore down on his mount, an enormous, snorting, unbarded mare. Beric was too far away to help. DeMaunt's sword flashed, and Lancelot moved aside, her wounded leg begging for mercy and rest. DeMaunt's sword flashed again, and it caught Lancelot on her shoulder, but caused no hurt.

"No, DeMaunt! This isn't what we wanted." Guinevere approached the fighters from the main gate, followed by the gray-haired Bagley DeMaunt. The queen's voice was insistent, and terrified. "Lancelot is not the enemy."

"She's the king's champion," the younger DeMaunt said. "Killing her is almost as good as killing him."

"Stop, son," the elder DeMaunt pleaded. "Lancelot's already hurt. She's no threat."

"You don't know her like I know her."

The conversation among the DeMaunts and Guinevere confused and disoriented Lancelot. What had she walked into?

The destrier's snort and the clank of the hot-headed DeMaunt's armor forced Lancelot to focus. Her shield was out of reach, but Arondight was all she needed. The destrier powered on at a gallop. If DeMaunt struck with his sword, he'd cut Lancelot in half. She could not run forever, and she was on the verge of passing out from loss of blood. She exhaled, centered herself, and avoided DeMaunt's blade as it *whooshed* past her head. She brought Arondight into the destrier's barrel where the stifle met its flank and the animal shrieked before stumbling and throwing DeMaunt. Lancelot hobbled to where DeMaunt lay on his back, stunned by the fall. Lancelot lifted Arondight in a killing pose.

"I beg you to spare my son, Lancelot. Please!"

Lancelot ignored the chieftain and prepared to strike.

"Guinevere!" the elder beseeched. "Speak to her. Tell her that my boy is crazy!"

"Lancelot, don't do it."

Guinevere penetrated Lancelot's urge to murder. Two knights tried to kill the dame warrior in the space of a warbler's song, but the queen's soft voice soothed the tension.

"Lancelot, you have a right to kill Sir Melvin," Guinevere said. "You have a right to defend yourself."

Seeing Lancelot's hesitation, Sir Melvin scuttled toward his weapon, but Lancelot gave chase and again she raised her sword.

"Lancelot!" The intensity of Guinevere's tone brought him up. "Wait. Hold off on your right. You've accomplished your mission."

Lancelot held her sword over her head, but kept it still.

"I'll return to Camelot with you. Sir Melvin and Lord DeMaunt have no hold on me here. I'm free to leave at any time."

Free to leave? Not held against her will? Not kidnapped? To Lancelot, nothing made sense about the day, but the melody of Guinevere's words brought Lancelot down from her lust for slaughter.

The young DeMaunt, humiliated, but his wits returning, glowed with hatred for Lancelot. "I'm not done with her!" He reached again for his sword.

"Son!" The elder DeMaunt feared his son's survival slipping away.

"No, Sir Melvin," Guinevere glanced at the soldiers on the

bridge. “Enough men have died. Rest now, gather your strength, and resume the fight at Camelot.”

Lancelot's breath caught at the suggestion.

“When?” the beaten man said. “In six months? A year? I want my satisfaction now.”

“A week.” Lancelot played along, trusting Guinevere, without grasping her meaning. Guinevere had intervened. Why? Besides, the bleeding champion wasn't sure how long she could last in front of Tirrum Monte's gate.

Bowing to Guinevere's persuasiveness, the younger DeMaunt grunted and backed away. His fate—or Lancelot's—was postponed seven days.

They'd meet again, and the next time, one of them would die.

* * *

Lord DeMaunt's sage-physician applied an antibiotic poultice to Lancelot's wound and sewed it up with catgut. Her wound was messy, but the blood loss was minimal. The dame knight ignored the pain and lightheadedness as she mounted Beric and led Guinevere on her palfrey across the Bridge of Swords. Sir Melvin kept out of sight, nursing his own wounds. Tirrum Monte's chieftain promised his son would appear at Camelot's tourney ground.

Lancelot could not ignore her curiosity. “What did you mean, Guinevere, when you said to Melvin, 'This isn't what we wanted.'”

“I only meant that we didn't want you to die, Lancelot. You're too important to the realm. Your death would be pointless. The loss of Viridiae's finest warrior in a private feud would break the country's heart. It would break my heart.”

Lancelot believed the queen, but doubts surfaced again, irritating her like a monk's hair shirt. She remembered a hurried conversation with Arturus the day before he married Guinevere. They joshed each other over wine and bread, and Lancelot said, “You don't deserve such a beauty.”

"I know," Arturus slurred, "but I must marry her."

"Why?"

"Because I love her," he said. "And because she is a threat to Camelot."

Lancelot brushed off the comment as a groom's nervousness, but now as she and Guinevere approached the crossroads town, Lancelot grasped Arturus' meaning. The fight with Sir Melvin was hard, and DeMaunt's treachery with the disguised knight was real, but the whole situation felt staged, as if the players were creating excuses for a bigger drama.

At Camelot, king and queen reunited in private. Arturus' ruse to explain Guinevere's absence worked, but Arturus' face paled at the news of Lancelot's fight with Melvin DeMaunt, as if a mortal fear had come true.

On the appointed day of reckoning with DeMaunt, Lancelot waited on the tourney ground. Her leg healing, and confident in her ability to defeat DeMaunt, she was nonetheless anxious for the first time since her earliest jousts. Persistent questions pushed her to the online archives. After reading the accounts of the days before the Round Table elected Arturus, she asked Guinevere to meet with her.

"DeMaunt has nursed a wound since the day he saw me," Guinevere said.

"And he's vowed revenge on Arturus since the day the king broke his promise to Lord DeMaunt," Lancelot said.

In the past, during private conversations, Lancelot and Guinevere often held hands or embraced before a warm fire. Not this night.

"Lord DeMaunt made Arturus king. In turn, Arturus made him promises he never kept," Guinevere said. "I made a promise too. One that I could never keep."

Promises, Lancelot thought, are the precursors to lies.

"I was here at Camelot, while my father participated in the negotiations," Guinevere said. She described Arturus' promise of land and position to the DeMaunt family. Lord DeMaunt brought his votes to Arturus, but the new king failed to keep his part of the bargain. "I was a teenager, uncertain of myself. Melvin DeMaunt was here too, with his father. But Melvin was confident, tall, strong, and I couldn't help myself. I pledged my love to him, but it was the pledge of a child. Later, when I broke off our engagement, he vowed to take me anyway, sometime, somehow."

"Sir Melvin was insulted, by you, and by Arturus at the tournament," Lancelot said. "Thus the kidnapping."

"Yes."

That was a lie, at least a partial lie, as Lancelot understood as she warmed up the next morning on Beric, waiting for DeMaunt to arrive. A fog had descended on the tourney ground, similar to the murky weather of the week before, but like an unwelcome sun, Lancelot felt the impact of Guinevere's secret ambition.

Arturus had made promises to the DeMaunts. He made promises to Guinevere's family as well. Three generations before, her great-grandfather had surrendered to Arturus the Great during the Civil Wars. The conflict had broken her family, but the hero of Viridiae was a generous man. As a reward, Guinevere's ancestor was brought into Arturus' inner circle. Her father, Leodegrance, told her of long-held hopes for the return of the family's power and prosperity. Both seemed as distant as the Range of Needles mountains, until it was clear that Guinevere was a great beauty. She was pursued by eligible aristocrats from across Viridiae. Arturus III fell in love with her, and she with him, though for different reasons.

The grounds were on a flat rise on the outskirts of the city that surrounded the citadel. The forested People's Preserve bordered the grounds, and moisture clung to the trees' branches, condensing into drips. The clink of armor plate announced a knight's arrival, but the sound was too complex, like the buzzing of hornets overwhelming the fizz of a single fly. Lancelot gripped Arondight as two mounted knights appeared, then four, then a dozen. Behind them marched a phalanx of men-at-arms. At their head was Melvin DeMaunt.

"My lord!" Lancelot faced Arturus. "What is this?"

"A traitor."

Arturus sat on the dais, Guinevere next to him. The king was pale as ever, but his jaw was set. Guinevere's glance shifted from Lancelot to Arturus to the challenging army approaching him. Word about the duel had leaked. Noblemen and women packed the grandstand, stunned by an apparition. The DeMaunt osprey sigil spread its claws on a red field. It was the family's war banner.

What did the DeMaunts want? Or more precisely, what did Melvin DeMaunt want?

"My lord! My king!" Lord Bagley DeMaunt rushed forward from his place in the grandstand. "I did all I could to dissuade my son from this. I thought I'd succeeded, but—he's gone mad."

"Mad with what, DeMaunt? Grief over my failures? Or rage over Guinevere's rejection?"

"Does it matter, my lord?" Guinevere said.

"It matters to me!" Arturus pounded his fist on his chair. "I know you think I'm weak, that I'm dying, and that the country is sick." He pointed at Sir Melvin, who'd stopped his advance. "He thinks by getting rid of me everything will be better. He's a fool. If he kills me, and you agree to marry him, the country will descend into chaos."

Lancelot saw two men in Arturus, one who recognized the limitations on his power, and one impatient with those limitations. Lancelot wasn't bound by either set. "My lord, let me fight him!"

"No, Lancelot. Now is the not the time—"

"I beg you, my lord. Let me end this before it begins."

"Lancelot—"

Before the king could finish his sentence, Lancelot prodded Beric and charged the enemy force. For a moment, DeMaunt didn't move, as if believing Lancelot was an envoy, or coming for a parley. But 10 lengths from DeMaunt, Lancelot screamed her war cry, raised Arondight and brought it down. She missed, but other DeMaunt knights and soldiers scattered, giving the combatants room.

"You're a traitor, DeMaunt! A filthy cheat who's trying to steal a country!"

"And you're a fool, Lancelot, blinded by your love for the queen, who thinks of you as nothing more than a pawn on a chessboard."

Lancelot heard the words, and they stung, but like a mosquito's bite, they were inconsequential. Lancelot cried out again, and the horse warriors charged one another, the pounding of the animals' hooves loud and hot. Arondight met DeMaunt's sword, the sound echoing through the fog, bouncing off the trees and the grandstand. They passed each other, reversing course at the same moment. They charged again, the horses set to collide, veering away at the last second, while both swords fell. Lancelot's blood lust was up, and this time, she gave it full reign. DeMaunt's sword glanced off Lancelot's helmet, while Arondight caught a piece of DeMaunt's mail, pulling him off his destrier.

Lancelot dismounted, determined to show that she would not win any fight unfairly, especially against a traitor. Her leg throbbed as she found purchase in the slippery grass and the two enemies' swords met in a terrible storm of blows, each one capable of inflicting instant death. DeMaunt parried all Lancelot's swings, as Lancelot did of DeMaunt's attacks, but Lancelot's foe slowed little by little. The breaths of both warriors came in gasps, but Lancelot was fired by love for her king and for Guinevere, even if the queen were not all she seemed.

DeMaunt raised his blade again, brought it down, and missed. Arondight, as if it had a will of its own, thrust into DeMaunt's side, and Lancelot drove it hard between DeMaunt's ribs, pushing it centimeter by centimeter until it cut the warrior's racing heart. Blood streamed down Arondight's fuller and DeMaunt collapsed, dead.

Lord DeMaunt ran up to take the body of his son in his arms. He wailed in grief.

Lancelot exulted in her victory, and she left Arondight where it could drink DeMaunt dry of blood. She turned to the men and women in the DeMaunt ranks. "Go home. Go home now before I slay every last one of you."

The army stepped back as one, as if fearing an attack by the king's champion would kill all of them in one swift stroke. A moment later, the fog enveloped them.

Lancelot limped to the grandstand, her leg wound reopened, her eyes focused on Arturus, forcing herself to keep her gaze on her king. She could not ignore Guinevere, nor the queen's tears, shed for whom, Lancelot did not know. Perhaps Lancelot was blind to something she couldn't quite fathom. In a way, she didn't care. She loved Arturus and Guinevere, Arturus because he was her king and her friend, and Guinevere because she was the loveliest, gentlest, most intelligent woman she had ever met.

CHAPTER 16: CHASE IN THE CALDERA

The next morning's dawn filled the ancient cave with light, and Percival woke quickly. After a brief cold meal, the group headed over a pass between two of the Backbone's granite vertebrae. The trail descended to a broad plain a day's walk in width. It was ringed by mountains.

"This is it," Galahad announced. "The caldera."

"A what?" Percival said.

"See those clouds?" Galahad pointed to puffs of white rising from the base of a natural stone wall. "Those are fumaroles, hissing like mythical dragons."

Percival heard nothing, not even the chirps of birds. The quiet was calming, and eerie.

Bors reigned in his horse. "You're telling us that this is an active volcano? There's grass and shrubs from wall to wall. Lichen is growing on the stones."

"The volcano hasn't erupted for thousands of years, as far as anyone knows," Galahad said. "But there's magma underneath our feet. The steam proves it."

"You mean it could erupt right now?" Percival said.

Galahad laughed. "We'd feel a warning, probably an earthquake. That's what the Old Civilization records said. You can credit Merlin for the discovery. He sent me the specific report on the volcanoes in the area."

Percival was impressed with Galahad's connections, but he was famous for his scholarship.

Meanwhile, Lancelot ranged out into the giant bowl, following a thin trail that led to hodgepodge of enormous stones in the center of the caldera. Next to the jumble was a cone-shaped structure studded with dwarf trees. Percival watched her shrink with distance as the Deer People and the expedition's staff took a break.

In the snap of a finger, Lancelot wheeled around and raced back. Beric kicked up a dust cloud. "Quickly! Follow me," Lancelot implored. "There's something there." She pointed at the boulders and cinder cone. She turned Beric around and galloped back.

Percival, Galahad, and Bors raced after her on their mounts. In two minutes, they were with Lancelot, who listened as the hooves of his companions' horses echoed.

"What is it, Lancelot?"

"Don't you hear it?"

Bors said, "I don't hear—No, wait."

"Almighty Gaia," Galahad said, his jaw dropping.

Percival strained to hear as the animals pawed the ground. Then his blood ran cold. It was the same sound he'd heard in the forested mountains where Lancelot had found him, ages ago.

"Gaia has blessed me again," Lancelot cried. "A questing beast!"

The cinder cone loomed above them. It was the height of Camelot's tallest tower and more, but walking around its base would take hours. The boulders, now as big as houses as Percival approached, lay partly buried, as if the ground was swallowing them. The four knights spread out, searching for a sign of the beast's lair. Lancelot discovered an area of hard-packed soil in front of a gap between two large monoliths. She drew Arondight.

"You're not going to kill it?" Galahad held his camera.

"Of course not, but I don't want to be a meal, either."

"What's that?" Bors said. "To the east?"

Percival strained to see Bors' target. Another dust cloud, perhaps a kilometer distant, receded. "Dust devil?" Percival had seen the spinning air vortexes in the eastern desert.

"I don't think so," Bors said.

Lancelot disappeared into the lair's entrance. An eerie light emanated from within. Percival and Bors followed.

The light came from Galahad's camera as he recorded the scene. The creature sprawled on its side, its long, scaled neck and blunt head stretched toward the entrance. Glittering objects lay all around. Each item was carefully arranged for an effect Percival could not suss out. He noticed a gap in the arrangement, as if the designer had removed an object in a hurry.

The creature's glassy eyes signaled its lifelessness. Even so, Percival was awed by its massive beauty.

"I think it's a juvenile or a yearling male." Galahad moved slowly, recording every millimeter of the beast. "Look here."

Galahad's floodlight focused on a long, broken blade embedded in the creature's neck. A wave of sadness nearly overwhelmed Percival. Below the blade, a pool of congealed blood soaked the ground. Percival recalled stabbing the questing beast in the forest. He hoped the creature hadn't died from the wound, but he was defending himself and Lancelot.

"Here's the other half." Lancelot knelt next to a cross-guard and partial blade covered in blood.

"One of its killers didn't get away." Bors stood over a body, clothed in the sewn hides and furs of the Deer People.

"This must be one of the hunters Jarn mentioned," Percival said.

"Look at the sword wound in his back," Lancelot said. "The beast didn't do that."

"The dust cloud," Bors said. "The others?"

"The other Viridians." Percival realized what happened. "Gaia's breath, they found it. The Grail was here. They killed the beast. Everyone knows the creatures love shiny things. It had the Grail. It was guarding it. The others found it with the help of the hunter. Maybe they kidnapped him. They killed him to cover their tracks, except we saw them trying to get away." Percival ran out of the lair and mounted his horse. Bors and Lancelot rushed after him.

"Are you coming, Galahad?" Lancelot said.

"I'll stay. I've got to record this atrocity. Jarn and the others will be here soon."

On their horses, Percival, Lancelot, and Bors strained to see the dirty cloud that marked the killers' escape, but they saw nothing. Spreading out, they looked for tracks, and Bors found them. Percival hoped the killers didn't know they'd been caught in a crime against nature. That would give him and his companions a chance to catch up. Out in the open plain of the caldera, however, he couldn't expect that kind of luck.

The trail of hoof prints and manure led to a cleft in the caldera that resembled a gate in a tumbledown castle's walls. Lancelot motioned the other two knights to dismount and tie up their horses. None of the three could see beyond the natural opening, and Lancelot feared an ambush. Creeping forward, Percival heard voices a few meters away, speaking as if unaware of the knights' presence.

"Two of them." Lancelot peered over a basalt rock the color of dried blood. "And two horses."

Percival chanced his own look. One of the horses, a dapple gray, carried a canvas pannier, perfect for transporting the Grail. His heart skipped a beat. "They're Viridian. Do you know them?"

"Never seen them before," Lancelot said.

Bors shook his head.

"Three against two," Lancelot whispered. "I say we take them on."

"Agreed," Bors said. He'd set aside his dislike of Lancelot for a good fight.

With hand signs, the three knights laid out their strategy. With a scream, Lancelot led the charge. Arondight flashed, ready for blood, but the footing was difficult, with small, loose rocks ready to trip an attacker. Arondight flew but missed. Percival raised his javelin and threw it through the smaller enemy's sternum, killing him. Bors brought up the rear, but he screamed in fright. A horse bore down on the fighters.

Percival's startled when he saw the rider: Sir Gawain, Lord Mordred's brother. Gawain bore down on Bors, who tripped over a stone. He landed on a second stone, rolling over, holding his hand over the injury inflicted by Odilia Malehaut. The Regarder hadn't healed as well as he'd claimed.

Lancelot was still engaged with her man, who was holding the dame knight off with an enormous broadsword. The sound of each warrior's parried blows sang off the caldera's walls.

Gawain spurred his horse to a gallop, aiming to run Percival down. The young knight had retrieved his javelin and blocked the mounted knight's swing. In the excitement, the horses from Gawain's party had scattered, including the animal with the pannier. Gawain saw his chance at escape. He wheeled his mount around and ran for the dappled gray. Percival's horse was on the other side of the natural gate. They'd had no time to bring the mounts through. Gawain caught the pack horse with the pannier and took off toward a copse of trees. His escape was assured.

In the meantime, Lancelot had disarmed his man, but the loser managed to jump on a horse and take off after Gawain.

"Lancelot! Gawain is getting away with the Grail." Percival ran back toward his mount.

Bors had stood up, sword in hand, but he was pale, and blood leaked from his side, either from his old injury or a new one. "Go on!" Bors winced with each word. "Find Gawain. I'll get back to Galahad."

Percival and Lancelot lost precious seconds chasing their horses before racing after Gawain. Doubts tugged at Percival as he galloped toward a thinning cloud of khaki-colored dust. Bors was a Regarder, Mordred's man, and Gawain was Mordred's relative. Did Bors hold back? Did he fake his hurt? Percival shook his head, unable to believe Bors had betrayed his companions. He and Lancelot did not get along, but that didn't make him a traitor when lives mattered. Gawain had attacked Bors, and it didn't look feigned. On the other hand, should he have left Bors alone to report what happened to Galahad? What would he say about the pannier and the possibility that the Grail had been found, but taken by a potential enemy of Arturus? The last phrase shocked Percival. Where had that idea come from?

He had no time to consider it. Lancelot had pulled ahead and when they reached the trees, the trail dipped down into a dry gully. In a flash, the knight Lancelot had disarmed jumped off a branch. He had a heavy stone in both hands, and he aimed for Lancelot's head. When the enemy landed on Beric's back, the horse lost its balance and the two fighters tumbled together to the dirt. They scrambled to their feet and faced each other.

Percival slowed to offer Lancelot help.

"What are you stopping for?" Lancelot snarled. "Gawain's got the Grail."

Lancelot could take care of herself, and Percival spurred his horse on. The steep sides of the gully funneled Gawain toward the sea. Before long, he was enveloped in a fog smelling of marine decay, and he feared his own ambush. He slowed to a trot, letting his mount feel its way down a watercourse.

Over the next hour, Percival lost hundreds of meters in elevation, but he saw no sign that Gawain had taken a different route. The fog turned into a mist, and he was soon soaked through. Finally, the stream bed leveled out and turned to sand. He had reached the sea. A few dozen meters away, the horse with the pannier chewed on lumpy grass. Percival spurred his horse. The pannier was empty.

A shaft of sunlight broke through the mist, and Percival saw a small boat with three people, two of them rowing with all their might. They made way for a three-masted vessel anchored a kilometer away. Percival didn't recognize it, but he was sure it wasn't the *Dolphin*.

Percival heard a horse behind him. Lancelot arrived, her hands caked with blood. Percival did not have to ask what happened. She looked at the boat and the masted vessel. Crew scrambled up the shrouds, getting ready to make sail.

"Gawain got away with the Grail?" Lancelot said.

Percival nodded, unable to hide his feelings of failure, even shame.

"Not to worry," Lancelot grinned. "The chase isn't over yet."

Percival returned her smile. She never gave up. Her confidence gave him heart.

CHAPTER 17: LADY MORGAUSE'S STORY

Dee shifted her weight. She couldn't find a comfortable position on Ganieda's polished floor. The yoga mat was no help, and neither was Percival's silence. She'd heard nothing from him for weeks, and the memory of his malnourished frame tormented her in her idle time. The difficulties with Lord Mordred's commission and the complexity of her feelings about him magnified her moodiness. Morgause's image kept crowding in as well, but she was a complete mystery. The weight of it all was nearly overwhelming. On top of everything, Ganieda insisted she spend more time honing her spiritual talents.

"Take a breath, Dee." Ganieda's cross-legged posture was perfect. "You can't succeed without taking in oxygen and letting out carbon dioxide."

"I'm holding my breath to avoid polluting the atmosphere with carbon."

"Don't be silly. Breathe in. Breathe out."

Willing herself to concentrate, Dee drew air in like a bellows at the bronze foundry where one of her friends cast a bust of Arturus. She really did want to develop her talents. She held the breath for a moment, then let it out at a slow and steady rate. The distracting pain in her seat grew less important and noticeable.

"Better," Ganieda said. "Remember the Wise Woman: 'Move not—'"

"'Move not the world; move yourself.'" Dee had memorized the 100 Aphorisms of Xochitl. Not all made sense, but they were useful for mental focus. The burning white sage helped, and Ganieda promised the mild tea of wormwood, jasmine, and dandelion root would enhance her invisible senses.

Unbidden, a phantom-like image of Eleanor appeared in her mind's eye, hands on hips, tsking at her daughter's superstitious nonsense. She once caught Dee reading Xochitl's *On the Matter of Theurgy*, the movement's founding text. It amounted to a code of conduct for practitioners. On the floor in front of Dee, as she toyed with a meditative practice, the book was opened to the 93rd Aphorism, “Taking life must be in the service of life.” Killing thrips and torturing spiders on her mother's property convinced her she had to master her power. If she didn't, her self-control might falter under stress. Dee remembered the troubled look on Eleanor's face, and how she appeared ready to scold her but didn't. A few days after Dee's classes started at university, Eleanor referred her to Ganieda.

“Mother taught us that science was the best way to truth and knowledge. She had no time for mysticism.”

“I love your mother,” Ganieda said. “My friendship with Eleanor was one reason I accepted you as a student. But she was, well, close-minded on the question.”

Dee would not admit it in front of Ganieda, but she agreed with her mentor.

“The thing science always misses is the connection among facts, and how they form a whole. I don't mean a system, such as the ecosystem of a forest. I mean the whole of the universe. Theurgists attempt to tap into this wholeness and use it to benefit the community.”

Dee thought a moment. “Why don't you and the other theurgists divine the location of the Grail? That would save everyone a lot of trouble.”

Ganieda laughed. “I love your naivete, Dee. We're not magicians.”

“Then why does theurgy have such a bad reputation?”

“Theurgists prefer to work quietly, behind the scenes. This makes people suspicious.” A look of sadness overcame Ganieda.

"Some, a very few, who practice our art, use it selfishly."

Did Ganieda mean Morgause? "I promise I won't do that, Ganieda."

"You're drifting again, Dee," Dee's mentor said, smiling. "Bring yourself back to the moment."

Ganieda was a patient teacher, in the theurgic world and in the artistic world. She advised Dee on the project for the Great Audience Hall, recommending different approaches to the composition, the palette, and the projection technology. One day, as they revised sketches of the mural, she advised Dee on how to handle Lord Mordred. "The relationship must be professional, Dee. It's easy to be awed by such a man, but you have a future to build. Getting too close to him could backfire."

"I'm not interested in anything else than finishing this commission." Dee wasn't sure she believed her own words.

"Men have a way of letting their power go to their heads. Remember the 48th Aphorism: 'A man's power tears a woman's flesh.'"

"Women can do the same thing."

"Indeed. Some men say women have far more power than they realize, and I agree. After all, more women practice theurgy than men. But it seems throughout history, men always manage to do more injury to women than women do to men. I don't want that to happen to you."

Dee appreciated Ganieda's concern, but her attraction to Mordred was undeniable. They hadn't seen each other since their meeting in the Great Audience Hall with Morgause, but Dee's thoughts turned more frequently to Mordred as the days passed. He had written her com notes with more ideas for the commission, along with 2-D images of his favorite light paintings. All the notes were professional in tone, but there was a respect in them that bordered on longing. Even the "Yours very truly" carried an emotional load. Was it a discrete message? Dee wanted to believe so.

On the opposite side of the coin, Mordred's mother was a puzzle. "What's Lady Morgause's story?"

Ganieda's face darkened. "Morgause is a frustrated, vindictive woman who manipulates her son for her own ends."

Dee was shocked. The critique didn't fit Dee's impression of Morgause, nor her teacher's apparent affection for the lady. One of the oldest photos on Ganieda's mantel showed her and Morgause at a birthday party. All smiles, they must have been only a little older than Dee. "I thought you and Morgause were friends."

"We were, a long time ago. We tore up the town together. We broke a lot of hearts, the pair of us." Ganieda fingered her theurgist's ring. "But Morgause's practice grew dark as the years passed, and we drifted apart. She frightened our mentor, old Delmorian, half to death when she managed to direct a thunderhead to drop three or four centimeters of hail on Camelot."

"You don't really believe she could do that?"

Ganieda smiled sadly. "I did a little research afterward and the sage-forecasters said there was a good chance for thunderstorms that day. But Delmorian believed it. She banned Morgause from Camelot's chapter of the Society soon after."

The story impressed Dee for Morgause's ability to take advantage of likelihoods. If you knew the signs, such as the shadowy streaks of rain falling from low clouds as they approached, you could appear to predict a storm, even conjure it. Morgause must've seen an opportunity and seized on it. "Why would Morgause want to frighten your teacher?"

"Delmorian wasn't frightened. She knew the tricks, but she couldn't tolerate Morgause's arrogance."

"You tolerated it."

"We were young. Delmorian was old. I was bound to take Morgause's side."

Dee had friends like that as well, mostly in college. So many of the professors were stuck in the Dark Days and needed to retire. A challenge to them at a lecture or a social event could be thrilling. It could even make a reputation, like being seen with a powerful man or woman.

Ganieda laughed at a thought, then pursed her lips. "We were probably a little too randy for our own good, too, but we were young, and the young knights in the Keep were so..." She shrugged and looked at her folded hands, hinting at guilt, regret, and nostalgia.

"Nothing wrong with that, as long as you're careful."

"I often wonder if the difference between success and failure is the ability to take advantage of the unexpected."

"Unexpected?" Dee glanced at Ganieda's belly. "You mean, you..."

"Not me. Morgause."

Dee still didn't get it. "Terminating isn't difficult. I mean, it's not easy, but..."

"That's not how Morgause saw it." Ganieda sighed. "You see, the father was the son of the most powerful man in Viridiae."

"You say that as if you think Morgause planned to get pregnant."

"That would be like her, but I never had proof. She behaved as if it were an accident."

Later, during the quiet of the guided meditation session, as she thought of Morgause's flinty eyes and widow's peak, things came into focus. Morgause was the mother of Arturus III's bastard son Mordred, sired before his marriage to Guinevere, but unacknowledged as his heir, even his issue.

"Ganieda, why didn't Arturus marry Morgause, if he was the father? That would be the honorable thing to do."

"It's amazing how people expect leaders to be paragons of virtue, when they have other things to weigh, such as threats to their position."

"You're saying Morgause saw her pregnancy as an opportunity to place herself in power, second only to Arturus, at least before Mordred came of age."

"Now you're seeing the situation more clearly."

"Arturus, however, didn't play along, and rebuffed her," Dee continued. "You have to admire Morgause. She's maneuvered Mordred into a position next to Arturus, despite the king's reservations. But why, Ganieda? Revenge?"

Ganieda lifted her hand. "Enough gossip. If you continue to

lose your concentration, Dee, we'll have to try the meditation exercise again tomorrow."

Dee doubted she could push away the revelations so easily. Her talent had appeared in childhood as flashes of insight. At first, when she learned of the DNA modification to her nervous system inherited from an Old Civilization ancestor, she thought of herself as a freak, abnormal, not quite human. During long talks late at night, Ganieda taught her to accept her legacy as a gift, and as she gradually internalized her reality, the geometry of the possible emerged from the white noise.

She perceived threads between prospects, all thin as spider silk, with some highlighted, like a spider's web speckled with dew. One filament extending into the future connected her and Mordred. It was more than the fulfillment of her commission. Her body warmed at the thought, even as an inner voice called for caution.

A set of threads linked Dee, Mordred, and Morgause, but the elder woman played with the connections like a puppeteer, and Dee could not see where the other strings led. Instinct marked these as important, but Dee had no facts to give her instinct substance. Mordred's own network intersected with his mother's, but she had her own web, independent of her son. This fit with Xochitl's 77th Aphorism, "Be like the lute-player, plucking more than one string at a time." Of course, Morgause had her hands in many things, but how did it matter to Dee? The mere fact that Dee perceived them argued for their significance.

"Dee, you're doing well." Thought-reading was a myth, but Ganieda had an amazing and chilling ability to read Dee. "Concentrate on one thing, if you can. Focus your energy on one image and look behind it."

Dee inhaled and exhaled. Metaphors got in the way of perception, like distracting jewels. She forced herself to ignore the thousands of fibers threatening to snag her. In a moment, an anxiety the color of daffodils filled Dee's sight. Instead of repelling her, she approached it, knowing she was safe in Ganieda's house. Something familiar was deeper within this environment, and Dee pushed away all distraction, even Ganieda's encouragement.

Percival! He'd caused a minor stir at court when he showed up at Grey Harbor. "I should punish him for disobedience," Arturus declared, "but he puts Viridiae's other knights to shame with his devotion." No one was surprised when he joined the Galahad expedition, but the lack of com communication as the ship sailed north irritated Dee. In this moment, as she explored her piece of the unseen realm, his appearance was a portent.

The more Dee explored her anxious feelings, the more she became alarmed. Her mind, exercising the instinct to impose order on chaos, showed her his face, and it was twisted with terror. She smelled salt and brine and blood and she heard his voice calling out to people around him, though the words were malformed. Danger surrounded him, and Dee was powerless. Unlike the attack by a troll in the woods when he was a teenager, he was beyond her reach.

"It's alright, Dee," Ganieda said. "There's nothing to be afraid of."

I am safe, Dee thought, but Percival is not. As she struggled to control her anxiety, a metallic, burning smell overwhelmed everything. A vulture flew into her field of vision, but it startled her: It had two heads!

"Percival!" Dee voiced her fear for the first time since her trance began. "They want to kill you!"

Ganieda reached out, touching Dee's arm. "Don't be afraid, Dee. Stay with your brother. Perceive what you will perceive."

Dee drew strength from her teacher. Percival's distressed visage faded, and a veil fell over the emotional scene, leaving a residue of sweat on Dee's neck and a fast-beating heart. Still in her trance, the world shrank until Mordred and Morgause reappeared. Mordred seemed thoughtful and calculating. Morgause was as determined as a hunter stalking her quarry. She stared at Dee as if she were a meal to be devoured. Her eyes were blood red...

Dee gasped. Breathing was hard, as if she were drowning, or

someone was choking her. Her body screamed for oxygen. Poisonous CO2 crowded out the life-giving element. Darkness enveloped her, but she remained awake. Her mind cleared, and she was in Ganieda's arms.

Dee's teacher cupped her face in her hands. “Dindrane, what did you see?”

The answer came as clear as a lightning strike. “Gaia protect him.”

“Protect who? Your brother?”

“Yes, but it's more than that.”

“How?” Ganieda was perplexed.

An image lingered in Dee's imagination. The two-headed vulture was feeding on a corpse. “They want the king dead.”

CHAPTER 18: A SEA BATTLE

Lancelot paced the water's edge, cursing Gawain and the escaping windship as the offshore breeze pushed it around a point. She and Percival had chased Mordred's brother across half the island. They had not seen the Grail itself, but they believed he had it, and that he was taking it home.

"He's won the race." Percival sat on a log, his face dark with defeat. "We should congratulate him."

Lancelot's years at court made her wiser about motives. "Gawain has the Grail, but that's not what he really wants. It isn't what his brother wants. Or Morgause."

"What does it matter that one knight or another has the Grail?" Percival said. "Gawain's ship is headed for Viridiae. He'll present the Grail to Arturus. The king will give it to Merlin, who will install it in the Great Machine, and health will return to the nation and the world."

"Maybe." Lancelot sat next to Percival. "Maybe he'll give it to someone else."

Percival was taken aback. "Sir Gawain is a loyal Viridian."

"I'm sure he is, but he's also a son of Morgause and brother to Mordred." Rumors said half-brother, but Lancelot didn't voice this speculation.

"I'm not following you, Lancelot."

"Does this help?" Lancelot reached into a pocket and pulled out a silver object. "I took it off Gawain's man, the man who tried to kill me just now."

Percival stared at the pin in the shape of the Lothian family crest. He cradled it in his hand. “It's the same as the pin I found near the cave in the badlands on Sir Kevin's expedition.”

“Same design, for sure.” Lancelot was thoughtful. “I think Mordred and his family have a very good private intelligence operation. At the very least, they have a fast operation. They found a way to get here sooner than us, secretly, but they nearly botched it. Trying to rape one of the Deer People, killing the beautiful questing beast, encountering the official expedition, and getting into a fight with the best knights in the realm. Despite their stupidity, one of them managed to get away with the Grail. That alone is worth congratulations.”

“You're still not making sense to me, Lancelot. Gawain's behavior is despicable, but if the Grail is returned to the Great Machine, doesn't that fulfill our mission?”

“I don't think the answer to that question is as simple as you think. Have you forgotten what happened to Sir Kevin's expedition? Could your misfortunes have been planned? Is it possible you survived despite Gawain's best efforts?”

“Are you accusing the Prime Minister's brother of murder?”

“Percival, you said you believed the expedition was betrayed. You found a pin in the form of the Lothian family crest near the cave where Sir Kevin thought he might find the Grail.” Lancelot retrieved the pin from the man near the caldera. “I found this on a man accompanying Gawain, who was trying very hard to get away from us.”

Percival grasped Lancelot's meaning. “If he put Viridiae first before his brother, he wouldn't have run from us.”

“Exactly.”

Lancelot had no clear idea what to do next. Neither she nor Percival knew where they were on the island, though Percival reported a very weak signal on his com system. Not enough to pull up a map, though it might be enough to send a message.

Shouts caught Lancelot's attention, and a party emerged from the brush and trees above the high tide line. Galahad, two of his staff, Nealla, Percival's friend among the Deer People, and Bors came through on horseback, along with some of the animals taken from Gawain's party. Behind Bors on the horse's rump was Gawain's man who had lost his Lothian pin to Lancelot.

Bors rode up to Percival. “I believe this belongs to you.” He handed Percival a bloody javelin. Percival dipped it in the salt water of the cove and rinsed it of blood.

“And I believe this belongs to you.” Bors pushed the bloody prisoner off the horse onto the sand. “Nice trussing job, Lancelot. I have a position for you at my farm, if you ever need it.”

“What about you?” Percival noted Bors' pale, pained face. He was badly hurt.

“I'll live.”

Lancelot approached the prisoner. “You're lucky. Unlike Gawain, I don't kill innocent beasts.”

The prisoner turned away his swollen face.

“What was the plan?” Lancelot showed the pin to the prisoner. “You might as well tell us.”

“He mumbled something about missing a rendezvous,” Galahad said. “Do you know what he's talking about?”

The prisoner spat in the sand.

Percival said, “It doesn't matter. Gawain got away with the Grail on a ship. It was waiting for him. Maybe that was the rendezvous.”

“You can have a rendezvous at sea,” Bors said. “Perhaps there was another meeting planned.”

“What do you think?” Lancelot eyed the prisoner, who would not meet her gaze. “I'd say he's sad at missing his cruise home.”

“I don't see the point of this.” Percival grew impatient. “We're marooned here.”

“We're not,” Galahad said. “Nealla says we're close to the bay where *Dolphin* anchored. It's only a few hours walk to the south. He knows the way. I told the rest of our party to meet us there. Jarn said he could get them to the campsite by evening.”

“Let's go then,” Lancelot said. “We have a ship to catch.”

* * *

The two parties arrived at the cove at sunset, and Galahad decided to leave most of the expedition's gear on the beach to save time. He loaded only the sample boxes, the scientific instruments, and the recording equipment for *Dolphin*. Lancelot and Percival described Gawain's ship to Captain Libb, who met them at the camp site.

"I know every ship from Koda to the Aztec Republic," Libb said. "Chances are it's a cargo vessel built for milk runs."

"*Dolphin*'s a cargo ship, too."

"She is, but she was built to run the Lucian blockade when the Empire went to war with the Aztecs. *Dolphin* can beat any square-rigger."

"Gawain has a head start," Percival said.

"But there's only one route to Viridiae, and Gawain wants to make best speed. It's just a matter of catching up."

It took two trips to move the expedition to the *Dolphin*, but they had to leave the man wounded in the Deer People's ambush behind. Jarn promised to care for him as if he were his own son.

"Our people have done you harm, Jarn," Galahad said. "They also killed a questing beast. I'm heartbroken over this. I will do what I can to make amends."

"I know you will make sure they are punished, Sir Galahad."

The two men shook hands. In the expedition's short time on Koda, Lancelot felt she had made new friends she might never see again. Percival embraced Nealla.

They reluctantly left the horses behind, including Lancelot's beloved Beric. She said a lingering goodbye to her. She had several warhorses, but she had a fondness for Beric. She would miss her intelligence and aggressiveness.

Once on board *Dolphin*, Libb's crew worked feverishly to weigh anchor and tow her out to sea. The darkness made the exit twice as dangerous as the entrance, but a full moon, a high tide, and a quiet swell in the bay worked in their favor. Once in the open sea, Libb ordered every stitch of canvas set. Gaia blessed *Dolphin* with gale force winds from the southwest, which he said was perfect for the chase.

Lancelot trusted Libb, but her sea legs had abandoned her. While Percival again celebrated the freedom of the Peaceful Sea, Lancelot retired to a bunk after an hour at her accustomed spot on the main hatch cover failed to quell her stomach. The illness wasn't as bad as the trip north, and she fell asleep, exhausted.

A pounding near her head startled her. She was dreaming of Guinevere when Percival slapped the wooden bulkhead above her.

"Lancelot, get up. We've spotted her."

Lancelot scrambled out of the bunk, her seasickness forgotten as a fight loomed. Libb invited her and Percival to the quarter-deck.

"We're gaining on her," Libb said, "but something's not right."

An hour later, they saw the light smoke rising from the ship. A sail at the top of the foremast flapped listless in the flagging wind.

Lancelot, Percival, Galahad, and Bors had retrieved their weapons. They prepared for a skirmish. None of them had fought on the water, and Lancelot hoped Gawain's crew was just as inexperienced. Surprise was impossible as a result of *Dolphin*'s slow walk toward Gawain's ship as the wind eased, but it was clear as it drew within 100 meters that no one aboard Gawain's ship would greet them.

"On deck!" The voice came from a lookout at the top of *Dolphin*'s mainmast. "I see bodies!"

"Might be an ambush," Bors said. "They realized they couldn't outrun us, so they'd make us think they were dead."

Lancelot's instincts argued otherwise. "Captain, can you bring us alongside slowly?"

"Like a toddler taking its first steps."

Lancelot grinned. She could feel her blood rising. "Come to momma."

Dolphin nudged the drifting ship. The vessels groaned like lovers as they rubbed against each other in the swell. Lancelot took a line hung from one of *Dolphin*'s yards and used it as a brace to step from one ship to the other. Nothing moved on the enemy's deck. The only sounds were loose blocks banging against the masts. Lancelot drew her pistols, but she found no targets.

Percival, Galahad, and Bors made their way over and scattered on the deck.

"Two bodies," Percival called out from the bow. "Both shot."

Lancelot descended into the officers' quarters. She found three men, one of them in the cook's apron, all dead from gunshots. The smoke had come from the cook stove, which was burning wood illegally.

Percival winced at the carnage. "Gawain's not among them?"

Lancelot shook her head. "I think the wood smoke gave them away to whoever attacked them."

"Is the Grail here?"

Lancelot suggested the four knights search the ship. They found seven bodies in all, accounting for a crew large enough to manage the ship with robot help. All the bots were stowed in their lockers. They were programmed to do so when com connections with their masters were broken.

"Unless Gawain hid it aboard, the Grail's not here," Percival joined Lancelot in the dead master's parlor.

"He wouldn't leave it behind, not deliberately."

"Maybe he fell overboard. Do you think he took it with him?"

Lancelot reassured Percival. "He's too careful for that." Where could Gawain be?

Galahad appeared at the parlor door. "Libb's spotted another ship. He's in a panic. He wants us back on *Dolphin*."

Trusting in Libb's judgment, the knights scrambled aboard. Every mariner was straining to see an odd shape on the horizon.

"Gaia protect us," Libb said. "It's a Lucian warship."

Lancelot gripped the hilt of Arondight. She hadn't fought Lucians directly for several years. Life at court kept you away from battlefields, although Camelot had not fought a major war with the Lucians since the reign of Arturus the Great. That said, skirmishes were plentiful along their border in the eastern desert.

The lands to the south of Viridiae were fragmented into weak, empty hinterlands with a few strong cities on the coast that left their northern neighbor alone. Still, bandits crossed the border into Viridian territory on a regular basis, and Lancelot went on punitive expeditions every few years. She had never fought or even witnessed a sea battle.

"What do we do?" Lancelot asked Libb.

"Nothing, for now. The wind has died to almost nothing, and making sail might get the Lucians' blood up. They're unpleasant with their blood up."

"So we wait for them to attack?" Percival said.

"We make like we're innocently attempting to help shipmates in need." Libb paced. The dead hulk of Gawain's ship drifted a pistol's shot away. "Sir Galahad, get all your people into their cabins. Hide your armor and weapons, but leave the instruments in view. We're a scientific expedition, studying the weather patterns and ocean currents."

Through a window in a cramped office next to the wheelhouse, Lancelot watched the Lucian galley make steady progress toward them, despite the lack of wind. It was a bireme. Two banks of oars on either side of the armored hull swept through the long swell. Two platforms extended from the deck over the oars, exposing banks of solar cells to the sun.

"I've studied the Lucians' naval technology," Galahad said. "The Lucians originally built warships with propellers, but oars precisely coordinated with robotics turned out to be more efficient. Their logic is a mystery."

"Why doesn't Viridiae have a navy?" Percival said.

"We've never had any trouble from the Peaceful Sea. The nearest nation of any power is Nihon on the other side of the ocean, and they prefer to keep to their coastal waters."

"We have to rethink that," Lancelot said. "I had no idea the Lucians sent warships this far north."

"Neither did I," Galahad said. "This is more than an ordinary patrol."

Lancelot was less interested in the Lucians' motivations than the ship's fighting capabilities. The extensions over the oars could double as fighting platforms. Was the heavy glass reinforced to protect the cells from the marines' boots? Was it slippery when covered with water or blood? Lancelot was almost willing to give up the Grail search to examine the craft.

On the quarterdeck, Libb spoke in whispers to two of his crew. As they disappeared into *Dolphin*'s hold, the Lucian galley shipped the oars on its port side, allowing her to move closer. The move was precise and mechanical.

"If you see any boarding robots, let me know," Libb said.

Lancelot nodded, though she was unsure what a boarding robot might look like.

"They're hailing us." Libb turned on the com speaker so Lancelot and the other knights could hear.

"Viridian vessel! This is LES Senator Antoninus. Identify yourself and your business."

Libb responded with his com call sign. "We are conducting scientific research in international waters on behalf of Camelot University."

"What is your business with the fishing vessel?"

The knights glanced at each other. Lancelot saw no fishing gear. Was that the cover story?

Libb keyed his com. "It appeared to be in distress. There are bodies aboard. Can you render assistance?" He keyed off. His hand trembled. He was frightened. A crewman, one of the two that went below deck, returned with a whispered message.

"Dolphin, *stand by to be boarded."*

Lancelot thought of Arondight, hidden in a utility closet along with the other knights' equipment. They'd bet the Lucians, if they came aboard, would perform a perfunctory search, if they searched at all. The captain of a single warship alone in international waters wouldn't risk an incident. On the other hand, Lucians were arrogant and stupid people. If Lancelot couldn't get to her weapons, she had her dagger strapped to her calf.

The galley lowered a boat to the gray water, and six men took their places. Galahad came into the office and lifted a pair of field glasses to his eyes. “Four rowers. The other two look like officers.”

“What is Libb going to do?” Lancelot felt helpless. Her fingers itched again for Arondight.

“Shit.” Galahad handed Lancelot the glasses. “At the bow, the man in the jacket.”

Thankful for something to do, Lancelot peered through the glasses. “Gaia's breath, it's Gawain.”

“Is he a prisoner?”

“I hope so. If not—” Lancelot thought of Mordred and his Regarders. He didn't want to contemplate the implications of Gawain's cooperation with the Lucians, if that was happening. Did Bors know something? Lancelot ducked into the wheelhouse to inform Libb. She lifted the glasses again.

“Who's that standing next to him?”

Libb lifted his own pair of binoculars. “I don't know. He's got plenty of gold braid. A high-ranking officer, probably. Wait. Crap. Your man is pointing at us. The officer just said something to an underling.”

Lancelot peered through her own field glasses. The deck of the *Senator Antoninus* teemed with sailors. A moment later, marines appeared on the fighting platform nearest *Dolphin*.

“This isn't good, Libb.”

“Yep.” Libb made a decision. He shouted to the two crew members standing by for his instructions.

A few seconds later, Lancelot heard a roar from deep within *Dolphin*. Its belly grumbled and the deck underneath Lancelot's feet lurched. Fearful that *Dolphin* was damaged or sinking, she tumbled out of the wheelhouse and saw the water churning underneath her ship. “Libb! What are you doing? Are we sinking?”

Libb pushed Lancelot aside, leaving another crew member at the ship's wheel. By now, all of the expedition, including Bors and Percival, were on the main deck, alarmed and horrified. Libb pushed through them into the hold. A puff of black smoke poured from a tube strapped to the foremast. Lancelot hadn't noticed it before. It was painted the same buff color as the mast, as if camouflaged.

The noise roared again. It reminded Lancelot of the questing beast, but the noise was regular, mechanical, like breathing and a heartbeat going hundreds of beats a minute.

A flash of sun on armor caught her attention. The marines on the *Antoninus* let loose a flight of arrows. Some were tipped with fire. They all landed short of *Dolphin*, but Lancelot knew the archers had the range. They sent another flight to the "fishing" boat. Two struck, and within moments, fire raged. The boat was doomed. Would *Dolphin* suffer the same fate?

Not if Libb could help it. *Dolphin* was moving away from the Lucian ship and picking up speed. The Lucian marines let loose another flight of arrows, and they fell in the spot where *Dolphin* had floated moments ago. The boat with the six men raced back to the *Antoninus*, and the crew struggled to haul it aboard quickly. As soon as it cleared the oars, the water churned with the oars' power.

Lancelot watched the wake grow behind *Dolphin*. The *Antoninus* was falling further behind. The truth dawned on him. "Libb, you've got a carbon-fueled engine."

"A particular kind that's fueled with a distilled oil called 'diesel.' I've attached it to a propeller." Libb grinned. "I told you *Dolphin* was once a blockade runner."

"Once Bors figures it out, he'll arrest you." Lancelot indicated the thick smoke pouring from the stack.

"I'm betting he won't if he gets out of this in one piece."

Lancelot wasn't so sure.

"We've got a head start," Libb said, "but the Lucians are brilliant sailors. They'll catch us if we're not careful."

"They're solar powered," Galahad said. "They can outlast a fossil fuel engine."

Lancelot was struck by Galahad's calm. "You knew about this, didn't you?"

"Libb showed me the engine in its compartment before we left Grey Harbor. I'd hoped we wouldn't have to use it. I hope they'll forgive us back home."

"They will if we survive." Lancelot glanced astern. "Right now, it's not looking good."

Libb stood with his hands on his hips. "The chances improve if we can hide or go where the Lucians can't."

"You're not making sense," Lancelot said.

Libb detailed his idea. Galahad agreed it was their best chance. Lancelot thought it was their only chance.

* * *

Dolphin set her course due east, straight for a range of mountains that poked above a bank of low clouds. The journey was agonizing. *Dolphin* churned forward, her bow breaking the waves at her head, but the *Antoninus* kept up. Her master was determined to catch the fleeing vessel. Though Lancelot winced at what the black smoke pouring from *Dolphin*'s stack might be doing to the planet's carbon load, she realized that they would be prisoners or worse without the belching monster in *Dolphin*'s hold.

An hour passed, and the *Antoninus* closed the distance. *Dolphin*'s crew nursed the engine, which complained so loudly that Lancelot had to run from its compartment holding her ears. She had never heard such a deafening mechanical cacophony, not even in the huge melees of knights in the national tournaments. To add insult to injury, the sun had come out, bathing the deck with spring-like warmth. Bors rested his eyes, while Percival kept his eyes astern. The expedition's other members spoke in low voices. Every movement of the crew was calm and efficient, as if they were chased by the Lucian Empire on a daily basis. The fact was, as long as *Dolphin* maintained her distance, the *Antoninus* could do nothing but stay with her quarry.

Then the mood changed. Lancelot saw a puff from *Antoninus*' bow and a miniature splash a few meters behind *Dolphin*. Others on deck noticed and strained to look. Another splash fell nearer. A small gun had fired, and its projectile had landed only a few meters from *Dolphin*'s stern.

"We're running out of time, Libb," Lancelot said.

"Quiet." Libb studied a com readout. "I'm looking for something." A line swept across the screen, leaving blobs of light behind. "There it is." He gave an order to the woman at the helm.

A bullet crashed into one of the *Dolphin*'s small boats. Everyone scrambled for cover.

Dolphin turned, almost imperceptibly, but she maintained her speed. Libb was running as fast as he could for a row of rocks at the base of a cliff. Lancelot wanted to object. She was caught between Libb's command of his ship and a boat full of Lucians with their blood up. She had no choice but to trust *Dolphin*'s captain. His life was at stake, as well as hers.

Libb smiled, and Lancelot understood. A cleft cut through the cliff, as if a giant had sliced through it with an ax. Libb took the wheel himself, and *Dolphin* lurched first to port then to starboard as he lined up his vessel. He ordered the female crew member to tell the engine crew to "open her up."

An arrow struck the wheelhouse inches from Libb's face. Lancelot ran to the deck. *Antoninus* had managed to close to arrow range. A fire arrow landed on the deck and in a furled sail above them. Expedition members quickly doused the deck arrow, exposing themselves to bullets and arrows, but the fire in the sail crept down the yard. Percival and another crew member raced up the shroud and edged out to the smoldering blaze. They doused it with lengths of canvas soaked in seawater. Another flight of arrows descended. One struck the yard next to Percival.

Lancelot urged Libb on. "Whatever you're planning, you'd better do it now."

"Shut up, I'm working." Libb kept his eyes on another readout. Without warning, a buzz sounded. "Gaia damn us, it's shoaled in."

"What are you saying?"

"The tide's going out and it's too shallow."

Lancelot wondered what she could do. In the interregnum after *Dolphin*'s initial escape, she had donned her breastplate and

Arondight. She was ready for a close-quarters fight, if necessary.

"Lancelot, I need you to go down to the engine room. Tell them to red line it. We've got one chance."

Lancelot had no idea what "red line" meant, but she followed Libb's order, dodging another hail of arrows and bullets from the *Antoninus*. Crew and expedition members scrambled to put out the fire arrows. Bors tended to a screaming expedition member with an arrow in his leg.

The engine room was a devil's den of noise and stink from the fuel. Lancelot could not imagine a fleet of boats in centuries past burning so much of the earth-destroying oil. She relayed Libb's order and returned to the main deck and clean air. At least she wouldn't suffocate in that hellhole.

Dolphin lurched forward as she strained toward the cleft in the rocks. The face of the cliff was close enough for Lancelot to stretch out and touch it. If *Dolphin* wrecked here, no one would ever sail through again. A small bay appeared behind the opening, but Lancelot knew what lay beneath the waves. As another group of arrows *plonked* onto the deck, she raised a death prayer to Gaia. If this was where she was meant to die, she prayed she could save Percival, Bors, her son Galahad, and all the others before she was taken.

Dolphin shuddered and her speed dropped. Lancelot fell forward. Only Libb had braced himself; he had no time to warn. "Come on, old girl. You've got it in you. Pour in on!" He leaned toward the tiny bay, as if his physical urging would push her through. The edges of the cleft loomed above *Dolphin*, like jaws of a predator clamping on a helpless rodent.

Dolphin surged forward. Libb yelped in joy. In seconds, *Dolphin* was through the cleft.

Lancelot reversed her gaze. *Antoninus*' oars splintered against the rocks flanking the entrance to the bay. The ship had followed *Dolphin*'s line, but the captain realized his mistake, and he tried to slow down before grounding. With broken oars flailing, *Antoninus* drifted helpless, though the outgoing tide carried her toward the open sea. The ship disappeared behind a cliff.

A cheer went up on *Dolphin*.

"How did we..." Lancelot's heart burst with relief.

Libb leaned against a bulkhead, tears brimming in his eyes. He'd seen his end, but his ship had saved him. "I told you *Dolphin* was built for blockade running. And she's done some smuggling. She's built to go into gunkholes like this one." He swept his eyes around the narrow inlet. "The depth seer isn't precise." He tapped on the electronics. "It can be a few centimeters off. We grounded, but the swell lifted us and the engine pushed us through. Gaia in heaven, I don't want to do that again."

Lancelot concurred. She thanked Gaia for her survival. She hoped she never saw another fight at sea again. Or any other ship. Except, perhaps, the *Dolphin*.

CHAPTER 19: THE GUNKHOLE

The *Dolphin* reminded Percival of a flesh and blood sea creature basking in the sun, except for the lack of sun. Within minutes of escaping the *Senator Antoninus*, the *Dolphin*'s crew discovered a leak caused by her grounding. The submerged stones shoved in several of her planks. *Dolphin*'s solar-powered pumps fell behind the incoming water, and Captain Libb beached his ship for repairs. An incessant drizzle proved good cover for the work.

Unlike the trip north, Libb did not want the inexperienced Percival's help with the repairs. The knight watched morosely from his seat on a bleached log. Curious, but frustrated, he wanted to learn how to set oakum in the seams between the fresh planks kept aboard for an emergency.

"I'm good with a sword and pistol, but I'm useless with a hammer and nails." Lancelot stretched out on the cobble underneath the overhang of a giant fir. "Still, I'm so bored I might volunteer to help Libb."

"He'll say no," Percival said. "You'll just be in the way."

"Sarcasm isn't like you, Percival. You're too young to be cynical."

"I've seen my share of the world." Percival pulled a sapling, which stubbornly clung to the ground.

Lancelot sighed. "Galahad is happy collecting things. Why don't you help him?"

The expedition leader ordered his staff to photograph and catalog some of the fauna in the bay's thick forest. The damp micro-climate had spawned some unusual forms. Percival shrugged. He was more interested in the boat than bugs.

Lancelot addressed Bors, who'd wandered by. "Well now, Sir Regarder and Farmer, what jobs have you taken on?"

Bors remained silent, unwilling to play along with Lancelot.

"About as much as Sir Percival and myself, I think. Here we are on our natural habitat—land instead of water, that is—and as useful to the expedition as our coms."

The high cliffs around the gunkhole effectively blocked what weak signals reached into the wilderness.

"How is your wound, Bors? You fought well at the caldera. I'd never know you had just one hand."

Bors' affect softened, as if he appreciated Lancelot's concern. "I'll take on ten knights, if called upon."

"Unlikely around here."

Percival marveled at how a fight of one kind or another always seemed on Dame Lancelot's mind.

"Perhaps we can reconnoiter," Lancelot said. "At least we can make sure no one is spying on us. What do you think, Percival?"

The idea was more attractive than imitating the bumps on the old log.

Lancelot brushed a fallen needle off her jacket. "Bors, I know we don't get along that well, and I'm not your boss, but—"

"I'll come along. It's better than stewing here. Libb says the repairs should be done by dark."

Lancelot was pleased, and Percival's mood lifted.

Several hours of diffuse daylight gave the three knights plenty of time to scout the surrounding area. Percival found a game trail that led into the forest. Streamers of gray-green lichen hung from branches. Moss grew thick as turf on the tree trunks. Time was arrested in the forest, a phenomenon Percival also noticed at sea, as *Dolphin* rode the disinterested rhythm of the swell. A squarish stone about knee height blocked their way. It marked a turn in the trail.

"That's not a natural shape for the local geology." Percival touched the pebbly surface. "Galahad says the stone around here is mostly volcanic."

"Poured concrete," Bors said. "I've seen similar shapes in the King's Forest, especially near the old roads. This one is good quality. It's lasted a millennium."

Percival let Lancelot lead the mini-expedition, with Bors in between them. Percival wondered if he should walk between his companions, because he could sense lingering tension. Lancelot and Bors had spoken only a few words to each other since they had nearly come to blows in Galahad's tent before the departure from Grey Harbor. Their communication was mostly limited to housekeeping on *Dolphin* and on the march to the caldera.

"Lancelot, I want to say something to you."

Bors' remark came out of nowhere, and the dame knight lifted her head, as if preparing for the unexpected. If Bors was still hostile to her and her relationship with Guinevere, he may have been looking for a time and place to act on his anger. The deep forest was a perfect place for a murder. Escape was easy. Percival blinked at his silly fantasy. These were his friends. All three had left their swords at camp, thinking they would be awkward in the brush. All three carried pistols, however. Percival noticed a small knife tucked into Lancelot's boot. He had his own knife, and he expected Bors had one as well.

"Water?" Lancelot handed Bors the canteen.

"Back at Grey Harbor, in Galahad's tent." Bors took a deep breath. "I said some things—"

Lancelot waved her hand. "Forgotten."

"I'd like to apologize."

Percival breathed out. There'd be no fight.

Lancelot relaxed. "Well, it was in the heat of the moment. We were drinking, and so on."

Bors nodded.

"Apology accepted. Enough said?" Lancelot clapped her hands, as if warding off an evil spirit. "Shall we move on?"

"There are things you should know about Guinevere. Things," Bors continued, "you probably won't like."

Percival perked up. Lancelot was taken aback by Bors' statement. What else about this taciturn man would surprise her?

Lancelot twisted the canteen lid tight and stowed it in her rucksack. "You know Bors, from the day we left Grey Harbor, I've been trying to figure out why you joined this expedition. I didn't believe your boredom excuse. You're the stereotypical farmer: honest, dependable, straightforward, with no patience for obfuscation or dissembling. That's why you've always preferred a quiet life on a nice, rather profitable farm, instead of Camelot."

Percival winced at Lancelot's hypocrisy. Court games didn't sit well with Lancelot either, but she tolerated backbiting and similar shenanigans to remain near Arturus and Guinevere.

"I'm a sworn knight, and a Regarder. Finding the Grail is part of my job."

"And you're Mordred's man, at least in principle." Lancelot responded. "Are you here to watch me, Percival and Galahad? You don't strike me as the informer type, though. Fess up, Regarder. What do you want? What's your secret?"

Bors folded his arms. "When Percival came round my place a few weeks ago, I told him that my wife and son had gone to visit relatives. They're in Carmelide. My wife is a cousin by marriage to the Leodegrance family, Guinevere's family."

"I know about her family," Lancelot said. "The local people still elect a chieftain to the Carmelide throne, though it hasn't existed as a real duchy for a hundred years, at least not since Arturus the Great defeated Guinevere's great-grandfather and stripped the family of nearly everything."

Percival had heard that ghosts of the family's resentment remained. The vestige reared its head during Round Table debates.

"The election was the big event while my wife was there," Bors said. "Do you know who was elected?"

Lancelot shrugged.

"I'm surprised you don't."

"It's not as though it matters."

"Guinevere is now Queen of the Carmelides."

Lancelot was unimpressed. "She's queen of a domain that's nothing more than a nostalgic dream. When did this happen?"

Bors gave a date.

"I'm pretty sure she was in Camelot that day."

Percival wondered if she was with Arturus, or Lancelot.

"She was elected *in absentia*," Bors continued. "The people have never got over how Arturus the Great humiliated the Leodegrance family. He stripped the clan's birthright and its independence. Guinevere's great-grandfather was loved. Giving the crown to his direct descendant was an act of homage."

Lancelot allowed that having Guinevere on hand for the election would've looked odd.

Bors added, "Her acceptance of the crown could be seen as seditious."

Lancelot's face reddened. "You're on thin ice, Bors."

"She's a powerful, intelligent, ambitious woman," Bors said. "And she's got an ax to grind. At least her family does."

Percival swallowed. He did not like where this was going. "Sir Bors, are you sure—"

"You've lost your mind," Lancelot interrupted. "Why would a family nurse a grudge for a century and plot revenge now?"

"Guinevere is in the perfect position to act, hypothetically."

Lancelot laughed. "Stick to raising pigs, Bors. Your audition for punditry on a news chan is a disaster."

Bors remained quiet, letting his idea sink in.

Percival felt the need to say something. "I don't understand. What would Her Majesty hope to gain by conspiring against Arturus? Restoration of her family's lands? That seems unlikely after so long."

"Certainly not restitution." Lancelot pointed her finger at Bors' chest. "That would break the treasury and upset a conservative like you. Besides, Carmelide is as rich now as it was then."

"I have more, Lancelot."

"You seem eager to spill your guts."

"I'm a loyal Viridian. I swore an oath as a Regarder to protect the earth in service to the people and the monarch." Bors looked into the distance. "Not all my brothers and sisters who wear Viridian green have the same values."

"More people unsheathing their knives?"

"Don't make fun of me, Lancelot. You aren't exactly the paragon of virtue, sleeping with the king's wife. I don't like it, but that's not what upset me back at Grey Harbor. I'll tell you what did upset me. You might be sleeping with a traitor. How do I know you aren't in league with her? You defend her with enough volume to be heard in Camelot. You know what people say, 'The louder you are, the more doubts you have.'"

"Listen to the homespun wisdom, Percival." Lancelot snickered.

In light of Bors' revelations about the new Queen of the Carmelides, Percival couldn't blame him for suspicion.

Lancelot said, "I don't go in for conspiracies, not that I believe anything you're telling me."

"Then think about this, Lancelot: I see the orders given by Mordred to the Regarders. He's not very good about compartmentalizing, as they taught in security class. He's a little too free with his desire for power."

"I often wonder if Mordred's ambition will get the better of him."

"He sent Gawain to disrupt Percival's expedition, and I know in my bones he sent Gawain to Koda. Mordred wants the Grail worse than Arturus, and not because he wants to save the nation, but because he believes the throne belongs to him."

Percival absorbed the news about Gawain. He was right all along, that Sir Kevin's expedition had been sabotaged. Nearly two dozen good men and women died because of it. He almost died. The revelation should've angered him, but in the context of Bors' implied accusations against Guinevere, he analyzed the situation dispassionately. "For Mordred to get what he wants, he needs inside help."

Lancelot understood, too. Percival could see it in her eyes. Guinevere aligning with Mordred—the Carmelides allied with the Lothians—would create a formidable political force. Not to mention a military force. Lancelot shook her head, as if dislodging an evil thought. "Like I said before, you're insane, Bors. Two and two do not always equal four at Government House."

"Maybe so, but ask yourself, does it ring true, or at least plausible?"

Percival stayed silent, unwilling to admit the idea's possibility out loud.

Lancelot wasn't quite ready either. "People have been spinning tales like this out of rumors and lies for thousands of years. That doesn't make any of them true."

"Suit yourself, Lancelot. But think about it. Gawain brings back the Grail, Mordred takes credit, and demands that a sick, weak, defeated Arturus give up the throne. Guinevere extracts a divorce. Mordred and Guinevere marry and reign as co-equal monarchs. Neat as a pin, eh?"

Lancelot had heard enough. She threw up her hands and walked off. She headed toward the *Dolphin*, leaving Bors to shout after her.

Percival followed his companions, but Bors' theory took over his thoughts. The plot did seem plausible, if unlikely, even stupid. Arturus was popular with the workaday Viridians, in spite of his infirmities and the slow decay of the country's environment, ostensibly because of the broken Great Machine. People groused, but Arturus' reign was relatively peaceful, efficient, and free of the worst kinds of corruption. Democracy was messy, but Arturus managed to lead the fractious Round Table into a semblance of consensus. He was a good man.

People who crave power, however, always find an excuse to act.

Lancelot bounded down the trail's switchbacks, with Bors a dozen meters behind. Percival struggled to keep up in the gathering darkness. Bors' anguished shout broke Percival's reverie. He picked up the pace, but lost sight of both knights. Another shout from Bors drew him toward the edge of a cliff, where the trail abruptly ended.

"Over here, Percival! We need help!"

Percival ran the dozen meters. Bors was on his belly. His right arm hung over the edge of the precipice. The stump of his left arm flailed to maintain balance. He didn't want to be pulled over. Percival peered over, and Lancelot hung by Bors' wrist. If she let go, she'd fall to her death.

Percival had nothing. No rope. No gear of any kind. He had no time to run for help. Bors could not hold Lancelot forever. She was calm, but Percival saw the fright in her eyes.

"Help me, Percival. Help Bors, or we'll both go."

Percival had only one option. He lay next to Bors. Thankfully, the ground sloped away from the cliff edge, giving the two men a little extra leverage. The lanky Percival managed to grab jacket fabric on the shoulder of the dame knight. Those weeks of hauling on lines aboard *Dolphin* had strengthened Percival's own shoulders, and he hauled with all his will. Bors pulled as well, his one good arm stronger to make up for the loss of his left hand. Centimeter by centimeter, they pulled Lancelot toward them, until she could bring her other arm up to grab a tree root sticking out into empty space. In a few seconds, Lancelot was sprawled on the forest floor with Percival and Bors.

"Gaia's blood, I thought I was dead." Tears leaked from her eyes.

"What in hell happened?" Percival said.

"I wasn't watching where I was going. One foot came down on nothing, and I went over. If Bors wasn't within a single pace..."

"Don't do that again, Lancelot." Bors flexed his fingers. "I can't afford to lose another arm."

Percival liked the joke, but none of them laughed. Death had brushed them, changing its mind at the last moment.

No one said anything for several moments as the evening deepened.

"I was thinking about an old girlfriend," Lancelot said.

"You're kidding me," Bors said.

"Arturus introduced us. He was a year ahead of me at The Keep. Neither of us liked academics, but we liked jousting and carousing on the weekends. At one of those parties, I introduced him to a woman in my cohort."

"Who was that?" Percival said.

"Morgause. Gaia's heart, they had a romance that burned out as as fast as it caught fire. Arturus broke it off—she was several years older than him—but he and I were fast friends after that. His mother was overprotective, and he loved a taste of freedom."

"You said you thought of an old girlfriend," Bors said.

"Arturus returned the favor by talking me up among his friends. I couldn't get a better endorsement. My new connections paid off later. But there was one woman who was head and shoulders above all the others."

"Her name?"

"Athena. She was broad-shouldered, grey-eyed, and multi-talented. She could weave gorgeous tapestries one day and crush a skull in battle the next."

Percival listened as Lancelot gave in to nostalgic memories of Athena. She and Lancelot spent long hours in the People's Preserve, hiking lesser-known trails and lying in each other's arms on the cool grass under a shade tree. Relationships among The Keep's cadets was strictly against the rules, but administrators and officers looked the other way if the lovers were discreet. The most painful day of Lancelot's life was Athena's graduation, when she learned of her first posting, a remote corner of Viridiae known as The Hook, a salient of land into Lucian territory. The two nations skirmished constantly over the disputed border.

"Three weeks later, Athena was killed in an ambush."

"I'm sorry," Percival said.

"Arturus was there. He was wounded badly enough to be awarded leave to Camelot. We talked about her on a bench in the People's Preserve."

"'She fought like hell, but she didn't have a chance.' That's what Arturus said."

In the darkness, Lancelot's voice broke. Athena was her first love, and she'd spent half a month's pay on a custom-made graduation gift she hoped would keep her in Athena's heart.

"I was glad Arturus was the one to tell me the story. I'd missed him too. He was my best friend. Still is, in my mind. But my life fell to dust when Athena departed for the most dangerous place within a thousand kilometers. My worst fears came true."

Lancelot sighed as she related the rest of the story to Percival and Bors.

"Arturus handed me a small canvas sheath decorated with intricate needlepoint. The image was a landscape with Camelot's citadel looming over the countryside. Arturus told me it was in her hand when she died of her wounds."

"A sheath?" Percival said. "You mean for a weapon?"

Lancelot pursed her lips. "It was stained with blood, probably Athena's. The sheath held my graduation gift to her. It was a steel knife with a green enameled hilt inlaid in gold with the Viridian eagle."

On the cliff above the Peaceful Sea where she had almost lost her life, Lancelot let her grief return, for memory's sake. "I still think of Athena from time to time, especially when I'm with Arturus. On the day of my commendation ceremony, when I swore fealty to Arturus, I met him in the royal apartments. I swore to him that I would protect him in a way I couldn't protect Athena. I told him I'd kill anyone who threatened him and my memory of first love."

Sitting between Bors and Percival, Lancelot removed the knife sheathed in her boot. It was Athena's knife.

Percival had nothing among his things that reminded him of Dee or his mother. He didn't have a lover back in Camelot, though his curiosity about Lina Catalpec, the girl in the gallery, hadn't abated. Lancelot's story brought tears to his eyes, and he thought himself a poor idiot who had nothing compared to Lancelot, or Bors, who had a wife and son. Percival cared about only one thing, finding the Grail and bringing it home.

"Listen." Lancelot's voice changed from regret to vigilance. Percival heard what she meant. It was much like the sound his mother made when she brushed her long hair. The cloud deck had lifted, revealing the moon and thousands of stars. They had enough light to see the trail again. The three knights followed the sound to a man-high shelf above a rocky beach. In a few dozen meters, they reached the shoreline, but not at the cove where the *Dolphin* was undergoing repairs.

Percival knew it was somewhere near, however, probably north. But the scene below him, Lancelot and Bors was arresting. Strewn on the rocks and pebbles, pounded by the waves, bodies floated, like so much flotsam produced by a winter storm. Among the uniformed corpses were pieces of the furnishings of life: doors off their hinges, blankets without beds, clothing, shields, lances, sail fabric, a sofa. Most were imprinted with the golden image of a laurel wreath and the initials “SPDL,” which stood for “Senatui ac Populo de Lucia” in the Lucian tongue.

Bors produced a battery-powered light.

“We could've used that on the trail.”

Bors shrugged. “What do you think happened here?”

Lancelot pointed out a half-sunken shape fifty meters off the beach. “The *Senator Antoninus*, I'd bet. I saw her crash on rocks at the entrance to *Dolphin*'s Cove. She must've floated in this direction and foundered.”

Bors walked down the beach, shining his light on bodies and debris. Percival tried to make out faces among the dead, but he didn't recognize any. The birds had feasted, though.

“I don't see any sign of Gawain or the Grail.”

“Gaia knows where he is,” Lancelot said. “The ship had at least one boat. He might've escaped.”

“Or he drowned, and took the Grail with him.”

Percival was tired. Bors had filled his mind with conspiracy theories, and they'd found the wreck of a Lucian warship with many, if not all, the crew dead. That was why Lancelot survived her fall. Death was sated on the souls of the Lucians. For the Viridians, it had left a warning. Omens were things for theurgists and the superstitious, but Percival couldn't suppress his anxiety about what awaited him in Camelot.

CHAPTER 20: MORDRED AND GUINEVERE?

Dindrane sent commands to the image projectors hovering above her in the Great Audience Hall. Workers had covered the original chemical painting with a special material that enhanced the three-dimensional aspects of light tapestries. Her work space was surrounded on three sides by black drapes hung from a tall scaffold, affording Dee privacy while she worked. She tapped and swiped her screen, and the projectors responded with splashes of color and animations of the figures.

Dee had decided on a scene depicting the presentation of a gift. She took inspiration from ancient stories of gifts given to kings and presidents, but projected the idea into the future. Dee planned the basic composition, but she was unsure of the details, even frightened of filling them in.

For three nights, dreams of Percival had troubled her. She'd wake as the morning twilight turned her room from near black to a dull gray, which was too much like the color of death. In the haze of semi-consciousness, fear, anger, and disappointment were followed by the kind of joy experienced anticipating a journey to a foreign land. Images of water and shouted words teetered on the edge of her senses, but when she opened her eyes, the impressions fizzled into nothing.

At first, she attributed the dreams to anxiety for her brother's safety. Only spotty reports about the expedition had made it to

Camelot, as if they had traveled to an unknown planet. On the second night, the dreams intensified, as if reflecting prey's fear of predator. On the third night, she awoke alarmed, and she rushed to her teacher, wondering what she should do.

Ganieda encouraged her to embrace the visions. "They're not about Percival. They're about you."

The dreams were connected to her painting and the fact that it represented an, as yet, unfocused future.

Mordred was the key to unlocking the puzzle. He stopped by nearly every day to watch her for a few minutes and offer praise. Over time, Dee regarded these words as small gifts that germinated. One time, they shared a laugh at a pompous courtier's expense. Mordred called him a "blowhard," and in his sarcasm, Dee saw how he wanted to open up. It moved her to touch him on the arm and laugh a little too loudly. In this way, she could return the favor of his admiration.

The simple pleasure of another's company evolved into stronger feelings. One evening, both worked late, and Mordred came for one of his visits. Dee had learned his moods, and for once, he'd left some of his normal restraint at the door. His eyes glittered, as if he was dying to tell her some news.

"What is it? Can you tell me?"

"It's news that could have a profound impact on our country and maybe the planet. I'm sorry that it's classified, or I would tell you all the details. I have to make sure it's true."

"I understand. 'Matters of state,' as you've said a dozen times."

Dee's rebuke disappointed Mordred."I'm teasing. Sorry. I have some news as well."

"Good news, I hope." Mordred sat on a stool.

"Yes and no. No one's heard from Galahad's expedition. The com system hardly works in the far north, but I got a message from Percival this morning."

Mordred's affect changed from someone who had a secret to reveal to someone determined to keep secrets. "He's fine, I hope."

"I assume so. His message was about the Grail."

At this, Mordred stiffened. "That's also a matter of national security."

"I know, but I've been having bad dreams about Percival, and I've been trying to contact him. One of my messages apparently got through, and he responded."

"What did he say?"

"There was only a few characters, but the message said 'Grail is gone.'"

"Nothing more?" Mordred looked askance, as if fearing a revelation.

"That was it. I took it to mean that the expedition had failed."

Mordred shrugged, a gesture tinged with relief. "It could mean anything. The message might even be garbled. I can tell you that Galahad's official transmissions, when we get them, are full of errors and radio noise the technicians can't penetrate. We need better communications planet-wide. That was another one of the lost achievements of the Old Civilization."

Mordred drew his hands over his face. He was working a problem in his mind. Dee found this incredibly attractive, even though she wished he could tell her more about his burden so that she could offer support, at least emotionally. Despite his dark reputation, Mordred was a highly intelligent man driven to achieve more than people expected. He wanted so much, though he rarely said anything that gave away his true desire. His habit of holding back his inner thoughts challenged Dee's desire to understand herself, not only her artistic talent, but her spiritual power.

Dee gave into temptation and recalled a form of telesthesia Ganieda introduced only the week before. She concentrated her mind on her subject's imaginary third eye, which Ganieda described as a hidden window into the soul. Mind-reading was impossible, but if the theurgist practiced concentration and openness, new knowledge about an individual's thoughts and feelings might present itself. The technique was intended as a way to grasp the meaning of an emotion difficult for the subject to articulate. The technique should only be used with men and woman who needed help, Ganieda taught, not as a way of spying on people. Voyeurism undermined theurgy's respectability, as well as violating a person's privacy.

Confident in her self-restraint, Dee promised herself she'd only glimpse Mordred's inner mind. As Dee relaxed, the waves of feeling from him coalesced. Among the expected anxieties and doubts of a man bred to lead, she discerned one that flattered her. He longed for her embrace.

Ganieda warned Dee to stay objective about knowledge gained this way, but she found that the energy of his thirst for her attracted like a magnet. Her resistance was as weak as a kitten. In fact, she didn't resist, but drew fire from it. She edged closer, and he reached out. In a moment, they kissed, but he pulled away.

"I'm sorry," he said. "We, I, shouldn't have done that."

Dee fell back on coyness to cover her intrusion. "Maybe you're right."

Mordred was perplexed. "But I thought—"

"Strictly speaking, I work for you. The law is clear on these kinds of relationships. You pay me to do a job, not become your lover."

"I didn't think of it that way."

"The boss never does." Dee hoped he picked up on her sarcasm.

Mordred's shoulders slumped in resignation. "It's been impossible for me to stay away from here. I look for any opportunity to walk by, even if I can't stop and say hello. I'm prime minister. I can't even have the hint of scandal or I'll never achieve ..." His voice trailed off.

Those secrets again. Telesthesia had revealed nothing about those.

"What would your mother say?" Dee half-expected Morgause to appear.

Mordred laughed. "She's my biggest supporter, and an anchor around my neck. She wants what I want, but for different reasons." He folded his arms, closing the discussion.

Dee was sorry she brought up Morgause. She had her own troubles with her mother, but Eleanor was a couple of hundred kilometers away. Even in a nation where communication was instant, if unreliable, Eleanor was not a constant presence, like Morgause was for Mordred. Dee sympathized with his amalgam of love and resentment.

Mordred gazed at the half-completed light painting, his mind, as Dee sensed it, a raging mass of plans and ambition. Almost no man among Camelot's thousands of men in her generation excited her, but here was a man who made her fingertips sweat. He was tall, broad-shouldered, and he had a destiny. As if on autopilot, she took a step toward him. She put her palm to his cheek, and his reaction excited her. Their second kiss compared to the first as a single berry compares to the sweetness of a whole field of berries.

She had no qualms about bringing him to her. Mordred was the kind of man she wanted, the kind that can take on any challenge, overcome it, and be greater for it. Other men were dalliances, nothing more than an evening's or a weekend's entertainment. When these men wanted to see her again, she said in no uncertain terms that they did not measure up. Mordred did, at least at that moment, and the waves of pleasure he provoked sealed her knowledge.

Will I regret what I've done, she asked herself.

Afterward, Mordred stared at Dee in the same way he'd earlier admired the painting. What would he say?

“We must be careful, Dee.”

“If you mean we have to be discreet, you'll get no argument from me. I don't need the trouble of gossips.”

“I've become entangled with women in the past who've seen me as a stepping stone,” Mordred said. “I don't want what happened to them to happen to you.”

Was that a threat? It didn't matter to Dee. She knew what she was doing. She thought so, anyway. “Keeping secrets is part of my theurgistic training.”

Mordred stroked Dee's long hair, and she leaned into his fingers. Dee felt as if they'd been lovers for months, maybe years. Layers of resistance between them peeled away, leaving emotions fresh as a new lamb. Dee's contentment warmed, and she could almost visualize the trust Mordred was handing her.

"If you vow again to keep my secrets," Mordred said, "I will tell you what I learned today."

"Do I need to repeat myself?"

"Don't take offense. I live in a world of betrayal and pretense. I have to be sure."

"Then I promise, with all my heart."

Mordred stepped away, still hesitating. He took a full breath, as if bracing himself. "I have the Grail."

The statement shocked Dee. "You mean, *the* Grail? The missing piece of the Great Machine?"

"Yes."

"How are you so sure? Is it here, in Camelot?"

"To be precise, Gawain has it, and he is on his way to the capital."

Dee had a thousand questions, but not all of her resistance to Mordred's charms had broken. She thought of Percival but kept her new worries to herself. Mordred's report made no sense. If Percival didn't have the Grail...

"How did Gawain find it?"

"I have my mother to thank. Some of her sources are better than the government's. I may have appointed Gawain to a government job, but he really works for her. She sent him to Koda by a mainland route. She had contacts along the way. The man practically killed himself getting there before Galahad and his ship of fools arrived."

Dee wanted to ask if that insult included her brother, but didn't.

"His journey back hasn't been a picnic either," Mordred added. "He deserves a medal."

"Are you really sure about the Grail, Mordred? Do you have pictures? A description?" The discovery of the true Grail would be an earthshaking event.

"Gawain is clever in his own way. He's sent me detailed photos via Morgause's network. I'm no expert, but the device looks genuine."

"Does Merlin know? Has he seen the pictures?"

"I haven't told him. I want to see the object for myself first."

"What about Arturus? Does he know?"

At this, Mordred's face darkened. "I'll tell him when he needs to know."

Mordred's answer frightened Dee. In the space of a few minutes, Mordred went from lonely politician to tender lover to a calculating noble willing to put his appetite for power on an equal footing with the interests of his country. Perhaps on a greater footing. To Dee's amazement, the change didn't dampen her desire for him. Her judgment was already at war with her heart.

But what of Percival and his quest to find the Grail and save the nation, as he promised Arturus? As the only human who truly knew her brother, Dee understood his ambition to be of the purest sort. He wanted nothing for himself, except perhaps ridding himself of the stain of killing his father with his own hand. Dee knew the anguish it caused, even if it was justified, and even though she was the one who finished the battle at the Lake of Souls with the *coup de grâce*.

She was torn by a blood loyalty to her brother and a new, untested love for Mordred.

Should she tell Percival what she knew, after swearing twice to Mordred she would keep his secret?

Tension filled the Great Audience Hall, and Mordred departed with a confused look, despite the tender kiss goodnight. Dee tried to work on her light painting, but the evening's revelations, happy and troubling, sapped her energy. She collected her things and headed for the palace parking lot and an automated car. The darkness of late night bothered her, even in a safe city such as Camelot.

* * *

Dee heard Guinevere call out in the corridor leading to the

parking lot. Dressed in a loose but modest robe and slippers, the king's wife looked as though she'd been unable to sleep. Dee could not avoid her.

"Working late says well of you, Dee, but I wouldn't make a habit of it. Your health will suffer."

"Thank you, my lady. In fact, I'm very tired. If you'll excuse me —"

"Won't you sit with me, just for a moment?"

Dee fought back a sigh. She'd had enough intrigue for one night.

A wooden bench with cushions was placed under a window, as if the architect knew that the long, dim corridor needed a place for rest. Motion detectors blinked red, then green. The entire palace was under constant surveillance.

"Mordred seems pleased with your work."

Dee's mind replayed the scene of an hour before. How much did Guinevere know? She remembered the queen's warning about Mordred and "careless women."

"I haven't seen the painting, so I only have his word to go on," Guinevere said. "But if it's half as good as the work I bought at the gallery show, I'm likely to be impressed."

"His lordship is checking on its progress frequently, and he seems happy so far."

"'Happy.' What a wonderful word. I wish I knew what it meant."

The strain on Guinevere's face marred her beauty. Dee had seen photos of her as a young woman. Middle age had done nothing but enhance her attractiveness. The chitchat chans frequently remarked on her grace and poise, while political commentators called her loyal, but enigmatic, even opaque. She seemed to need a friend, but Dee was only a temporary addition to the court.

"You don't look well, my lady. Should I call one of your attendants?"

"Do you know the story of Elizabeth, one of the ancient queens of the British Islands?"

Guinevere's question was a *non sequitur* for Dee, but she went along. “Ganieda has mentioned her once or twice.”

“She was queen 1,500 years ago. The sage-historians have managed to piece together her story. She was an extraordinary woman. In Camelot and in Viridiae, women can hold any office, own and run a company, even fight on the battlefield.” An unspoken thought crossed Guinevere's brow. “Our social equality with men is as normal as the sunrise.”

“I know this wasn't always true.”

“Before the Dissolution, women had almost no power, relative to men. In Elizabeth's time, 500 years earlier, they had even less, but she became queen of a small country and set it on a course to become one of the most powerful nations on earth. For a time, at least.”

“I shall have to read more on Elizabeth, but I don't understand your point, ma'am.”

“She was born to it. She was educated to be a queen, though the chances of her assuming the British throne were minuscule. Circumstances conspired to put her there. And she loved it.”

“You are a queen. And you're a great help to Arturus.” It felt like the right thing to say.

Guinevere seemed not to hear. “She assumed the throne as an unmarried woman, and then she decided never to marry and she never had children. It was unheard of in those days. What strength she must have had! I'd give almost anything to meet her and ask her how—” Guinevere stopped cold, afraid to go further.

“Ask her what, ma'am?”

“She was independent all her life, even though she was surrounded by people, mostly men, mind you, or comparatively powerless women.”

“She must've been terribly lonely.”

Guinevere's voice grew firm. “But she wanted to be queen. She wanted to be the best of monarchs. She didn't need any man or any other person to be a partner, despite constant pressure to find one.”

“You have a partner.”

"Who is that?" Guinevere looked at Dee as if the younger woman could read her mind.

"The king, of course." Dee didn't understand who else she might've meant.

"Oh." Guinevere's face flashed sheepishness, as if she'd made a *faux pas*.

"What do partners really want, Dindrane Rathkeale? They say they will share with you everything in equal parts, but do they, when push comes to shove? Are people who call themselves 'partners' really just one of those vampires in the old myths, all sweet talk but sucking you dry?"

The questions left Dee nonplussed. A part of her wanted to respond somehow, but Guinevere was asking a riddle. "I hope you're not talking about King Arturus. He's doing his best, despite—"

"Despite the troubles bedeviling him and the country." Guinevere's affect turned quizzical. "Have you ever wondered what a different person on the throne might do?"

Dee's heart skipped. Was it an innocent question, or was Guinevere laying a trap? Truthfully, Dee hadn't thought about it. In casual conversation, people wondered about the succession, because Guinevere and Arturus had no children. Mordred was in line, she knew, but the throne wasn't automatically passed from father to son, as in the old monarchies. As representatives of the people, the Round Table elected a leader. It just so happened that in Viridiae's short history, the new king was the old king's first son. It was a coincidence, nothing more. Dee tried to remember what happened in the ancient world when the succession wasn't clear. It came to her: civil war. But things were different in Viridiae, weren't they?

Dee's mind turned. Hadn't she heard Ganieda say something about Guinevere and the Duchy of Camiliard? She struggled to remember. "I'm not a political person, my lady. That's a question for lawyers or politicians."

Mordred's ambitious nature came into focus for Dee. He and Guinevere were similar in that way. Did they want the same thing?

Guinevere patted Dee's hand. “Artists are lucky. They can focus on making beautiful things and ignore the pettiness of court life.” The queen sighed. “Elizabeth was an educated woman, another rarity in those days. She spoke five languages. She could've been a brilliant scholar. But destiny chose a different path for her.”

Dee flashed back to her gallery opening. Guinevere and Mordred were together that night, ostensibly on their way to dinner. What did they discuss? Policy? Art? Something else?

“Should we make our own paths?” Guinevere said. “Or should we accept what Gaia has presented?”

The shadowy corridor encouraged black thoughts in Dee's mind. Mordred had revealed a powerful secret to her. He had control of an object that meant everything to Viridiae's survival. It was a symbol of the nation's health, as well as a practical device. Arturus had fought—through men and women such as Percival and Lancelot—to retrieve it and reinstall it in the Great Machine. Mordred may have the same ultimate ambition, but he had other motives and goals. Dee was convinced of it.

Was Guinevere hinting at the same thing? Was her plan troubling her so much that she wanted to reveal her conflicted heart to a nobody? Dee was now caught in a web spun by two spiders, the prime minister and the king's wife. Perspiration beaded on her temples as the clarity of her predicament revealed itself.

There was one difference. Mordred was excited by what his discovery of the Grail meant. Guinevere, in contrast, appeared ambivalent. She had not decided whether to follow through with whatever she and Mordred had contrived. Dee's curiosity almost overcame her trepidation, but she feared overstepping her bounds.

Dee had her own ambitions. Daily contact with the second most powerful man in Viridiae, a man who wanted her as his lover, put Dee into a powerful position. If she played her cards right, she could be the most admired artist in Camelot. Or the most respected theurgist. Or both. She'd have to nurse her relationship with Mordred, like a careful gardener taking advantage of a spring shower.

Mordred complained about women who used him as a stepping stone. Did they discard him, or did he discard them? And now that Guinevere hinted at the choice in front of her, Dee wondered if she was a friend, or an enemy. If Dee said the wrong thing, or met the wrong person, her freedom, even her life, might be in danger.

It was thrilling, and frightening.

It certainly meant Percival's life was in danger.

The thought of her brother brought Dee back to earth. Percival probably didn't know Gawain had found the Grail. He'd hate the thought of facing Arturus empty-handed, even if he, Galahad, and the rest had done their best. Mordred didn't want Arturus to know his secret, and he was capable of doing anything to keep it. If she helped Percival, or warned him, Mordred might retaliate. Her life might be ruined. Not even Ganieda could overcome a public condemnation by Viridiae's prime minister. Dee might have to retire to the forest, like her mother. The thought upset her.

"My dear," Guinevere said, "now you're the one who looks ill."

"I'm sorry, ma'am," Dee said. "It's late, and I have many things to think about."

CHAPTER 21: BELL'S HAM

Percival begged Captain Libb to bend on as much canvas as possible to *Dolphin*'s yards. He wanted to catch every breath of wind. Every second counted. Every nautical mile mattered. The message from Dee was cryptic: "The spider has its prey." Her text had come through within minutes of *Dolphin* coming into range of Viridiae's com system, and Percival puzzled over it for hours. He was glad to hear from her, but she had been trying to reach him for days, because a backlog of messages poured in. Each was the same, sent every few hours, as if she was desperate. Was she the prey, or the spider?

Galahad could not make sense of it, nor could Lancelot or Bors. Percival was not sure if any of his daily messages after Gawain's had reached Dee, because she had never responded, and once *Dolphin* was far out to sea after her successful repairs, electronic communication was impossible. Dee was not one for sending Percival jokes or riddles, which made the message all the more enigmatic. Percival turned it over and over in his mind, thinking of the days when he and Dee would roam the woods with their mother, who would point out the flora and fauna. Dee liked spiders in particular, and she once spent hours watching an orb weaver build a web and wrap a victim with a shroud of white silk.

Then it came to him. The spider was a hunter. All the photos and descriptions of the Grail showed it as a sphere with a silvery hue, which Galahad's discovery of the False Grail in Perditon proved to be true. If the ball was the Grail, and the hunter was

Gawain...

"That's a stretch of logic," Galahad said after Percival explained his reasoning.

"Maybe the spider is something else," Bors said. "Or maybe the message was garbled. Why doesn't she just say, 'The Grail is here.'"

"She's at court," Lancelot said. "She may think she's being watched, or that she has to be discreet to protect herself. Or Percival."

"Mordred has something to do with this," Bors said. Over the days of the return voyage, the farmer knight had shared his knowledge and his suspicions about Mordred and Guinevere's goals. The other three knights had resisted, Lancelot included, but Bors' case grew stronger with each passing moment, though Guinevere's involvement still seemed far-fetched, at least to Lancelot.

"Have you been able to get in touch with Dee?" Lancelot said to Percival.

"She's not responding to my pings. I'm getting worried."

"You should be." Every instinct told Lancelot to act quickly. "I think we should behave as if Gawain has returned to Viridiae and he has the Grail. I also think we should assume that his first loyalty is to his mother and brother, not the country. We don't have any proof, but we need to intercept him before he gets to Mordred, assuming he isn't already in Camelot."

Two more days passed before the *Dolphin* tied up at Grey Harbor's wharf. A quick canvas of the waterfront's denizens confirmed no ships with Gawain or other knights had arrived in the past week. They guessed Gawain would find the shortest, fastest route to Camelot. Acquiring fresh horses, Percival and Lancelot raced for the most northerly port in Viridiae, while Galahad and Bors headed for likely towns inland. The chances of intercepting Gawain were slim, but they had to try.

* * *

Percival and Lancelot had almost nothing to go on, beyond a vague hypothesis about the shortest route to Camelot. Percival had spent long hours talking with *Dolphin*'s crew, and they often told stories of the waterfront in the tiny port of Bell's Ham. No one knew where the name came from, but it was a pig sty, one mariner declared. If you were a sailor, and you needed a job that paid in cash, or you were on the run from the Regarders, a dive bar or a flophouse in Bell's Ham was the place to go. Lancelot agreed. She could easily imagine Gawain laying low in such a place.

Riding hard, the two knights made it to the burg in two days, stopping only for fresh horses. The crew of *Dolphin* had been generous in their description. The decrepit waterfront skirted part of a bay that might have been pretty, if it weren't for the half-dead trees that climbed the hills above the shore. A few rust-streaked two- and three-masted ships slumped in the water, surrounded by skirts of floating debris. The bay was a throwback to the days before the Dissolution, when humans used the sea as a dumping ground. Time had forgotten Bell's Ham.

"Smells like a rancid armpit," Lancelot said.

Percival led the way down a street, his horse picking its way around heaves of cracked concrete. With no plan of action, except for keeping their eyes open, he and Lancelot stopped at a tavern called the Uncorked Growler. A sign displayed a tipped-over bottle dripping the last of its contents. Even in their mud-speckled clothes, they stood apart from the scattering of patrons in the shadows.

"I'm hungry." Lancelot perused a three-item menu scrawled on a slate with chalk.

"Are you sure about a meal here?"

"Probably not as deadly as the characters in the booths."

They ordered plates of cold meat and mugs of ale.

Percival relished the beef, served with fresh bread and a crisp apple. The ale was good too. The gangrenous appearance of the

Uncorked Growler was deceiving.

"I have a question." Lancelot addressed the bar maid, a woman called Jan with graying hair in a bun. "Where can a woman with security experience get a job around here?"

Percival glanced at Lancelot, puzzled.

"What kind of experience?" Jan wiped the bar with a wet cloth.

As Lancelot explained her background, most of it lies, Percival took in the booths and tables. The Growler was larger on the inside than it seemed from the outside, and Percival noted a rear entrance that likely led to an alley. It was an escape route, just in case.

Percival stretched his legs, the long ride catching up to him with aching muscles unused in the weeks at sea. He closed his eyes for a second, and when he opened them, a man in a cloth cap faced him. The shadow from his cap's bill hid his eyes, but Percival sensed menace.

"You're not from here." Only one side of the man's mouth moved, as if the other were paralyzed.

"Yes, we're visitors." Percival said. "New to town, actually. We're planning to stick around for a few days, maybe find some work."

"Security, huh?" The man grinned.

"Maybe, if the pay's good."

"The only security you'll get is by turning around and going back the way you came."

"No trouble today, Darragh, please," Jan said.

Lancelot had finished her chat with Jan and regarded the dingy customer. "You're obviously not from the Chamber of Commerce."

"I can smell a Regarder a mile off," Darragh said.

"In this stench?" Lancelot wrinkled her nose.

Darragh did not take the bait. "If you're not careful, you'll be rotting in a shallow grave before the sun goes down."

"Look, friend." Percival wanted to diffuse the situation. "You're an intelligent person. I won't lie to you. We're not Regarders, but we are looking for someone."

"I'm not an informer. If any of these boys and girls saw me inform, they'd cut my throat."

"What's the harm in hearing us out? There might be a reward in it."

"I told you I'm not an informer." Darragh's eyes shifted, belying his interest in a payout.

"Don't say anything. Just nod if you've seen this man." Percival showed Darragh a photo of Gawain. Percival held his com toward him as discreetly as possible.

The man hardly moved. "What if I have?"

Percival's heart skipped a beat. Darragh hadn't said No, though he hadn't said Yes. Percival couldn't keep his hand from shaking. He wasn't cut out for cloak and dagger investigating.

A cleaning bot skittered by their feet.

Lancelot rescued Percival. "If we walk out together, Darragh, and you take us to him, I'll see that you get a year's salary deposited into your personal bank account."

The man squinted. "I know you."

Lancelot blinked. "I get a lot of that. I'm certain we haven't met."

"Whoever you are," Darragh said below his breath, "I can get double from the Lucians for telling them I saw a couple of out-of-place strangers looking for Prince Mordred's brother."

Lancelot grinned and grabbed Darragh's arm. She dragged him out the door, smiling politely to the other patrons. "Percival, pay our host."

Percival waved his com over the reader and followed Lancelot. She had pinned Darragh against a post.

"Let me introduce myself, Mr Darragh Spy-for-the-King's-Enemies. I'm Dame Lancelot du Lac, late of King Arturus III's confidence, and possessed of knowledge on how to skin you alive." She held Athena's jeweled dagger to the spy's throat. "Now, do you know where Gawain is or not?"

Darragh's eyes widened in recognition, and he nodded at a pace calculated to extend his life. The dagger's razor-sharp point touched the skin above his throbbing carotid artery.

"Good," Lancelot said. "If you're telling the truth, I'll give you half the reward I promised."

Darragh's eyes sagged.

"And I'll let you live."

Darragh's next nod was more enthusiastic.

Percival couldn't believe their luck. Finding Gawain's trail was one chance in a million, and by all rights, Gawain should've been long gone, perhaps at Camelot by now. Something was wrong, but Percival had no idea what it might be.

Sheathing her blade in her boot, Lancelot twisted Darragh's arm behind him and urged him to lead the way. The sidewalk was pot-holed and crumbly, and an on-shore breeze carried a miasma from the bay. After five or six blocks, Darragh indicated one of a dozen flophouses on each side of a narrow avenue. They entered one called "The Deluxe." Lancelot saluted the toothless old man at the desk as Darragh led them down to the basement. At the end of dark hallway, Darragh stopped at a water-stained door. "He's in there."

Percival reached for the handle, but Lancelot stopped him. She said to Darragh, "How do we know we're not walking into an ambush?"

"You don't, but I like money, and you've got it. Why should I give up that chance?"

Lancelot pursed her lips, and she kicked in the door.

"Wait!" Darragh said. "What about my reward?"

"Invoice me."

Ignoring Lancelot, Percival rushed into the closet, his own dagger out, expecting to be waylaid. Instead, he saw a man on a cot. Bloody bandages covered part of his face and both of his hands. In the dim light of a weak bulb, he was pale and thin. Lancelot ripped off the blanket to uncover weapons.

The figure pleaded. "No, please. You got what you wanted. Leave me alone."

Percival tried to place the man, then he realized who he was. "Gawain?" It was impossible to believe it was the same man who had nearly killed him, as well as Lancelot and Bors, at the caldera on Koda.

Gawain opened his one, unbandaged eye, which leaped from Percival to Lancelot and back. “No, please. I was only doing—” He halted.

“Where's the Grail?” Lancelot growled.

“Don't tell my brother. Or my mother. Please.”

Percival and Lancelot glanced at each other.

Gawain whimpered as his misery forced a tear from his eye. “I was on my way home. I almost made it. Then they found me.”

“I don't understand,” Percival said. “Who found you?”

“They tied me up and beat me. I didn't want to tell them. I was afraid of Mordred and what he might do. What would Mother do?”

“Damn it, man,” Lancelot barked. “Where's the Grail?”

Gawain breathed easier as he remembered. “I came ashore. I wanted to rest a while before going to Camelot. Nobody recognized me. Everything was fine. Then they cornered me, and they brought me here. I'm sorry, Mordred,” he cried to the moldy ceiling, “but it hurt so much.”

“You had the Grail, Gawain, but you lost it,” Percival said.

“I hid it. It would be stupid to carry it around.” With his arms, Gawain made a shape about the size of the rucksack carrying the Grail. “But they made me tell them where I hid it.”

“Who's 'they'?” Lancelot demanded.

“Are they still here, Gawain?” Percival began to lose heart.

Gawain thought a moment. “I doubt it. They're probably over the border by now.”

“Speak clearly, Gawain.” Lancelot's face was red with frustration. “What border?”

“What border would you expect? The Lucian Empire!”

The revelation knocked Percival back on his heels. “They were Lucians? How did they know?”

“I don't know. Gaia help me.” Tears flowed freely from Gawain's eye. “Mordred will kill me. Mother will kill me. The Grail was the key to the whole thing. Everything depended on it.”

Lancelot's face lost its color. “The coup attempt?”

Gawain cried out in terror. “But I haven't told them. You can't tell them. They'll flay me alive!”

Percival's mind was a mass of emotions: disappointment at losing the Grail yet again, fear that hundreds of kilometers away in Camelot, King Arturus was in danger, worry that Dee was caught up in the intrigue. “What should we do, Lancelot?”

“Get up,” Lancelot lifted Gawain bodily to his feet. “We'll give you a lift home.”

“But, what about—”

“Shut up.” Lancelot glanced at the door, where Darragh watched. “If you want your reward sooner, take us back to the Growler. I don't want to get lost in this hellhole of a town. Percival will keep an eye on you.”

At the Growler, the knights collected their horses, purchasing a third for Gawain at a stable a few doors away. Percival sent a message to Galahad and Bors to set up a rendezvous.

“Here's your money.” Lancelot transferred credits to an account Darragh supplied. “Enjoy a drink on me.”

“Are you sure he deserves it?” Percival asked as the trio passed the last of the shacks on the main road.

“No, but that's not why I paid him.”

Percival drew a blank.

“Darragh the non-informer had me deposit his silver in a bank I recognized from security briefings. It's famous among the criminal class for laundering digital currency, no questions asked.”

“So he is working for the Lucians,” Percival said. “Should we tell someone?”

“He doesn't work for the Lucians. At least they don't work with that bank.”

“I don't get it.”

“The loyal officers of that institution deal strictly with Viridians. Darragh is working for someone in Camelot.”

Whoever that is, Percival guessed, already knows what happened today in Bell's Ham.

CHAPTER 22: LADY MORGAUSE'S THREAT

The public car's abrupt slowdown startled Dee out of her reverie. She was on her way to the palace to work on her commission. She'd watched the shipping reports for the arrival of *Dolphin,* and she relaxed when it tied up with all passengers and crew accounted for. She'd ignored Percival's calls and texts, thinking she'd done enough to get him in trouble. He was probably under surveillance. He'd decide what to do next on his own. New trouble appeared on the street, however, when the car halted in front of Morgause. Dee took in a sharp breath.

Leaving her bodyguard on the sidewalk, Morgause climbed in and took the seat facing the younger woman. "What a pleasant surprise." The elder's affect suggested the encounter was less of a surprise than she claimed.

"Likewise, my lady." Dee hoped her tone was properly deferential. Truth was, she was afraid of Mordred's mother.

"I've enjoyed public transportation so much more now that the public cars pick up at a moment's notice if they have an empty seat. I constantly run into friends."

"I'm glad you consider me a friend, my lady."

Morgause did not share her destination or purpose. Instead, she glanced out the window at the stone and glass buildings in Camelot's business district before turning a studied gaze on Dee. "Friends come in different categories, wouldn't you agree?"

"Yes, ma'am."

"There's the kind who are there for you whenever you need them. Loyal to the core."

Morgause had a menace to her, despite her silvery hair and trim build. Her theurgist's ring was prominent on her left hand.

"Then there's the kind who call you a friend, but when your back is turned, they care about no one but themselves." Morgause's eyes flashed.

"I don't understand what you mean."

Morgause returned stony silence, but her features softened. "My son is in love with you."

Dee's tongue went dry. Morgause's observation reeked of distrust.

"He talks about you frequently, or at least about your work. At first, I thought it was just an infatuation. I regret sometimes that I've been hard on him. I steered him away from most women, though he needed a release now and then, as do most men of power. None of his dalliances captured his heart. He thinks differently of you. He seems a little happier, not quite so serious."

Dee squirmed as Morgause examined her as if she were a specimen under a jar.

"How did you do it?"

"Excuse me?"

"What theurgist's trick did you use? I know all the love and sex charms and potions. I made Mordred immune to them."

Dee's blood pressure rose. Ethical theurgists frowned on chemical manipulations. "I haven't used any tricks."

Morgause absorbed the sentence, perhaps judging whether it was a lie or not. "Do you love him, then?"

Dee was uncertain how to answer. After their first kiss and lovemaking, Dee thought she might be in love with him. As the emotional high wore off, she wasn't as sure. She admired Mordred for his intelligence and charisma. His presence elicited a level of awe in Dee she found appealing. His willingness to trust her with his feelings charmed her. "With all due respect, my lady, it's none of your business."

"You mistake me, Dindrane Rathkeale." Morgause hissed. "I didn't track you down for a private chat to discuss maudlin emotions. I want to know what you want."

"Madam?"

"I know that you messaged your brother after my foolish son revealed our plans. You tricked him somehow, and he thinks it's love." Morgause rolled her eyes. "I've protected him too long, and now he doesn't know witchery from the real thing."

Dee doubted Morgause knew anything about love except bitter rejection.

"If you don't love him, who are you working for?"

"I'm not a spy, if that's what you mean. I only want my brother to be safe. And I care about my country and my king."

"Don't insult my intelligence. It's always family first, eh?" Morgause laughed. "Maybe that's why he loves you. He understands you, perhaps better than I do. Maybe better than you understand yourself."

The main palace gate loomed in the car's windshield, much to Dee's relief.

Morgause took Dee's chin in her hand. Her skin was soft, but the grip was painful. Dee wanted to bite the woman's fingers.

"You listen to me," the elder woman snarled. "Say anything to Mordred about our talk, and I'll flay you and your brother alive. If you hurt my son, I'll get even more creative with a punishment. If he learns the Grail—"

Morgause stopped herself, but Dee sensed her fear. The elder grinned and let Dee's chin go. "You're good. You almost got me to tell you *my* secret. Won't happen, not with me. I know the theurgist's ways."

A realization came to Dee in a flash. Morgause thought she had the Grail in hand, but she lost it somehow. She and her son needed the object to legitimize their attempt to depose Arturus. If she did not have it, whatever plans she had would fail, and she wanted success more than anything. Instead, she planned to move forward anyway.

Before Dee had a chance to think through a next step, the public car's door opened. Mordred greeted them, first taking his mother's hand, then Dee's. His smile for his mother was practiced. His smile for Dee was authentic.

Dee could not help but return the feeling. Her hand in his spread warmth through her body as if she'd caught a luscious disease. But the illness interfered with Dee's intellect like a net catches a bird. She was in love with Mordred, and it terrified her.

"What news, my son?"

Mordred waited until they were out of earshot of the guards at the gate. "Everything is in place, Mother."

Morgause stole a look at Dee.

"Ms Rathkeale is sympathetic to our cause, are you not?"

Dee wasn't sure where she stood, in a political sense. She cared only for the safety of Percival, but Mordred the politician's inclusion of her in the conspiracy ratcheted up her fear, which fought with her growing affection for Mordred the man like tournament knights. She was not a traitor to the king, but under the gaze of Morgause, she nodded in agreement with Mordred without much conviction. Others, maybe the king himself, would not give her the benefit of the doubt if Mordred and Morgause's plan failed.

"I'm so glad," Mordred said. "I've also received a message from Gawain."

"Gawain?" Morgause was surprised.

"He confirms he has the Grail, and that he'll bring it here within hours."

The information confused Dee. Hadn't Morgause just hinted that Mordred's brother did not have the object?

Morgause looked equally nonplussed. "I have more news, and it may call for an unpleasant decision. I believe Percival, Galahad, Bors and Lancelot have discovered us, and they are planning to —" The elder thought a moment. "—intercept Gawain and take the Grail from him. They want to deprive you of your birthright, Mordred."

Dee's eyes fell to the ground. Should she pretend to be loyal to Mordred more than Percival? Would it help or harm her brother?

"How many of the Regarders do you have at hand?" Morgause said.

"A squadron."

“I know the route the four knights are taking. Send them to meet them.”

“And do what?” For the first time Dee could remember, Mordred appeared uncertain.

“Whatever is necessary to protect our success.”

Morgause meant that the Regarder knights should kill them. Percival's life was under threat even more, and Dee could not act for fear of discovery.

“That is not what we planned, Mother. The Grail would be our ticket. The people are tired of Arturus' weakness. The Round Table's endless debate and inaction is destroying the nation.”

“You are Arturus' heir in everything but name. You are his son by my womb. You're destined to be King of Viridiae, Mordred. My life is dedicated to making that happen. I've risked everything for you!”

“You're risking civil war.”

“A few dead knights is a small price to pay for achieving our dreams, your dreams, Mordred. You are the Prince of Lothia. It's a small step to become King of Viridiae.”

Morgause's speech lit a fire in Mordred's eyes. How many times had she delivered this appeal? From the day she first held him to her breast? Dee had nothing to counter her argument, and even if she tried, she feared what Mordred might do to her if he thought she would betray him. They may be in love, but the gauze of emotion was thin.

“Send ten Regarders to meet Percival and the others,” Morgause said. “Arrest them, and if they resist, do whatever is necessary to stop them. They are a threat to you and to Viridiae. If they've taken the Grail from Gawain, they are thieves and traitors.”

Percival a traitor? Morgause's lie infuriated Dee, but she could do nothing. Mordred, however, had more strength. Despite the certitude in his eyes, Dee saw a strain of doubt. A seed of hesitation had sprouted, and Dee ransacked her mind for a way to make it grow.

“My love.” Dee said the words, knowing they were mostly, if

not wholly true. She saw how quickly he responded with a soft look. "If you are ready to take this kind of risk, you must be certain of everything. The Lady Morgause's sources could be wrong —"

"My sources—"

"Unlikely, but possible," Dee continued. "Why not take an hour, or even 30 minutes, to check for yourself? You have the resources of an entire nation. Use them, as you would if you were king today."

Morgause looked at Dee as if she were a Lucian whore.

Mordred touched Dee's cheek with the back of his forefinger. "It's hard to decide on the best course of action when my advisers are so beautiful and wise."

Morgause huffed in disgust.

Mordred said, looking at neither his mother nor Dee, "I will ask a few questions. Until then, come to my office for tea."

Dee had no idea what to do next. She had bought some time, but nothing more. Begging a moment to relieve herself, she opened her com to send a message to Percival. Morgause openly admitted surveilling Dee, but she had to take the chance. However, when she sent the message, an error message appeared: "Unreachable." Her com had worked fine before. Was she blocked, somehow?

Maybe a third party could help. Whom could she trust? No one inside the palace, that was certain. Dee had many friends from school in the art community, but none she could give a message to relay to Percival. Except one: her teacher, Ganieda.

Dee had learned so much from the elder. Dee had arrived at Ganieda's doorstep a child in a young woman's body. She had powers she didn't understand and even suppressed, but Ganieda had shown her how to accept them. With acceptance came control and, Ganieda promised, mastery. Ganieda also taught her how to channel that power into her art so that it would never tempt her to interfere with the affairs of men and women in authority, except when the need was greatest. Dee had toyed with her powers, as she did in the Great Audience Hall when she tried telesthesia on Mordred.

Dee believed in Ganieda's teachings about turning a mistake of a dozen generations in the past into a gift for the present and future. Manipulating humanity's DNA for vanity's sake was wrong, but good could come from it. Dee knew her country and her king was in danger, as well as Percival, but did she have the strength to intervene on their behalf? She hoped she wouldn't be tested.

She sent a message to Ganieda, hoping it wouldn't be intercepted, and that Ganieda would act before Morgause or Mordred could stop her. With surprising quickness, as if she expected Dee's communication, Ganieda responded with a promise to do whatever she could. The response gave her pupil confidence.

Dee emerged into a scene of urgency outside Mordred's suite of offices. Two uniformed Regarders in light armor saluted the prime minister and strode off. Morgause regarded Dee with a half-grin.

Mordred said, "I don't see a reason to wait any longer. I've sent my soldiers to intercept Percival and the others. Gawain might be with them, and he may have the Grail. I can't risk losing it. In the meantime, we're moving forward with our rescue of Viridiae."

"Rescue?" Dee was mystified. "You mean coup."

Morgause glared. "We have no time to waste."

Dee feared her plan was already falling apart. Even a few minutes' warning could save Percival's life, as well as the others. Mordred passed through a set of double-doors that led to a courtyard, where the mounted Regarders were waiting for their commander's final instructions. Dee and Morgause followed him, eyes aflame.

Outdoors, the weather had turned sour. A shower with drops the size of small beads pelted them. A dozen mounted knights with swords, pistols and lances were in danger of a soak. Morgause covered her head with the hood of her cloak. As Mordred and the captain spoke, Dee saw the horses' uneasiness. She had to delay the troop as long as possible, but make it look as though the delay was natural. As she had demonstrated at the Lake of Souls, she had the power to mold the atmosphere within her immediate presence, and Ganieda explained how to channel this energy with more discipline. Dee relaxed and let her imagination direct the innumerable molecules of the air.

A wind came up, blowing directly into the horses' faces, fanning the fire of their nervousness until the riders could not keep them in check. The raindrops grew bigger, falling in a cascade that frightened the animals until the sergeant ordered the riders to dismount or else they might be thrown and hurt. Dee saw all this in her mind's eye. Her physical eyes were closed tight. Her hands were at her side. Her feet were planted as if rooted solidly in the gravel of the courtyard.

"Dindrane Rathkeale!" The shout, at once fearful and angry, emanated from Morgause like a banshee. Dee heard the wail, but she took its energy and funneled it into the squall. Dee would not let Morgause's threats get in her way. She was her adversary, not her son. Mordred was busy keeping clear of the panicking horses while grooms and riders fought to keep them from bolting.

In the midst of this, Dee heard a voice. "*Call for your brother. In your heart, call for Percival.*"

The voice was Ganieda's, but it came from within Dee, not from anywhere in the palace walls.

"*Call for your brother, Dee, before it's too late!*"

As the rain soaked her to the skin, and the wind whipped her coattail like a fall leaf, she reached out to Percival, directing her thoughts toward the sea. She'd felt his new found love of the ocean and its freedom, and she let her heart ride this wave of joy in his direction. Less with words and more with love and concern, she entreated, "*Percival, my dearest brother, beware. Beware the son and his mother!*"

CHAPTER 23: WARNING FROM A DISTANCE

Percival rode hard for Camelot. Lancelot, Galahad, and Bors were on his heels, with Gawain sandwiched between them. Couriers brought their weapons and armor from *Dolphin* to a rendezvous, while Lancelot and Galahad ordered fresh war horses from Joyous Gard and Corbenic Manor. Lancelot complained about missing Beric, left on Koda, but Percival was satisfied with his mount. The retainers polished the knights' armor, sharpened their swords, and reloaded their pistols. Percival sat ramrod straight in his saddle. All four looked the part of patriots on a mission to save their country.

Gawain, ashamed of his capture, was not given arms or a war horse, though his strong mare kept the pace.

Galahad recommended a shorter route to Camelot that followed an ancient winding road. Chunks of pulverized asphalt marked the trail. The group approached a pass through a range of hills and Percival, always 10 or 15 lengths ahead, pulled hard on his reigns at the crest. Before him lay a wide valley. Camelot was only a few dozen kilometers away.

As he leaned forward, a command to his excited horse on his lips, the hairs on the back of his neck stood on end, as if an electrical charge had sprung from the ground. His mount did not react, but Percival shook his head to clear his mind. He was so focused on riding east to the capital that he hardly thought of anything else, except Dee. He urged his horse ahead, but the animal took only two steps before Percival reigned it in again.

Lancelot pulled up, brow sweaty but eyes bright and alert as a hawk's. “What is it? What's wrong?”

“I don't know. I feel like someone's here.” Percival strained to see what bothered him.

Galahad and Bors arrived, asking for news.

“Percival thinks we might have unseen friends. I suggest you reconnoiter.”

Galahad and Bors trotted into the bush on their flanks.

“Have you heard anything from your sister?” Lancelot said. “Anything on the com?”

“No.” Percival thought carefully. “But...”

Galahad and Bors reported no signs of followers or an ambush.

“It's just nervousness.” Lancelot peered down the road. “We're getting close to home.”

The remark sparked a memory. Once, when Percival and Dee were children, Percival had became lost in the forest surrounding their mother's house in the mountains. He panicked when he lost his way in the twilight. Cold and lonely, he started crying. A voice touched him. He sensed, but did not hear his name arriving like a newly hatched spider floating on the thinnest thread of silk. The feeling calmed him, and he saw a path through the woods that led the way home.

Now, on the road to Camelot, Percival said, “It's Dee. She's calling for me.”

“What?” Lancelot said. “There's no one on the road. I can see a kilometer onward.”

“She's a theurgist, remember?”

“The stories are true, then,” Galahad said. “Your sister has enormous power.”

“I don't know about the stories,” Percival said, “but Dee and I know each other like we have the same soul.”

Lancelot focused on the business at hand. “Is she saying anything?”

Percival closed his eyes, partly to close off Lancelot's demanding tone. He listened hard for meaning to his sensations, which permeated his whole body. It tingled, as if hoarfrost was forming on his arms and face. Percival's eyes snapped open. “It's a warning. Somebody's coming for us.”

“Who?” Lancelot said.

“I'm not sure.” The feeling was vague enough for doubts to creep in. “A mother and son?”

“Whoever it is, we might have walked into an ambush, if it weren't for Dee.”

Bors yanked on the cord leading to Gawain's horse, bringing it forward. The captured knight was exhausted, but attentive. “What do you know about this, Gawain? Have you sent a message to Mordred?”

“Exactly how would I do that? You smashed my com under a rock.”

“Don't be an ass—”

“We don't have time for arguments,” Percival said. “I think we have to be ready.”

“Look there, on the other side of the valley.” Galahad pointed. “The dust cloud.”

“That's it. That's what Dee's warning us about.”

“We've been discovered,” Lancelot said. “Can't say I'm surprised.”

“Recommendations?” Galahad said.

“We go down to meet them, whoever they are.” Lancelot dismounted. “We're going to leave Gawain here.”

“But I—”

“Shut up.” Lancelot pulled Gawain off the horse while the others dismounted. “If there's going to be a fight, I don't want to be responsible for you.” Lancelot ordered a rope from one of the retainers who had caught up with the vanguard. In a moment, Gawain was made fast to the trunk of a young tree. “That'll hold you long enough for us to deal with the visitors. We'll come back for you.”

“You're sure we're coming back,” Bors said.

“Of course we are.” Lancelot shrugged. “If we don't, our friends across the valley will find Gawain.”

Gawain's face showed a dislike for both possibilities.

“They're coming out of the trees onto the plain,” Galahad said.

“Time for some fun,” Lancelot said.

Percival spurred his horse as Lancelot climbed into her saddle. Bors drank a deep draft of water while Galahad chewed on an energy biscuit.

The four knights slowed to a trot, watching as the dust cloud resolved into a dozen figures, all in armor. A fight was almost a certainty. Dee's message was clearer: A force from Camelot was on its way to meet the expedition knights.

What Percival did not expect was the tall man with dark hair on the lead horse. Mordred, Prince of Lothia, was in command.

* * *

Percival halted a few meters from Mordred, who rode at the head of his troopers. The four expedition knights positioned themselves about five meters apart, arranged in a shallow crescent, with the ends slightly closer to the Regarders than the middle. Lancelot believed the formation made them appear more menacing and took away some of the Regarders' advantage in numbers.

The Regarders eyed their prospective opponents nervously. Mordred had not thought to array his troop in any kind of fighting order. He did not feel threatened by Percival and the others.

“Mr Prime Minister, it's an honor to see you here.” Percival wasn't quite sure what to say. “How can we help you?”

“You can start by handing over the Grail.”

Percival glanced at Galahad.

“When we see the king, sir,” Galahad said, “I will be sorry to formally report to His Majesty that the Grail was not where we expected to find it. It is still… missing. I'm sure you saw my preliminary report. The expedition was a failure.”

“Lying is beneath you, Sir Galahad. I happen to know that you have the Grail in your possession."

"I assure you, my lord, that I do not. None of us have it."

Mordred's face showed disbelief.

"Cut to the quick, Sir Mordred." Bors spoke as if talking to an insect. "Why do you want it so badly? You could've waited for us to bring it to Camelot, assuming we had it."

Mordred's eyes narrowed. "I wanted to make sure it was safe. You know its importance to the nation."

"You mean to your own criminal ambition, and that of the queen." Bors nearly spat out the words.

Mordred's eyes flashed. "I don't care how you speak about me, but be careful what you say about the king's wife."

"Why? Because she might be your own someday?"

The Regarder troopers glanced at each other, then at Mordred. Percival wanted to take advantage of their unease. Lancelot was chomping at the bit.

"My lord," Galahad said, "I say on my honor that we do not have the Grail, nor do we know where it is with any certainty."

"I don't believe you. My mother said—" Mordred stopped himself, as if fearful of revealing a secret.

"The Lady Morgause probably lied to you, my lord." Lancelot said. "It wouldn't be the first time a woman lied to a man, or a mother to her son."

Mordred's eyes shifted, as if considering the possibility. "Why would she do that?"

"To keep your plan in play, perhaps," Galahad said. "To make you think all was well."

Percival thought this made sense.

"Maybe to do something she hasn't told you about," Bors said. "Or maybe just to save her own skin."

Galahad continued, "Morgause has an interest in the Grail as well, as an object of authority at least. She may even know who took it from Gawain. Oh yes, my lord, he achieved his mission, Gaia bless him, but he lost it when he got to Bell's Ham. We're pretty sure we know who has it now, at least in the abstract."

"Speak, man." Mordred barked.

“The Lucians, you idiot.” The words shot from Lancelot as if she'd fired her pistol.

“That's not possible.”

“Ask your brother.”

“Gawain? Is he here?”

“He's safe.” Lancelot's voice was full of contempt. “He's up the hill with the rest of our party. Harmless as a flea.”

“He's a member of the King's Regarders. I demand that you release him to me.”

Lancelot shook her head. “So that you can disappear him, if not kill him outright?”

“He's my brother. Why in hell would I do that?”

“To cover up your crime,” Percival said. “And the crimes of others.”

“Such as your mother's,” Bors sneered.

“All of you are talking nonsense,” Mordred said. “I want the Grail for the same reason you do. I want to save the country. Dindrane supports me, Percival.”

The statement shocked Percival. “That's a lie. She'd never work against His Majesty. What have you said to her?”

“You don't know your own sister, Percival. She understands the necessity of strong leadership.”

Percival shook his head. “She's a loyal Viridian. Maybe she just said that to you to protect herself.” Percival words hung in the air. Had Mordred compromised her somehow? “Have you threatened her? Have you hurt her?”

“I could never do that.” Mordred's softer tone surprised Percival. “Dindrane is the loveliest creature I have ever met.”

Did Mordred have true feelings for Dee? Was it a trick to distract him?

“Be strong, my friend,” Lancelot said to Percival. “Love shows terrible truths and deceives in the same instant.”

“Dindrane and I are of the same mind,” Mordred said.

“No, my lord.” Lancelot said. “You have no thought for anyone but yourself. You came to take the Grail as a way to legitimize a coup against our elected sovereign. You are a traitor. We're going to arrest you."

Mordred laughed hard. "We outnumber you three-to-one. Exactly how do you plan to take me without dying uselessly?"

Percival did not want to die. Dee had warned him of Mordred's coming. If she believed in Mordred's cause, she would not have done so. She worried he might be injured or killed. He wanted to live as a way to honor her risk for him. "If we die, Sir Mordred, it will be in service to our country."

As if on cue, Lancelot and Bors moved to their left and right, respectively. Percival and Galahad put further distance between each other. In a moment, the four knights appeared to surround Mordred and his knights, who were clustered around him.

"You are the traitors!" Mordred's voice had the telltale edge of fear, but he meant to keep control of his troopers. "Arrest all of them. They are hiding the Grail, and I mean to find it."

The expedition knights walked, then trotted their horses in a circle around the trapped Regarders, whooping and hollering. Placing Mordred at their center, the confused and anxious troopers drew their pistols at their captain's order, but they had difficulty picking a target among the cantering knights long enough for a shot to make sense. Slowly, Percival and the expedition knights tightened their circle. Mordred shouted at his men and women to act, but they were disoriented by the tightening noose of the expedition knights, who compressed them into a tighter bunch. None of the Regarders wanted to fire on a fellow knight, even ones their commander-in-chief had labeled traitors, and they had lost any room to slash with their swords without striking each other or their master.

One of the Regarders' horses lost its footing and leaned hard into another horse. Like a row of dominoes, three animals fell, scattering the rest. Lancelot lunged toward Mordred, but the prime minister moved away. Several shots were fired, by whom in which direction, Percival couldn't tell. He was in a battle with a female knight who was either fighting for her master or fighting to escape. The answer came when Percival pulled his animal to his left and the warrior raced by, heading back to Camelot.

The other Regarders had no stomach for death at the hands of the most powerful knights in the country, and they ran after their compatriot. Mordred screamed at them to return, but only the sergeant and the captain remained beside him.

"Well, now," Lancelot said, offering no indication she had even broken a sweat, "it's four against three. Better odds, I'd say. Is anyone hurt? Fine. Gaia has blessed us this day. Lord Mordred, let's collect your brother and go home."

Mordred saw his chance. The moment of relaxation gave him the precious seconds to wheel his horse around and spur it toward Camelot and freedom. The sergeant and captain followed suit, and at the last moment, the sergeant fired his pistol. The bullet whizzed by Percival's ear. Galahad laid his pistol on his leveled arm, squeezed the trigger, and the sergeant dropped off his horse. Mordred and the captain disappeared into the treeline.

Lancelot galloped after them.

Percival said, "Sir Bors, Sir Galahad, I suggest you bring the expedition home with Gawain. I'm going after Lancelot. If Mordred makes it to Camelot before I can..." He didn't want to think about the consequences.

"I know," Galahad said. "Your sister."

Percival nodded in thanks and took off at a gallop.

CHAPTER 24: AMBUSH AND DEATH

Percival rode on as the sun fell behind the hills on the western edge of the valley, the darkness magnified by the forests on either side of the road. Mordred and his captain could easily turn around and ambush him, though they'd have to contend with Lancelot first. She was the best fighter in Viridiae, but that was no guarantee against a lucky shot or a lame horse.

Mordred had only one place to go: Camelot. Percival knew he and Morgause planned to depose Arturus and take control of Viridiae. How many nobles, knights, or soldiers had they recruited? What of Dindrane? The way Mordred talked, she was part of the conspiracy. But Percival wouldn't accept that possibility. As he spurred his horse on the trail, he teased out the multiple emotions in her message to him at the pass. One was love for Mordred. The other was ambivalence over what she should do, except to warn her brother.

What of Guinevere? To tell the truth, Percival was intimidated by her. She was confident and demanding in a quiet way. She was important to Percival because she was the king's wife. Mordred had not mentioned her in the valley, but he bristled when Bors brought up the possibility that the queen was also a part of the conspiracy. Lancelot winced at Bors' comment. She had been unable to deny that Bors' hypothesis made logical sense, but the proof was thin. Guinevere—at least her family—had plenty of reason to hate the Arturii dynasty, and she was in a position to exact revenge. But Dee told Percival once that Guinevere didn't like Mordred or the Lothians, and Guinevere had expressed admiration, if not passionate love, for the king. Where was she in this mess?

Percival's horse halted, breaking his train of thought. The horse could see better than the rider in the dark, and something was in its way. The night insects were subdued, the sky was moonless, and the thin starlight offered no help. Percival heard, rather than saw, movement ahead, and then behind. Before he could react, hands pulled him off the horse. They dragged him into the brush. More hands restrained him from fighting back. He called out for Lancelot before scaly fingers covered his mouth.

"Quiet, or we'll blow your brains out."

"Lancelot!" Percival yelled through the rough hand. Cold steel was at his temple.

"You're already dead, but we'd like to make your passing humane. Don't tempt us otherwise."

The rescue in the King's Forest as he stumbled back from Kevin's expedition flashed in Percival's mind. This time, however, Lancelot was after Mordred and wouldn't come back for him, even if she'd heard his cries. Percival would have to find a way out of this, and time was wearing thin.

"My friend's hand is tired," the voice said. "He's going to let go. At your first peep, I'm pulling the trigger."

The fingers released, and Percival kept quiet. His initial panic subsided, and he made out three figures, two beside him, and one standing above. He was the one who spoke. The coarse, horny palm of his captor gave their identities away. Three trolls had captured him.

In his haste to follow Lancelot, Percival had made a huge tactical mistake, riding alone in hostile territory. Who would've thought the forest in his own country would harbor enemies? Lancelot might be in the same position.

"I am Sir Percival Rathkeale, a knight of the Round Table."

The statement elicited no obvious reaction, though Percival thought he perceived a grin on the part of the standing buck.

"One fish caught," the troll said. "One that got away."

The troll meant Lancelot. "There are more of us."

"On the other side of the valley, Sir Percival." The troll sat on a low stone. His knobby knees bent comically toward his massive head. "We watched the whole thing."

"They'll come looking for me."

"Why would they? They're preoccupied, and they expect you to meet up with Dame Lancelot."

Bandit trolls weren't uncommon. The story Bors told at his farm was only one example. But these creatures weren't bandits. "Who are you?"

"Just a trio of 'dirty trolls.' That's what you smoothies always call us."

"I've told you my name—"

"And I should pay you the courtesy of telling you mine." The buck sighed. "I am called 'Trell.'"

"And your friends?"

"The less you know, the better. Besides, you'll be dead soon, so the knowledge won't matter much."

"I don't understand. You could've killed me ten minutes ago. Am I a hostage? What are you waiting for?"

"We could be getting ready to torture you, flay you alive or something, before eating your entrails."

Percival gulped. His mother, Eleanor, had told him troll fables as a boy. They were meant to teach him to stay alert in strange surroundings. He never thought they were true stories.

"You smoothies are all the same. You believe every story you're told about things you don't bother to understand."

Percival had to agree. He half-believed the fables, though these three trolls defied the stereotype.

"I haven't killed you because we haven't been ordered to kill you, unless we have to."

"Who ordered—"

The troll with the gun pressed it into Percival's rib. The knight couldn't see more than three meters around. He had no idea where the road was. The night was pitch dark. Running now would be suicidal. Trolls were said to have good night vision.

"I want to ask you a question, Sir Percival."

Percival sensed genuine curiosity. Trell had offered a chance to play for time. "I'll try to answer."

"Why are you people so crazy about the Grail?"

The question struck Percival as odd. Didn't everyone, even trolls, understand that the Grail was key to the kingdom's survival? "Because we need it to repair the Great Machine. We need it to keep the earth from overheating, from going back to the time before the Dissolution, when the world fell apart."

"That's a schoolboy answer. Why do you really want the Grail?"

The troll's retort made no sense to Percival. The creatures weren't supposed to care about normal people's concerns. "You're asking the strangest questions."

Trell shrugged. "I could kill you now and find someone else to enlighten me."

"I'll try to answer your question, but you have to tell me why you took me in the first place. You won't gain much by killing me."

"Ah, that's where you're wrong, my noble friend. Our patron promised us food, shelter, freedom from harassment, and future favors, if we stopped you and Lancelot."

"You failed with her."

"But not with you. 'The Lady Morgause will reward you handsomely if any of the four knights are killed.' That's what the fellow said, the one who hired us."

Percival's jaw dropped, first because of Morgause's name, and second because Trell was so free with it. Both Morgause and her agent knew that the trolls would stay quiet, and even if they were captured and they talked, no one would believe that the mother of Viridiae's prime minister would hire trolls for a contract on a loyal knight's head, much less four of them. After all that had happened since Koda and Bell's Ham, Percival had no trouble accepting Trell's story. It also meant Percival had only a short time to live.

"I don't understand something," Percival said, his hands

sweating. “When did you get this contract?”

“It was pretty hasty, I admit. We were contacted only a few hours ago. Double the usual rate, the agent said.”

Morgause had done this kind of thing before. “I still don't get why she would attack me.”

“I don't really care. All I know is that my friends and I will eat well for the next week or two.”

The truth hit Percival. Trell was insurance, in case Mordred didn't succeed in stopping the expedition knights. Mordred planned to kill Percival and the others once he had the Grail, because they would expose the conspiracy. But Lancelot's tactics and Mordred's arrogance got in the way. Morgause was in the best position to judge whether her son would be successful or not. She hedged her bet.

“I'm getting tired and hungry.” Trell smacked his lips. “The lady's agent paid in advance, in hard coin and supplies. There's a feast for us back at camp. Are you going to answer my question or not, knight?”

Percival wasn't sure what to say. He'd given the expected answer, and Trell wasn't impressed.

“You smoothies are going to a hell of a lot of trouble to find a piece of machinery for a thousand-year-old machine. Someone's stringing you along. We ought to know. We're the product of lies and deception going back at least as long.”

Percival remembered how Viridians dealt with the random mutations that appeared in their children. The young knight wondered if it was worth opening up to the creature, whom he was taught was sub-human, even anti-human, like the invisible anti-matter the sage-physicists talked about. At best, it would buy a few more minutes of life. At worst... he wasn't sure if there was a counter-argument.

“I killed a man, once, an important man,” Percival said. “I guess I'm trying to make up for it.”

Trell laughed. “Is that all? People kill all the time. That doesn't send folks looking for mythological gadgets.”

“He was my father.”

Trell stood. "I guess that's important to a smoothie like yourself. I'm not impressed, though. I don't know who my father is, or my mother. I do know they left me like trash in the King's Forest until my foster found me. I was lucky. Did you know that most troll infants die of exposure before they're found? I'll bet they didn't tell you that in whatever school you went to."

No, they hadn't, Percival admitted.

"My stomach feels empty as a Regarder's heart. Let's go, Sir Percival."

"But—" Before he could object further, the two unnamed trolls lifted him off the ground. They marched on a narrow trail down a ravine. Percival's senses, sharpened by the dilemma of run and be killed, or submit and be killed, took in every leaf of salal and whiff of pine, even in the pitch darkness. He missed the familiar feeling of his javelin and his sword. Both were taken from him when he was dragged from the road. His mind raced for a solution to his predicament, but the trolls on either side of him held him tightly, and Trell kept his pistol trained on Percival's back. Hope was draining away. After a hundred paces or so, they stopped at a small stream that cut through the ravine's bottom.

Trell faced him, while the two others stepped away from Percival. As they loosened their grips, Percival felt a kind of liberation. He had no options. He thought of his father, Sir Adnan deGrosse, and the helmet at the foot of his bed. Maybe Percival was paying his penalty for killing his father, even though he was defending his king. Gaia had a way of keeping things in balance. She always had her way, eventually.

"Sir Percival, it's been a pleasure knowing you. I don't take any joy in doing this. I just want to eat."

Percival closed his eyes, waiting for the bullet. All at once, a warmth enveloped him, like a blanket, or an embrace by Dee. Death was not so hard. It was even pleasant. He relaxed and opened his eyes. He was still in the forest, but a whirlwind had come up, filling the air with dust and debris that slapped his bare skin like a swarm of bees. Strangely, he heard nothing, until a scream pierced his consciousness. The air glowed purple, as if the molecules of oxygen and nitrogen had taken on new properties, and in the dispersed light he saw Trell with the others, bent backwards against themselves, like a spider Dee nearly killed on a log when they were children. In an instant, the trolls' spines snapped like twigs. The whirlwind subsided as fast as it had risen. Percival stood there in disbelief. He was untouched.

Perce! Run!

The voice was as clear as if Dee was next to him. But she wasn't anywhere in sight. Only the twisted bodies of the trolls were Percival's company. He spied the trail out of the ravine, and he ran. He feared the trolls' mangled bodies would repair themselves and they would track him down. After a few hundred meters, gasping for breath, he found the road, illuminated by the moon. Nothing had followed him. He knew the way to Camelot, but it would take a half-day to reach it by foot. Having no other plan, he stumbled toward the city, kicking up dust with his scuffed boots, until he spotted his horse, the one he'd borrowed for the journey from Bell's Ham. Miraculously, his sword and javelin were still aboard.

Exhausted, but determined, he took off at a gallop. He was still an hour or so behind Lancelot. Percival worried she had run into her own ambush, and he kept an eye out for a riderless horse or a body on the side of the road. Percival reached a crossroads, and it turned out to be the road to Bors' farm. A short distance in the opposite direction was the cutoff through the People's Preserve. With luck, the trail might save precious time.

Once he got to the city, where would he find Mordred, and maybe Lancelot? Percival cleared his mind as best he could, and he thought of Dee. Silently, he asked a question, and hoped for an answer before Lancelot was dead.

CHAPTER 25: FIGHT IN THE PALACE

Lancelot's agony increased with each bounce in her saddle. She did the best she could to immobilize her right arm after the surprise attack by the trolls as she chased Mordred on the road back to Camelot. As they tried to pull her off her horse, one twisted her arm behind her, and she almost heard the ligament in her elbow tear. Another troll slashed her with a knife. She could only rest her arm on the leather behind the pommel as it swelled. She had nothing to wrap it with and no time to wrap it. Blood dripped down the horse's flank.

The injury meant she could not even lift Arondight if she were attacked again. To add to her troubles, she'd lost track of Mordred, but she believed he'd head to the palace compound, where he'd find allies and his powerful lady mother. He might find Guinevere as well. The thought pained Lancelot, remembering Bors' accusations and speculation.

The road in the small hours was dead quiet, with nothing to suggest that the prime minister of Viridiae was planning anything as evil as overthrowing the king. Lancelot's com battery was exhausted, which always left her feeling isolated, a sensation worse than the pain in her arm. She needed help, but she couldn't trust anyone. The moon cast deep shadows, and the only sound was the horse's shoes on the pavement.

Lancelot arrived at the palace gate, but to her astonishment, no guard stood at attention, waiting for visitors. Even in the small hours, people came in and out of the building; the king had a penchant for late-night meetings. The absence of any soul on the street, at the gate, or on the ceremonial square inside the gate alarmed Lancelot. She felt an impending sense of disaster.

A solitary lamp illuminated the square.

Lancelot had no idea where Mordred might be in the sprawling complex of government buildings surrounding the square. One-handed, she tied her horse to a hitching post next to a government car, as inert as the world around her. Not even night insects broke the silence. Had everyone simply run away?

Blinking through her lightheadedness, Lancelot didn't believe it. She imagined Mordred and Morgause ordering everyone indoors, ostensibly for their safety, but truly for their own. But why hadn't even a token resistance formed? Why wouldn't they leave soldiers or allies at the gate? Had something changed drastically since Lancelot left for Koda? She couldn't imagine what it might be.

Arondight at her side—she couldn't bear the thought of leaving it behind—Lancelot was relieved when her punched-in code still allowed her inside the palace. The door unlocked with an audible *snap*. The electricity was still on, but lights outside and inside the stone and wood building were few and far between. Lancelot wished the moon could somehow illuminate the dingy darkness of hallways and empty offices, though slivers of ghostly light made their way inside, as if guiding Lancelot toward an unseen treasure.

A sound caught her ear, a *tap* or a *clap*, reminding her of a footfall. Her own booted footsteps echoed down a long corridor leading to the Great Audience Hall. Another echo drew her forward, and she stepped under an expansive, arched entrance. Moonlight poured into the basilica's clerestory. Above the columns marching down its flanks, masked by semi-darkness, the figures of frescoes appeared indifferent and aloof. One part of the western wall was covered in scaffolding draped in black cloth. Lancelot guessed this was Dee's work space. A flicker of curiosity formed, and Lancelot stepped toward the scaffold.

Again, she heard a *tap*. The sound was hard and glassy this time. Lancelot peered into the darkness toward the monarch's ceremonial throne, and she saw a man sitting on the steps, holding his sword point down on the marble, occasionally bringing it up a few centimeters and pushing it down, as if trying to stab the earth. She was too far away to identify the figure. It could've been an ordinary soldier, a knight, or even Arturus.

With the lightest step possible, Lancelot moved toward the man, and when he lifted his head, she saw it was Mordred.

"So, I'm not alone, after all," the prime minister said.

"Can that be true?"

"It's as if they've all been kidnapped, or they're hiding somewhere, waiting for the second end of the world."

Lancelot swallowed. A few of the sage-scientists said if the Grail was not found, or Merlin and his researchers couldn't find a way to get the Great Machine working again, the Earth would roast like a marshmallow over a flame. "I don't think the world is ending."

"Did you see anyone on your way in?" Mordred said.

"Not a soul. Not in the city. Not in the compound."

"They're not dead. We'd smell them." Mordred lifted his sword and dropped the point on the floor. The sound was a mix of *clang* and *thud*. The steel made a discernible gouge in the stone.

"I don't know what happened, Lord Mordred, but I know my duty. I'm arresting you for attempted treason." Lancelot reached out her hand. "Give me your sword, and I won't bind your hands."

Mordred spied Lancelot's lame arm and smirked. "You really are as stupid as they say."

"What?"

"All vim and bluster and blind as a bat with its beady eyes gouged out. You see nothing of what's going on around you. You've cornered hypocrisy, like a child who's taken all the candy out of the jar for herself."

Lancelot believed Mordred had lost his mind.

"You've all got the intelligence of a midge. You've all failed. You've failed me."

Mordred stood, reaching with both arms to the ceiling a dozen meters overhead, his sword in his right hand, the fingers of his left outstretched. "I WANT TO BE KING!"

The shouted words, full of pain and longing, caromed off the basilica's walls for a full five seconds, fading with each bounce, like a dream upon waking.

"I wanted the Grail. It was my charm, my credential, my key to this city and to the nation. You and your worthless son, Galahad, were supposed to bring it back. You failed me."

The charge put Lancelot on the defense. Mordred was still the prime minister, the second most powerful man in Viridiae. "We failed Arturus. We nearly succeeded, but Gawain got there first."

"Gawain, my feckless, sniveling brother, forever trying to get on the good side of his mother, my mother, whose sole aim in life is to interfere in the business of others. He lost the Grail to the Lucians. He failed. She succeeded in interfering, but ultimately she failed, or I'd be sitting there." Mordred pointed at the empty ceremonial chair.

Lancelot could only listen while Mordred raved.

"Even Arturus failed me." The Prince of Lothia laughed. "He wasn't even here for me to depose."

"Mordred, if you come with me in peace, I'm sure Arturus—"

"Will what? Show mercy? You're such a damned fool, Lancelot." Mordred stared at the throne, a simple thing with four legs that rose above the seat to support armrests and an open back decorated with the Viridian national crest. With its stripped-down design, the artisan had used its symbolism to make it the most precious object in the room.

"I can still win," Mordred continued, "even if it's for a moment." The knight climbed the short flight of stairs to the broad platform on which stood the throne, illuminated by moonlight.

"I can't let you do that, Mordred." Even though Mordred's contemplated act might be meaningless with no witnesses save his enemy, Lancelot felt that letting Mordred take the seat would mean she had failed to protect the king, her friend.

Lancelot's arm throbbed, and blood leaked onto her hand.

Mordred ignored Lancelot's warning. He stood before the

throne, as if all his hopes and dreams were bound into his next act. He leaned forward, but Arondight's blade blocked his way.

Lancelot held the sword with her left hand. "Come with me, Lord Mordred. Don't make this mistake."

Mordred glared at Lancelot's steel as if it were diseased. With a roar, he knocked it aside with his own blade and bolted for the chair. His fingers nearly grasped the arm of the chair, before Lancelot pushed him aside. Her arm screamed in pain. Both knights lost their balance and tumbled down the three steps. Scrambling to their feet, they faced off.

"Lord Mordred, I'm arresting you in the name of the Great Charter and the Viridian people." Lancelot swallowed. She had never fought another knight one-handed, or with her left arm. She'd trained to do it, but she was never good at it. "I don't want to hurt you."

Mordred bared his teeth and swung his sword hard. Lancelot moved back, out of the way, and she ran to one of the side aisles, where darkness concealed her.

"Come out and fight me, Lancelot!"

Hiding behind a column, Lancelot considered her next move.

"I always knew you were a coward at heart, Lancelot. Guinevere told me so, but we all know about it. Sneaking around like teenagers behind the king's back. That's the way of the craven."

As she kept her target in sight, Lancelot understood Mordred's game. He hoped to get under her skin and shame her into doing something rash. "Who's the coward, Mordred? Using your mother as a means to take the throne by stealth." Lancelot swallowed hard before saying her next words. "Arturus is sick, just like the country. If you were patient, maybe you could be king the honorable way."

Mordred stepped like a cat on the hunt, peering into each corner, trying to pinpoint the direction of Lancelot's voice. Unlike the mouse, for whom stillness is the best defense, the dame knight also moved to keep Mordred from zeroing in on her.

"Arturus is ill, but he lingers," Mordred said. "He may live a dozen years more, and I'll be an old man. I won't wait. In ancient times, I would've been his heir, if he only acknowledged me. Instead, he keeps me under his thumb."

"You're the prime minister of the most powerful country on the continent, save for Lucana." Lancelot was thoughtful enough to know not to lie to Mordred. "How is that a judgment against you?"

"Ever heard of keeping your enemies close, Lancelot?"

Lancelot found her next move. The combatants drew near to Dee's work space. Struggling to stay hidden while removing her boots and socks, she pushed aside the drape, feeling the cold marble floor on the soles of her feet. A human's bare foot had the same whorls and ridges that gave the hand its grip, and Lancelot glided through the hidden space behind the curtains to a place where Mordred stood. She had one problem: To surprise Mordred, she had to let him out of her sight for a few seconds.

It was a mistake that almost killed her.

Seeing the sleeve of his jacket, she believed she was behind him. She lunged through the gap in the drapes, but the open jacket hung on a bench, as if the owner had forgotten it. She heard the *whirr* of Mordred's blade before she saw it, and if she hadn't moved a millimeter to the left, Mordred would've opened her skull like a melon. With the good purchase of her feet on the smooth floor, she swung around with Arondight, but Mordred met the blow, and Lancelot was sure the *clang* was heard in the Lucian capital.

From then on, the fight was close and desperate. Mordred wanted to end it, there and then, and so did Lancelot, but she was on the defensive, parrying blow after blow. Her right arm was useless, and her left arm quickly tired. Each parry and counter-thrust made cuts in the hard steel until edges resembled serrated blades rather than smooth. Both fighters breathed hard with each spin and duck from thrown chairs or torn hangings. The fight revolved around the throne as if it were the sun and the two fighters were orbiting planets bent on crashing into one another.

The one great thing about shoes is that they protect the feet.

Lancelot later recalled thinking that shoemaking would've been a good trade for her, because she liked working with leather in her non-existent spare time. She thought this as the small toe on her left foot caught in the divit in the marble made by Mordred's sword as he lamented his failures. The twist caused pain as a toe bone snapped, which broke her concentration, and she winced. As she fell, she let go of Arondight, which skittered out of reach. Mordred saw this and pressed the advantage. With Lancelot's guard down, Mordred drew back his sword and readied himself for the killing thrust toward Lancelot's heart.

"Mordred! No!"

Mordred's concentration broke, and he looked toward the back of the hall, his sword held high.

Percival stood at the arched entrance, at the opposite end of the long hall, javelin in his hand. Lancelot thought she should move, but when she instinctively moved her right arm, the agony made her cry out.

"Put down your sword, Mordred," Percival said. "Don't make things worse."

Mordred grinned. "Two enemies killed in one night. Perhaps I can salvage something from this loss."

Lancelot's and Mordred's eyes met, and she had seen that look only once or twice before. It was the madness of blood lust, when the thing that separates a human from an animal flees.

Mordred lifted his sword. Lancelot swore she heard a rushing sound, like a flock of pigeons lifting off the palace courtyard, or a bumblebee zooming past her ear. Out of the corner of her eye, she saw the javelin, flying straight for her eye, like they say you can see the pistol ball coming at you before it kills you. The javelin was moving far more slowly, but too fast for Mordred to react. It entered his shoulder at the collarbone, and Lancelot heard the crack.

Mordred gasped and fell, the embedded spear ripping at his flesh. Percival stood over Mordred. "Yield or I'll kill you."

Mordred's lust faded. Blood drained from his face, but Lancelot knew that face well from meetings in the lists: The battle may be lost, but I'm not finished. The prime minister lay on his side within arm's reach of the throne. He nodded once.

"Stop this fight! I order you to stop immediately."

Lancelot focused on the archway. Below it stood Arturus.

In the pale light of the moon, Arturus rushed to the trio of knights.

"You stupid, foolish man," Arturus said to Mordred. "All your ambition and sharp mind gone to waste."

Mordred leaned back, his head on the lower step of the central platform. He closed his eyes.

"No, Mordred, you can't die, not yet," Arturus said. "I need every man, every general with any experience and brains to win."

Percival turned to Arturus. "My lord, Mordred is a traitor. He wanted to take your throne."

"At some other time, I'd have him tried for treason," Arturus said. "Not this time, at least not now."

"I'm sorry, Majesty. I don't understand."

"You will, soon enough. In the meantime, we have more important things to worry about." Arturus knelt on one knee beside the prostrate Mordred and the worried Lancelot.

"You see, dear Percival, the Lucians have invaded."

CHAPTER 26: THREAT FROM THE EAST

All Viridians with com access received a message broadcast by the government. Civilians were told to remain indoors and to douse all lights. The War Ministry ordered men-at-arms on duty and on leave to muster outside the eastern suburb of Nespelem. The citadel told knights to join them in full armor and weapons.

Thousands of men-at-arms and knights milled in a five-hectare pasture on the edge of Nespelem, turning the pastoral quiet of a town that supplied milk and cheese to the capital into a military outpost. But the martial atmosphere failed to mask the chaos. Units, partial units, and individual soldiers meandered with no leadership. The palace guards gathered in a corner with nothing but their ceremonial pikes. Peasants and burghers drifted in from the countryside, ready to defend their country. More were coming, but it would take days for some to arrive. Among the volunteers were men and women who hadn't wielded a sword, loosed an arrow, or fired a pistol in decades.

A miasma of desperation hung over the king's pavilion as Percival and the other expedition knights, save for Lancelot, presented themselves to an adjutant. Percival recognized most of the general staff, which surrounded a table with a map. Political advisers pored over documents. Intelligence officers studied photographs taken by drones.

"I don't see Mordred," Percival said.

"He's probably under guard, maybe in the citadel." Bors looked over a tablet. "The muster list says I'm here, but I don't have any orders."

"Where is Lancelot?" Galahad said.

A shout came from the back of the pavilion. Every soldier and knight in the tent came to attention, even the gray-haired generals. The civilians stopped their conversations. The rustle of papers and tap of keys fell silent.

An aide held open a flap of canvas as King Arturus stepped through. He wore a tailored suit and a sash that indicated his role as war chief. Despite his thinning frame and loose skin, Arturus had a determination to his mouth and a fire in his eyes that gave soldiers confidence. Arturus was a warrior at heart, and if he was worried about losing his country, he didn't show it.

"Ladies and gentlemen, I apologize for the earlier disorder, but we are now getting a clearer picture of what's happened in the last 18 hours."

Percival looked around for Lancelot, but she had not appeared. Neither had Guinevere. Was she also under arrest?

"As you know," Arturus continued, "the Lucian Empire loves to poke its nose into our business."

A few people in the crowd chuckled.

"Good," Galahad said, under his breath. "Show courage and be calm."

"This time, however, the Lucians have decided to poke more than their nose into our country. They've pushed through the door and into the mud room, you might say."

Few people smiled this time.

"The knights and men-at-arms in our northwestern command fought bravely, but they were overwhelmed by the Sixth and Seventh Legions under a General Dardarius. This is not a raid, as we've seen in the past. It's a full-scale invasion, supported by drones and naval units in the Colum River."

Percival swallowed. He was not old enough to remember the last major war with Lucana.

"The Lucians are marching in force through the Satus Pass, which is remote and lightly defended. We suspect another legion, possibly the Eleventh, is coming down the river to land here." He pointed to spot on the map due south of Camelot.

"My lord! Why invade now?"

"Ah, Sir Galahad. I'm so pleased to see you back safely from the expedition. I apologize that I will not be able to hear your report for a while." Arturus clasped his hands at his belt. "We don't know the answer to your question, to be perfectly honest. The Lucian empress has made her expansionist ambitions clear. Our ancestor Arturus stopped the empress' grandfather at our borders, which have held firm for almost a century. Empress Vetrania is apparently unsatisfied with the status quo."

The empress had a reputation for murder and corruption.

"We certainly weren't prepared for an invasion," Bors said. "Isn't that true, Majesty?"

A murmur rose in the crowd. Percival sensed hostility. Bors was being rude.

"Your criticism is welcome and encouraged, Sir Bors. I'm inclined to agree with you and this situation warrants a full investigation, once we've dealt with the emergency."

Percival was growing impatient. His home had been invaded by the most powerful nation in the hemisphere, and he wanted to fight back. "What do we do now, Majesty?"

"We are gathering as many forces as we can here in Nespelem to meet Dardarius at a point on a tributary of the Colum River. He must cross there if he plans to attack Camelot."

What of Merlin, Percival wondered.

As if answering, Arturus said, "Our science adviser Merlin, who also counsels us on new weapons, will remain at the Great Machine for now, until he is called upon."

"Two legions. Ten thousand men and women" Galahad rubbed his chin. "I don't think we have more than five thousand nearby, maybe six, if we gather a few more in the next day or two. When do we march?"

"Tomorrow at dawn, Galahad."

Nearly everyone protested that they could never be ready in time. The generals asked for more time, more weapons, and more supplies. Soldiers and officers listening outside the tent complained in whispers. Percival did not complain. He was ready to move at a moment's notice.

"We can't wait. We fight with what we have." Arturus' voice barely rose in volume, but the crowd quieted. "If we do nothing, the Lucians will sack Camelot in three days. We all know what the Lucians are capable of. Mercy is not in their order of battle. We stop them here—" he pointed to the river ford "—or we lose Viridiae. Is that clear?"

After a moment of quiet, the crowd reconciled with reality.

"But first, we have another matter of state business." Arturus lowered his eyes slightly. Sadness almost overcame him. "One of our closest advisers is accused of treason."

Arturus glanced at the place in the tent wall where he had entered. The flap opened and Mordred stepped through. Defiant and proud, his hands were bound. He was pale, unsteady on his feet, and his hair was matted with dried sweat. He wore a t-shirt over his powerful torso, but a red stain on his shoulder the size of an officer's brass button marred the white fabric. A man followed Mordred with a wheelchair, and Percival guessed that Mordred would not allow Arturus to humiliate him by arriving like an invalid.

"By now," Arturus started, "you've heard the basics of Mordred's conspiracy."

As the expedition knights made their way to Nespelem, the government had released a statement, and the media in Camelot expanded on it. Arturus was tipped off about an impending coup attempt, and Regarders loyal to Viridiae and the Round Table were waiting for Mordred to move on the throne when the news came of the Lucian invasion. By sheer luck, Mordred had left the capital to meet the returning Grail expedition, though it was unclear why. When Mordred returned, the palace grounds were empty. Arturus had issued a curfew and ordered all active duty military to Nespelem, including the palace guard.

Lady Morgause and the prime minister were placed under arrest pending an investigation. Lancelot and Percival had wounded Mordred in a fight to stop the coup. In Arturus' presence, Mordred had admitted his treason, the palace statement said.

The crowd stared at Mordred with the contempt reserved for traitors. On the same day the nation faced its greatest security crisis in a century, he had tried to make himself king. In the murmuring of the assembly, Percival heard people wonder if Mordred was conspiring with the Lucians. What had Vetrania offered him, beyond the crown of Viridiae?

For his part, Mordred stared forward, his head high. He believed he was doing the right thing for his country. That was Percival's impression at least. The young knight, though he felt disgust at Mordred's treachery, couldn't help a touch of admiration for a man willing to risk so much for his beliefs.

Arturus took three steps toward Mordred. The king's face was stony, but Percival perceived sadness, and then pity.

"Lord Mordred, in Viridiae, the accused are innocent until proven guilty, but I have certain traditional powers due a monarch. I have signed the documents stripping you of your office and appropriating your lands until the courts have disposed of your case."

Mordred was still as a statue.

"I can never trust you in my house again." Arturus took a deep breath. "But I told you in the Great Audience Hall that Viridiae needs every soldier."

Arturus reached beneath his sash and removed a short-bladed dirk. Percival blinked, alarmed at what Arturus might do in front of the entire country. The king took another step toward Mordred, who could easily have attacked the king, despite his shackles. The whole room tensed. Slowly, deliberately, Arturus sliced through the hemp bindings around Mordred's hands. The former prime minister of Viridiae's eyes glistened with tears, but Percival could not tell if they were tears of joy, or of anger.

"Mordred, I'm releasing you in hopes that you are the man you say you are, absolutely loyal to Viridiae, and a true enemy to the Lucian Empire. You are one of my best field generals, and you would do no one any good locked in a cell."

The throng was silent as the grave. What would Mordred do?

He could attack Arturus' person right there, perhaps even kill him. He could run for his freedom, perhaps to Dardarius and the Lucian cohorts. He could stand still and do nothing. For a moment, that's what Percival thought might happen, but after a long pause, Mordred stepped over to an empty space in the front of the crowd. People made room for him, as if he were toxic, but no one said anything or did anything. Arturus had made his wishes known.

"Thank you, Lord Mordred," Arturus said. "We are more confident of victory with your presence."

Percival realized that Mordred would also bide his time until he could try again for the throne.

"Now we must appoint a new prime minister," Arturus said. "Sir Galahad, would you step forward?"

Arturus announced that he had appointed Galahad his new chief administrator. Standing with his hand on the pommel of Secace, Galahad did not look surprised, as if he had known Arturus planned this. Galahad had received a secret communication from the palace on his way to Nespelem.

Sir Bors was given command of a unit of Regarders.

Percival was assigned to Arturus' personal guard at Lancelot's recommendation.

Lancelot and Guinevere were still not among the crowd. Mounting his horse, Percival decided to search for the two women. It took nearly an hour. He finally found one of Guinevere's gentlemen in waiting who directed Percival to a dirt road on the far end of the trampled pasture. At the fence, he found Lancelot, leaning against a post and staring down the empty road. Her arm was wrapped in a bandage, and her foot was in a temporary cast.

"Lancelot," Percival said. "what happened to your foot?"

"I broke my dignity." In truth, she had broken her toe in the fight with Mordred. "You didn't help."

Percival's jaw dropped. He had saved Lancelot's life. Then he remembered the incident with the questing beast in the King's Forest. Lancelot had found him, but Percival had stopped the beast with Arondight. Lancelot was angry at the time.

In the pasture at Nespelem, Lancelot shook her head. “My remark was unfair, Percival. I'm grateful to you, beyond words. How did you find me, by the way?”

Percival told a short version of his skirmish with the trolls, leaving out Dee's intervention. “When I got to the palace grounds, I saw your horse outside the audience hall. I followed the blood trail inside. A child could've found you.”

“Good thing I left a trail. I might be dead and Mordred king if you hadn't sniffed me out.”

Percival nodded, mostly to change the subject. “Was the queen with you today?”

“The king has sent her home to Carmelide.”

Percival was not surprised. “Is she exiled?”

Lancelot grinned at Percival, who saw that the elder knight had been crying. “Call it a trial separation, if you like, young man. They need to be apart. She's… not trusted here.”

“The king must be heartbroken.”

“I'm going to tell you a state secret, Percival. It seems everyone has their own spy network in this city. Arturus' personal agents found correspondence between Mordred and Guinevere that implicated her in Mordred's plans. Fortunately for the queen, she tipped Arturus off before he got the report. An hour later, who knows what might've happened.”

Percival was stunned. Like Mordred, Guinevere was also a traitor, if what Lancelot said was true. On the other hand, Guinevere had informed on Mordred. She was as loyal as any subject. Nothing about palace life seemed normal or good to Percival. How could anyone want power if you always had to look over your shoulder? If he moved this way or that, thorns would slice him into ribbons. Lancelot was hooked as well, but by a different thorn.

“You love her, don't you, Lancelot?”

The dame knight didn't hesitate. “She's betrayed my king, but I love her like my own breath. She's taken it away, and I doubt I'll ever get it back.”

"What are you going to do now?"

Lancelot drew herself up, and brushed off dust from the fence post. "What do you expect, Sir Percival? I'm off to kill a few Lucians."

Lancelot limped toward the king's pavilion, Percival at her side. Even wounded, she was still Viridiae's greatest fighter. Percival was lucky to have her as a friend.

EPILOG

Percival remembered his vow to King Arturus: Find the Grail and heal the nation. Two expeditions later, Percival reflected on his failure to fulfill his promise. Did it matter? What if Gawain had managed to deliver the Grail to Mordred? Did Percival care if Mordred used the device's recovery as an excuse to claim the throne, as long as the Great Machine was repaired? Mordred and Arturus wanted the same thing, which was to restore the health of Viridiae and the earth. A verdant planet was a gift that transcended people and countries. Percival remembered the troubling words of an Old Civilization sage, "The end justifies the means."

In his heart of hearts, Percival didn't believe in what those words represented. In Viridiae, people had agreed to live together according to certain rules, and Mordred disobeyed those rules. What was the point of a healthy land if people couldn't trust each other? Would Gaia smile on that? The Lord Prince of Lothia might have good reasons for his actions, but that didn't give him any special rights or privileges. Percival still believed he could find the Grail and keep his promise to Arturus, but he wanted to do it in a way that followed the law. Maybe that was boring, naive, or stupid, but playing by the rules was the only way he wanted to win. It was a matter of self-respect.

First, however, Viridiae had to defeat the Lucian invaders. They were a more immediate threat to Viridiae's survival. The Lucians had lain a hellish trap, and the Viridians had no choice but to walk into it. Percival might die in battle and never fulfill his vow. Why did the Lucians want the Grail so badly? They risked a secret mission deep into Viridian territory to steal it.

There were other Great Machines, all performing a similar function. Was the one in Lucana failing as well? Percival pushed the frightening thought from his mind. What if two Grails were needed, but only one existed? Before he could find the Grail that belonged in the mountains west of Perditon, he and Arturus' army had to stop the Lucian legions. And before they met at the ford in the river south of Camelot, he needed to see his sister, Dee.

Percival found her in the Great Audience Hall poring over a color palette on her tablet. Their embrace was long and both fought back tears, though for different reasons. Arturus knew the consequences of failure, and he told everyone at Nespelem that they were under no obligation to sacrifice their lives for a desperate cause. Though many believed they were in their last days, virtually no one left the camp. However, Percival spied Gawain slinking away in the darkness.

Percival said, “Why are you crying, Dee?”

“Because I'm happy to see you, you idiot.” Dee cupped her brother's cheek in her hand. “I was worried I might not see you again alive. Mordred and Morgause were ready to do anything to get what they wanted.”

Percival took Dee's hand. “When we were on the road, I thought I heard you call out a warning. Not in words, so much. Just a feeling.”

“It might've been me. Once I saw that you were in danger, all I could think about was the time we faced our father at the Lake of Souls. At first, I did everything I could think of to delay Mordred, but I only infuriated him. When he tore one of his Regarders off his saddle, and took off toward you, I cried to Heaven.”

“Some people think you're a sorceress.”

“Ganieda offered her help. She was the one who sensed the hidden trolls. She protected Lancelot, but she was exhausted by the time you were captured. She looks older every day. That left me to help you. I concentrated so hard I thought I was floating in midair. I saw you in my mind. I just held you there, like a doll. It was only for a moment.”

"It was long enough."

"Then I killed the trolls. It had to be done." Dee's tears flowed freely. "It wasn't easy."

"I understand."

"I don't think you do. The trolls and I are like cousins, except I have a gift in each of my body's cells that can serve people, while they are cursed. I'm going to use that gift. I'm going to be a theurgist."

"I feel blessed that you're my sister. I don't like Camelot and its backstabbing politics. I just want to find the Grail and defend my country."

"And now you're going off to war," Dee said. "I hope I didn't waste my time. I can't warn you or protect you every time a sword or a bullet is headed your way."

"Will you warn Mordred?"

Dee looked at Percival, puzzled.

"He's been paroled by Arturus. The king wants him to fight, though I don't understand how Arturus can trust him."

"I think he can. Even if Mordred wants to be king, he doesn't want to be a Lucian client. He loves this country, I know it."

"People say you're his lover."

"So what if I am? I can make whatever choice in men or women I want. I choose him, for now."

"Your friends are going to get you into trouble one of these days."

"Maybe, but first I want to finish this job." Dee touched a key on her tablet, and the projectors fired light onto the specially prepared surface of the wall.

Dee described the results so far as studies and cartoons, with only hints of the colors and subtle animations that made light tapestries mesmerizing, but Percival was astounded. Even in its skeletal state, he was witnessing the birth of a masterpiece, and not just because it was his sister's creation. For a moment, he forgot to breathe.

"It's amazing, Dee. I knew you were good, but this..."

The painting was about three times longer than tall, reminding Percival of the screens showing tournaments in the taverns on nearly every corner of Camelot's weave of streets. A parade of walking and riding figures, male and female, processed toward a seated figure on a platform. Percival took the figure to be a leader, perhaps a king. The scene was joyous and sensual. It was a celebration of some kind, or a ritual gift-giving, because in front of the king knelt a man holding a tray decorated with twisting questing beasts and prancing knights. A blank place was waiting to be filled with the gift.

"It's a scene from an old story, right? But I can't tell which one."

"It is and it isn't. I took some inspiration from ancient stories, but I want to keep the details to myself for now."

"You can tell me. I'm your brother."

"To be honest, I'm not exactly sure how the story is going to turn out. That's why none of the figures have their faces."

It was true. They only had hints of eyes, noses and mouths, but Percival thought he recognized a few of the parading courtiers, maybe even himself.

"I'm almost hesitant to ask, but this isn't just an imaginary scene. This is from the future."

"Accurate non-mathematical predictions of the future are impossible, Perce. We've talked about it before. My painting is not a foretelling, but it's the most likely outcome, in my opinion."

"Of what? The quest for the Grail?"

"Yes, but remember it's an impression. I could be wrong. The possibility of an invasion by the Lucians never crossed my mind. There's lots of variables that could derail my idea. I might even have to start over."

"It's what you think should happen, as much as will happen."

"All I can say is that these are real people, alive today, and they are celebrating a great accomplishment. I'm certain of it."

Percival didn't understand the emotional and spiritual realm of artists and theurgists. "Are you in this picture? A lot of artists like to do that."

"I don't know yet, Perce. Sometimes, I think I'm one of the figures. Sometimes I think I'm far away. The threads of the future, including my future, haven't yet been woven."

The painting's unfinished state was a perfect metaphor for the state of things. Dee was on her way to making one of the great works of Viridian art. Percival wanted desperately to fulfill his vow to find the Grail, but he had no idea when he could pursue it again, assuming he survived the war. Viridiae, which he once believed was as solid and stable as his mother on her land near the King's Forest, had an uncertain future. Of one thing, he was sure. He wanted to see the finished painting, and understand his place in Viridiae's future.

SPECIAL PREVIEW: PRISONER OF WAR

***Chapter 1 of* War for the Green Land, *Book 2 of* The Future History of the Grail**

Sir Percival Rathkeale scraped morsels of oat gruel from the bottom of a bowl and fed them to a wounded man. Like miniature vultures, flies circled the putrefying wound on the man's leg. The insects had found plenty of illness and death to feed upon in the weeks since Percival watched thousands of his fellow Viridians die at the River Colum.

The flap of the tent flew open, and a centurion in his crested helmet and red ochre fatigues barged in. "I'm looking for someone named Rathkeale."

Percival stood up, his heavily muscled shoulders filling his blood-stained shirt. "That's Sir Percival to you."

Fire in his eyes, the centurion held himself back. The name tape said "Cantwell." He held the rank of tribune. That meant he was on the general staff. "You're wanted."

"By whom and why?"

Tribune Cantwell spoke in a thick accent. "None of your fucking business. I'm to fetch you, that's all."

"Are you sending me home?" Percival doubted Cantwell understood sarcasm, even if it contained a hint of desperation. Some Viridian families had ransomed relatives. His mother might try to ransom him.

Cantwell grinned. "You've got the least chance of getting out of here alive, Rathkeale."

"I'd like to finish feeding these warriors." Percival gestured to the dozens of injured, some moaning, some motionless.

Cantwell slapped away the bowl in Percival's hand. "You're done. Are you coming or do you want to join them?"

Breaking Cantwell's gaze, Percival told the Viridian soldier at his feet, "I'll come back and change your dressing, if this nice man lets me."

Cantwell grabbed Percival by the back of the neck and pushed him through the tent opening. Percival stumbled into the mud, but he checked his urge to fight back. For all he knew, the Lucian was taking him to the execution grounds.

Cantwell pointed Percival to the makeshift gate at the end of a lane between two areas of lean-tos, salvaged field tents, and milling prisoners in rags. Camp smoke drifted into the cloudy sky. Surveillance cameras on tall poles followed their movements. The captives watched Percival with a mixture of pity and fear. He recognized a few. They had left the hospital, thanks in part to Percival's ministrations, and they nodded in respect. Percival found it hard to return their gratitude, for he felt more like a coward than a nurse. After all, hadn't he run from the battle like a frightened dog?

Cantwell waved at the guards, who opened the gate, letting the prisoner and his escort through. They walked toward the gallows, where crows tore at the faces of three Viridian bodies. An electric cart waited to take the corpses to the incineration pit. Percival's mouth went dry. Was he next? He could not think of any transgression. No Lucian officer or guard had warned him of anything.

His racing mind flashed to the battle. Screams of dying men, women, and horses filled his ears. On the field, he met blow for blow from each opponent, once slicing open a man's belly, spilling intestines like they were macabre sausages. Percival killed three Lucians, including an officer. Were the Lucians about to take their revenge?

He blinked in relief as Cantwell led him past the gallows to another tent. Four legionnaires guarded the pavilion, and Percival noticed the sigil of Dardarius, the Lucian's commanding general, on their breast armor. The legionnaires belonged to Dardarius' personal guard.

"You there, in the tent," Cantwell bellowed. "I found your lackey." The Lucian pushed Percival forward. He raised the flap.

Inside, the windowless walls danced with shadows. A single lamp illuminated the face of a man. Arturus, dressed in the sack cloth tunic worn by ordinary Lucian slaves, stood tall, but with a slight tremble. The king's eyes glistened in the weak light.

Disbelieving his own eyes, Percival fell to one knee. "Majesty."

Arturus stepped forward and placed his hands on Percival's upper arms, urging the knight to rise. The monarch of Viridiae studied Percival as if he hadn't seen him for a thousand years. He embraced Percival as he might a lost brother. "Sir Percival, I cannot tell you what a blessing from Gaia it is to see you again."

"Likewise, Your Majesty, but—" Percival could not find the words to express his surprise and delight. With Arturus came hope. "We heard nothing. The Lucians would never answer our questions. There were rumors, but ..." He couldn't finish the sentence.

"I wouldn't blame you if you thought I was dead." Arturus collected himself. "For a while, I thought I was dead, despite Dardarius' promises."

"Promises?"

Arturus gestured to a pair of chairs next to a table with bread, cheese, and wine. "I'm a hostage, surety for my country's good behavior and a trade for Merlin."

Merlin? Why Merlin? How could he be more important than the king? "Have they hurt you, sire?" Percival's hands warmed with anger to think that Merlin was more important than the king. "The last time I saw you, you were in chains in front of Dardarius."

"No. I'm more fortunate than others." He glanced in the direction of the gallows.

"Majesty, what is happening? More prisoners die every day. Ten thousand surrendered. It's been two weeks. There's five or six thousand now. There's no food and water and we're living in our own shit. We can't take much more. I've been working in the hospital. We have one doctor, and she's overwhelmed."

"I suspect Dardarius is consolidating his gains in Viridiae before taking us back to Lucana."

"Us?"

Worry creased Arturus' forehead, as if he was imagining the next days and weeks. "Dardarius wants to treat me according to my rank." Arturus chuckled to hide embarrassment. "He has a certain practical honor when he isn't killing people. I asked to have an aide attend me. I asked for you."

Percival startled. Of all Viridiae's soldiers, including men and women of far greater influence than he, Arturus had chosen him.

"I didn't forget the day of the battle. All of us saw the inevitable and ran for our lives, but you said you'd stay beside me. You were the only one, Percival. Did you know that? That took bravery, because if there was anyone the Lucians wanted dead, it was me. Anyone around me would've died too. As it turns out, they really wanted Merlin."

"Why?"

"He has knowledge they want, and it's connected to the stolen Grail, but I don't know the details."

Percival hadn't thought much about the Grail since the battle, feeling his quest to find it was as much a failure as his performance at the River Colum.

"What about Camelot, my lord? We hear rumors it's destroyed. We didn't believe them."

Arturus fingered his plastic tumbler of wine. "The walls still stand, but Dardarius is preparing a final assault."

"Our people will defend it to the last man and woman."

"No, they won't."

Percival's mouth gaped. In the space of two minutes, he'd found the king he thought was dead, and learned that Camelot with its nine towers and tree-lined streets would soon be a pile of ashes. His heart thumped at so much loss in so short a time.

Arturus saw his distress and grasped his arm. “Listen to me, Percival. There's information in what the Lucians haven't told me.”

“I don't understand.”

“Have you seen or heard from Mordred? Anything from Lancelot, Galahad, or Bors?”

The mention of Lancelot brought back a moment from the battle. She was surrounded by a dozen mounted Lucians. Her war cry was so powerful, Lucian ears leaked blood. Arms and heads flew off with each swipe of her sword Arondight. Percival never saw a scratch on her, but like the other knights listed by Arturus, she vanished in the awe-inspiring chaos of flesh and mud.

“We've seen no bodies, and they're not among the prisoners or the wounded.”

Arturus smiled. “Dardarius would've told me if my leading commanders were dead or captured. I'm willing to bet that most or all of them escaped. I just hope they made it back to Camelot and save as many people as they can before the Lucians wreck the place.” Arturus paused. “I know you have a special connection to your sister, Dindrane. Can you tell me anything?”

Percival had sensed nothing since last seeing Dee in Camelot a lifetime ago.

“I'm truly sorry about that. I hope she's safe.”

“If Mordred and the others are alive, would they try to rescue us?”

“That would be stupid, and Galahad is not an idiot. I left him in command after Mordred tried to depose me, but the people admire Mordred. They'll give him the benefit of the doubt, particularly now. He won't attack for the time being, given our losses.”

“What about us?”

Arturus rubbed his chin. “Tell me more about our brethren.”

“The Lucians have separated the wealthy from the less-so. Some have already been ransomed. The prisoners who haven't fallen sick are losing hope. Everyone is frightened.”

Arturus folded his hands, as if praying. “Things are going to get worse before they get better, far worse. I know that I will be taken to Lucana's capitol as a hostage. You will be with me. The dead and perhaps dying will be left here. Maybe those most likely to pay ransom. Those who can walk will go with us. Those that survive will be enslaved.”

Percival thought of the wounded man whom he had fed morsels of gruel. What was the point of saving his life if he was to become a slave? The knight's emotions descended into despair, as he counted all the things he had lost in the past days. He'd lost his country, his sense of self-worth, and his sense of honor. The only thing he'd recovered was his king, who happened to be his only friend. If they could survive whatever was coming, maybe there was a chance at seeing home again.

AUTHOR'S NOTE

Thank you so much for reading *Fall of the Green Land*, the first book in my fantasy trilogy, *The Future History of the Grail*. Like many young boys, I thrilled at the King Arthur stories, starting with T.H. White's *The Once and Future King*, published in 1958, the year before I was born. I also loved any movie with Arthurian themes. I'll never forget watching John Boorman's 1981 classic *Excalibur* at a theatre in Seattle's Northgate Mall in 1981. Frankly, I found these versions of Arthur, Guinevere, Lancelot, and all the other Arthurian personalities far more compelling than other rising interpretations of medieval fantasy, such as Dungeons & Dragons. The inventions of Geoffrey of Monmouth, Sir Thomas Malory, and various French and German storytellers are timeless, universal and cross-cultural, available to any modern storyteller willing to take them on.

Today's challenge is finding a new approach to the characters. I've written science fiction novels that take place in a relatively near future affected by climate change, which is one of my major themes. I believe humanity faces an existential threat from a warming climate, and I wanted to speculate on how people might adapt in the next century or two. For this new project, I wondered how could I combine the Arthurian legends with the reality of an unfolding environmental disaster. Most modern interpretations of the Arthurian stories place them in a historical past or a more-or-less realistic present. I decided to project my Arthurian characters into the future, a thousand years, to be exact. To my knowledge, very few writers have tried this. I'll leave it to you to decide whether I was successful.

Figuring out the problems with this strategy took some research. Of course, I watched *Excalibur* again. I also picked up a few volumes from Powell's Books in Portland, Ore. The books included *Arthurian Myth & Legend: An A-Z of People and Places*, a reference I went to again and again. I also purchased John Matthews' *The Arthurian Tradition* and *The Grail Tradition*, which provided invaluable structural and plot help, as well as explaining the original spiritual meaning of the Grail legend. *Life in a Medieval Village*, by Frances and Joseph Gies, provided some ideas about setting. A video lecture series by Prof. Dorsey Armstrong of Purdue University was priceless in helping me understand the Arthurian narrative tradition. The series is part of the Great Courses, which I accessed through the Seattle Public Library. And then there are countless online articles and websites. A good list of sites is available at the Best of Legends. I found the lyrics for the traditional songs used in chapter 14 of *Fall of the Green Land* and chapter 21 of *Return of the Green Land* at the Traditional Music Library. I also took inspiration for the characters and culture of the Lucians from Shakespeare's *Julius Caesar* and the HBO series *Rome*. And what would writers on deadline do without Wikipedia?

Of course, I had enormous help with the project along the way. Editor Melanie Austin helped with structure and characters. My wife Edith Follansbee proved again that I have a habit of forgetting to insert certain words, thinking that people won't notice them if they've gone missing. My friends at South Seattle Fiction Writers read early drafts. More friends at Two-Hour Transport in Seattle suffered through readings of my works-in-progress. Numerous friends and relatives volunteered as beta readers, not knowing what they were getting into. Thank you all!

I'd like to hear your feedback. Please take a moment to review my book on Amazon, Goodreads, or your favorite book review site. You can follow me on Facebook (@AuthorJGFollansbee), Twitter (@Joe_Follansbee), and Instagram (@jgfollansbee). You can also follow me on my personal blog. Tell your friends!

The three novels in the *Future History of the Grail* are intended to be read in sequence. *Fall of the Green Land* is followed by *War for the Green Land* and finally by *Return of the Green Land.* Of course, you can read them in whatever sequence you like, as long as you read them.

Thanks again!

–J.G. Follansbee, Summer 2020

MORE BOOKS BY J.G. FOLLANSBEE

Tales From a Warming Planet
The Mother Earth Insurgency
Carbon Run
City of Ice and Dreams
Restoration

The Fyddeye Guides
The Fyddeye Guide to America's Maritime History
The Fyddeye Guide to America's Lighthouses

Young Adult Historical Fiction
Bet: Stowaway Daughter

Maritime History
Shipbuilders, Sea Captains, and Fishermen: The Story of the Schooner Wawona
Blowing Out the Stink: Life on a Lumber and Cod Schooner, 1897-1947

ABOUT THE AUTHOR

J.G. Follansbee is an award-winning writer of thrillers, fantasy and science fiction novels and short stories with climate change themes. An author of maritime history and travel guides, he has published articles in newspapers, regional and national magazines, and regional and national radio networks, including National Public Radio. He's also worked in the high-tech and non-profit worlds. He lives in Seattle and blogs at https://jgfollansbee.com/blog/.

www.ingramcontent.com/pod-product-compliance
Lightning Source LLC
LaVergne TN
LVHW010604100826
845148LV00014B/2848
* 9 7 8 1 7 3 5 4 6 5 6 7 8 *